W9-BST-717

STERN MEN

Books by Elizabeth Gilbert

Pilgrims

Stern Men

STERN MEN

ELIZABETH GILBERT

HOUGHTON MIFFLIN COMPANY
BOSTON • NEW YORK
2000

Library of Congress Cataloging-in-Publication Data

Gilbert, Elizabeth, date.
Stern men / Elizabeth Gilbert.
p. cm.
ISBN 0-395-83622-0
I. Title.

PS3557.I3415 S74 2000
813'.54—dc21 99-046756

Book design and drawings by Anne Chalmers
Typefaces: Janson Text, Copperplate 31ab

Printed in the United States of America
QUM 10 9 8 7 6 5 4 3 2 1

To Michael Cooper —

for playing it cool

In an aquarium at Woods Hole in the summer of 1892, a conch was placed in the same tank with a female lobster, which was nearly ten inches long, and which had been in captivity about eight weeks. The conch, which was of average size, was not molested for several days, but at last, when hard pressed by hunger, the lobster attacked it, broke off its shell, piece by piece, and made quick work of the soft parts.

—*The American Lobster: A Study of Its Habits and Development*
Francis Hobart Herrick, Ph.D., 1895

STERN
MEN

Prologue

Twenty miles out from the coast of Maine, Fort Niles Island and Courne Haven Island face off—two old bastards in a staring contest, each convinced he is the other's only guard. Nothing else is near them. They are among nobody. Rocky and potato-shaped, they form an archipelago of two. Finding these twin islands on a map is a most unexpected discovery; like finding twin towns on a prairie, twin encampments on a desert, twin huts on a tundra. So isolated from the rest of the world, Fort Niles Island and Courne Haven Island are separated from each other by only a fast gut of seawater, known as Worthy Channel. Worthy Channel, nearly a mile wide, is so shallow in parts at low tide that unless you knew what you were doing—unless you *really* knew what you were doing—you might hesitate to cross it even in a canoe.

In their specific geography, Fort Niles Island and Courne Haven Island are so astonishingly similar that their creator must have been either a great simpleton or a great comic. They are almost exact duplicates. The islands—the last peaks of the same ancient, sunken mountain chain—are made from the same belt of quality black granite, obscured by the same cape of lush spruce. Each island is approximately four miles long and two miles wide. Each has a handful of small coves, a number of freshwater ponds, a scattering of rocky beaches, a single sandy beach, a single great hill, and a single deep harbor, held possessively behind its back, like a hidden sack of cash.

On each island, there is a church and a schoolhouse. Down by the harbor is a main street (called, on each island, Main Street), with a tiny cluster of public buildings—post office, grocer, tavern. There are no paved roads to be found on either island. The houses on the islands are much alike, and the boats in the harbors are identical. The islands share the same pocket of interesting weather, significantly warmer in the winter and cooler in the summer than any coastal town, and they often find themselves trapped within the same spooky bank of fog. The same species of fern, orchid, mushroom, and wild rose can be found on both islands. And, finally, these islands are populated by the same breeds of birds, frogs, deer, rats, foxes, snakes, and men.

The Penobscot Indians left the first human records on Fort Niles and Courne Haven. They found the islands an excellent source of sea fowl eggs, and the ancient stone weapons of these early visitors still show up in certain coves. The Penobscot didn't long remain so far out in the middle of the sea, but they did use the islands as temporary fishing stations, a practice picked up handily in the early seventeenth century by the French.

The first permanent settlers of Fort Niles and Courne Haven were two Dutch brothers, Andreas and Walter Van Heuvel, who, after taking their wives and children and livestock out to the islands in June of 1702, laid claim to one island for each family. They called their settlements Bethel and Canaan. The foundation of Walter Van Heuvel's home remains, a moss-covered pile of rock in a meadow on what he called Canaan Island—the exact site, in fact, of Walter's murder at the hands of his brother just one year into their stay. Andreas also killed Walter's children on that day and took his brother's wife over to Bethel Island to live with his family. Andreas was frustrated, it is said, that his own wife was not bearing him children fast enough. Eager for more heirs, he'd set out to claim the only other woman around. Andreas Van Heuvel broke his leg some months later, while building a barn, and he died from an ensuing infection. The women and children were soon rescued by a passing English patrol ship and taken to the stockade at Fort Pemaquid. Both women were pregnant at the time. One delivered a healthy son, whom she named Niles. The other woman's child died in delivery, but the mother's life was saved by Thaddeus Courne, an English doctor. Somehow this event gave rise to the names of the two islands: Fort Niles and Courne Haven—two very pretty places that would not be settled again for another fifty years.

The Scots-Irish came next, and they stayed. One Archibald Boyd, along with his wife, his sisters, and their husbands, took over Courne Haven in 1758. They were joined during the next decade by the

Cobbs, Pommeroys, and Strachans. Duncan Wishnell and his family started a sheep farm on Fort Niles in 1761, and Wishnell soon found himself surrounded by neighbors called Dalgleish, Thomas, Addams, Lyford, Cardoway, and O'Donnell, as well as some Cobbs who'd moved over from Fort Niles. The young ladies of one island married the young men of the other, and the family names began floating back and forth between the two places like loose buoys. By the mid-1800s, new names appeared, from new arrivals: Friend, Cashion, Yale, and Cordin.

These people shared much the same ancestral background. And because there were not many of them out there, it's not surprising that, in time, the inhabitants came to resemble one another more and more. Rampant intermarriage was the culprit. Fort Niles and Courne Haven somehow managed to avoid the fate of Malaga Island, whose population became so inbred that the state had to finally step in and evacuate everyone, but the blood lines were still extremely thin. In time, there developed a distinctive form (short, tightly muscled, sturdy) and face (pale skin, dark brows, small chin), which came to be associated with both Courne Haven and Fort Niles. After several generations, it could be fairly said that every man looked like his neighbor and every woman would have been recognized by her ancestors on sight.

They were all farmers and fishermen. They were all Presbyterians and Congregationalists. They were all political conservatives. During the Revolutionary War, they were colonial patriots; during the Civil War, they sent young men in blue wool jackets to fight for the Union in distant Virginia. They did not like to be governed. They did not like to pay taxes. They did not trust experts, and they were not interested in the opinions or the appearance of strangers. Over the years, the islands were, on different occasions and for various reasons, incorporated into several inland counties, one after another. These political mergers never ended well. Each arrangement ultimately became unsatisfactory to the islanders, and by 1900 Courne Haven and Fort Niles were left to form an independent township. Together, they created the tiny domain of Skillet County. But that, too, was a temporary arrangement. In the end, the islands themselves split; the men on each island, it seemed, felt best and safest and most autonomous when left completely alone.

The population of the islands continued to grow. Toward the end of the nineteenth century, there came a muscular expansion, with the advent of the granite trade. A young New Hampshire industrialist named Dr. Jules Ellis brought his Ellis Granite Company to both islands, where he soon made a fortune by excavating and selling the glossy black rock.

Courne Haven, in 1889, hit its peak, achieving a record population of 618. This number included Swedish immigrants, who had been hired by the Ellis Granite Company as raw-muscled quarry labor. (Some of the granite on Courne Haven was so rifted and coarse that it was good only for making cobblestones, easy work for unskilled laborers like the Swedes.) That same year, Fort Niles boasted a society of 627 souls, including Italian immigrants, who'd been hired as skilled carvers. (Fort Niles had some fine, mausoleum-grade granite—beautiful granite to which only Italian craftsmen could do justice.) There was never much work for the native islanders in the granite quarries. The Ellis Granite Company much preferred hiring immigrants, who were less expensive and easier to control. And there was little interaction between the immigrant workers and the locals. On Courne Haven, some local fishermen married Swedish women, and there appeared a streak of blonds in that island's population. On Fort Niles, however, the pale, dark-haired Scottish look remained unsullied. Nobody on Fort Niles married the Italians. It would have been unacceptable.

The years passed. Trends in fishing changed, from lines to nets and from cod to hake. The boats evolved. The farms grew obsolete. A town hall was built on Courne Haven. A bridge was built over Murder Creek on Fort Niles. Telephone service arrived in 1895, through a cable run under the sea, and by 1918 several homes had electricity. The granite industry dwindled and was finally driven into extinction by the advent of concrete. The population shrank, almost as quickly as it had ballooned. Young men moved off the islands to find work in big factories and big cities. Old names started vanishing from the rolls, slowly leaking away. The last of the Boyds died on Courne Haven in 1904. There were no O'Donnells to be found on Fort Niles after 1910, and—with each decade of the twentieth century—the number of families on Fort Niles and Courne Haven diminished further. Once sparsely inhabited, the islands became sparse once again.

What the two islands needed—what they always needed—was good blood between them. So far away from the rest of the nation, so similar in temperament, lineage, and history, the residents of Courne Haven and Fort Niles should have been good neighbors. They needed one another. They should have tried to serve each other well. They should have shared resources and burdens and benefited from all manner of cooperation. And perhaps they could have been good neighbors. Perhaps their destiny did not have to be one of conflict. Certainly there was peace between the two islands for the first two centuries or so of settlement. Perhaps if the men of Fort Niles and Courne Haven had remained simple farmers or deep-sea fishermen, they would have been excellent neighbors. We have no way of knowing what might have been, though, because they ultimately became lobstermen. And that was the end of good neighbors.

Lobsters do not recognize boundaries, and neither, therefore, can lobstermen. Lobstermen seek lobsters wherever those creatures may roam, and this means lobstermen chase their prey all over the shallow sea and the cold-water coastline. This means lobstermen are constantly competing with one another for good fishing territory. They get in each other's way, tangle each other's trap lines, spy on each other's boats, and steal each other's information. Lobstermen fight over every cubic yard of the sea. Every lobster one man catches is a lobster another man has lost. It is a mean business, and it makes for mean men. As humans, after all, we become that which we seek. Dairy farming makes men steady and reliable and temperate; deer hunting makes men quiet and fast and sensitive; lobster fishing makes men suspicious and wily and ruthless.

The first lobster war between Fort Niles Island and Courne Haven Island began in 1902. Other islands in other bays of Maine have had their lobster wars, but none was waged so early as this one. There was scarcely even a lobster industry in 1902; the lobster had not yet become a rare delicacy. In 1902, lobsters were common, worthless, even an annoyance. After bad storms, hundreds and thousands of the creatures washed up on the shores and had to be cleared away with pitchforks and wheelbarrows. Laws were passed forbidding affluent households from feeding their servants lobster more than three days a week. At that moment in history, lobstering was merely something island men did to supplement their income from farming or vessel fishing. Men had been lobstering on Fort Niles and Courne Haven for only thirty years or so, and they still fished in coats and ties. It was a new industry.

So it is remarkable that anyone could have felt sufficiently invested in the lobster industry to start a war over it. But that is exactly what happened in 1902.

The first Fort Niles–Courne Haven lobster war began with a famous and reckless letter written by Mr. Valentine Addams. By 1902, Addamses were to be found on both islands; Valentine Addams was a Fort Niles Addams. He was known to be intelligent enough, but famously high-strung and maybe the slightest bit mad. It was in the spring of 1902 that Valentine Addams wrote his letter. It was addressed to the Presiding Chairman of the Second International Fisheries Conference in Boston, a prestigious event to which Addams had not been invited. He sent neatly written copies of his letter to several of the Eastern Seaboard's major fishing newspapers. And he sent a copy to Courne Haven Island on the mail boat.

Valentine wrote:

> Sirs!
>
> I must sadly and dutifully report a hateful new crime perpetrated by deceitful members of our local lobster fishing ranks. I have termed this crime Short Lobster Stocking. I refer to the practice by which some unscrupulous lobstermen will covertly pull up an honest lobsterman's pots during the night and exchange the honest man's Large Lobsters for a batch of the unscrupulous man's worthless young Short Lobsters. Consider the consternation of the honest fisherman, who pulls up his pots in daylight, only to discover worthless Short Lobsters within! I have been confounded by this practice again and again at the hands of *my own neighbors* from the Nearby Island of Courne Haven! Please consider addressing your commission to the detainment and punishment of these Courne Haven Island Short Lobster Bandits. (Whose names I list for your agents herein.)
>
> I remain your grateful reporter,
>
> Valentine Addams

In the spring of 1903, Valentine Addams wrote a letter to the Third International Fisheries Conference, again held in Boston. This conference, even larger than that of the year before, included dignitaries from the Canadian Provinces and from Scotland, Norway, and Wales. Addams again had not been invited. And why should he have been? What business would a common fisherman like him have at such a gathering? This was a meeting of experts and legislators, not an occasion for the airing of local grievances. Why should he have been invited, with all the Welsh and Canadian dignitaries, and all the successful Massachusetts wholesalers, and all the renowned game wardens? But what of that? He wrote, in any case:

Gentlemen!

With all my respect, sirs, please convey the following to your fellows: A pregnant she-lobster carries some 25,000 to 80,000 eggs on her belly, known to us fishermen as "berries." As an article of food, these salty egg berries were once a popular addition to soups. You will recall that the eating of this article of food was officially discouraged some years ago, and that the practice of collecting for sale any berried she-lobster was outlawed. Sensible, sirs! This was for the sound purpose of solving the Eastern Shores' Lobster Problem and conserving the Eastern Shores' Lobster. Gentlemen! By this date you must surely have heard that some scoundrel lobster fishermen have evaded the law by scraping the valuable berries off the creature's belly. The unscrupulous fishermen's motive is to keep this good breeding lobster for their personal sale and profit!

Gentlemen! Scraped as such into the sea, these lobster eggs do not become healthy lobster fry, but, rather, become 25,000 to 80,000 bits of bait for hungry schools of cod and sole. Gentlemen! Look to those greedy fish bellies for the scores of lobsters vanished from our shores! Look to those unscrupulous Berry-Scraping Lobstermen for our diminishing lobster population! Gentlemen! The Scriptures ask, "Shall the flocks and the herds be slain for them, to suffice them? Or shall all the fish of the sea be gathered together for them, to suffice them?"

I have it on excellent authority, Sirs, that On My Neighboring Island of Courne Haven, *every fishing man* practices berry-scraping! The State's gaming agents stand unwilling to arrest or detain these Courne Haven thieves — for they are thieves! — despite my reports. I intend to commence immediately confronting these scoundrels myself, delivering such punitive measures as I shall deem suitable, representing the certainty of my sound suspicions and the good name of your Commission. Gentlemen!

I remain your willing agent, Valentine R. Addams.

(And I include herewith the names of Courne Haven Scoundrels.)

The very next month, Courne Haven Harbor's only pier burned down. Valentine Addams was suspected by several Courne Haven lobstermen of having participated in the act, a suspicion Addams did not much allay by being present at the Courne Haven fire, standing in his peapod boat just off the shore at dawn, shaking his fist and yelling, "Portuguese whores! Look at the Catholic beggars now!" as the Courne Haven lobstermen (who were no more Portuguese or Catholic than Valentine Addams himself) fought to save their boats. Not many days following this, Addams was found in Fineman's Cove, having been weighted down to the bottom of the sea by two fifty-pound sacks of rock salt. A clam digger discovered the body.

The fish and game agent ruled the drowning a suicide. Fair enough. In its way, the death was a suicide. Burning the single pier of a neighboring island is as suicidal an action as a man can take. Everyone knew that. No sane man on Fort Niles Island could reasonably begrudge the Courne Haven fishermen their retaliatory gesture, violent though it may have been. Still, it created a problem. Addams left behind an awkwardly pregnant widow. If she stayed on Fort Niles Island, she would be a great inconvenience to her neighbors, who would have to support her. As it turned out, that was what she intended to do. She would be dead weight on Fort Niles, a drain on a community whose working families could scarcely support themselves. Fear of this burden caused resentment over Valentine Addams's death. What was more, the drowning of a man with the very rock salt he had used to preserve his stinking bait was more than a little insulting. Recourse would be sought.

As retaliation, the men of Fort Niles Island rowed over to Courne Haven Island one night and painted a thin coat of tar on the seats of every dinghy anchored in its harbor. That was merely a rude joke, done for laughs. But they then sliced all the buoys they could find that marked lobster traps in the Courne Haven fishing territory, causing the pot wrap lines to snake down through the heavy water, and the tethered traps to vanish forever. It was the full destruction of the community's industry—what little lobster industry there was, of course, in 1903—for the entire season.

Fair enough.

After this, it was quiet for a week. Then a popular man from Fort Niles Island, Joseph Cardoway, was caught outside a mainland tavern by a dozen Courne Haven lobstermen, who beat him with long oak fishing gaffs. When Cardoway healed from the beating, his left ear was missing, his left eye was blinded, and his left thumb dangled, loose and useless as an ornament, from his muscle-torn hand. The attack outraged all of Fort Niles. Cardoway was not even a fisherman. He ran a small mill on Fort Niles and was an ice-cutter. He had nothing to do with lobster fishing, yet he'd been crippled because of it. Now the lobster war reached its full heat.

The fishermen of Courne Haven Island and Fort Niles Island fought for a decade. They fought from 1903 to 1913. Not steadily, of course. Lobster wars, even back then, are not steady fights. They are slow territory disputes, with spasmodic acts of retaliation and withdrawal. But during a lobster war, there is constant tension, constant danger of losing gear to another man's knife. Men become so consumed in defending their livelihood that they essentially eradicate that livelihood. They spend so much time fighting, spying, and challenging that they have little time left to actually fish.

As in any conflict, some contestants in this lobster war became more involved than others. On Fort Niles, the men of the Pommeroy family were most entangled in territory disputes, and, as a consequence, were effectively destroyed by the strife. They were impoverished. On Courne Haven, the fishermen in the Burden family were effectively destroyed, as well; they neglected their labor in order to undermine the efforts of, for instance, the Pommeroy family on Fort Niles. On both islands, the Cobbs were very nearly destroyed. Henry Dalgliesh found himself so demoralized by the war that he simply packed up his family and moved from Courne Haven Island to Long Island, New York, where he became a constable. Anyone who grew up on Fort Niles or Courne Haven during this decade was raised in poverty. Any Pommeroy, Burden, or Cobb who grew up during this decade was raised in extreme poverty. And hatred. For them, it was a true famine.

As for the widow of the murdered Valentine Addams, she gave birth in 1904 to twin boys: a foul-mannered baby whom she named Angus and a fat, listless baby whom she named Simon. The Widow Addams was not much more rational than her dead husband had been. She would not tolerate the words "Courne Haven" spoken in her presence. On hearing them, she would keen as if she herself were being murdered. She was a force of vindictiveness, a bitter woman whose anger aged her, and she prodded her neighbors to perform bold acts of hostility against the fishermen on the other side of Worthy Channel. She propped up her neighbors' rage and resentment if ever they let it sag. Partly because of her exhortations, partly because of the inevitable pace of any conflict, the widow's twin sons were a full ten years old before the lobster war their father had begun was fully over.

There was only one fisherman among those on both islands who did not take part in these events, a Fort Niles fisherman by the name of Ebbett Thomas. After the burning of the Courne Haven pier, Thomas quietly took all his lobster pots from the water. He cleaned them and stored them, with their gear, safe in his cellar. He pulled his boat from the water, cleaned it, and stored it on shore, covered with a tarp. There had never been a lobster war before this, so one wonders how he was able to anticipate the destructive events to come, but he was a man of considerable intuition. Ebbett Thomas apparently suspected, with a smart fisherman's awareness of bad weather rising, that it might be wiser to sit this one out.

After safely hiding his lobster gear, Ebbett Thomas walked up the single great hill of Fort Niles Island to the offices of the Ellis Granite Company and applied for a job. This was practically unheard of—a local seeking work in the quarries—but Ebbett Thomas nonetheless managed to get work at the Ellis Granite Company. He managed to talk Dr. Jules Ellis himself—the founder and owner of the company—into hiring him. Ebbett Thomas became the foreman of the Ellis Granite Company's Box Shop, supervising the construction of the wooden crates and boxes in which pieces of finished granite were shipped from the island. He was a fisherman, and his ancestors had all been fishermen, and his descendants would all be fishermen, but Ebbett Thomas did not put his fishing boat back in the water until ten years had passed. It was his considerable intuition that enabled him to weather this difficult episode without suffering the economic ruin visited on his neighbors. He kept to himself and he kept his family at a distance from the whole mess.

Ebbett Thomas was an unusual man for his time and place. He had no education, but he was bright and, in his way, worldly. His intelligence was recognized by Dr. Jules Ellis, who thought it a shame that this intelligent man was confined to a small, ignorant island and to a miserable life of fishing. Dr. Ellis often thought that, under different circumstances, Ebbett Thomas might have been a sound businessman, perhaps even a professor. But Ebbett Thomas was never granted different circumstances, so he lived out his days on Fort Niles, accomplishing little except to fish well and for a decent profit, always staying free of the petty disputes of his neighbors. He married his third cousin, an inestimably practical woman named Patience Burden, and they had two sons, Stanley and Len.

Ebbett Thomas lived well, but he did not live long. He died of a stroke at the age of fifty. He didn't live long enough to see Stanley, his firstborn, get married. But the real pity is that Ebbett Thomas didn't live long enough to meet his granddaughter, a girl by the name of Ruth, born to Stanley's wife in 1958. And that is a shame, because Ebbett Thomas would have been fascinated by Ruth. He might not have particularly understood his granddaughter, but he surely would have regarded her life with some measure of curiosity.

1

> Unlike some crustaceans, who are coldly indifferent to the welfare of their offspring, the mamma lobster keeps her little brood about her until the youthful lobsterkins are big enough to start in life for themselves.
>
> —*Crab, Shrimp, and Lobster Lore*
> William B. Lord
> 1867

THE BIRTH OF RUTH THOMAS was not the easiest on record. She was born during a week of legendary, terrible storms. The last week of May 1958 did not quite bring a hurricane, but it was not calm out there, either, and Fort Niles Island got whipped. Stan Thomas's wife, Mary, in the middle of this storm, endured an unusually hard labor. This was her first child. She was not a big woman, and the baby was stubborn in coming. Mary Thomas should have been moved to a hospital on the mainland and put under the care of a doctor, but this was no weather for boating around a woman in hard labor. There was no doctor on Fort Niles, nor were there nurses. The laboring woman, in distress, was without any medical attention. She just had to do it on her own.

Mary whimpered and screamed during labor, while her female neighbors, acting as a collective of amateur midwives, administered comfort and suggestions, and left her side only to spread word of her condition across the island. The fact was, things didn't look good. The oldest and smartest women were convinced from early on that Stan's wife was not going to make it. Mary Thomas wasn't from the island, anyway, and the women didn't have great faith in her strength. Under the best of circumstances, these women considered her somewhat pampered, a little too fine and a little too susceptible to tears and shyness. They were pretty sure she was going to quit on them in the middle of her labor and just die of pain right there, in front of everyone. Still, they fussed and interfered. They argued with one another over the best treatment, the best positions, the best advice. And when they briskly returned to their homes to collect clean towels or ice for the woman in labor, they passed the word among their husbands that things at the Thomas house were looking very grave indeed.

Senator Simon Addams heard the rumors and decided to make his famous peppery chicken stock, which he believed to be a great healer, one that would help the woman in her time of need. Senator Simon was an aging bachelor who lived with his twin brother, Angus, another aging bachelor. The men were the sons of Valentine Addams, all grown up now. Angus was the toughest, most aggressive lobsterman on the island. Senator Simon was no kind of lobsterman at all. He was terrified of the sea; he could not set foot in a boat. The closest Simon had ever come to the sea was one stride wide of the surf on Gavin Beach. When he was a teenager, a local bully tried to drag him out on a dock, and Simon had nearly scratched that kid's face off and nearly broken that kid's arm. He choked the bully until the boy fell unconscious. Senator Simon certainly did not like the water.

He was handy, though, so he earned money by repairing furniture and lobster traps and fixing boats (safely on shore) for other men. He was recognized as an eccentric, and he spent his time reading books and studying maps, which he purchased through the mail. He knew a great deal about the world, although not once in his life had he stepped off Fort Niles. His knowledge about so many subjects had earned him the nickname Senator, a nickname that was only half mocking. Simon Addams was a strange man, but he was acknowledged as an *authority*.

It was the Senator's opinion that a good, peppery chicken soup could cure anything, even childbirth, so he cooked up a nice batch for Stanley Thomas's wife. She was a woman he dearly admired, and he was worried about her. He brought a warm pot of soup over to the Thomas home on the afternoon of May 28. The female neighbors let him in and announced that the little baby had already arrived. Everyone was fine, they assured him. The baby was hearty, and the mother was going to recover. The mother could probably use a touch of that chicken soup, after all.

Senator Simon Addams looked into the bassinet, and there she was:

little Ruth Thomas. A girl baby. An unusually pretty baby, with a wet, black mat of hair and a studious expression. Senator Simon Addams noticed right away that she didn't have the red squally look of most newborns. She didn't look like a peeled, boiled rabbit. She had lovely olive skin and a most serious expression for an infant.

"Oh, she's a dear little baby," said Senator Simon Addams, and the women let him hold Ruth Thomas. He looked so huge holding the new baby that the women laughed—laughed at the giant bachelor cradling the tiny child. But Ruth blew a sort of a sigh in his arms and pursed her tiny mouth and blinked without concern. Senator Simon felt a swell of almost grandfatherly pride. He clucked at her. He jiggled her.

"Oh, isn't she just the dearest baby," he said, and the women laughed and laughed.

He said, "Isn't she just a peach?"

Ruth Thomas was a pretty baby who grew into a very pretty girl, with dark eyebrows and wide shoulders and remarkable posture. From her earliest childhood, her back was straight as a plank. She had a striking, adult presence, even as a toddler. Her first word was a very firm "No." Her first sentence: "No, thank you." She was not excessively delighted by toys. She liked to sit on her father's lap and read the papers with him. She liked to be around adults. She was quiet enough to go unnoticed for hours at a time. She was a world-class eavesdropper. When her parents visited their neighbors, Ruth sat under the kitchen table, small and silent as dust, listening keenly to every adult word. One of the most common sentences directed at her as a child was "Why, Ruth, I didn't even see you there!"

Ruth Thomas escaped notice because of her watchful disposition and also because of the distracting commotion around her in the form of the Pommeroys. The Pommeroys lived next door to Ruth and her parents. There were seven Pommeroy boys, and Ruth was born right at the end of the run of them. She pretty much vanished into the chaos kicked up by Webster and Conway and John and Fagan and Timothy and Chester and Robin Pommeroy. The Pommeroy boys were an *event* on Fort Niles. Certainly other women had produced as many children in the island's history, but only over decades and only with evident reluctance. Seven babies born to a single exuberant family in just under six years seemed almost epidemic.

Senator Simon's twin brother, Angus, said of the Pommeroys, "That's no family. That's a goddamn litter."

Angus Addams could be suspected of jealousy, though, as he had no family except his eccentric twin brother, so the whole business of other people's happy families was like a canker on Angus Addams. The Senator, on the other hand, found Mrs. Pommeroy delightful. He was charmed by her pregnancies. He said that Mrs. Pommeroy always looked as if she was pregnant because she couldn't help it. He said she always looked pregnant in a cute, apologetic way.

Mrs. Pommeroy was unusually young when she married — not yet sixteen — and she enjoyed herself and her husband completely. She was a real romp. The young Mrs. Pommeroy drank like a flapper. She loved her drinking. She drank so much during her pregnancies, in fact, that her neighbors suspected she had caused brain damage in her children. Whatever the cause, none of the seven Pommeroy sons ever learned to read very well. Not even Webster Pommeroy could read a book, and he was the ace of smarts in that family's deck.

As a child, Ruth Thomas often sat quietly in a tree and, when the opportunity arose, threw rocks at Webster Pommeroy. He'd throw rocks back at her, and he'd tell her she was a stinkbutt. She'd say, "Oh, yeah? Where'd you read that?" Then Webster Pommeroy would drag Ruth out of the tree and kick her in the face. Ruth was a smart girl who sometimes found it difficult to stop making smart comments. Getting kicked in the face was the kind of thing that happened, Ruth supposed, to smart little girls who lived next door to so many Pommeroys.

When Ruth Thomas was nine years old, she experienced a significant event. Her mother left Fort Niles. Her father, Stan Thomas, went with her. They went to Rockland. They were supposed to stay there for only a week or two. The plan was for Ruth to live with the Pommeroys for a short time. Just until her parents came back. But some complicated incident occurred in Rockland, and Ruth's mother didn't come back at all. The details weren't explained to Ruth at the time.

Eventually Ruth's father returned, but not for a long while, so Ruth ended up staying with the Pommeroys for months. She ended up staying with them for the entire summer. This significant event was not unduly traumatic, because Ruth really loved Mrs. Pommeroy. She loved the idea of living with her. She wanted to be with her all the time. And Mrs. Pommeroy loved Ruth.

“You’re like my own daughter!” Mrs. Pommeroy liked to tell Ruth. “You’re like my own goddamn daughter that I never, ever had!”

Mrs. Pommeroy pronounced the word *daughtah*, which had a beautiful, feathery sound in Ruth’s ears. Like everyone born on Fort Niles or Courne Haven, Mrs. Pommeroy spoke with the accent recognized across New England as Down East—just a whisper off the brogue of the original Scots-Irish settlers, defined by an almost criminal disregard for the letter *r*. Ruth loved the sound. Ruth’s mother did not have this beautiful accent, nor did she use words like *goddamn* and *fuck* and *shit* and *asshole*, words that delightfully peppered the speech of the native lobstermen and many of their wives. Ruth’s mother also did not drink vast quantities of rum and then turn all soft and loving, as Mrs. Pommeroy did every single day.

Mrs. Pommeroy, in short, had it all over Ruth’s mother.

Mrs. Pommeroy was not a woman who would hug constantly, but she certainly was one to nudge a person. She was always nudging and bumping into Ruth Thomas, always knocking her around with affection, sometimes even knocking her over. Always in a loving way, though. She knocked Ruth over only because Ruth was still so small. Ruth Thomas hadn’t got her real size yet. Mrs. Pommeroy knocked Ruth on her ass with pure, sweet love.

“You’re like my own goddamn daughter that I never had!” Mrs. Pommeroy would say and then nudge and then—*boom*—down Ruth would go.

Daughtah!

Mrs. Pommeroy probably could have used a daughter, too, after her seven handfuls of sons. She surely had a genuine appreciation of daughters, after years of Webster and Conway and John and Fagan and so on and so on, who ate like orphans and shouted like convicts. A daughter looked pretty good to Mrs. Pommeroy by the time Ruth Thomas moved in, so Mrs. Pommeroy had an informed love for Ruth.

But more than anyone else, Mrs. Pommeroy loved her man. She loved Mr. Pommeroy madly. Mr. Pommeroy was small and tight-muscled, with hands as big and heavy as door knockers. His eyes were narrow. He walked with his fists on his hips. He had an odd, scrunched-up face. His lips were always smooched in a half-kiss. He frowned and squinted, like someone performing difficult mathematics in his head. Mrs. Pommeroy adored him. When she passed her husband in the house hallways, she'd grab at his nipples through his undershirt. She'd tweak his nipples and yell, "Tweaky!"

Mr. Pommeroy would yell, "Whoop!"

Then he'd grab her wrists and say, "Wanda! Quit that, will you? I really hate it."

He'd say, "Wanda, if your hands weren't always so warm, I'd throw you out of the damn house."

But he loved her. In the evenings, if they were sitting on the couch listening to the radio, Mr. Pommeroy might suck on a single strand of Mrs. Pommeroy's hair as if it were sweet licorice. Sometimes they'd sit together quietly for hours, she knitting woolen garments, he knitting heads for his lobster traps, a bottle of rum on the floor between them from which they both drank. After Mrs. Pommeroy had been drinking for a while, she liked to swing her legs up off the floor, press her feet against her husband's side, and say, "Feet on you."

"No feet on me, Wanda," he'd say flatly, not looking at her, but smiling.

She'd keep pressing on him with her feet.

"Feet on you," she'd say. "Feet on you."

"Please, Wanda. No feet on me." (He called her Wanda although her true name was Rhonda. The joke was on their son Robin, who — in addition to having the local habit of not pronouncing *r* at the end of a word — could not say any word that started with *r*. Robin couldn't say his own name for years, no less the name of his mother. What's more, for a long time everyone on Fort Niles Island imitated him. Over the whole spread of the island, you could hear the great strong fishermen complaining that they had to mend their *wopes* or fix their *wigging* or buy a new short-wave *wadio*. And you could hear the great strong women asking whether they could borrow a garden *wake*.)

Ira Pommeroy loved his wife a great deal, which was easy for everyone to understand, since Rhonda Pommeroy was a true beauty. She wore long skirts, and she lifted them when she walked, as if she imagined herself fancy in Atlanta. She wore a persistent expression of amazement and delight. If someone left the room for even a moment, she'd arch her brows and say charmingly, "Where have you *been?*" when the person returned. She was young, after all, despite her seven sons, and she kept her hair as long as a young girl's. She wore her hair swung up and around her whole skull, in an ambitious, glossy pile. Like everyone else on Fort Niles, Ruth Thomas thought Mrs. Pommeroy a great beauty. She adored her. Ruth often pretended to be her.

As a girl, Ruth's hair was kept as short as a boy's, so when she pretended to be Mrs. Pommeroy, she wore a towel knotted around her head, the way some women do after a bath, but hers stood for Mrs. Pommeroy's famous glossy pile of hair. Ruth would enlist Robin Pommeroy, the youngest of the boys, to play Mr. Pommeroy. Robin was easy to boss around. Besides, he liked the game. When Robin played Mr. Pommeroy, he arranged his mouth into the same smooch his dad often wore, and he stomped around Ruth with his hands heavy on his hips. He got to curse and scowl. He liked the authority it gave him.

Ruth Thomas and Robin Pommeroy were always pretending to be Mr. and Mrs. Pommeroy. It was their constant game. They played it for hours and weeks of their childhood. They played it outside in the woods, nearly every day throughout the summer that Ruth lived with the Pommeroys. The game would start with pregnancy. Ruth would put a stone in her pants pocket to stand for one of the Pommeroy brothers, unborn. Robin would purse his mouth all tight and lecture Ruth about parenthood.

"Now listen me," Robin would say, his fists on his hips. "When that baby's bawn, he won't have any teeth. Heah that? He won't be weddy to eat that hard food, like what we eat. Wanda! You have to feed that baby some juice!"

Ruth would stroke the baby stone in her pocket. She'd say, "I think I'm about to have this baby right now."

She'd toss it on the ground. The baby was born. It was that easy.

"Would you just look at that baby?" Ruth would say. "That's a big one."

Each day, the first stone to be born was named Webster, because he was the oldest. After Webster was named, Robin would find another stone to represent Conway. He'd give it to Ruth to slip into her pocket.

"Wanda! What's that?" Robin would then demand.

"Would you just look at that," Ruth would answer. "Here I go, having another one of those goddamn babies."

Robin would scowl. "Listen me. When that baby's bawn, his foot bones'll be too soft for boots. Wanda! Don't you go stick any boots on that baby!"

"I'm naming this one Kathleen," Ruth would say. (She was always eager for another girl on the island.)

"No way," Robin would say. "That baby's gonna be a boy, too."

Sure enough, it would be. They'd name that stone Conway and toss him down by his big brother, Webster. Soon, very soon, a pile of sons would grow in the woods. Ruth Thomas delivered all those boys, all summer long. Sometimes she'd step on the stones and say, "Feet on you, Fagan! Feet on you, John!" She birthed every one of those boys every single day, with Robin stomping around her, hands heavy on his hips, bragging and lecturing. And when the Robin stone itself was born at the end of the game, Ruth sometimes said, "I'm throwing out this lousy baby. It's too fat. It can't even talk right."

Then Robin might take a swing, knocking the towel-hair off Ruth's head. And she might then whip the towel at his legs, giving him red slashes on his shins. She might knock a fist in his back if he tried running. Ruth had a good swing, when the target was slow, fat Robin. The towel would get wet from the ground. The towel would get muddied and ruined, so they'd leave it and take a fresh one the next day. Soon, a pile of towels would grow in the woods. Mrs. Pommeroy could never figure that one out.

Say, where'd those towels go? Hey! What about my towels, then?

The Pommeroys lived in the big house of a dead great-uncle who had been a relative of both of them. Mr. and Mrs. Pommeroy were related even before they were married. They were cousins, each conveniently named Pommeroy before they fell in love. ("Like the goddamn Roosevelts," Angus Addams said.) To be fair, of course, that's not an unusual situation on Fort Niles. Not many families to choose from anymore, so everyone's family.

The dead Pommeroy great-uncle was therefore a shared dead great-uncle, a common dead great-uncle. He'd built a big house near the church, with money made in a general store, back before the first lobster war. Mr. and Mrs. Pommeroy had doubly inherited the home. When Ruth was nine years old and stayed with the Pommeroys for the summer, Mrs. Pommeroy tried to get her to sleep in that dead uncle's bedroom. It was under a quiet roof and had one window, which spied on a massive spruce tree, and it had a soft wooden floor of wide planks. A lovely room for a little girl. The only problem was that the great-uncle had shot himself right there in that room, right through his mouth, and the wallpaper was still speckled with rusty, tarnished blood freckles. Ruth Thomas flatly refused to sleep in that room.

"Jesus, Ruthie, the man's dead and buried," Mrs. Pommeroy said. "There's nothing in this room to scare anybody."

"No," Ruth said.

"Even if you see a ghost, Ruthie, it would just be my uncle's ghost, and he'd never hurt you. He loved all children."

"No, thank you."

"It's not even blood on the wallpaper!" Mrs. Pommeroy lied. "It's fungus. It's from the damp."

Mrs. Pommeroy told Ruth that she had the same fungus on her bedroom wallpaper every now and again, and that she slept just fine. She said she slept like a cozy baby every night of the year. In that case, Ruth announced, she'd sleep in Mrs. Pommeroy's bedroom. And, in the end, that's exactly what she did.

Ruth slept on the floor next to Mr. and Mrs. Pommeroy's bed. She had a large pillow and a mattress of sorts, made from rich-smelling wool blankets. When the Pommeroys made any noise, Ruth heard it, and when they had giggly sex, she heard that. When they snored through their boozy sleeping, she heard that, too. When Mr. Pommeroy got up at four o'clock every morning to check the wind and leave the house for lobster fishing, Ruth Thomas heard him moving around. She kept her eyes shut and listened to his mornings.

Mr. Pommeroy had a terrier that followed him around everywhere, even in the kitchen at four o'clock every morning, and the dog's nails ticked steady on the kitchen floor. Mr. Pommeroy would talk quietly to the dog while making his breakfast.

"Go back to sleep, dog," he'd say. "Don't you want to go back to sleep? Don't you want to rest up, dog?"

Some mornings Mr. Pommeroy would say, "You following me around so you can learn how to make coffee for me, dog? You trying to learn how to make my breakfast?"

For a while, there was a cat in the Pommeroy house, too. It was a dock cat, a huge coon-cat that had moved up to the Pommeroys' because it hated the terrier and hated the Pommeroy boys so much that it wanted to stay near them at all times. The cat took the terrier's eye out in a fight, and the eye socket turned into a stink and mess of infection. So Conway put the cat in a lobster crate, floated the crate on the surf, and shot at it with a gun of his father's. After that, the terrier slept on the floor beside Ruth Thomas every night, with its mean, stinking eye.

Ruth liked sleeping on the floor, but she had strange dreams. She dreamed that the ghost of the Pommeroys' dead great-uncle chased her into the Pommeroys' kitchen, where she searched for knives to stab him with but could find nothing except wire whisks and flat spatulas to defend herself. She had other dreams, where it was storming rain in the Pommeroys' back yard, and the boys were wrestling with each other. She had to step around them with a small umbrella, covering first one boy, then another, then another, then another. All seven Pommeroy sons fought in a tangle, all around her.

In the mornings, after Mr. Pommeroy had left the house, Ruth would fall asleep again and wake up a few hours later, when the sun was higher. She'd crawl up into bed with Mrs. Pommeroy. Mrs. Pommeroy would wake up and tickle Ruth's neck and tell Ruth stories about all the dogs her father had owned, back when Mrs. Pommeroy was a little girl exactly like Ruth.

"There was Beadie, Brownie, Cassie, Prince, Tally, Whippet . . ." Mrs. Pommeroy would say, and eventually Ruth learned the names of all the bygone dogs and could be quizzed on them.

Ruth Thomas lived with the Pommeroys for three months, and then her father returned to the island without her mother. The complicated incident had been resolved. Mr. Thomas had left Ruth's mother in a town called Concord, New Hampshire, where she would remain indefinitely. It was made pretty clear to Ruth that her mother would not be returning home at all. Ruth's father took Ruth out of the Pommeroy house and back next door, where she was able to sleep in her own bedroom again. Ruth resumed her quiet life with her father and found that she did not much miss her mother. But she very much missed sleeping on the floor beside the bed of Mr. and Mrs. Pommeroy.

Then Mr. Pommeroy drowned.

All the men said Ira Pommeroy drowned because he fished alone and he drank on his boat. He kept jugs of rum tied to some of his trap lines, bobbing twenty fathoms down in the chilled middle waters, halfway between the floating buoys and the grounded lobster traps. Everyone did that occasionally. It wasn't as if Mr. Pommeroy had invented the idea, but he had refined it greatly, and the understanding was that he'd wrecked himself from refining it too greatly. He simply got too drunk on a day when the swells were too big and the deck was too slippery.

He probably went over the side of his boat before he even knew it, losing his footing with a quick swell while pulling up a trap. And he couldn't swim. Scarcely any of the lobstermen on Fort Niles or Courne Haven could swim. Not that being able to swim would have helped Mr. Pommeroy much. In the tall boots, in the long slicker and heavy gloves, in the wicked and cold water, he would have gone down fast. At least he got it over with quickly. Knowing how to swim sometimes just makes the dying last longer.

Angus Addams found the body three days later, when he was fishing. Mr. Pommeroy's corpse was bound tightly in Angus's lines, like a swollen, salted ham. That's where he'd ended up. A body can drift, and there were acres of ropes sunk in the water around Fort Niles Island that could act like filters to catch any drifting corpses. Mr. Pommeroy's drift stopped in Angus's territory. The seagulls had already eaten out Mr. Pommeroy's eyes.

Angus Addams had pulled up a line to collect one of his traps, and he'd pulled up the body, too. Angus had a small boat, with not much room for another man on board, alive or dead, so he'd tossed dead Mr. Pommeroy into the holding tank on top of the living, shifting lobsters he'd caught that morning, whose claws he'd pegged shut so they wouldn't rip each other into a slop of pieces. Like Mr. Pommeroy, Angus fished alone. At that time in his career, Angus didn't have a sternman to help him. At that point in his career, he didn't feel like sharing his catch with a teenage helper. He didn't even have a radio, which was unusual for a lobsterman, but Angus did not like being chattered at. Angus had dozens of traps to haul that day. He always fished through his chores, no matter what he found. And so, despite the corpse he'd fished up, Angus went ahead and pulled his remaining lines, which took several hours. He measured each lobster, as he was supposed to do, threw the small ones back, and kept the legal ones, pegging their claws safely shut. He tossed all the lobsters on top of the drowned body in the cool tank, out of the sun.

Around three-thirty in the afternoon, he headed back to Fort Niles. He anchored. He tossed Mr. Pommeroy's body into his rowboat, where it was out of his way, and counted the catch into the holding crates, filled his bait buckets for the next day, hosed off the deck, hung up his slicker. When he was finished with these chores, he joined Mr. Pommeroy in the rowboat and headed over to the dock. He tied his rowboat to the ladder and climbed up. Then he told everyone exactly whom he'd found in his fishing grounds that morning, dead as any idiot.

"He was all stuck in my wopes," Angus Addams said grimly.

As it happened, Webster and Conway and John and Fagan and Timothy and Chester Pommeroy were at the docks when Angus Addams unloaded the corpse. They'd been playing there that afternoon. They saw the body of their father, laid out on the pier, puffed and eyeless. Webster, the oldest, was the first to see it. He stammered and gasped, and then the other boys saw it. They fell like terrified soldiers into a crazy formation, and broke right into a run home, together, in a bunch. They ran up from the harbor, and they burst, fast and weeping, past the roads and the collapsing old church to their house, where their neighbor Ruth Thomas was fighting with their littlest brother, Robin, on the steps. The Pommeroy sons drew Ruth and Robin up into their run, and the eight of them shoved into the kitchen at the same time and rushed into Mrs. Pommeroy.

Mrs. Pommeroy had expected this news ever since her husband's boat was found, three nights before, without her husband anywhere near it, floating far off course. She already knew her husband was dead, and she'd guessed that she would never recover his body. But now, as her sons and Ruth Thomas hurled themselves into the kitchen, their faces stricken, Mrs. Pommeroy knew that the body had been found. And that her sons had seen it.

The boys knocked into Mrs. Pommeroy and took her down to the floor as though they were mad brave soldiers and she was a live grenade. They covered and smothered her. They were grieving, and they were a real weight upon her. Ruth Thomas had been knocked over, too, and was sprawled out, confused, on the kitchen floor. Robin Pommeroy, who did not yet get it, was circling the pile of his sobbing brothers and his mother, saying, "What? What?"

What was a word Robin could say very easily, unlike his own name, so he said it again.

"What? What? Webster, what?" he said, and he must have wondered at this poor snarl of boys and at his mother, so silent under them. He was far too little for such a report. Mrs. Pommeroy, on the floor, was quiet as a nun. She was cloaked in her sons. When she struggled to stand up, her boys came up with her, stuck on her. She picked her boys off her long skirts as if they were brambles or beetles. But as each boy dropped off to the floor, he crawled back on her again. They were all hysterical. Still, she stood quietly, plucking them from her.

"Webster, what?" Robin said. "What, what?"

"Ruthie," Mrs. Pommeroy said, "go on home. Tell your father."

Her voice had a thrilling, beautiful sadness. *Tell yah fathah* . . . Ruth thought it the prettiest sentence she had ever heard.

Senator Simon Addams built the coffin for Mr. Pommeroy, but the Senator did not attend the funeral, because he was deadly afraid of the sea and never attended the funeral of anyone who had drowned. It was an unsustainable terror for him, no matter who the dead person was. He had to stay away. Instead, he built Mr. Pommeroy a coffin of clean white spruce, sanded and polished with light oil. It was a lovely coffin.

This was the first funeral that Ruth Thomas had attended, and it was a fine one, for a first funeral. Mrs. Pommeroy was already showing herself to be an exceptional widow. In the morning, she scrubbed the necks and fingernails of Webster, Conway, John, Fagan, Timothy, Chester, and Robin. She worked their hair down with a fancy tortoise-shell comb dipped in a tall glass of cold water. Ruth was there with them. She could not stay away from Mrs. Pommeroy in general, and certainly not on an important day like this. She took her place at the end of the line and got her hair combed with water. She got her nails cleaned and her neck scrubbed with brushes. Mrs. Pommeroy cleaned Ruth Thomas last, as though the girl were a final son. She left Ruth's scalp hot and tight from the combing. She made Ruth's nails shine like coins. The Pommeroy boys stood still, except for Webster, the oldest, who was tapping his fingers nervously against his thighs. The boys were very well behaved that day, for the sake of their mother.

Mrs. Pommeroy then performed some brilliant work on her own hair, sitting at the kitchen table before her bedroom dresser mirror. She wove a technically complicated plait and arranged it around her head with pins. She oiled her hair with something interesting until it had the splendid sheen of granite. She draped a black scarf over her head. Ruth Thomas and the Pommeroy boys all watched her. She had a real gravity about her, just as a dignified widow should. She had a true knack for it. She looked spectacularly sad and should have been photographed that day. She just was that beautiful.

Fort Niles Island was required to wait more than a week to stage the funeral, because it took that long to get the minister to come over on the *New Hope*, the mission boat. There was no permanent ministry on Fort Niles anymore, nor on Courne Haven. On both islands, the churches were falling down from lack of use. By 1967, there wasn't a large enough population on either Fort Niles or Courne Haven (just over a hundred souls on the two islands) to sustain a regular church. So the citizens shared a minister of God with a dozen other remote islands in a similar predicament, all the way up the coast of Maine. The *New Hope* was a floating church, constantly moving from one distant sea community to another, showing up for brief, efficient stays. The *New Hope* remained in harbor only long enough to baptize, marry, or bury whoever needed it, and then sailed off again. The boat also delivered charity and brought books and sometimes even the mail. The *New Hope*, built in 1915, had carried several ministers during its tenure of good work. The current minister was a native of Courne Haven Island, but he was scarcely ever to be found there. His work sometimes took him all the way up to Nova Scotia. He had a far-flung parish, indeed, and it was often difficult to get his attention promptly.

The minister in question was Toby Wishnell, of the Wishnell family of Courne Haven Island. Everyone on Fort Niles Island knew the Wishnells. The Wishnells were what was known as "high-line" lobstermen, which is to say that they were terrifically skilled and inevitably wealthy. They were famous lobstermen, superior to every fishing man. They were rich, supernatural fishermen, who had even managed to excel (comparatively) during the lobster wars. The Wishnells always tore great masses of lobster from any depth of water, in any season, and they were widely hated for it. It made no sense to other fishermen how many lobsters the Wishnells claimed as their own. It was as if the Wishnells had a special arrangement with God. More than that, it was as if the Wishnells had a special arrangement with lobsters as a species.

Lobsters certainly seemed to consider it an honor and a privilege to enter a Wishnell trap. They would crawl over other men's traps for miles of sea bottom just to be caught by a Wishnell. It was said that a Wishnell could find a lobster under a rock in your grandmother's flower garden. It was said that families of lobsters collected in the very walls of Wishnell homes, like rodents. It was said that Wishnell boys were born with tentacles, claws, and shells, which they shed during the final days of nursing.

The Wishnells' luck in fishing was obscene, offensive, and inherited. Wishnell men were especially gifted at destroying the confidence of Fort Niles men. If a Fort Niles fisherman was inland, doing business for a day in, say, Rockland, and he met a Wishnell at the bank or at the gas station, he would inevitably find himself behaving like an idiot. Losing all self-control, he would demean himself before the Wishnell man. He would grin and stammer and congratulate Mr. Wishnell on his fine new haircut and fine new car. He would apologize for his filthy overalls. He would foolishly try to explain to Mr. Wishnell that he'd been doing chores around his boat, that these filthy rags were only his work clothes, that he'd be throwing them out soon, rest assured. The Wishnell man would go on his way, and the Fort Niles fisherman would rage in shame for the rest of the week.

The Wishnells were great innovators. They were the first fishermen to use light nylon ropes instead of the old hemp ropes, which had to be painstakingly coated in hot tar to keep them from rotting in the seawater. The Wishnells were the first fishermen to haul traps with mechanized winches. They were the first fishermen, in fact, to use motorized boats. That was the way with the Wishnells. They were always first and always best. It was said that they bought their bait from Christ Himself. They sold huge catches of lobsters every week, laughing at their own sickening luck.

Pastor Toby Wishnell was the first and only man born into the Wishnell family who did not fish. And what an evil and well-conceived insult that was! To be born a Wishnell—a lobster magnet, a lobster *magnate*—and piss away the gift! To turn away the spoils of that dynasty! Who would be idiot enough to do such a thing? Toby Wishnell, that's who. Toby Wishnell had given it all up for the Lord, and that was seen over on Fort Niles as intolerable and pathetic. Of all the Wishnells, the men of Fort Niles hated Toby Wishnell the most. He absolutely galled them. And they fiercely resented that he was their *minister.* They didn't want that guy anywhere near their souls.

"There's something about that Toby Wishnell he ain't telling us," said Ruth Thomas's father, Stan.

"It's faggotry, is what it is," said Angus Addams. "He's pure faggot."

"He's a dirty liar. And a born bastard," Stan Thomas said. "And it may be faggotry, too. He may just be a faggot, too, for all we know."

The day that young Pastor Toby Wishnell arrived on the *New Hope* to attend to the funeral of drowned, drunk, swollen, eyeless Mr. Pommeroy was a handsome early autumn day. There were high blue skies and keen winds. Toby Wishnell looked handsome, too. He had an elegant frame. He wore a lean black wool suit. His trousers were tucked into heavy, rubber fishermen's boots to guard against the muddied ground.

There was something unreasonably fine about Pastor Toby Wishnell's features, something too pretty about his cleancut chin. He was polished. He was cultivated. What's more, he was blond. Somewhere along the way, the Wishnells must have married some of the Swedish girls born to the Ellis Granite Company workers. This happened back at the turn of the century, and the soft blond hair had stuck around. There was none of it on Fort Niles Island, where nearly everyone was pale and dark. Some of the blond hair on Courne Haven was quite beautiful, and the islanders were rather proud of it. It had become a quiet issue between the two islands. On Fort Niles, blonds were resented wherever they were seen. Another reason to hate Pastor Toby Wishnell.

Pastor Toby Wishnell gave Ira Pommeroy a most elegant funeral. His manners were perfect. He walked Mrs. Pommeroy to the cemetery, holding her arm. He guided her to the edge of the newly dug grave. Ruth Thomas's Uncle Len had dug that grave himself over the last few days. Ruth's Uncle Len, always hard up for money, would take any job. Len was reckless and didn't generally give a damn throughout life. He had also offered to keep the body of drowned Mr. Pommeroy in his root cellar for a week, despite the protests of his wife. The corpse was sprinkled heavily with rock salt to cut the smell. Len didn't care.

Ruth Thomas watched Mrs. Pommeroy and Pastor Wishnell head to the grave. They were in perfect step with each other, as matched in their movements as ice skaters. They made a good-looking couple. Mrs. Pommeroy was trying bravely not to cry. She held her head tilted back, daintily, like a nosebleeder.

Pastor Toby Wishnell delivered his address at the graveside. He spoke carefully, with traces of his education.

"Consider the brave fisherman," he began, "and the jeopardy of his sea . . ."

The fishermen listened without a flinch, regarding their own fishermen's boots. The seven Pommeroy boys stood in a descending line beside their mother, as still as though they'd been pegged to the ground, except for Webster, who shifted and shifted on his feet as if he were about to race. Webster hadn't stood still since first seeing his father's body laid out on the pier. He'd been moving and tapping and shifting nervously ever since. Something had happened to Webster that afternoon. He had become goosey, fidgety, and unnerved, and his reaction wasn't going away. As for Mrs. Pommeroy, her beauty troubled the silent air around her.

Pastor Wishnell recalled Mr. Pommeroy's skills on the sea and his love of boats and children. Pastor Wishnell regretted that such an accident could befall so skilled a sailor. Pastor Wishnell recommended that the gathered neighbors and loved ones avoid speculating on God's motives.

There were not many tears. Webster Pommeroy was crying, and Ruth Thomas was crying, and Mrs. Pommeroy was touching the corners of her eyes every so often, but that was it. The island men were silent and respectful, but their faces did not suggest personal devastation at this event. The island wives and mothers shuffled and stared actively, reckoning the grave and reckoning Mrs. Pommeroy and reckoning Toby Wishnell and, finally, reckoning their own husbands and sons quite frankly. It was a tragedy, they were surely thinking. Hard to lose any man. Painful. Unfair. Yet beneath such sympathetic thoughts each of these women was probably thinking, *But it was not my man.* They were almost fully occupied with relief. How many men could drown in a year, after all? Drownings were rare. There were almost never two drownings in a year in such a small community. Superstition suggested that Mr. Pommeroy's drowning had made all the other men immune. Their husbands would be safe for some time. And they would not lose any sons this year.

Pastor Toby Wishnell asked those gathered to remember that Christ Himself was a fisherman, and that Christ Himself promised a reception for Mr. Pommeroy in the full company of trumpeting angelic hosts. He asked that those gathered, as a community of God, not neglect the spiritual education and guidance of Mr. Pommeroy's seven young sons. Having lost their earthly father, he reminded those present, it was now ever more imperative that the Pommeroy boys not lose their heavenly Father as well. Their souls were in the care of this community, and any loss of faith by the Pommeroy boys would surely be seen by the Lord as the fault of the community, for which He would punish its people accordingly.

Pastor Wishnell asked those gathered to consider the witness and testimony of Saint Matthew as a warning. He read from his Bible, "But whoso shall offend one of these little ones which believe in me, it were better for him that a millstone were hanged about his neck, and that he were drowned in the depth of the sea."

Behind Pastor Wishnell was the sea itself, and there was Fort Niles harbor, glittering in the hard afternoon light. There was the *New Hope* mission boat, anchored among the squatty fishing boats, gleaming prominently and looking lean and long by comparison. Ruth Thomas could see all this from where she stood, on the slope of a hill, next to Mr. Pommeroy's grave. With the exception of Senator Simon Addams, everyone on the island had come to the funeral. Everyone was there, near Ruth. Everyone was accounted for. But down on the Fort Niles dock stood an unfamiliar big blond boy. He was young, but he was bigger than any of the Pommeroy boys. Ruth could tell his size even at that significant distance. He had a big head shaped something like a paint can, and he had long, thick arms. The boy was standing perfectly still, with his back to the island. He was looking out to sea.

Ruth Thomas became so interested in the strange boy that she stopped crying over Mr. Pommeroy's death. She watched the strange boy during the entire funeral service, and he did not move. He faced the water for the full duration, his arms by his side. He stood there, still and quiet. It was only long after the funeral, when Pastor Wishnell walked down to the dock, that the boy moved. Without speaking to the pastor, the big blond boy climbed down the ladder of the pier and rowed Pastor Wishnell back to the *New Hope.* Ruth watched with the greatest interest.

But that all happened after the funeral. In the meantime, the service continued smoothly. Eventually, Mr. Pommeroy, idling in his long and leggy spruce box, was packed down in the dirt. The men dropped clods of earth upon him; the women dropped flowers upon him. Webster Pommeroy fidgeted and paced in place and looked as if he might start running any minute now. Mrs. Pommeroy let go of her composure and cried prettily. Ruth Thomas watched in some anger as the drowned husband of her favorite person in the entire world was buried.

Ruth thought, *Christ! Why didn't he just swim for it instead?*

. . .

Senator Simon Addams brought Mrs. Pommeroy's sons a book that night, in a protective canvas bag. Mrs. Pommeroy was making supper for her boys. She was still wearing her black funeral dress, which was made of a material heavy for the season. She was scraping the root hairs and rough skin from a bucket of her garden's carrots. The Senator brought her a small bottle of rum, as well, which she said she thought she wouldn't be having any of, but she thanked him all the same.

"I've never known you to turn down a drink of rum," Senator Simon Addams said.

"All the fun's out of drinking for me, Senator. You won't be seeing me drink anymore."

"There was fun in drinking once?" the Senator asked. "There ever was?"

"Ah . . ." Mrs. Pommeroy sighed and smiled sadly. "What's in the sack?"

"A gift for your boys."

"Will you have supper with us?"

"I will. Thank you very much."

"Ruthie!" Mrs. Pommeroy said, "bring the Senator a glass for his rum."

But young Ruth Thomas had already done so, and she'd brought him a chunk of ice, too. Senator Simon rubbed Ruth's head with his big, soft hand.

"Shut your eyes, Ruthie," he told her. "I've got a gift for you."

Ruth obediently shut her eyes for him, as she always had, ever since she was a very small girl, and he kissed her on the forehead. He gave her a big smack. That was always his gift. She opened her eyes and smiled at him. He loved her.

Now the Senator put the tips of his two index fingers together. "OK, Ruthie. Cut the pickle," he said.

Ruth made scissors of the fingers on her right hand and snipped through his fingers.

"Get the tickle!" he exclaimed, and he tickled her ribs. Ruth was too old for this game, but the Senator loved it. He laughed and laughed. She smiled indulgently. They sometimes performed this little routine four times a day.

Ruth Thomas was eating supper with the Pommeroys that night, even though it was a funeral night. Ruth nearly always ate with them. It was nicer than eating at home. Ruth's father wasn't much for cooking a hot meal. He was clean and decent enough, but he didn't keep much of a home. He wasn't against having cold sandwiches for dinner. He wasn't against mending Ruth's skirt hems with a staple gun, either. He ran that kind of house and had done so ever since Ruth's mother left. Nobody was going to starve or freeze to death or go without a sweater, but it wasn't a particularly cozy home. So Ruth spent most of her time at the Pommeroys', which was much warmer and easier. Mrs. Pommeroy had invited Stan Thomas over for dinner that night, too, but he'd stayed at home. He was thinking that a man shouldn't take a supper off a woman freshly grieving the funeral of her husband.

The seven Pommeroy boys were murderously glum at the dinner table. Cookie, the Senator's dog, napped behind the Senator's chair. The Pommeroys' nameless, one-eyed dog, locked in the bathroom for the duration of the Senator's visit, howled and barked in outrage at the thought of another dog in his home. But Cookie didn't notice. Cookie was beat tired. Cookie followed the lobster boats out sometimes, even when the water was rough, and she was always very nearly drowning. It was awful. She was only a year-old mutt, and she was crazy to think she could swim against the ocean. Cookie had been pulled by the current once nearly to Courne Haven Island, but the mail boat happened to pick her up and bring her back, almost dead. It was awful when she swam out after the boats, barking. Senator Simon Addams would edge near the dock, as close to it as he dared, and would beg Cookie to come back. Begging and begging! The young dog swam in small circles farther and farther out, sneezing off the spray from the outboard motors. The sternmen in the chased boats would throw hunks of herring bait at Cookie, yelling, "Git on outta heh!"

Of course the Senator could never go out after his dog. Not Senator Simon, who was as afraid of water as his dog was inspired by it. "Cookie!" he'd yell. "Please come on back, Cookie! Come on back, Cookie! Come on back now, Cookie!"

It was hard to watch, and it had been happening since Cookie was a puppy. Cookie chased boats almost every day, and Cookie was tired every night. This night was no exception. So Cookie slept, exhausted, behind the Senator's chair during supper. At the end of Mrs. Pommeroy's supper, Senator Simon caught the last morsel of pork on his plate with his fork tines and waved his fork behind him. The pork dropped to the floor. Cookie woke up, chewed the meat thoughtfully, and went back to sleep.

Then the Senator pulled from the canvas sack the book he'd brought as a gift for the boys. It was a huge book, heavy as a slab of slate.

"For your boys," he told Mrs. Pommeroy.

She looked it over and handed it to Chester. Chester looked it over. Ruth Thomas thought, *A book for those boys?* She had to feel sorry for someone like Chester, with such a massive book in his hand, staring at it with no comprehension.

"You know," Ruth Thomas told Senator Simon, "they can't read."

Then she said to Chester, "Sorry!" thinking that it wasn't right to bring up such a fact on the day of a boy's father's funeral, but she didn't know for certain whether the Senator knew that the Pommeroy boys couldn't read. She didn't know if he'd heard of their affliction.

Senator Simon took the book back from Chester. It had been his great-grandfather's book, he said. His great-grandfather had purchased the book in Philadelphia the only time that good man had ever left Fort Niles Island in his entire life. The cover of the book was thick, hard, brown leather. The Senator opened the book and began to read from the first page.

He read: "Dedicated to the King, the Lords Commissioner of the Admiralty, to the Captains and Officers of the Royal Navy, and to the Public at Large. Being the most accurate, elegant, and perfect edition of the whole works and discoveries of the celebrated circumnavigator Captain James Cook."

Senator Simon paused and looked at each of the Pommeroy boys. "Circumnavigator!" he exclaimed.

Each boy returned his look with a great lack of expression.

"A circumnavigator, boys! Captain Cook sailed the world all the way around, boys! Would you like to do that someday?"

Timothy Pommeroy stood up from the table, walked into the living room, and lay down on the floor. John helped himself to some more carrots. Webster sat, drumming his feet nervously against the kitchen tile.

Mrs. Pommeroy said politely, "Sailed around the whole world, did he, Senator?"

The Senator read more: "Containing an authentic, entertaining, full, and complete history of Captain Cook's First, Second, and Third Voyages."

He smiled at Mrs. Pommeroy. "This is a marvelous book for boys. Inspiring. The good captain was killed by savages, you know. Boys love these stories. Boys! If you wish to be sailors, you will study James Cook!"

At that time, only one of the Pommeroy boys was any kind of a sailor. Conway was working as a substitute sternman for a Fort Niles fisherman named Mr. Duke Cobb. A few days every week, Conway left the house at five in the morning and returned late in the afternoon, reeking of herring. He pulled traps and pegged lobsters and filled bait bags, and received ten percent of the profits for his work. Mr. Cobb's wife packed Conway his lunch, which was part of his pay. Mr. Cobb's boat, like all the boats, never went much farther than a mile or two from Fort Niles. Mr. Cobb was certainly no circumnavigator. And Conway, a sullen and lazy kid, was not shaping up to be a great circumnavigator, either.

Webster, the oldest boy, at fourteen, was the only other Pommeroy old enough to work, but he was a wreck on a boat. He was useless on a boat. He went nearly blind with seasickness, dying from headaches and vomiting down his own helpless sleeves. Webster had an idea of being a farmer. He kept a few chickens.

"I have a little joke to show you," Senator Simon said to Chester, the nearest boy. He spread the book on the table and opened it to the middle. The huge page was covered with tiny text. The print was dense and thick and faint as a small pattern on old fabric.

"What do you see here? Look at that spelling."

Terrible silence as Chester stared.

"There's no letter *s* anywhere, is there, son? The printers used *f* instead, didn't they, son? The whole book is like that. It was perfectly common. It looks funny to us, though, doesn't it? To us, it looks as if the word *sail* is the word *fail.* To us, it looks as if every time Captain Cook *sailed* the boat, he actually *failed* the boat! Of course, he didn't fail at all. He was the great circumnavigator. Imagine if someone told you, Chester, that someday you would *fail* a boat? Ha!"

"Ha!" said Chester, accordingly.

"Have they spoken to you yet, Rhonda?" Senator Simon asked Mrs. Pommeroy suddenly, and shut the book, which slammed like a weighty door.

"Have who, Senator?"

"All the other men."

"No."

"Boys," Senator Simon said, "get out of here. Your mother and I need to talk alone. Beat it. Take your book. Go outside and play."

The boys sulked out of the room. Some of them went upstairs, and the others filed outside. Chester carried the enormous, inappropriate gift of Captain James Cook's circumnavigations outdoors. Ruth slipped under the kitchen table, unnoticed.

"They'll be coming by soon, Rhonda," the Senator said to Mrs. Pommeroy when the room had cleared. "The men will come by soon for a talk with you."

"Fine."

"I wanted to give you some warning. Do you know what they'll be asking you?"

"No."

"They'll ask if you're planning on staying here, on the island. They'll want to know if you're staying or if you're planning to move inland."

"Fine."

"They probably wish you'd leave."

Mrs. Pommeroy said nothing.

From her vantage point under the table, Ruth heard a splash, which she guessed was Senator Simon's pouring a fresh dollop of rum on the ice in his glass.

"So, do you think you'll stay on Fort Niles, then?" he asked.

"I think we'll probably stay, Senator. I don't know anybody inland. I wouldn't have anywhere to go."

"And whether you do or do not stay, they'll want to buy your man's boat. And they'll want to fish his fishing ground."

"Fine."

"You should keep both the boat and the ground for the boys, Rhonda."

"I don't see how I can do that, Senator."

"Neither do I, to tell you the truth, Rhonda."

"The boys are so young, you see. They aren't ready to be fishermen so young, Senator."

"I know, I know. I can't see either how you can afford to keep the boat. You'll need the money, and if the men want to buy it, you'll have to sell. You can't very well leave it on shore while you wait for your boys to grow up. And you can't very well go out there every day and chase men off the Pommeroy fishing ground."

"That's right, Senator."

"And I can't see how the men will let you keep the boat or the fishing ground. Do you know what they'll tell you, Rhonda? They'll tell you they just intend to fish it for a few years, not to let it go to waste, you see. Just until the boys are big enough to take over. But good luck taking it back, boys! You'll never see it again, boys!"

Mrs. Pommeroy listened to all this with equanimity.

"Timothy," Senator Simon called, turning his head toward the living room, "do you want to fish? Do you want to fish, Chester? Do you boys want to be lobstermen when you grow up?"

"You sent the boys outside, Senator," Mrs. Pommeroy said. "They can't hear you."

"That's right, that's right. But do they want to be fishermen?"

"Of course they want to be fishermen, Senator," Mrs. Pommeroy said. "What else could they do?"

"Army."

"But forever, Senator? Who stays in the Army forever, Senator? They'll want to come back to the island to fish, like all the men."

"Seven boys." Senator Simon looked at his hands. "The men will wonder how there'll ever be enough lobsters around this island for seven more men to make a living from them. How old is Conway?"

Mrs. Pommeroy informed the Senator that Conway was twelve.

"Ah, they'll take it all from you, for sure they will. It's a shame, a shame. They'll take the Pommeroy fishing ground, split it among them. They'll buy your husband's boat and gear for a song, and all that money will be gone in a year, from feeding your boys. They'll take over your husband's fishing territory, and your boys will have a hell of a fight to win it back. It's a shame. And Ruthie's father probably gets the most of it, I'll bet. Him and my greedy brother. Greedy Number One and Greedy Number Two."

Under the table, Ruth Thomas frowned, humiliated. Her face got hot. She did not entirely understand the conversation, but she felt deeply ashamed, suddenly, of her father and of herself.

"Pity," the Senator said. "I'd tell you to fight for it, Rhonda, but I honestly don't know how you can. Not all by yourself. Your boys are too young to stage a fight for any territory."

"I don't want my boys fighting for anything, Senator."

"Then you'd better teach them a new trade, Rhonda. You'd better teach them a new trade."

The two adults sat silently for some time. Ruth hushed her breathing. Then Mrs. Pommeroy said, "He wasn't a very good fisherman, Senator."

"He should have died six years from now, instead, when the boys were ready for it. That's really what he should have done."

"Senator!"

"Or maybe that wouldn't have been any better. I honestly don't see how this could have worked out at all. I've been thinking about it, Rhonda, ever since you had all those sons in the first place. I've been trying to figure out how it would settle in the end, and I never did see any good coming of it. Even if your husband had lived, I suppose the boys would have ended up fighting among themselves. Not enough lobsters out there for everyone; that's the fact. Pity. Fine, strong boys. It's easier with girls, of course. They can leave the island and marry. You should have had girls, Rhonda! We should have locked you in a brood stall until you started breeding daughters."

Daughtahs!

"Senator!"

There was another splash in a glass, and the Senator said, "And another thing. I came to apologize for missing the funeral."

"That's all right, Senator."

"I should have been there. I should have been there. I have always been a friend to your family. But I can't take it, Rhonda. I can't take the drowning."

"You can't take the drowning, Senator. Everyone knows that."

"I thank you for your understanding. You are a good woman, Rhonda. A good woman. And another thing. I've come for a haircut, too."

"A haircut? Today?"

"Sure, sure," he said.

Senator Simon, pushing back his chair to get up, bumped into Cookie. Cookie woke with a start and immediately noticed Ruth sitting under the kitchen table. The dog barked and barked until the Senator, with some effort, bent over, lifted the corner of the tablecloth, and spotted Ruth. He laughed. "Come on out, girl," he said, and Ruth did. "You can watch me get a haircut."

The Senator took a dollar bill from his shirt pocket and laid it on the table. Mrs. Pommeroy got the old bed sheet and her shears and comb from the kitchen closet. Ruth pushed a chair into the middle of the kitchen for Simon Addams to sit on. Mrs. Pommeroy wrapped the sheet around Simon and his chair and tucked it around his neck. Only his head and boot tips showed.

She dipped the comb in a glass of water, wetted down the Senator's hair against his thick, buoy-shaped head, and parted it into narrow rows. She cut his hair one share at a time, each segment flattened between her two longest fingers, then cropped off on a neat bias. Ruth, watching these familiar gestures, knew just what would happen next. When Mrs. Pommeroy was finished with the haircut, the sleeves of her black funeral dress would be topped with the Senator's hair. She would dust his neck with talcum powder, bundle the sheet, and ask Ruth to take it outdoors and shake it. Cookie would follow Ruth outside and bark at the whipping sheet and bite at the tumbling clumps of damp hair.

"Cookie!" Senator Simon would yell. "Come on back in here now, baby!"

Later, of course, the men did visit Mrs. Pommeroy.

It was the following evening. Ruth's father walked over to the Pommeroy house because it was right next door, but the other men drove over in the unregistered, unlicensed trucks they kept for carting their trash and children around on the island. They brought blueberry cakes and casseroles as offerings from their wives and stayed in the kitchen, many of them leaning on the counters and walls. Mrs. Pommeroy made the men polite pots of coffee.

On the grass outside, below the kitchen window, Ruth Thomas was trying to teach Robin Pommeroy how to say his name or any word beginning with *r.* He was repeating after Ruth, fiercely pronouncing every consonant but the impossible one.

"ROB-in," Ruth said.

"WOB-in," he insisted. "WOB-in!"

"RAZZ-berries," Ruth said. "RHU-barb. RAD-ish."

"WAD-ish," he said.

Inside, the men offered suggestions to Mrs. Pommeroy. They'd been discussing a few things. They had some ideas about dividing the traditional Pommeroy fishing ground among them for use and care, just until one of the boys showed interest and skill in the trade. Until any one of the Pommeroy boys could maintain a boat and a fleet of traps.

"RUBB-ish," Ruth Thomas instructed Robin, outside the kitchen window.

"WUBB-ish," he declared.

"RUTH," she said to Robin. "RUTH!"

But he wouldn't even try that one; *Ruth* was much too hard. Besides, Robin was tired of the game, which only served to make him look stupid. Ruth wasn't having much fun, anyhow. The grass was full of black slugs, shiny and viscous, and Robin was busy slapping at his head. The mosquitoes were a mess that night. There hadn't been weather cold enough to eliminate them. They were biting Ruth Thomas and everyone else on the island. But they were really shocking Robin Pommeroy. In the end, the mosquitoes chased Robin and Ruth indoors, where they hid in a front closet until the men of Fort Niles began to file out of the Pommeroy house.

Ruth's father called for her, and she took his hand. Together, they walked to their home next door. Stan Thomas's good friend Angus Addams came with them. It was past dusk and getting cold, and once they were inside, Stan made a fire in the parlor wood stove. Angus sent Ruth upstairs to the closet in her father's bedroom to fetch the cribbage board, and then he sent her to the sideboard in the living room to fetch the good decks of cards. Angus set up the small, antique card table next to the stove.

Ruth sat at the table while the two men played. As always, they played quietly, each determined to win. Ruth had watched these men play cribbage hundreds of times in her young life. She knew how to be silent and useful so that she wouldn't be sent away. She fetched them beers from the icebox when fresh beers were needed. She moved their pegs along the board for them so that they wouldn't have to lean forward. And she counted aloud to them as she moved the pegs. The men said little.

Sometimes Angus would say, "Have you ever seen such luck?"

Sometimes he'd say, "I've seen better hands on an amputee."

Sometimes he'd say, "Who dealt this sorry rag?"

Ruth's father beat Angus soundly, and Angus put down his cards and told them a terrible joke.

"Some men are out fishing one day for sport, and they're drinking too much," he began. Ruth's father put down his cards, too, and sat back in his chair to listen. Angus narrated his joke with the greatest of care. He said, "So, these fellas are out fishing and they're really having a time and drinking it up. They're getting awful stewed. In fact, these fellas get to drinking so bad that one of them, the one named Mr. Smith, he falls overboard and drowns. That ruins everything. Hell! It's no fun having a fishing party when a man drowns. So the men drink some more booze, and they set to feeling pretty miserable, because nobody wants to go home and tell Mrs. Smith her husband is drowned."

"You're terrible, Angus," Ruth's father interrupted. "What kind of joke is that for tonight?"

Angus continued. "Then one of the guys has a great idea. He suggests maybe they ought to hire Mr. Smooth-Talking-Jones to go break the bad news to Mrs. Smith. That's right. It seems there's a fella in town, name of Jones, who's famous for being a real smooth talker. He's perfect for the job. He'll tell Mrs. Smith about her husband, but he'll tell her so nice, she won't even care. The other guys think, *Hey, what a great idea!* So they go find Smooth-Talking-Jones, and he says he'll do the job, no problem. So Smooth-Talking-Jones puts on his nicest suit. He puts on a tie and a hat. He goes over to the Smith house. He knocks on the door. A woman answers. Smooth-Talking-Jones says, 'Pardon me, ma'am, but ain't you the Widow Smith?' "

At this, Ruth's father laughed into his beer glass, and a thin spray of foam flew from his mug to the table. Angus Addams held up his hand, palm out. Joke wasn't finished. So he finished it.

"The lady says, 'Why, I am Mrs. Smith, but I ain't no widow!' And Smooth-Talking-Jones says, 'The fuck you ain't, sweetheart.' "

Ruth toyed with that word in her mind: *Sweethaht, sweet-hot . . .*

"Oh, that's terrible." Ruth's father rubbed his mouth. He was laughing, though. "That's terrible, Angus. Jesus Christ, what a rotten joke to tell. I can't believe you'd tell a joke like that on a night like this. Jesus Christ."

"Why, Stan? You think it sounds like someone we know?" Angus said. Then he asked, in a strange falsetto, "Ain't you the Widow Pommeroy?"

"Angus, that is terrible," Ruth's father said, laughing even harder.

"I'm not terrible. I'm telling jokes."

"You're terrible, Angus. You're terrible."

The two men laughed and laughed, and then settled down a bit. Eventually, Ruth's father and Angus Addams commenced playing cribbage once more and grew quiet.

Sometimes Ruth's father said, "Christ!"

Sometimes Ruth's father said, "I should be *shot* for that play."

At the end of the night, Angus Addams had won one game and Stan Thomas had won two. Some money was exchanged. The men put away the cards and dismantled the cribbage board. Ruth returned the board to the closet in her father's bedroom. Angus Addams folded up the card table and set it behind the sofa. The men moved into the kitchen and sat at the table. Ruth came back down, and her father patted her bottom and said to Angus, "I don't imagine Pommeroy left his wife enough money to pay you for that nice coffin your brother built."

Angus Addams said, "You kidding me? Pommeroy didn't leave any money. There's no money in that goddamn family. Not enough money for a pissant funeral, I can tell you that. Not enough money for a coffin. Not even enough money to buy a ham bone to shove up his ass so the dogs could drag his body away."

"How interesting," Ruth's father said, completely deadpan. "I'm not familiar with that tradition."

Then it was Angus Addams who was laughing. He called Ruth's father terrible.

"I'm terrible?" Stan Thomas said. "*I'm* terrible? You're the terrible one."

Something in this kept them both laughing. Ruth's father and Mr. Angus Addams, who were excellent friends, called each other terrible people all that night long. Terrible! Terrible! As if it was a kind of reassurance. They called each other terrible, rotten, deadly people.

They stayed up late, and Ruth stayed up with them, until she started crying from trying to keep herself awake. It had been a long week, and she was only nine. She was a sturdy kid, but she'd seen a funeral and heard conversations she didn't understand, and now it was past midnight, and she was exhausted.

"Hey," Angus said. "Ruthie? Ruthie? Don't cry, then. What? I thought we were friends, Ruthie."

Ruth's father said, "Poor little pie."

He took her up into his lap. She wanted to stop crying, but she couldn't. She was embarrassed. She hated crying in front of anyone.

Still, she cried until her father sent her into the living room for the deck of cards and let her sit on his lap and shuffle them, which was a game they used to play when she was small. She was too old to be sitting in his lap and shuffling cards, but it was a comfort.

"Come on, Ruthie," Angus said, "let's have a smile out of you."

Ruth tried to oblige, but it wasn't a particularly good smile. Angus asked Ruth and her father to do their funniest joke for him, the one he loved so much. And they did.

"Daddy, Daddy," Ruth said in a fake little-girlie voice. "How come all the other children get to go to school and I have to stay home?"

"Shut up and deal, kid," her father growled.

Angus Addams laughed and laughed.

"That's terrible!" he said. "You're both terrible."

2

After discovering that he is imprisoned, which he does very speedily, the lobster seems to lose all his desire for the bait, and spends his time roaming around the pit, hunting for a means of escape.

—*The Lobster Fishery of Maine*
John N. Cobb, Agent of the United States Fish Commission
1899

NINE YEARS passed.

Ruth Thomas grew into a teenager, and she was sent away to a private school for girls, located in the far-off state of Delaware. She was a good student but not the firecracker she should have been, with her brains. She worked exactly as hard as it took for her to get adequate grades, and not one bit harder. She resented having been sent away to school, although clearly something had to be done with her. At that moment in the century, in the 1970s, Fort Niles Island educated its children only through the age of thirteen. For most of the boys (future lobstermen, that is), this was plenty. For the others—bright girls and boys with bigger ambitions—special arrangements had to be made. Generally, this meant they were sent to the mainland to live with families in Rockland and attend public high school there. They came back to the island only on long vacations or over the summer. Their dads checked up on them during trips to Rockland, when it was time to sell the lobster catch.

This was the system that Ruth Thomas would have preferred. Attending high school in Rockland was the normal path, and it was what she'd expected. But an exception was made for Ruth. An expensive exception. A private education was arranged for her, far away from home. The idea, according to Ruth's mother, who was now living in Concord, New Hampshire, was to expose the girl to something other than lobster fishermen, alcoholism, ignorance, and cold weather. Ruth's father sullenly and silently gave his permission, so Ruth had no choice. She went to the school, but she made her protest known. She read the books, learned the math, ignored the other girls, and got it over with. Every summer, she returned to the island. Her mother suggested other summer activities, such as going to camp or traveling or finding an interesting job, but Ruth refused with a finality that left no room for negotiation.

It was Ruth Thomas's firm position that she belonged nowhere but on Fort Niles Island. This was the position she took with her mother: she was truly happy only on Fort Niles; Fort Niles was in her blood and soul; and the only people who understood her were the residents of Fort Niles Island. None of this, it must be said, was entirely true.

It was important to Ruth in principle that she feel happy on Fort Niles, although, for the most part, she was pretty bored there. She missed the island when she was away from it, but when she returned, she immediately found herself at a loss for diversion. She made a point of taking a long walk around the shoreline the minute she came home ("I've been thinking about this all *year!*" she would say), but the walk took only a few hours, and what did she think about on that walk? Not much. There was a seagull; there was a seal; there was another seagull. The scenery was as familiar to her as her bedroom ceiling. She took books down to the shore, claiming that she loved to read near the pounding surf, but the sad fact is that many places on this Earth offer better reading environments than wet, barnacle-covered rocks. When Ruth was away from Fort Niles, the island became endowed with the characteristics of a distant paradise, but when she returned to it, she found her home cold and damp and windy and uncomfortable.

Still, whenever she was on Fort Niles, Ruth wrote letters to her mother, saying, "Finally I can breathe again!"

More than anything, Ruth's passion for Fort Niles was an expression of protest. It was her resistance against those who would send her away, supposedly for her own good. Ruth would have much preferred to determine what was good for her. She had great confidence that she knew herself best and that, given free rein, would have made more correct choices. She certainly wouldn't have elected to send herself to an elite private school hundreds of miles away, where girls were concerned primarily with the care of their skin and horses. No horses for Ruth, thank you. She was not that kind of girl. She was more rugged. It was boats that Ruth loved, or so she constantly said. It was Fort Niles Island that Ruth loved. It was fishing that Ruth loved.

In truth, Ruth had spent time working with her father on his lobster boat, and it had never been a terrific experience. She was strong enough to do the work, but the monotony killed her. Working as a sternman meant standing in the back of the boat, hauling up traps, picking out lobsters, baiting traps and shoving them back in the water, and hauling up more traps. And more traps and more traps. It meant getting up before dawn and eating sandwiches for breakfast and lunch. It meant seeing the same scenery again and again, day after day, and rarely venturing more than two miles from shore. It meant spending hour upon hour alone with her father on a small boat, where the two of them never seemed to get along.

There were too many things for them to argue about. Stupid things. Ruth's father used to eat his sandwich and throw the lunch bag right in the ocean, and that would drive Ruth crazy. He would throw his soda can in after it. She'd yell at him for this, and he'd sulk, and the rest of the trip would be tense and silent. Or he might get fed up and spend the whole trip scolding and berating her. She didn't work fast enough; she didn't handle the lobsters carefully enough; she was going to step in that pile of rope one of these days and get pulled overboard and drown if she didn't pay closer attention. That kind of thing.

On one of their early trips, Ruth warned her father about a barrel drifting up on his "port side," and he laughed in her face.

"Port side?" he said. "This isn't the Navy, Ruth. You don't need to worry about port and starboard. The only direction you need to worry about is staying out of my way."

Ruth seemed to get on his nerves even when she wasn't trying to, although sometimes she did so on purpose, just to pass the time. One wet summer day, for instance, they pulled up string after string of traps and found no lobsters. Ruth's father got more and more agitated. He was catching nothing but seaweed, crabs, and urchins. Eight or nine strings later, however, Ruth pulled a good-sized male lobster out of a trap.

"Dad, what's this?" she asked innocently, holding up the lobster. "I've never seen one of these before. Maybe we can take it into town and sell it to somebody."

"That's not funny," her father said, although Ruth herself thought it was pretty good.

The boat stank. It was cold even in the summer. In bad weather, the boat deck jumped and popped, and Ruth's legs ached from the strain of keeping her balance. It was a small boat and had barely any shelter. She had to pee in a bucket and empty it overboard. Her hands were always freezing, and her father would yell if she took a break to warm her hands around the hot exhaust pipe. He never worked with gloves, he said, even in December. Why couldn't she handle the cold in the middle of July?

Yet when Ruth's mother asked Ruth what she wanted to do with her summer, Ruth invariably replied that she wanted to work on a lobster boat.

"I want to work with my dad," Ruth said. "I'm really only happy out on the water."

As for her relations with the other islanders, she may not have been as perfectly understood by them as she told her mother. She loved Mrs. Pommeroy. She loved the Addams brothers, and they loved her. But because of her long spells in Delaware getting educated, she was pretty much forgotten by everyone else, or, worse, disowned. She was no longer like them. Truth to tell, she'd never been all that much like them in the first place. She'd always been an inward-looking child, not, say, like the Pommeroy boys, who screamed and fought and made perfect sense to everyone. And now that Ruth passed most of her time someplace very far off, she talked differently. She read an awful lot of books. And, to many of her neighbors, she seemed stuck up.

Ruth graduated from boarding school in late May of 1976. She had no plans for the future except to return to Fort Niles, where she so obviously belonged. She made no move to attend college. She never even looked at the college brochures scattered around her school, never responded to the advice of her teachers, never gave any notice to the shy hints of her mother.

In that May of 1976, Ruth Thomas turned eighteen. She was five feet six inches tall. She had shiny hair that was almost black, and it came to her shoulders; she wore it in a ponytail every day. Her hair was so thick, she could sew a button on a coat with it. Her face was roundish, her eyes were wide apart, and she had an inoffensive nose and long, pretty eyelashes. Her skin was darker than anyone else's on Fort Niles, and she tanned to a smooth, even brown. She was muscular and a little heavy for her height. She had a bigger rear end than she wanted, but she didn't fuss about it too much, because the last thing she wanted to sound like was those girls at school in Delaware who fussed over their figures annoyingly, uninterruptedly, odiously. She was a heavy sleeper. She was independent. She was sarcastic.

When Ruth returned to Fort Niles at the independent, sarcastic age of eighteen, she did so in her father's lobster boat. He picked her up at the bus station in the rotten truck he kept parked down by the ferry landing, the truck he used for his business and shopping whenever he came to town, which was approximately every two weeks. He picked Ruth up, accepted a slightly ironic kiss from her, and immediately announced that he was dropping her off at the grocery store to pick up supplies while he had a goddamn talk with his goddamn wholesaler, the miserable bastard. ("You know what we need out there," he said. "Just spend fifty bucks.") Then he told Ruth the reasons that his goddamn wholesaler was a miserable bastard, all of which she had heard before in careful detail. She drifted out of the conversation, such as it was, and considered how odd it was that her father, who had not seen her in several months, did not think to ask about her graduation ceremony. Not that she cared. But it was odd.

The boat ride back to Fort Niles took more than four hours, during which Ruth and her father did not converse much, because the boat was loud and because she had to slip around in the stern to make sure that the boxes of groceries didn't tip over or get wet. She thought about her plans for the summer. She had no plans for the summer. While loading the boat, her father had informed her that he'd hired a sternman for the season—Robin Pommeroy, of all people. Ruth's father had no work for his daughter. Although she griped at him for leaving her out, she was secretly pleased not to be working for him again. She would have acted as his sternman strictly on principle, had he asked, but she would have been miserable out there. So it was a relief. Still, it meant she had nothing to do with her time. She was not sufficiently confident of her abilities as a sternman to approach any other fisherman and ask for a job, even if she had really, really wanted one, which she really, really did not. Besides, as her father had also informed her, everyone on Fort Niles already had help. All the partnerships had been negotiated. Weeks before Ruth showed up, every old man on Fort Niles had found a young man to do the muscle work in the back of the boat.

"Maybe you can pick up if other kids get sick or fired," her father shouted to her suddenly, midway through the journey back to Fort Niles.

"Yeah, maybe I'll do that," Ruth shouted back.

She was already thinking ahead to the next three months and—who was she kidding?—to the rest of her life, which had absolutely no shape to it. *Good God!* she thought. She was facing backward, sitting on a box of canned goods. Rockland was long since out of sight on this misty day, and the other islands, inhabited or not, that they passed so slowly and so *loudly* looked as small and brown and wet as lumps of shit. Or so Ruth thought. She wondered whether she could get another job on Fort Niles, although the idea of a job on Fort Niles that didn't involve lobstering was something of a joke. *Ha-ha.*

What the hell am I going to do with my time? Ruth thought. She felt an awful and familiar sense of boredom rise within her as the boat chugged and bumped over the cold Atlantic bay. As far as she could see, there was nothing for her to do, and she knew exactly what that meant. Nothing to do meant hanging around with the few other islanders who had nothing to do. Ruth could see it coming. She was going to spend her summer hanging around with Mrs. Pommeroy and Senator Simon Addams. She could see it coming clearly. It wasn't so bad, she told herself. Mrs. Pommeroy and Senator Simon were her friends; she was fond of them. They'd have lots to talk about. They'd ask her all about her graduation ceremony. It wouldn't be so boring, really.

But the uneasy, unpleasant sense of approaching boredom remained in Ruth's belly, like seasickness. Finally she drove the boredom—*already!*—down by composing in her mind a letter to her mother. She would write it that night, in her bedroom. The letter would begin, "Dear Mom: As soon as I stepped back onto Fort Niles, all the tension drained out of my body and I took the first deep breaths I have taken in months and months. The air smelled like hope!"

That's exactly what she would say. Ruth decided this on her father's lobster boat precisely two hours before Fort Niles was even in sight, and she spent the rest of the trip mentally composing the letter, which was most poetic. The exercise cheered her up a good deal.

Senator Simon Addams was seventy-three years old that summer, and he had a special project going. It was an ambitious and eccentric project. He was going to search for an elephant's tusk that, he believed, was buried in the mudflats at Potter Beach. The Senator thought there might even be two tusks buried out there, though he'd announced that he would be happy to find just one.

Senator Simon's conviction that 138 years of seawater would not have impaired such strong material as pure ivory provided him with the necessary confidence for his search. He knew the tusks must be somewhere. They may have been separated from their skeleton and from each other, but they would not have decomposed. They could not have dissolved. They were either buried in the sand far out at sea or they had washed up on a beach. And the Senator believed they may well have found their way to Fort Niles Island. Those rare elephant tusks may have been swept by currents — as wreckage had been swept for centuries — right up on Potter Beach. Why not?

The tusks the Senator sought were from an elephant that had been a passenger aboard the 400-ton steamboat *Clarice Monroe*, a vessel that went down right outside Worthy Channel in late October of 1838. It was a famous event at the time. The steamer, a wooden side-wheeler, caught fire just after midnight, during a sudden snowstorm. The fire itself may have been caused by so simple a mishap as a tipped lamp, but the storm winds caught and spread it before it could be contained, and the deck of the steamer was quickly blanketed in flame.

The captain of the *Clarice Monroe* was a drinker. The fire was almost certainly not his fault, but it was his undoing. He panicked shamefully. Without waking the passengers or crew, he ordered the one sailor on watch to lower a single lifeboat, in which he, his wife, and the young sailor rowed away. The captain left the doomed *Clarice Monroe*, his passengers, and his cargo to burn. The three survivors in the rowboat became lost in the storm, rowed for a full day, lost the power to row any further, and drifted for one day more. When they were picked up by a merchant marine vessel, the captain was dead of exposure, his wife had lost her fingers, feet, and ears to frostbite, and the young sailor had completely lost his mind.

Without her captain, the *Clarice Monroe*, still burning, had drifted against the rocks off Fort Niles Island, where she broke up among the waves. There were no survivors among the ninety-seven passengers. Many of the corpses drifted over to Potter Beach, piling up in the brine and mud alongside the charred and battered wooden wreckage of the steamboat. The men of Fort Niles gathered the corpses, wrapped them in burlap, and stored them in the icehouse. Some were identified by family members who came to Fort Niles throughout the month of October on ferry boats to collect their brothers and wives and mothers and children. Those unfortunates who were not claimed were buried in the Fort Niles cemetery, under small granite markers inscribed, simply, DROWNED.

But the steamboat had lost other cargo.

The *Clarice Monroe* had been transporting, from New Brunswick down to Boston, a small circus made up of several remarkable items: six white show horses, several trick monkeys, a camel, a trained bear, a pack of performing dogs, a cage of tropical birds, and an African elephant. After the ship broke up, the circus horses tried to swim through the snowstorm. Three drowned, and the other three reached the shores of Fort Niles Island. When the weather cleared the next morning, everyone on the island turned out to see the three magnificent white mares gingerly picking their way across the snowy boulders.

None of the other animals made it. The young sailor from the *Clarice Monroe*, found in the rowboat with his dead captain and the captain's devastated wife, driven to delirium by exposure to the storm, said upon his rescue — insisted! — that he had seen the elephant jump over the railing of the burning wreck and swim strongly through the waves, its tusks and trunk lifted high above the churning, icy water. He swore he had seen the elephant swimming through the salty snow as he himself rowed away from the wreck. He saw the elephant swim and swim and then, sounding one last mighty trumpet, sink beneath the waves.

The sailor, as noted, was out of his mind at the time of his rescue, but there were those who believed his story. Senator Simon Addams had always believed it. He'd heard the story from his earliest childhood and had been fascinated by it. And it was the tusks of that circus elephant which the Senator now sought to recover, 138 years later, in the spring of 1976.

He wanted to put at least one tusk on display at the Fort Niles Museum of Natural History. In 1976, the Fort Niles Museum of Natural History did not exist, but the Senator was working on it. He'd been collecting artifacts and specimens for the museum for years, storing them in his basement. The whole idea was his. He had no backers, and he was the sole curator. He believed a tusk would make a most impressive centerpiece to his collection.

The Senator, obviously, couldn't search for the tusks himself. He was a sturdy old man, but he was in no condition to dig around in the mud all day. Even if he were younger, he would not have had the courage to wade out into the loose soup of seawater and shifting mudflats that extended from Potter Beach. He was much too afraid of the water. So he had taken on an assistant, Webster Pommeroy.

Webster Pommeroy, who was twenty-three that summer, had nothing else to do anyway. Every day, the Senator and Webster would head down to Potter Beach, where Webster would look for the elephant's tusks. It was a perfect task for Webster Pommeroy, because Webster Pommeroy was not capable of doing anything else. His meekness and seasickness prevented his becoming a lobsterman or a sternman, but his problems went deeper than that. Something was wrong with Webster Pommeroy. Everyone saw it. Something had happened to Webster the day he saw his father's corpse—eyeless and puffy—sprawled out on the Fort Niles dock. Webster Pommeroy, at that moment, broke; fell to bits. He stopped growing, stopped developing, nearly stopped speaking. He turned into a twitchy and nervous and deeply troubled local tragedy. At twenty-three, he was as slim and small as he'd been at fourteen. He seemed to be forever cast in a boy's frame. He seemed to be forever trapped in that moment of recognizing his dead father.

Senator Simon Addams had a sincere concern for Webster Pommeroy. He wanted to help the boy. The boy broke the Senator's heart. He felt the boy needed a *vocation*. It took the Senator several years to discover Webster's worth, though, because it was not immediately clear what, if anything, Webster Pommeroy could do. The Senator's only idea was to enlist the young man in his project for the Museum of Natural History.

The Senator initially sent Webster to the homes of neighbors on Fort Niles, requesting that they donate to the museum any interesting artifacts or antiques, but Webster was a shy and miserable failure at the task. He would knock on a door, but when the neighbor opened it, he was likely to stand there, mute, nervously tapping his feet. Every local housewife was disturbed by his behavior. Webster Pommeroy, standing on the doorstep, looking as if he was about to cry, was not a born solicitor.

The Senator next tried to enlist Webster in building a holding shed in the Addamses' back yard to house the Senator's growing collection of items suitable for the museum. But Webster, while conscientious, was not a natural carpenter. He was neither strong nor handy. His tremors made him useless in the construction work. Worse than useless, indeed. He was a danger to himself and others, because he was always dropping saws and drills, always hammering his fingers. So the Senator took Webster off the building detail.

Other tasks the Senator created were similarly unsuitable for Webster. It was beginning to look as though Webster could do nothing. It took nearly nine years for the Senator to discover what Webster was good at.

It was mud.

Down at Potter Beach was a veritable pasture of mud, revealed fully only at low tide. During the lowest tides, it was more than ten acres of mud, wide and flat and smelling of rancid blood. Men had periodically dug clams in this mud, and they frequently turned up hidden treasures—ancient boat parts, wooden buoys, lost boots, odd bones, bronze spoons, and extinct iron tools. The muddy cove apparently was a natural magnet for lost objects, and so it was that the Senator conceived the idea of searching the flats for the elephant's tusks. Why would they not be there? Where else would they be?

He asked Webster whether he was interested in wading through the mud, like a clam digger, seeking artifacts in a systematic manner. Could Webster examine the shallower areas of the Potter Beach mudflats, perhaps, wearing high boots? Would that distress Webster too greatly? Webster Pommeroy shrugged. He didn't seem distressed. And so it was that Webster Pommeroy began his career of searching the mudflats. And he was brilliant at it.

As it turned out, Webster Pommeroy could move through any mud. He could negotiate mud that was nearly up to his chest. Webster Pommeroy could move through mud like a vessel made for the task, and he found marvelous treasures—a wristwatch, a shark's tooth, a whale's skull, a complete wheelbarrow. Day after day, the Senator would sit on the dirty rocks by the shore and watch Webster's progress. He watched Webster search through the mud every day of the summer of 1975.

And when Ruth Thomas came home from boarding school in late May of 1976, the Senator and Webster were at it again. With nothing else to do, with no work and no friends of her age, Ruth Thomas developed the hobby of walking down to the Potter Beach mudflats every morning to watch Webster Pommeroy scour the mud. She would sit with Senator Simon Addams on the beach for hours at a time, watching. At the end of each day, the three would walk back to town together.

They made a strange threesome—the Senator and Ruth and Webster. Webster was a strange one in any company. Senator Simon Addams, an unusually large man, had a misshapen head; it looked as if it had been kicked in at one time and had healed poorly. He teased himself about his odd fat nose. ("I have nothing to do with the shape of my nose," he liked to say. "It was a birthday present.") And he frequently wrung his great doughy hands. He had a strong body but was subject to severe bouts of fear; he called himself a champion coward. He often looked as if he was afraid someone was about to come around the corner and smack him. This was quite the opposite of Ruth Thomas, who often looked as if she was about to smack the next person who came around the corner.

Sometimes, as Ruth sat on the beach, looking at huge Senator Simon and tiny Webster Pommeroy, she wondered how she had become involved with these two weak, weird men. How had they become her good friends? What would the girls back in Delaware think if they knew of this little gang? She was not embarrassed by the Senator and Webster, she assured herself. Whom would she be embarrassed around, all the way out there on Fort Niles Island? But those two were odd ones, and anyone from off the island who might have caught a glimpse of the threesome would have thought Ruth odd, too.

Still, she had to admit, it was fascinating to watch Webster crawl around in the mud, looking for a tusk. Ruth had not a shred of faith that Webster would find an elephant's tusk, but it was entertaining to watch him work. It was really something to see.

"That's dangerous, what Webster's doing out there," the Senator would say to Ruth as they watched Webster head deeper and deeper into the mud.

It was indeed dangerous, but the Senator had no intention of interfering, even as Webster sank into the loosest, most collapsing, most embracing mud, his arms submerged, feeling about for artifacts in the blind muck. The Senator was nervous and Ruth was nervous, but Webster moved stoically, without terror. Such moments, in fact, were the only times his twitchy body was ever still. He was calm in the mud. He was never afraid in the mud. Sometimes he too seemed to be sinking.

He would pause in his search, and the Senator and Ruth Thomas would see him slowly descending. It was frightful. It did look at times as if they were about to lose him.

"Should we go after him?" the Senator would suggest, meekly.

"Not in that fucking deathtrap," Ruth would say. "Not me."

(Ruth had developed something of a mouth by the time she was eighteen years old. Her father often commented on it. "I don't know where you got that goddamn mouth of yours," he'd say, and she would reply, "Now there's a goddamn mystery.")

"Are you sure he's all right?" the Senator would ask.

"No," Ruth would say. "I think he may be going under. But I'm not going after him, and neither are you. Not in that fucking deathtrap."

No, not her. Not out there, where forgotten lobsters and clams and mussels and sea worms grew to godless size, and where Christ only knew what else hovered about. When the Scottish settlers first came to Fort Niles, they had leaned over those very mudflats from huge rocks and had dug out, with gaffs, living lobsters as big as any man. They had written of this in their journals; descriptions of pulling out hideous five-foot monster lobsters, ancient as alligators and caked with mud, grown to repulsive extremes from centuries of unmolested hiding. Webster himself, sifting with his bare, blind hands, had found in this mud some petrified lobster claws the size of baseball mitts. He had dug out clams the size of melons, urchins, dogfish, dead fish. No way was Ruth Thomas going in there. No way.

So the Senator and Ruth would have to sit and watch Webster sink. What could they do? Nothing. They sat in tense silence. Sometimes a gull would fly overhead. Other times, there was no movement at all. They watched and waited, and occasionally felt panic simmering in their hearts. But Webster himself never panicked in the mud. He would stand, sunk past his hips, and wait. He seemed to be waiting for something unknown that, after a long period, he would find. Or perhaps it would find him. Webster would begin to move through the sinking mud.

It was not clear to Ruth how he did this. From the beach, it looked as though a rail had risen from below to reach Webster's bare feet, and he was now standing safely on this rail, which was taking him, slowly and smoothly, away from a dangerous spot. It looked, from the beach, like a clean, gliding rescue.

Why was he never stuck? Why was he never cut by clams, glass, lobsters, mollusks, iron, stone? All the hidden dangers in the mud seemed to shift politely aside to let Webster Pommeroy pass. Of course, he wasn't always in danger. Sometimes he would dawdle around in the shallow, ankle-deep mud near the shore, staring down, expressionless. That could get boring. And when it got too boring, Senator Simon and Ruth, sitting on the rocks, would talk to each other. For the most part, they talked about maps and explorations and shipwrecks and hidden treasure, the Senator's favorite topics of conversation. Especially shipwrecks.

One afternoon, Ruth told the Senator that she might try to find work on a lobster boat. This wasn't entirely true, although it was exactly what Ruth had written to her mother in a long letter the day before. Ruth *wanted* to want to work on a lobster boat, but the actual desire was not there. She mentioned the idea to the Senator only because she liked the sound of it.

"I've been thinking," she said, "of finding work on a lobster boat."

The Senator instantly grew annoyed. He hated to hear Ruth talk of setting foot on any boat. It made him nervous enough when she went to Rockland with her father for the day. All during the times of Ruth's life when she'd worked with her dad, the Senator had been upset. He imagined, every day, that she would fall over and drown or the boat would sink or there'd be a terrible storm that would wash her away. So when Ruth brought up the idea, the Senator said he would not tolerate the risk of losing her to the sea. He said he would expressly forbid Ruth to work on a lobster boat.

"Do you want to *die?*" he asked. "Do you want to drown?"

"No, I want to make some money."

"Absolutely not. Absolutely *not.* You do not belong on a boat. If you need money, I'll give you money."

"That's hardly a dignified way to make a living."

"Why do you want to work on a boat? With all your brains? Boats are for idiots like the Pommeroy boys. You should leave boating to them. You know what you really should do? Go inland and stay there. Go live in Nebraska. That's what I'd do. Get away from the ocean."

"If lobstering is good enough for the Pommeroy boys, it's good enough for me," Ruth said. She didn't believe this, but it sounded principled.

"Oh, for heaven's sake, Ruth."

"You've been encouraging the Pommeroy boys to be sailors forever, Senator. You're always trying to get them fishing jobs. You're always telling them they should be circumnavigators. I don't see why you shouldn't give me a little encouragement, every now and again."

"I do give you encouragement."

"Not to be a fisherman."

"I will kill myself if you become a fisherman, Ruth. I will kill myself every single day."

"What if I wanted to be a fisherman, though? What if I wanted to be a sailor? What if I wanted to join the Coast Guard? What if I wanted to be a circumnavigator?"

"You don't want to be any circumnavigator."

"I might want to be a circumnavigator."

Ruth did not want to be a circumnavigator. She was making small talk. She and the Senator spent hours talking nonsense like this. Day after day. Neither one paid too much mind to the nonsense-speak of the other. Senator Simon patted his dog's head and said, "Cookie says, 'What's Ruth talking about, a circumnavigator? Ruth doesn't want to be a circumnavigator.' Didn't you say that, Cookie? Isn't that right, Cookie?"

"Stay out of this, Cookie," Ruth said.

A week or so later, the Senator brought up the topic again while the two of them watched Webster in the mudflats. This is how the Senator and Ruth had always talked, in long, eternal circles. They had, in fact, only one conversation, the one they'd been having from the time Ruth was about ten years old. They went round and round. They covered the same ground again and again, like a pair of schoolgirls.

"Why do you need experience on a fishing boat, for heaven's sake?" Senator Simon said. "You're not stuck on this island for life like the Pommeroys. They're poor slobs. Fishing is all they can do."

Ruth had forgotten that she'd even mentioned getting work on a fishing boat. But now she defended the idea. "A woman could do that job as well as anyone."

"I'm not saying a woman couldn't do it. I'm saying nobody should do it. It's a terrible job. It's a job for jerks. And if everyone tried to become a lobsterman, pretty soon all the lobsters would be gone."

"There're enough lobsters out there for everyone."

"Absolutely not, Ruthie. For heaven's sake, who ever told you that?"

"My dad."

"Well, enough lobsters for him."

"What's that supposed to mean?"

"He's Greedy Number Two. He'll always get his."

"Don't call my father that. He hates that nickname."

The Senator patted his dog. "Your dad is Greedy Number Two. My brother is Greedy Number One. Everyone knows that. Even Cookie here knows that."

Ruth looked out at Webster in the mudflats and did not reply. After a few minutes, Senator Simon said, "You know, there are no lifeboats on lobster boats. It's not safe for you."

"Why should they have lifeboats on lobster boats? Lobster boats aren't much bigger than lifeboats in the first place."

"Not that a lifeboat can really save a person . . ."

"Of course a lifeboat can save a person. Lifeboats save people all the time," Ruth asserted.

"Even in a lifeboat, you'd better hope to get rescued soon. If they find you floating around in your lifeboat in the first hour after a shipwreck, of course, you'll be fine . . ."

"Who's talking about shipwrecks?" Ruth asked, but she knew very well that the Senator was always about three minutes away from talking about shipwrecks. He'd been talking to her about shipwrecks for years.

The Senator said, "If you are not rescued in your lifeboat in the first hour, your chances of being rescued at all become very slim. Very slim, indeed, Ruthie. Slimmer with every hour. After a whole day lost at sea in a lifeboat, you can assume that you won't be rescued at all. What would you do then?"

"I'd row."

"You'd row. You would *row*, if you were stuck on a lifeboat and the sun was going down, with no rescue in sight? You would *row*. That's your plan?"

"I guess I'd have to figure something out."

"Figure what out? What is there to figure out? How to row to another continent?"

"Jesus, Senator. I'm never going to be lost at sea in a lifeboat. I promise you."

"Once you're in a shipwreck," the Senator said, "you will be rescued only by chance—if you are rescued at all. And remember, Ruthie, most shipwreck survivors are injured. It's not as if they jumped off the edge of a boat in calm water for a little swim. Most shipwreck survivors have broken legs or ghastly cuts or burns. And what do you think it is that kills you in the end?"

Ruth knew the answer. "Exposure?" she guessed wrongly, just to keep the conversation going.

"No."

"Sharks?"

"No. Lack of water. Thirst."

"Is that right?" Ruth asked politely.

But now the subject of sharks had arrived, the Senator paused. Finally he said, "In the tropics, the sharks come right up into the boat. They bring their snouts into the boat, like dogs sniffing around. But barracudas are worse. Let's say you've been wrecked. You're clinging to a piece of wreckage. A barracuda comes over and sinks his teeth into you. You can rip him off, Ruthie, but his head will stay attached to you. Like a snapping turtle, Ruthie. A barracuda will hold on to you long after he's dead. That's right."

"I don't worry about barracudas too much around here, Senator. And I don't think you should worry about barracudas, either."

"Well, how about your bluefish, then? You don't have to be in the tropics for bluefish, Ruthie. We've got packs of bluefish right out there." Senator Simon Addams waved past the mudflats and Webster, pointing to the open Atlantic. "And bluefish hunt in packs, like wolves. And stingrays! Shipwreck survivors have said that giant rays came right up under their boat and spent the whole day there, hovering. They used to call them blanket fish. You could find rays out there bigger than your little lifeboat. They ripple along under your boat like the shadow of death."

"That's very vivid, Senator. Well done."

The Senator asked, "What kind of sandwich is that, Ruthie?"

"Ham salad. Want half?"

"No, no. You need it."

"You can have a bite."

"What's on there? Mustard?"

"Why don't you have a bite, Senator?"

"No, no. You need it. I'll tell you another thing. People lose their minds in a lifeboat. They lose their ideas about time. They might be out there in an open boat for twenty days. Then they get rescued, and they're surprised to find that they can't walk. Their feet are rotting from waterbite, and they have open sores from sitting in pools of saltwater; they have injuries from the wreck and burns from the sun; and they're surprised to find, Ruthie, that they can't walk. They never have any understanding of their situation."

"Delirium."

"That's right. Delirium. Exactly. Some men in a lifeboat get a condition called 'shared delirium.' Let's say there are two men in a boat. They both lose their minds the same way. One man says, 'I'm going over to the tavern for a beer,' and steps over the side and drowns. The second man says, 'I'll join you, Ed,' and then he steps over the side and drowns, too."

"With the sharks lurking."

"And the bluefish. And here's another common shared delusion, Ruthie. Say there are only two men in a lifeboat. When they do get rescued, they'll both swear that there was a third man with them the whole time. They'll say, 'Where's my friend?' And the rescuers will tell them, 'Your friend is in the bed right next to you. He's safe.' And the men will say, 'No! Where's my other friend? Where's the other man?' But there never was any other man. They won't believe this. For the rest of their lives they'll wonder: Where's the other man?"

Ruth Thomas handed the Senator half of her sandwich, and he ate it quickly.

"In the Arctic, of course, they die from the cold," he continued.

"Of course."

"They fall asleep. People who fall asleep in lifeboats never wake up."

"Of course they don't."

Other days, they talked about mapmaking. The Senator was a big fan of Ptolemy. He bragged about Ptolemy as if Ptolemy were his gifted son.

"Nobody altered Ptolemy's maps until 1511!" he'd say proudly. "Now that's quite a run, Ruth. Thirteen hundred years, that guy was the expert! Not bad, Ruth. Not bad at all."

Another favorite topic of the Senator's was the shipwreck of the *Victoria* and the *Camperdown*. This one came up time after time. It didn't need a particular trigger. One Saturday afternoon in the middle of June, for instance, Ruth was telling the Senator about how much she'd hated the graduation ceremony at her school, and the Senator said, "Remember the wreck of the *Victoria* and the *Camperdown*, Ruthie!"

"OK," Ruth said, agreeably, "if you insist."

And Ruth Thomas did remember the wreck of the *Victoria* and the *Camperdown*, because the Senator had been telling her about the wreck of the *Victoria* and the *Camperdown* since she was a toddler. This wreck was even more disturbing for him than the *Titanic*.

The *Victoria* and the *Camperdown* were the flagships of the mighty British Navy. In 1893, they collided with each other in open daylight on calm seas because a commander issued a foolish order during maneuvers. The wreck agitated the Senator so much because it had occurred on a day when no boat should have sunk, and because the sailors were the finest in the world. Even the boats were the finest in the world, and the officers were the brightest in the British Navy, but the boats went down. The *Victoria* and the *Camperdown* collided because the fine officers—fully knowing that the order they had received was a foolish one—followed it out of a sense of duty and died for it. The *Victoria* and the *Camperdown* proved that anything can happen on the sea. No matter how calm the weather, no matter how skilled the crew, a person in a boat was never safe.

In the hours after the collision of the *Victoria* and the *Camperdown*, as the Senator had been telling Ruth Thomas for years, the sea was filled with drowning men. The propellers of the sinking ship chewed through the men horribly. They were chopped to pieces, he had always emphasized.

"They were chopped to pieces, Ruthie," the Senator said.

She didn't see how this related to her story about graduation, but she let it go.

"I know, Senator," she said. "I know."

The next week, back at Potter Beach, Ruth and the Senator got to talking again about shipwrecks.

"What about the *Margaret B. Rouss?*" Ruth asked, after the Senator had been quiet for a long time. "That shipwreck ended pretty well for everyone."

She offered up this ship's name carefully. Sometimes the name *Margaret B. Rouss* would calm the Senator down, but sometimes it would agitate him.

"Jesus Christ, Ruthie!" he exploded. "Jesus Christ!"

This time it agitated him.

"The *Margaret B. Rouss* was filled with lumber, and it took forever to sink! You know that, Ruthie. Jesus Christ! You know it was an exception. You know it's not usually that easy to be shipwrecked. And I'll tell you another thing. It is not pleasant to be torpedoed under any conditions, with any cargo, no matter what happened to the crew of the goddamn *Margaret B. Rouss.*"

"And what did happen to the crew, Senator?"

"You know full well what happened to the crew of the *Margaret B. Rouss.*"

"They rowed forty miles—"

"—forty-five miles."

"They rowed forty-five miles to Monte Carlo, where they befriended the Prince of Monaco. And they lived in luxury from that point forward. That's a happy story about a shipwreck, isn't it?"

"An unusually easy shipwreck, Ruthie."

"I'll say."

"An exception."

"My father says it's an exception when any boat sinks."

"Well, isn't he a smartie? And aren't you a smartie, too? You think because of the *Margaret B. Rouss* it's safe for you to spend your life working on the water in someone's lobster boat?"

"I'm not spending my life on any water, Senator. All I said was maybe I could get a job spending three months on the water. Most of the time I'd be less than two miles from shore. I was just saying I want to work on the water for the summer."

"You know it's exceedingly dangerous to put any boat on the open sea, Ruth. It's very dangerous out there. And most people aren't going to be able to row any forty-five miles to any Monte Carlo."

"I'm sorry I brought it up."

"In most conditions, you'd be dead from exposure by then. There was a shipwreck in the Arctic Circle. The men were in lifeboats for three days, up to their knees in icy water."

"Which shipwreck?"

"I do not recall the name."

"Really?" Ruth had never heard of a shipwreck the Senator did not know by name.

"The name doesn't matter. The wrecked sailors landed on an

Icelandic island eventually. They all had frostbite. The Eskimos tried to revive their frozen limbs. What did the Eskimos do, Ruthie? They rubbed the men's feet vigorously with oil. Vigorously! The men were screaming, begging the Eskimos to stop. But the Eskimos kept on vigorously rubbing the men's feet with oil. I can't recall the name of the shipwreck. But you should remember that when you get on a boat."

"I'm not planning on sailing to Iceland."

"Some of those men on the Icelandic island fainted from the pain of the vigorous rubbing, and they died right there."

"I'm not saying that shipwrecks are good, Senator."

"Every one of those men eventually needed amputations."

"Senator?"

"To the knee, Ruthie."

"Senator?" Ruth said again.

"They died from the pain of the rubbing."

"Senator, please."

"The survivors had to stay in the Arctic until the next summer, and the only thing they had for food was blubber, Ruth."

"Please," she said.

Please. *Please.*

Because there was Webster, standing before them. He was coated in mud up to his skinny waist. He had tight curls sweated into his hair and dashes of mud across his face. And he was holding an elephant's tusk flat across his filthy, outstretched hands.

"Oh, Senator," Ruth said. "Oh, my God."

Webster laid the tusk on the sand before the Senator's feet, as one would lay a gift before a regent. Well, the Senator had no words for this gift. The three people on the beach—the old man, the young woman, the tiny, muddy young man—regarded the elephant tusk. No one moved until Cookie rose up stiffly and slouched toward the thing with suspicion.

"No, Cookie," Senator Simon said, and the dog assumed the posture of a Sphinx, her nose stretched toward the tusk as if to smell it.

At last, in an apologetic and hesitant way, Webster said, "I guess he was a small elephant."

Indeed, the tusk was small. Very small for an elephant that had grown to a mighty size during 138 years of myth. The tusk was slightly longer than one of Webster's arms. It was a slim tusk, with a modest arc. At one end was a dull point, like a thumb. At the other end was the ragged edge of its break from the skeleton. There were deep black, cracked grooves in the ivory.

"He was just a small elephant, I guess," Webster repeated, because the Senator had not yet responded. This time, Webster sounded almost desperate. "I guess we thought it would be bigger, right?"

The Senator stood up, as slowly and stiffly as if he'd been sitting on the beach for 138 years, waiting for the tusk. He stared at it some more, and then he put his arm around Webster.

"That's a good job, son," he said.

Webster sank to his knees, and the Senator eased himself down beside him and put his hand on the boy's lank shoulder.

"Are you disappointed, Webster?" he asked. "Did you think that I would be disappointed? It's a beautiful tusk."

Webster shrugged, and his face looked stricken. A breeze came up, and Webster gave a thin shiver.

"I guess it was just a small elephant," he repeated.

Ruth said, "Webster, it's a terrific elephant tusk. You did a good job, Webster. You did a great job."

Then Webster gave two hard sobs.

"Oh, come on, now, boy," the Senator said, and his voice, too, was choked. Webster was crying. Ruth turned her head. She could still hear him, though, making those sad noises, so she stood up and walked away from the rocks toward the spruce trees lining the shore. She left Webster and the Senator sitting on the beach for a good long time while she wandered among the trees, picking up sticks and breaking them. The mosquitoes were after her, but she didn't care. She hated to see people crying. Every once in a while she looked toward the beach, but she could see that Webster was still sobbing and the Senator was still comforting him, and she wanted no part of it.

Ruth sat herself down, with her back to the beach, on a mossy log. She lifted a flat rock in front of her, and a salamander scooted out, giving her a start. Maybe she'd become a veterinarian, she thought absently. She'd recently read a book, given to her by the Senator, about the breeding of bird dogs, and she had found it rather beautiful. The book, written in 1870, had the loveliest language. She'd been moved almost to tears by a description of the best Chesapeake labrador the author had ever seen, one that had retrieved a downed seabird by leaping over crashing ice floes and swimming far out past the point of invisibility. The dog, whose name was Bugle, had returned to shore, nearly frozen to death, but carrying the bird ever so gently in its soft mouth. Not a mark on it.

Ruth stole a glance over her shoulder back to Webster and the Senator. Webster appeared to have stopped crying. She wandered down to the shoreline, where Webster was sitting, staring ahead grimly. The Senator had taken the tusk to a warm pool of tidewater to rinse it off. Ruth Thomas went over, and he straightened up and handed her the tusk. She dried it on her shirt. It was light as bone and yellow as old teeth, its hollow inside packed with mud. It was warm. She hadn't even seen Webster find it! All those hours of sitting on the beach watching him search the mud, and she had not seen the moment when he found it!

"You didn't see him find it, either," she said to the Senator. He shook his head. Ruth weighed it in her hands. "Unbelievable," she said.

"I didn't think he would actually find it, Ruth," the Senator said, in a desperate whisper. "Now what the hell am I supposed to do with him? Look at him, Ruth."

Ruth looked. Webster was trembling like an old engine in idle.

"Is he upset?" she asked.

"Of course he's upset! This project kept him going for a year. I don't know," the Senator whispered in panic, "what to do with the boy now."

Webster Pommeroy got up and came to stand beside Ruth and the Senator. The Senator straightened to his full height and smiled widely.

"Did you clean it off?" Webster asked. "Does it look n-n-nicer?"

The Senator spun around and hugged tiny Webster Pommeroy close to him. He said, "Oh, it's splendid! It's gorgeous! I'm so proud of you, son! I am so proud of you!"

Webster sobbed again, and recommenced crying. Ruth, reflexively, shut her eyes.

"Do you know what I think, Webster?" Ruth heard the Senator ask. "I think it is a magnificent find. I really do. And I think we should bring it to Mr. Ellis."

Ruth's eyes flew open in alarm.

"And do you know what Mr. Ellis is going to do when he sees us coming with this tusk?" the Senator asked, his huge arm draped over Webster's shoulder. "Do you know, Webster?"

Webster did not know. He shrugged pathetically.

The Senator said, "Mr. Ellis is going to grin. Isn't that right, Ruthie? Won't that be something? Don't you think Mr. Ellis will love this?"

Ruth did not answer.

"Don't you think so, Ruthie? Don't you?"

3

Lobsters, by instinctive force,
Act selfishly, without design.
Their feelings commonly are coarse,
Their honor always superfine.

— *The Doctor and the Poet*
J. H. Stevenson
1718–1785

MR. LANFORD ELLIS lived in Ellis House, which dated back to 1883. The house was the finest structure on Fort Niles Island, and it was finer than anything on Courne Haven, too. It was built of black, tomb-grade granite in the manner of a grand bank or train station, in only slightly smaller proportions. There were columns, arches, deep-set windows, and a glinting tile lobby the size of a vast, echoing Roman bath house. Ellis House, on the highest point of Fort Niles, was as far away from the harbor as possible. It stood at the end of Ellis Road. Rather, Ellis House stopped Ellis Road abruptly in its tracks, as if the house were a big cop with a whistle and an outstretched, authoritative arm.

As for Ellis Road, it dated back to 1880. It was an old work road that had connected the three quarries of the Ellis Granite Company on Fort Niles Island. At one time, Ellis Road had been a busy thoroughfare, but by the time Webster Pommeroy, Senator Simon Addams, and Ruth Thomas made their way along the road toward Ellis House, on that June morning in 1976, it had long since fallen into disuse.

Alongside Ellis Road ran the dead length of the Ellis Rail, a two-mile track, dating from 1882, that had been laid down to carry the tons of granite blocks from the quarries to the sloops waiting in the harbor. Those heavy sloops steamed away to New York and Philadelphia and Washington for years and years. They moved in slow formation down to cities that always needed paving blocks from Courne Haven Island and more monument-grade granite from Fort Niles Island. For decades, the sloops carried off the granite interior of the two islands, returning, weeks later, packed with the coal needed to power the excavation of still more granite, to scour out more deeply the guts of the islands.

Beside the ancient Ellis Rail lay an orange-rusted scattering of Ellis Granite Company quarry tools and machine parts — peen hammers and wedges and shims and other tools — that nobody, not even Senator Simon, could identify anymore. The great Ellis Granite Company lathe was rotting in the woods nearby, bigger than a locomotive engine car, never to be moved again. The lathe sat miserably in the murk and vines as if it had been consigned there as punishment. Its 140 tons of clockwork gears were weathered together in an angry lockjaw grip. Rusted pythonic lengths of cable lurked in the grass all around.

They walked. Webster Pommeroy and Senator Simon Addams and Ruth Thomas walked up Ellis Road, next to the Ellis Rail, toward Ellis House, bearing the elephant tusk. They were not smiling, not laughing. Ellis House was not a place any of them frequented.

"I don't know why we're bothering," Ruth said. "He's not even going to be here. He's still in New Hampshire. He won't be here until next Saturday."

"He came to the island early this year," the Senator said.

"What are you talking about?"

"This year, Mr. Ellis arrived on April eighteenth."

"You're kidding me."

"I'm not kidding you."

"He's been here? He's been here the whole time? Since I got back from school?"

"That's right."

"Nobody told me."

"Did you ask anybody? You shouldn't be so surprised. Everything is different now at Ellis House from the way it used to be."

"Well. I guess I should know that."

"Yes, Ruthie. I suppose you should."

The Senator fanned mosquitoes off his head and neck as he walked, using a fan he'd made from fern fronds.

"Is your mother coming to the island this summer, Ruth?"

"No."
"Did you see your mother this year?"
"Not really."
"Oh, is that right? You didn't visit Concord this year?"
"Not really."
"Does your mother like living in Concord?"
"Apparently. She's been living there long enough."
"I'll bet her house is nice. Is it nice?"
"I've told you about a million times that it's nice."
"Do you know that I haven't seen your mother in a decade?"
"And you've told me that about a million times."
"So you say she's not coming to visit the island this summer?"
"She never comes," Webster Pommeroy said abruptly. "I don't know why everybody keeps talking about her."

That stopped the conversation. The threesome did not talk for a long while, and then Ruth said, "Mr. Ellis really came out here on April eighteenth?"

"He really did," the Senator said.

This was unusual news, even astonishing. The Ellis family came to Fort Niles Island on the third Saturday of June, and they had been doing so since the third Saturday of June 1883. They lived the rest of the year in Concord, New Hampshire. The original Ellis patriarch, Dr. Jules Ellis, had started the practice in 1883, moving his growing family to the island in the summers to get away from the diseases of the city, and also to keep an eye on his granite company. It was not known to any of the locals what kind of doctor Dr. Jules Ellis was, exactly. He certainly didn't act like a physician. He acted rather like a captain of industry. But that was during a different era, as Senator Simon liked to point out, when a man could be many things. This was back when a man could wear many hats.

None of the natives on Fort Niles liked the Ellis family, but it was an odd point of pride that Dr. Ellis had elected to build Ellis House on Fort Niles and not on Courne Haven, where the Ellis Granite Company was also at work. This point of pride had little actual value; the islanders should not have been flattered. Dr. Jules Ellis had chosen Fort Niles for his home not because he liked that island better. He had selected it because, by building Ellis House on the island's high, east-facing cliffs, he could keep an eye on both Fort Niles and Courne

Haven, right across Worthy Channel. He could live atop one island and watch the other carefully and also enjoy the advantage of keeping an eye on the rising sun.

During the reign of Dr. Jules Ellis, summertime would bring quite a crowd to Fort Niles Island. In time, there were five Ellis children arriving every summer, together with numerous members of the extended Ellis family, a continuing rotation of well-dressed Ellis summer guests and business associates, and a summer household staff of sixteen Ellis servants. The servants would bring the Ellis summer household necessities up from Concord on trains and then over on boats. On the third Saturday of June, the servants would appear at the docks, unloading trunks and trunks of summer china and linens and crystal and curtains. In photographs, these piles of trunks resemble structures in themselves, looking like awkward buildings. This enormous event, the arrival of the Ellis family, lent great importance to the third Saturday of June.

The Ellises' servants also brought across on boats several riding horses for the summer. Ellis House had a fine stable, in addition to a well-cultivated rose garden, a ballroom, an icehouse, guest cottages, a lawn tennis court, and a goldfish pond. The family and their friends, on Fort Niles Island for the summer, indulged themselves in sundry forms of recreation. And at the end of the summer, on the second Saturday of September, Dr. Ellis, his wife, his five children, his riding horses, his sixteen servants, his guests, the silver, the china, the linens, the crystal, and the curtains would leave. The family and servants would crowd onto their ferry, and the goods would be packed into the towering stacks of trunks, and everything and everyone would be shipped back to Concord, New Hampshire, for the winter.

But all this was long ago. This mighty production had not taken place for years.

By Ruth Thomas's nineteenth summer, in 1976, the only Ellis who still came to Fort Niles Island was Dr. Jules Ellis's eldest son, Lanford Ellis. He was ancient. He was ninety-four years old.

All of Dr. Jules Ellis's other children, save one daughter, were dead. There were grandchildren and even great-grandchildren of Dr. Ellis who might have enjoyed the great house on Fort Niles, but Lanford Ellis disliked and disapproved of them, and he kept them away. It was his right. The house was entirely his; he alone had inherited it. Mr.

Lanford Ellis's one surviving sibling, Vera Ellis, was the only family member for whom he cared, but Vera Ellis had stopped coming to the island ten summers earlier. She considered herself too frail to make the trip. She considered herself in poor health. She had spent many happy summers on Fort Niles, but preferred now to rest in Concord, the year round, with her live-in companion to care for her.

So, for ten years, Lanford Ellis had been spending his summers in Fort Niles alone. He kept no horses and invited no guests. He did not play croquet or take boating excursions. He had no staff with him at Ellis House except one man, Cal Cooley, who was both groundskeeper and assistant. Cal Cooley even cooked the old man's meals. Cal Cooley lived in Ellis House throughout the year, keeping his eye on things.

Senator Simon Addams, Webster Pommeroy, and Ruth Thomas walked on toward Ellis House. They walked side by side, Webster holding the tusk against one of his shoulders as if it were a Revolutionary War musket. On their left ran the stagnant Ellis Rail. Deep in the woods on their right stood the morbid remains of the "peanut houses," the tiny shacks built by the Ellis Granite Company a century earlier to house its Italian immigrant workers. There were once over three hundred Italian immigrants packed into these shacks. They were not welcome in the community at large, although they were allowed to have the occasional parade down Ellis Road on their holidays. There used to be a small Catholic church on the island to accommodate the Italians. No more. By 1976, the Catholic church had long since burned to the ground.

During the reign of the Ellis Granite Company, Fort Niles was like a real town, busy and useful. It was like a Fabergé egg—an object encrusted in the greatest detail. So much crowded on to such a small surface! There had been two dry-goods stores on the island. There had been a dime museum, a skating rink, a taxidermist, a newspaper, a pony racetrack, a hotel with a piano bar, and, across the street from each other, the Ellis Eureka Theater and the Ellis Olympia Dance Hall. Everything had been burned or wrecked by 1976. *Where had it all gone?* Ruth wondered. *And how had everything fit there, in the first place?* Most of the land had returned to woods. Of the Ellis empire, only two buildings remained: the Ellis Granite Company Store and Ellis House. And the company store, a three-story wooden structure down by the harbor, was vacant and falling in on itself. Of course, the quarries were there, holes in the earth over a thousand feet deep—smooth and oblique—now filled with spring water.

Ruth Thomas's father called the peanut houses in the back of the woods "guinea huts," a term he must have learned from his father or grandfather, because the peanut houses were empty even when Ruth's father was a boy. Even when Senator Simon Addams was a boy, the peanut houses were emptying out. The granite business was dying by 1910 and dead by 1930. The need for granite ran out before the granite itself did. The Ellis Granite Company would have dug in the quarries forever, if there had been a market. The company would have dug the granite until both Fort Niles and Courne Haven were gutted. Until the islands were thin shells of granite in the ocean. That's what the islanders said, anyway. They said the Ellis family would have taken everything, but for the fact that no one any longer wanted the stuff from which the islands were made.

The threesome walked up Ellis Road and slowed down only once, when Webster saw a dead snake in their path and stopped to poke it with the tip of the elephant tusk.

"Snake," he said.

"Harmless," said Senator Simon.

At another point, Webster stopped walking and tried to hand the tusk to the Senator.

"You take it," he said. "I don't want to go up there and see any Mr. Ellis."

But Senator Simon refused. He said Webster had found the tusk and should get the credit for his find. He said there was nothing to fear in Mr. Ellis. Mr. Ellis was a good man. Although there had been people in the Ellis family to fear in the past, Mr. Lanford Ellis was a decent man, who, by the way, thought of Ruthie as practically his own granddaughter.

"Isn't that right, Ruthie? Doesn't he always give you a big grin? And hasn't he always been good to your family?"

Ruth did not answer. The three continued walking.

They did not speak again until they reached Ellis House. There were no open windows, not even any open curtains. The hedges outside were still wrapped in protective material against the vicious winter winds. The place looked abandoned. The Senator climbed the broad, black granite steps to the dark front doors and rang the bell. And knocked. And called. There was no answer. In the noose-shaped driveway was parked a green pickup truck, which the three recognized as Cal Cooley's.

"Well, it looks like old Cal Cooley is here," the Senator said.

He walked around to the back of the house, and Ruth and Webster followed. They walked past the gardens, which were not gardens anymore so much as unkempt brush piles. They walked past the tennis court, which was overgrown and wet. They walked past the fountain, which was overgrown and dry. They walked toward the stable, and found its wide, sliding door gaping open. The entrance was big enough for two carriages, side by side. It was a beautiful stable, but it had been so long out of use that it no longer even had a trace of the smell of horses.

"Cal Cooley!" Senator Simon called. "Mr. Cooley?"

Inside the stable, with its stone floors and cool, empty, odorless stalls, was Cal Cooley, sitting in the middle of the floor. He was sitting on a simple stool before something enormous and was polishing the object with a rag.

"My God!" the Senator said. "Look what you've got!"

What Cal Cooley had was a huge piece of a lighthouse, the top piece of a lighthouse. It was, in fact, the magnificent glass-and-brass circular lens of a lighthouse. It was probably seven feet tall. Cal Cooley stood up from his stool, and he was close to seven feet tall, too. Cal Cooley had thick, combed-back blue-black hair and oversized blue-black eyes. He had a big square frame and a thick nose and a huge chin and a deep, straight line right across his forehead that made him look as if he'd run into a clothesline. He looked as if he might be part Indian. Cal Cooley had been with the Ellis family for about twenty years, but he hadn't seemed to age a day, and it would have been difficult for a stranger to guess whether he was forty years old or sixty.

"Why, it's my good friend the Senator," Cal Cooley drawled.

Cal Cooley was originally from Missouri, a place he insisted on pronouncing *Missourah.* He had a prominent Southern accent, which—although Ruth Thomas had never been to the South—she believed he had a tendency to exaggerate. She believed, for the most part, that Cal Cooley's whole demeanor was phony. There were many things about Cal Cooley that she hated, but she was particularly offended by his phony accent and his habit of referring to himself as Old Cal Cooley.

As in "Old Cal Cooley can't wait for spring," or "Old Cal Cooley looks like he needs another drink."

Ruth could not tolerate this affectation.

"And look! It's Miss Ruth Thomas!" Cal Cooley drawled on. "She is always such an oasis to behold. And look who's with her: a savage."

Webster Pommeroy, muddied and silent under Cal Cooley's gaze, stood with the elephant's tusk in his hand. His feet shifted about quickly, nervously, as if he were preparing to race.

"I know what this is," Senator Simon Addams said, approaching the huge and magnificent glass that Cal Cooley had been polishing. "I know exactly what this is!"

"Can you guess, my friend?" Cal Cooley asked, winking at Ruth Thomas as if they had a wonderful shared secret. She looked away. She felt her face get hot. She wondered if there was some way she could arrange her life so that she could live on Fort Niles forever without ever seeing Cal Cooley again.

"It's the Fresnel lens from the Goat's Rock lighthouse, isn't it?" the Senator asked.

"Yes, it is. Exactly right. Have you ever visited it? You must have been to Goat's Rock, eh?"

"Well, no," the Senator admitted, flushing. "I can never go out to a place like Goat's Rock. I don't go on boats, you know."

Which Cal Cooley knew perfectly well, Ruth thought.

"Is that so?" Cal asked innocently.

"I have a fear of water, you see."

"What a terrible affliction," Cal Cooley murmured.

Ruth wondered whether Cal Cooley had ever been severely beaten up in his life. She would have enjoyed seeing it.

"My goodness," the Senator marveled. "My goodness. How did you ever acquire the lighthouse from Goat's Rock? It's a remarkable lighthouse. It's one of the oldest lighthouses in the country."

"Well, my friend. We bought it. Mr. Ellis has always fancied it. So we bought it."

"But how did you get it here?"

"On a boat and then a truck."

"But how did you get it here without anyone knowing about it?"

"Does nobody know about it?"

"It's gorgeous."

"I am restoring it for Mr. Ellis. I am polishing every individual inch and every single screw. I've already been polishing for ninety hours, I estimate. I expect that it will take me months to finish. But won't it gleam then?"

"I didn't know the Goat's Rock lighthouse was for sale. I didn't know you could *buy* such a thing."

"The Coast Guard has replaced this beautiful artifact with a modern device. The new lighthouse doesn't even need an attendant. Isn't that remarkable? Everything is all automated. Very inexpensive to operate. The new lighthouse is completely electric and perfectly ugly."

"This *is* an artifact," the Senator said. "You're right. Why, it's suitable for a museum!"

"That's right, my friend."

Senator Simon Addams studied the Fresnel lens. It was a beautiful thing to see, all brass and glass, with beveled panes as thick as planks, layered over one another in tiers. The small section that Cal Cooley had already disassembled, polished, and reassembled was a gleam of gold and crystal. When Senator Simon Addams passed behind the lens to look at the whole thing, his image became distorted and wavy, as though seen through ice.

"I have never seen a lighthouse before," he said. His voice was choked with emotion. "Not in person. I have never had the opportunity."

"It's not a lighthouse," Cal Cooley corrected fastidiously. "It is merely the lens of a lighthouse, sir."

Ruth rolled her eyes.

"I have never seen one. Oh, my goodness, this is such a treat for me, such a treat. Of course, I've seen pictures. I've seen pictures of this very lighthouse."

"This is a pet project for me and Mr. Ellis. Mr. Ellis asked the state whether he could buy it, they named a price, and he accepted. And, as I say, I have been working on this for approximately ninety hours."

"Ninety hours," the Senator repeated, staring at the Fresnel lens as if he had been tranquilized.

"Built in 1929, by the French," Cal said. "She weighs five thousand pounds, my friend."

The Fresnel lens was perched on its original brass turntable, which Cal Cooley now gave a slight push. The entire lens, at that touch, began to spin with a freakish lightness—huge, silent, and exquisitely balanced.

"Two fingers," Cal Cooley said, holding up two of his own fingers. "Two fingers is all it takes to spin that five-thousand-pound weight. Can you believe it? Have you ever seen such remarkable engineering?"

"No," Senator Simon Addams answered. "No, I have not."

Cal Cooley spun the Fresnel lens again. What little light was in that stable seemed to throw itself at the great spinning lens and then leap away, bursting into sparks across the walls.

"Look how it eats up the light," Cal said. He somehow pronounced *light* so that it rhymed with *hot*.

"There was a woman on a Maine island once," the Senator said, "who was burned to death when the sunlight went through the lens and hit her."

"They used to cover the lenses with dark gunnysacks on sunny days," Cal Cooley said. "Otherwise, the lenses would have set everything on fire; they're that strong."

"I have always loved lighthouses."

"So have I, sir. So has Mr. Ellis."

"During the reign of Ptolemy the Second, there was a lighthouse built in Alexandria that was regarded as one of the wonders of the ancient world. It was destroyed by an earthquake in the fourteenth century."

"Or so history has recorded," said Cal Cooley. "There is some debate on that."

"The earliest lighthouses," the Senator mused, "were built by the Libyans in Egypt."

"I am familiar with the lighthouses of the Libyans," said Cal Cooley, evenly.

The Goat's Rock lighthouse antique Fresnel lens spun and spun in the vast empty stable, and the Senator stared at it, captivated. It spun more and more slowly, and quietly whispered to a stop. The Senator was silent, hypnotized.

"And what do *you* have?" Cal Cooley asked, finally.

Cal was regarding Webster Pommeroy, holding the elephant's tusk. Webster, caked with mud and looking most pathetic, clung desperately to his small find. He did not answer Cal, but his feet were tapping nervously. The Senator did not answer, either. He was still entranced by the Fresnel lens.

And so Ruth Thomas said, "Webster found an elephant's tusk today, Cal. It's from the wreck of the *Clarice Monroe*, 138 years ago. Webster and Simon have been looking for it for almost a year. Isn't it wonderful?"

And it was wonderful. Under any other circumstances, the tusk would have been recognized as an undeniably wonderful object. But not in the shadow of Ellis House, and not in the presence of the intact and beautiful brass-and-glass Fresnel lens crafted by the French in 1929. The tusk seemed suddenly foolish. Besides, Cal Cooley, with his height and demeanor, could diminish anything. Cal Cooley made his ninety hours of polishing seem heroic and productive, while—without saying a word, of course—making a year of a lost boy's life searching through the mud seem a depressing prank.

The elephant's tusk suddenly looked like a sad little bone.

"How very interesting," Cal Cooley said, at length. "What a perfectly interesting project."

"I thought Mr. Ellis might like to see it," the Senator said. He had snapped out of his gaze at the Fresnel lens and was now giving Cal Cooley a most unattractive look of supplication. "I thought he might grin when he sees the tusk."

"He may."

Cal Cooley did not commit.

"If Mr. Ellis is available today . . ." the Senator began, and then trailed off. The Senator did not wear a hat, but if he were a hat-wearing man, he would have been working the hat brim in his anxious hands. As it was, he was just wringing his hands.

"Yes, my friend?"

"If Mr. Ellis is available, I would like to talk to him about it. About the tusk. You see, I think this is the kind of object that may finally convince him of our need for the Natural History Museum on the island. I'd like to ask Mr. Ellis to consider granting me the use of the Ellis Granite Company Store building for the Natural History Museum. For the island. For education, you know."

"A museum?"

"A Natural History Museum. Webster and I have been collecting artifacts now for several years. We have quite a large collection."

Which Cal Cooley knew. Which Mr. Ellis knew. Which everybody knew. Ruth was now officially furious. Her stomach hurt. She could feel herself frowning, and she willed herself to keep her forehead smooth. She refused to show any emotion in front of Cal Cooley. She willed herself to look impassive. She wondered what a person would have to do to get Cal Cooley fired. Or killed.

"We have many artifacts," the Senator said. "I recently acquired a pure white lobster, preserved in alcohol."

"A Natural History Museum," Cal Cooley repeated, as though he were considering the notion for the very first time. "How intriguing."

"We need a space for the museum. We already have the artifacts. The building is large enough that we could continue to collect artifacts as time went on. For instance, it might be the place to display this Fresnel lens."

"You aren't saying you want Mr. Ellis's *lighthouse?*" Cal Cooley looked absolutely aghast.

"Oh, no. No! No, no, no! We don't want anything from Mr. Ellis except permission to use the company store building. We would rent it, of course. We could offer him some money every month for it. He might appreciate that, you know, since the building hasn't been used for anything in years. We don't need any *money* from Mr. Ellis. We don't want to take his *possessions.*"

"I certainly hope you aren't asking for money."

"You know what?" Ruth Thomas said. "I'm going to wait outside. I don't feel like standing here anymore."

"Ruth," Cal Cooley said with concern. "You look agitated, sweetheart."

She paid him no heed. "Webster, you want to come with me?"

But Webster Pommeroy preferred to race his feet in place beside the Senator, holding his hopeful tusk. So Ruth Thomas walked out of the stable alone, back through the abandoned pastures, toward the rock cliffs facing east and Courne Haven Island. She hated to watch Simon Addams grovel before Mr. Lanford Ellis's caretaker. She had seen it before and couldn't stand it. So she walked to the edge of the cliff and picked lichen off some rocks. Across the channel, she could clearly see Courne Haven Island. A heat mirage floated above it, like a mushroom cloud.

This would be the fifth time Senator Simon Addams had formally visited Mr. Lanford Ellis. The fifth time that Ruth Thomas knew of, that is. Mr. Ellis never granted the Senator a meeting. There may have been other visits that Ruth hadn't been told about. There may have been more hours spent waiting in the front yard of

Ellis House for nothing, more incidents of Cal Cooley explaining, with insincere apologies, that he was sorry, but Mr. Ellis was not feeling well and would not be receiving guests. Each time, Webster had come along, each time carrying some discovery or find with which the Senator hoped to convince Mr. Ellis of the necessity of a Natural History Museum. The Natural History Museum would be a public place, the Senator was always ready to explain with sincerity and heart, where the people of the island—for only a dime's admission!—could explore the artifacts of their singular history. Senator Simon had a most eloquent speech prepared for Mr. Ellis, but he had never had a chance to deliver it. He had recited the speech to Ruth several times. She listened politely, although each time it broke her heart a little.

"Plead less," she always suggested. "Be more assertive."

It was true that some of Senator Simon's artifacts were uninteresting. He collected everything and was not much of a curator, not one for picking among objects and discarding the worthless ones. The Senator thought all old objects had worth. On an island, people rarely throw anything away, so, essentially, every basement on Fort Niles Island was already a museum—a museum of obsolete fishing gear or a museum of the possessions of dead ancestors or a museum of the toys of long-grown children. But nowhere was this sorted or catalogued or explained, and the Senator's desire to create a museum was a noble one.

"It's the common objects," he constantly told Ruth, "that become rare. During the Civil War, the most common object in the world was a blue wool Union soldier's coat. A simple blue coat with brass buttons. Every soldier in the Union had one. Did the soldiers save those after the war, as souvenirs? No. Oh, they saved the general's dress uniforms and the handsome cavalry britches, but nobody thought to save the simple blue jackets. The men came home from war and wore the jackets to work in the fields, and when the jackets fell apart, their wives made rags and quilt squares from them, and today a common Civil War jacket is one of the most rare things in the world."

He would explain this to Ruth as he put an empty cereal box or an unopened can of tuna in a crate marked FOR POSTERITY.

"We cannot know today what will be of value tomorrow, Ruth," he would say.

"Wheaties?" she would reply, incredulous. "Wheaties, Senator? *Wheaties?*"

So it was not surprising that the Senator had run out of room in his house for his growing collections. And it was not surprising that the Senator would get the idea to seek access to the Ellis Granite Company Store, which had been standing vacant for forty years. It was a rotting, useless space. Still, Mr. Ellis had never once given the Senator an answer or a nod or any acknowledgment, other than to defer the entire subject. It was as though he were waiting the Senator out. It was as though Lanford Ellis expected to outlive the Senator, at which point the matter would be settled without the inconvenience of decision.

The lobster boats were still in the channel, working and circling. From her perch on the cliffs, Ruth saw the boat of Mr. Angus Addams and the boat of Mr. Duke Cobb and the boat of her father. Beyond them, she could see a fourth boat, which may have belonged to someone on Courne Haven Island; she couldn't identify it. The channel was so littered with lobster trap buoys, it looked like a scatter of confetti on a floor or dense litter on a highway. Men set their traps nearly on top of one another in that channel. It was risky, fishing there. The border between Courne Haven Island and Fort Niles Island had never been established, but nowhere was it more in contention than in Worthy Channel. Men from both islands defined and defended their ground hard, always pushing toward each other. They cut away each other's traps and waged collective assaults toward the opposite island.

"They'll drop their traps on our front goddamn doorsteps, if we let them in," said Angus Addams.

On Courne Haven Island they said the same of Fort Niles fishermen, of course, and both statements were true.

On this day, Ruth Thomas thought the Courne Haven boat was hovering a little close to Fort Niles, but it wasn't easy to be sure, even from above. She tried counting strings of buoys. She picked a blade of grass and made a whistle with it, pressed between her thumbs. She played a game with herself, pretending that she was seeing this view for the first time in her life. She shut her eyes for a long moment, then opened them slowly. The sea! The sky! It was beautiful. She did live in a beautiful place. She tried to look down on the lobster boats as if she did not know how much they cost and who owned them and how they smelled. How would this scene look to a visitor? How would Worthy Channel look to a person from, say, Nebraska? The boats would look like toys, adorable and sturdy as bathtub boats, manned by hardworking Down

East characters who dressed in picturesque overalls and gave each other friendly waves across their bows.

Ya can't get thah from heah . . .

Ruth wondered whether she would enjoy lobster fishing more if she had her own boat, if she were the captain. Maybe it was just working with her father that was so unpleasant. She couldn't imagine, though, whom she would enlist as a sternman. She ran over the names of all the young men from Fort Niles and quickly confirmed that, yes, they were all idiots. Every last drunken one of them. Incompetent, lazy, surly, inarticulate, funny-looking. She had no patience for any of them, with the possible exception of Webster Pommeroy, whom she pitied and worried over like a mother. But Webster was a damaged young man, and he was certainly no sternman. Not that Ruth was any lobsterman. She couldn't kid herself about that. She didn't know much about navigation, nothing about maintaining a boat. She'd shrieked "Fire!" to her father once when she saw smoke coming out of the hold; smoke that was actually steam from a ruptured hose.

"Ruth," he'd said, "you're cute, but you're not very smart."

But she *was* smart. Ruth had always had a sense of being smarter than anyone around her. Where had she got that idea? Who had ever told her such a thing? God knew, Ruth would never publicly admit this sense of hers. It would sound appalling, horrible, to admit what she believed about her own smartness.

"You think you're smarter than everyone else." Ruth had often heard this accusation from her neighbors on Fort Niles. A few of the Pommeroy boys had said it to her, as had Angus Addams and Mrs. Pommeroy's sisters and that old bitch on Langly Road whose lawn Ruth had mowed one summer for two dollars a pop.

"Oh, please," was Ruth's standard reply.

She couldn't deny it with more conviction than this, though, because she did, in fact, think she was considerably smarter than everyone else. It was a feeling, centered not in her head, but in her chest. She felt it in her very lungs.

She was certainly smart enough to figure out how to get her own boat if she wanted one. If that was what she wanted, she could get it. Sure. She was certainly no dumber than any of the men from Fort Niles or Courne Haven who made a good living by lobstering. Why not? Angus Addams knew a woman on Monhegan Island who fished alone and made a good living. The woman's brother had died and left his boat to her. She had three kids, no husband. The woman's name was Flaggie. Flaggie Cornwall. She made a good go of it. Her buoys, Angus reported, were painted bright pink, with yellow heart-shaped dots. But Flaggie Cornwall was tough, too. She cut away other men's traps if she thought they were messing with her business. Angus Addams quite admired her. He talked about her often.

Ruth could do that. She could fish alone. She wouldn't paint her buoys pink with yellow hearts, though. *Jesus Christ, Flaggie, have some self-respect!* Ruth would paint her buoys a nice, classic teal. Ruth wondered what kind of name Flaggie was. It must be a nickname. Florence? Agatha? Ruth had never had a nickname. She decided that if she became a lobsterman—a lobsterwoman? lobster*person?*—she'd figure out a way to make a great living at it without getting up so goddamn early in the morning. Honestly, was there any reason a smart fisherman had to wake up at four A.M.? There had to be a better way.

"Are you enjoying our view?"

Cal Cooley was standing right behind Ruth. She was startled but didn't show it. She turned slowly and gave him a steady look.

"Maybe."

Cal Cooley did not sit down; he stood there, directly behind Ruth Thomas. His knees almost touched her shoulders.

"I sent your friends home," he said.

"Did Mr. Ellis see the Senator?" Ruth asked, already knowing the answer.

"Mr. Ellis isn't himself today. He could not see the Senator."

"That makes him not himself? He never sees the Senator."

"That may be true."

"You people have no idea how to act. You have no idea how rude you are."

"I don't know what Mr. Ellis thinks about these people, Ruth, but I sent them home. I thought it was too early in the morning to be dealing with the mentally handicapped."

"It's four o'clock in the afternoon, you prick." Ruth liked the way that sounded. Very calm.

Cal Cooley stood behind Ruth for some time. He stood behind her like a butler, but more intimate. Polite, but too near. His nearness created a constant feeling that she did not appreciate. And she did not like speaking to him without seeing him.

"Why don't you sit down?" she said, at last.

"You want me to sit next to you, do you?" he asked.

"That's entirely up to you, Cal."

"Thank you," he said, and he did sit down. "Very hospitable of you. Thank you for the invitation."

"It's your property. I can't be hospitable on your property."

"It's not my property, young lady. It's Mr. Ellis's property."

"Really? I always forget that, Cal. I forget it's not your property. Do you ever forget that, too?"

Cal did not answer. He asked, "What's the little boy's name? The little boy with the tusk."

"He's Webster Pommeroy."

Which Cal Cooley knew.

Cal stared out at the water and recited dully: "Pommeroy the cabin boy was a nasty little nipper. Shoved a glass up in his ass and circumcised the skipper."

"Cute," Ruth said.

"He seems like a nice child."

"He's twenty-three years old, Cal."

"And I believe he is in love with you. Is this true?"

"My God, Cal. That is truly relevant."

"Listen to you, Ruth! You are so educated these days. It is such a pleasure to hear you using such big words. It is rewarding, Ruth. It makes us all so pleased to see that your expensive education is paying off."

"I know you try to rile me, Cal, but I'm not sure what you gain from it."

"That's not true, Ruth. I don't try to rile you. I'm your biggest supporter."

Ruth laughed sharply. "You know something, Cal? That elephant tusk really is an important find."

"Yes. You said as much."

"You didn't even pay attention to the story, an interesting story, about an unusual shipwreck. You didn't ask Webster how he found it. It's an incredible story, and you didn't pay any attention at all. It'd be annoying if it wasn't so damn typical."

"That's not true. I pay attention to everything."

"You pay a great deal of attention to some things."

"Old Cal Cooley is incapable of not paying attention."

"You should have paid more attention to that tusk, then."

"I am interested in that tusk, Ruth. I'm actually holding it for Mr. Ellis so that he can look at it later. I think he'll be very interested indeed."

"What do you mean, holding it?"

"I'm holding it."

"You *took* it?"

"As I've said, I'm holding it."

"You took it. You sent them away without their tusk. Jesus Christ. Why would a person do something like that?"

"Would you like to share a cigarette with me, young lady?"

"I think you people are all pricks."

"If you would like to smoke a cigarette, I won't tell anybody."

"I don't fucking *smoke*, Cal."

"I'm sure you do lots of bad things you don't tell anybody about."

"You took that tusk out of Webster's hands and sent him away? Well, that's a downright horrible thing to do. And typical."

"You sure do look beautiful today, Ruth. I meant to tell you that immediately, but the opportunity did not arise."

Ruth stood up. "OK," she said, "I'm going home."

She started to walk off, but Cal Cooley said, "As a matter of fact, I believe you need to stay."

Ruth stopped walking. She didn't turn around, but she stood still, because she knew from his tone what was coming.

"If you're not too busy today," Cal Cooley said, "Mr. Ellis would like to see you."

They walked toward Ellis House together. They walked silently beyond the pastures and the ancient gardens and up the steps to the back verandah and through the wide French doors. They walked through the broad and shrouded living room, down a back hall, up the modest back stairs—the servants' stairs—along another hall, and finally reached a door.

Cal Cooley stood as though to knock, but, instead, stepped back. He walked a few more paces down the hallway and ducked into a recessed doorway. When he gestured for Ruth to follow, she did. Cal Cooley put his big hands on Ruth's shoulders and whispered, "I know you hate me." And he smiled.

Ruth listened.

"I know you hate me, but I can tell you what this is all about if you want to know."

Ruth did not reply.

"Do you want to know?"

"I don't care what you tell me or don't tell me," Ruth said. "It doesn't make any difference in my life."

"Of course you care. First of all," Cal said, in a hushed voice, "Mr. Ellis simply wants to see you. He's been asking after you for a few weeks, and I've been lying. I've told him that you were still at school. Then I said you were working with your father on his boat."

Cal Cooley waited for Ruth to respond; she didn't.

"I should think you'd thank me for that," he said. "I don't like to lie to Mr. Ellis."

"Don't, then," Ruth said.

"He's going to give you an envelope," Cal said. "It has three hundred dollars in it."

Again, Cal waited for a response, but Ruth did not oblige, so he continued. "Mr. Ellis is going to tell you that it's fun money, just for you. And, to a certain extent, that's true. You can spend it on whatever you like. But you know what it's really for, right? Mr. Ellis has a favor to ask of you."

Ruth remained silent.

"That's right," Cal Cooley said. "He wants you to visit your mother in Concord. I'm supposed to take you there."

They stood in the recessed doorway. His big hands on her wide shoulders were as heavy as dread. Cal and Ruth stood there for a long time. Finally, he said, "Get it over with, young lady."

"Shit," Ruth said.

He dropped his hands. "Just take the money. My suggestion to you is not to antagonize him."

"I never antagonize him."

"Take the money and be civil. We'll figure out the details later."

Cal Cooley stepped out of the doorway and walked back to the first door. He knocked. He whispered to Ruth, "That's what you wanted, right? To know? No surprises for you. You want to know everything that's going on, right?"

He threw open the door, and Ruth stepped inside, alone. The door closed behind her with a beautiful brushing sound, like the swish of expensive fabric.

She was in Mr. Ellis's bedroom.

The bed itself was made, as seamlessly as though it were never used. The bed was made up as though the bedding had been produced at the same time as the piece of furniture itself and had been tacked or glued to the woodwork. It looked like a display bed in an expensive store. Bookcases were everywhere, holding rows of dark books, each precisely the same shade and size as its neighbors, as though Mr. Ellis owned one volume and had had it repeated throughout the room. The fireplace was lit, and there were heavy duck decoys on the mantel. The musty wallpaper was interrupted by framed prints of clippers and tall ships.

Mr. Ellis was near the fire, sitting in a large, wing-back chair. He was very, very old and very thin. A plaid lap rug was pulled high over his waist and tucked around his feet. His baldness was absolute, and his skull looked thin and cold. He held out his arms to Ruth Thomas, his palsied palms upward and open. His eyes were swimming in blue, swimming with tears.

"It's nice to see you, Mr. Ellis," Ruth said.

He grinned and grinned.

4

In traveling over the bottom in search of its prey, the lobster walks nimbly on its delicate legs. When taken out of the water, it can only crawl, owing to the heavy weight of the body and the claws, which the slender legs are now unable to sustain.

— *The American Lobster: A Study of Its Habits and Development*
Francis Hobart Herrick, Ph.D.
1895

THAT NIGHT, when Ruth Thomas told her father she had been to Ellis House, he said, "I don't care who you spend your time with, Ruth."

Ruth had gone looking for her father immediately after she left Mr. Ellis. She walked down to the harbor and saw that his boat was in, but the other fishermen said he'd long been done for the day. She tried him at their house, but when she called for him, there was no answer. So Ruth got on her bicycle and rode over to the Addams brothers' house to see whether he was visiting Angus for a drink. And so he was.

The two men were sitting on the porch, leaning back in folding chairs, holding beers. Senator Simon's dog, Cookie, was lying on Angus's feet, panting. It was late dusk, and the air was shimmering and gold. Bats flew low and fast above. Ruth dropped her bicycle in the yard and stepped up on the porch.

"Hey, Dad."

"Hey, sugar."

"Hey, Mr. Addams."

"Hey, Ruth."

"How's the lobster business?"

"Great, great," Angus said. "I'm saving up for a gun to blow my fucking head off."

Angus Addams, quite the opposite of his twin brother, was getting leaner as he grew older. His skin was damaged from the years spent in the middle of all kinds of bad weather. He squinted, as if looking into a field of sun. He was going deaf after a lifetime spent too near loud boat engines, and he spoke loudly. He hated almost everyone on Fort Niles, and there was no shutting him up when he felt like explaining, in careful detail, why.

Most of the islanders were afraid of Angus Addams. Ruth's father liked him. When Ruth's father was a boy, he'd worked as a sternman for Angus and had been a smart, strong, ambitious apprentice. Now, of course, Ruth's father had his own boat, and the two men dominated the lobster industry of Fort Niles. Greedy Number One and Greedy Number Two. They fished in all weather, with no limits on their catch, with no mercy for their fellows. The boys on the island who worked as sternmen for Angus Addams and for Stan Thomas usually quit after a few weeks, unable to take the pace. Other fishermen—harder drinking, fatter, lazier, stupider fishermen (in Ruth's father's opinion)—made easier bosses.

As for Ruth's father, he was still the handsomest man on Fort Niles Island. He had never remarried after Ruth's mother left, but Ruth knew he had liaisons. She had some ideas about who his partners were, but he never spoke about them to her, and she preferred not to think about them too much. Her father was not tall, but he had wide shoulders and thin hips. "No fanny at all," he liked to say. He weighed the same at forty-five as he had at twenty-five. He was fastidiously neat about his clothing, and he shaved every day. He went to Mrs. Pommeroy once every two weeks for a haircut. Ruth suspected that something may have been going on between her father and Mrs. Pommeroy, but she hated the thought of it so much that she never pursued it. Ruth's father's hair was dark, dark brown, and his eyes were almost green. He had a mustache.

Ruth, at eighteen, thought her father was a fine enough person. She knew he had a reputation as a cheapskate and a lobster hustler, but she also knew that this reputation had grown fertile in the minds of island men who commonly spent the money from a week's catch on one night in a bar. These were men who saw frugality as arrogant and offensive. These were men who were not her father's equal, and they knew it and resented it. Ruth also knew that her father's best friend was a bully and a bigot, but she had always liked Angus Addams, anyway. She did not find him to be a hypocrite, in any case, which put him above many people.

For the most part, Ruth got along with her father. She got along with him best when they weren't working together or when he wasn't trying to teach her something, like how to drive a car or mend rope or navigate by a compass. In such situations, there was bound to be yelling. It wasn't so much the yelling that Ruth minded. What she didn't like was when her father got quiet on her. He got real quiet, typically, on any subject having to do with Ruth's mother. She thought he was a coward about it. His quietness sometimes disgusted her.

"You want a beer?" Angus Addams asked Ruth.

"No, thank you."

"Good," Angus said. "Makes you fat as all goddamn hell."

"It hasn't made you fat, Mr. Addams."

"That's because I work."

"Ruth can work, too," Stan Thomas said of his daughter. "She's got an idea to work on a lobster boat this summer."

"The two of you been saying that for damn near a month now. Summer's almost over."

"You want to take her on as a sternman?"

"You take her, Stan."

"We'd kill each other," Ruth's father said. "You take her."

Angus Addams shook his head. "I'll tell you the truth," he said. "I don't like to fish with anyone if I can help it. Used to be, we fished alone. Better that way. No sharing."

"I know you hate sharing," Ruth said.

"I fucking do hate sharing, missy. And I'll tell you why. In 1936, I only made three hundred and fifty dollars the entire goddamn year, and I fished my balls off. I had close to three hundred dollars in expenses. That left me fifty to live on the whole winter. And I had to take care of my goddamn brother. So, no, I ain't sharing if I can help it."

"Come on, Angus. Give Ruth a job. She's strong," Stan said. "Come on over here, Ruth. Roll up your sleeves, baby. Show us how strong you are."

Ruth went over and obediently flexed her right arm.

"She's got her crusher claw here," her father said, squeezing her muscle. Then Ruth flexed her left arm, and he squeezed that one, saying, "And she's got her pincher claw here!"

Angus said, "Oh, for fuck's sake."

"Is your brother here?" Ruth asked Angus.

"He went over to the Pommeroy house," Angus said. "He's all goddamn worried about that goddamn snot-ass kid."

"He's worried about Webster?"

"He should just goddamn adopt the little bastard."

"So the Senator left Cookie with you, did he?" Ruth asked.

Angus growled again and gave the dog a shove with his foot. Cookie woke up and looked around patiently.

"At least the dog's in loving hands," Ruth's father said, grinning. "At least Simon left his dog with someone who'll take good care of it."

"Tender loving care," Ruth added.

"I hate this goddamn dog," Angus said.

"Really?" Ruth asked, wide-eyed. "Is that so? I didn't know that. Did you know that, Dad?"

"I never heard anything about that, Ruth."

"I hate this goddamn dog," Angus said. "And the fact that I have to feed it corrodes my soul."

Ruth and her father started laughing.

"I hate this goddamn dog," Angus said, and his voice rose as he recited his problems with Cookie. "The dog's got a goddamn ear infection, and I have to buy it some goddamn drops, and I have to hold the dog twice a day while Simon puts the drops in. I have to *buy* the goddamn drops when I'd rather see the goddamn dog go deaf. It drinks out of the toilet. It throws up every goddamn day, and it has never once in its entire life had a solid stool."

"Anything else bothering you?" Ruth asked.

"Simon wants me to show the dog some goddamn affection, but that runs contrary to my instinct."

"Which is?" Ruth asked.

"Which is to stomp on it with heavy boots."

"You're terrible," Ruth's father said, and bent over laughing. "You're terrible, Angus."

Ruth went into the house and got herself a glass of water. The kitchen of the Addams house was immaculate. Angus Addams was a slob, but Senator Simon Addams cared for his twin brother like a wife, and he kept the chrome shining and the icebox full. Ruth knew for a fact that Senator Simon got up at four in the morning every day and made Angus breakfast (biscuits, eggs, a slice of pie) and packed sandwiches for Angus's lunch on the lobster boat. The other men on the island liked to tease Angus, saying they wished they had things so good at home, and Angus Addams liked to tell them to shut their fucking mouths and, by the way, they shouldn't have married such lazy fat goddamn whores in the first place. Ruth looked out the kitchen window to the back yard, where overalls and long underwear swayed, drying. There was a loaf of sweetbread on the counter, so she cut herself a piece and walked back out to the porch, eating it.

"None for me, thanks," Angus said.

"Sorry. Did you want a piece?"

"No, but I'll take another beer, Ruth."

"I'll get it on my next trip to the kitchen."

Angus raised his eyebrows at Ruth and whistled. "That's how educated girls treat their friends, is it?"

"Oh, brother."

"Is that how Ellis girls treat their friends?"

Ruth did not reply, and her father looked down at his feet. It became very quiet on the porch. Ruth waited to see whether her father would remind Angus Addams that Ruth was a Thomas girl, not an Ellis girl, but her father said nothing.

Angus set his empty beer bottle on the floor of the porch and said, "I'll get it my own self, I guess," and he walked into the house.

Ruth's father looked up at her. "What'd you do today, sugar?" he asked.

"We can talk about it at dinner."

"I'm eating dinner here tonight. We can talk about it now."

So she said, "I saw Mr. Ellis today. You still want to talk about it now?"

Her father said evenly, "I don't care what you talk about or when you talk about it."

"Does it make you mad that I saw him?"

That's when Angus Addams came back out, just as Ruth's father was saying, "I don't care who you spend your time with, Ruth."

"Who the hell is she spending her time with?" Angus asked.

"Lanford Ellis."

"Dad. I don't want to talk about it now."

"Those goddamn bastards again," Angus said.

"Ruth had a little meeting with him."

"Dad—"

"We don't have to keep secrets from our friends, Ruth."

"Fine," Ruth said, and she tossed her father the envelope Mr. Ellis had given her. He lifted the flap and peered at the bills inside. He set the envelope on the arm of his chair.

"What the hell is that?" Angus asked. "What is that, a load of cash? Mr. Ellis give you that money, Ruth?"

"Yes. Yes, he did."

"Well, you fucking give it back to him."

"I don't think it's any of your business, Angus. You want me to give the money back, Dad?"

"I don't care how these people throw their money around, Ruth," Stan Thomas said. But he picked up the envelope again, took out the bills, and counted them. There were fifteen bills. Fifteen twenty-dollar bills.

"What's the goddamn money for?" Angus asked. "What the hell is that goddamn money for, anyhow?"

"Stay out of it, Angus," Ruth's father said.

"Mr. Ellis said it was fun money for me."

"Funny money?" her father asked.

"Fun money."

"Fun money? Fun money?"

She did not answer.

"This sure is fun so far," her father said. "Are you having fun, Ruth?"

Again, she did not answer.

"Those Ellis people really know how to have fun."

"I don't know what it's for, but you get your fanny over there and give it back," Angus said.

The three sat there with the money looming between them.

"And another thing about that money," Ruth said.

Ruth's father passed his hand over his face, just once, as though he suddenly realized he was tired.

"Yes?"

"There's another thing about that money. Mr. Ellis would really like it if I used some of it to go visit Mom. My mother."

"Jesus Christ!" Angus Addams exploded. "Jesus Christ, you were gone all goddamn year, Ruth! You only just goddamn got back here, and they're trying to send you away again!"

Ruth's father said nothing.

"That goddamn Ellis family runs you all over the goddamn place, telling you what to do and where to go and who to see," Angus continued. "You do every goddamn thing that goddamn family tells you to do. You're getting to be just as bad as your goddamn mother."

"Stay out of it, Angus!" Stan Thomas shouted.

"Would that be fine with you, Dad?" Ruth asked, gingerly.

"Jesus Christ, Stan!" Angus sputtered. "Tell your goddamn daughter to stay here, where she goddamn belongs."

"First of all," Ruth's father said to Angus, "shut your goddamn mouth."

There was no second of all.

"If you don't want me to see her, I won't go," Ruth said. "If you want me to take the money back, I'll take the money back."

Ruth's father fingered the envelope. After a brief silence, he said to his eighteen-year-old daughter, "I don't care who you spend your time with."

He tossed the envelope of money back to her.

"What's the problem with you?" Angus Addams bellowed at his friend. "What's the problem with all you goddamn people?"

As for Ruth Thomas's mother, there was certainly a big problem with her.

The people of Fort Niles Island had always had problems with Ruth Thomas's mother. The biggest problem was her ancestry. She was not like all the people on Fort Niles Island whose families had been in place there forever. She was not like all the people who knew exactly who their ancestors were. Ruth Thomas's mother was born on Fort Niles, but she wasn't exactly *from* there. Ruth Thomas's mother was a problem because she was the daughter of an orphan and an immigrant.

Nobody knew the orphan's real name; nobody knew anything at all about the immigrant. Ruth Thomas's mother, therefore, had a genealogy that was cauterized at both ends—two dead ends of information. Ruth's mother had no forefathers, no foremothers, no recorded family traits by which to define herself. While Ruth Thomas could trace back two centuries of her father's ancestors without leaving the Fort Niles Island cemetery, there was no getting past the orphan and the immigrant who began and completed her mother's blunt history. Her mother, unaccounted for as such, had always been looked at askance on Fort Niles Island. She'd been produced by two mysteries, and there were no mysteries in anyone else's history. One should not simply appear on Fort Niles with no family chronicle to account for oneself. It made people uneasy.

Ruth Thomas's grandmother — her mother's mother — had been an orphan with the uninspired, hastily invented name of Jane Smith. In 1884, as a tiny baby, Jane Smith was left on the steps of the Bath Naval Orphans' Hospital. The nurses collected her and bathed her and bestowed upon her that ordinary name, which they decided was as good a name as any. At the time, the Bath Naval Orphans' Hospital was a relatively new institution. It had been founded just after the Civil War for the benefit of children orphaned by that war; specifically for the children of naval officers killed in battle.

The Bath Naval Orphans' Hospital was a rigorous and well-organized institution, where cleanliness and exercise and regular bowels were encouraged. It is possible that the baby who came to be known as Jane Smith was the daughter of a sailor, perhaps even a naval officer, but there were no clues whatsoever on the baby to indicate this. There was no note, no telling object, no distinctive clothing. Just a healthy enough baby, swaddled tightly and set quietly on the orphanage steps.

In 1894, when the orphan called Jane Smith turned ten, she was adopted by a certain gentleman by the name of Dr. Jules Ellis. Jules Ellis was a young man, but he had already made a good name for himself. He was the founder of the Ellis Granite Company, of Concord, New Hampshire. Dr. Jules Ellis, it seemed, always took his summer holidays on the Maine islands, where he had several lucrative quarries in operation. He liked Maine. He believed the citizens of Maine to be exceptionally hardy and decent; therefore, when he decided it was time to adopt a child, he sought one from a Maine orphanage. He thought that would vouchsafe him a hearty girl.

His reason for adopting a girl was as follows. Dr. Jules Ellis had a favorite daughter, an indulged nine-year-old named Vera, and Vera insistently asked for a sister. She had several brothers, but she was bored to death with them, and she wanted a girl playmate for companionship over those long, isolated summers on Fort Niles Island. So Dr. Jules Ellis acquired Jane Smith as a sister for his little girl.

"This is your new twin sister," he told Vera on her tenth birthday.

Ten-year-old Jane was a big, shy girl. On her adoption, she was given the name Jane Smith-Ellis, another invention that she accepted with no more protest than she had shown the first time she was christened. Mr. Jules Ellis had put a great red bow on the girl's head the day he presented her to his daughter. Photographs were taken on that day; in them, the bow looks absurd on the big girl in the orphanage dress. The bow looks like an insult.

From that time forward, Jane Smith-Ellis accompanied Vera Ellis everywhere. On the third Saturday of every June, the girls traveled to Fort Niles Island, and on the second Saturday of every September, Jane Smith-Ellis accompanied Vera Ellis back to the Ellis mansion in Concord.

There is no reason to imagine that Ruth Thomas's grandmother was ever considered for a moment to be the actual *sister* of Miss Vera Ellis. Although adoption made the girls legal siblings, the thought that they deserved equal respect in the Ellis household would have been farcical. Vera Ellis did not love Jane Smith-Ellis as a sister, but she fully relied on her as a servant. Although Jane Smith-Ellis had the responsibilities of a handmaid, she was, by law, a member of the family, and consequently received no salary for her work.

"Your grandmother," Ruth's father had always said, "was a slave to that goddamn family."

"Your grandmother," Ruth's mother had always said, "was fortunate to have been adopted by a family as generous as the Ellises."

Miss Vera Ellis was not a great beauty, but she had the advantage of wealth, and she passed her days exquisitely dressed. There are photographs of Miss Vera Ellis perfectly outfitted for swimming, riding, skating, reading, and, as she grew older, for dancing, driving, and marrying. These turn-of-the-century costumes were intricate and heavy. It was Ruth Thomas's grandmother who kept Miss Vera Ellis tight in her buttons, who sorted her kidskin gloves, who tended to the plumes of her hats, who rinsed her stockings and lace. It was Ruth Thomas's grandmother who selected, arranged, and packed the corsets, slips, shoes, crinolines, parasols, dressing gowns, powders, brooches, capes, lawn dresses, and hand purses necessary for Miss Vera Ellis's summer sojourn on Fort Niles Island every year. It was Ruth Thomas's grandmother who packed Miss Vera's accoutrements for her return to Concord every autumn, without misplacing a single item.

Of course, Miss Vera Ellis was likely to visit Boston for a weekend, or the Hudson Valley during October, or Paris, for the further refinement of her graces. And she needed to be attended to in these circumstances as well. Ruth Thomas's grandmother, the orphan Jane Smith-Ellis, served well.

Jane Smith-Ellis was no beauty, either. Neither woman was excellent to behold. In photographs, Miss Vera Ellis at least bears a remotely interesting expression on her face — an expression of expensive haughtiness — but Ruth's grandmother shows not even that. Standing behind the exquisitely bored Miss Vera Ellis, Jane Smith-Ellis shows nothing in her face. Not smarts, not a determined chin, not a sullen mouth. There is no spark in her, but there is no mildness, either. Merely deep and dull fatigue.

In the summer of 1905, Miss Vera Ellis married a boy, from Boston, by the name of Joseph Hanson. The marriage was of little significance, which is to say that Joseph Hanson's family was good enough, but the Ellises were much better, so Miss Vera retained all power. She suffered no undue inconvenience from the marriage. She never referred to herself as Mrs. Joseph Hanson; she was forever known as Miss Vera Ellis. The couple lived in the bride's childhood home, the Ellis mansion in Concord. On the third Saturday of every June, the couple followed the established pattern of moving to Fort Niles Island and, on the second Saturday of every September, moving back to Concord.

What's more, the marriage between Miss Vera Ellis and Joe Hanson did not in the least change Ruth's grandmother's life. Jane Smith-Ellis's duties were still clear. She was, naturally, of service to Miss Vera on the wedding day itself. (Not as a bridesmaid. Daughters of family friends and cousins filled those roles. Jane was the attendant who dressed Miss Vera, managed the dozens of pearl buttons down the back of the dress, hooked the high wedding boots, handled the French veil.) Ruth's grandmother also accompanied Miss Vera on her honeymoon to Bermuda. (To collect umbrellas at the beach, to brush sand from Miss Vera's hair, to arrange for the wool bathing suits to dry without fading.) And Ruth's grandmother stayed on with Miss Vera after the wedding and honeymoon.

Miss Vera and Joseph Hanson had no children, but Vera had weighty social obligations. She had all those events to attend and appointments to keep and letters to write. Miss Vera used to lie in bed each morning, after picking at the breakfast Ruth's grandmother had delivered on a tray, and dictate—in an indulgent imitation of a person with a real job dictating to a real employee—the responsibilities of the day.

"See if you can take care of that, Jane," she would say.

Every day, for years and years.

The routine would surely have continued for many more years but for a particular event. Jane Smith-Ellis became pregnant. In late 1925, the quiet orphan whom the Ellises had adopted from the Bath Naval Orphans' Hospital was pregnant. Jane was forty-one years old. It was unthinkable. Needless to say, she was unmarried, and no one had considered the possibility that she might take a suitor. Nobody in the Ellis family, of course, had thought of Jane Smith-Ellis for a moment as a woman for intimacy. They'd never expected her to acquire a friend, no less a lover. It was nothing they had ever given thought to. Other servants were constantly getting entangled in all manner of idiotic situations, but Jane was too practical and too necessary to get in trouble. Miss Vera could not spare Jane long enough for Jane to *find* trouble. And why would Jane look for trouble in the first place?

The Ellis family, indeed, had questions about the pregnancy. They had many questions. And demands. How had this come to pass? Who was responsible for this disaster? But Ruth Thomas's grandmother, obedient though she generally was, told them nothing except one detail.

"He is Italian," she said.

Italian? *Italian?* Outrageous! What were they to surmise? Obviously, the man responsible was one of the hundreds of Italian immigrant workers in the Ellis Granite Company's quarries on Fort Niles. This was incomprehensible to the Ellis family. How had Jane Smith-Ellis found her way to the quarries? Even more bewildering, how had a worker found his way to *her?* Had Ruth's grandmother visited the peanut houses, where the Italians lived, in the middle of the night? Or—horrors!—had an Italian worker visited the Ellis House? Unthinkable. Had there been other encounters? Perhaps years of encounters? Had there been other lovers? Was this a lapse, or had Jane been living a perverse double life? Was it a rape? A whim? A love affair?

The Italian quarry workers spoke no English. They were constantly being replaced, and, even to their immediate supervisors, they were nameless. As far as the quarry foremen were concerned, the Italians may as well have had interchangeable heads. Nobody thought of them as individuals. They were Catholic. They had no social commerce with the local island population, no less with anyone connected to the Ellis family. The Italians were largely ignored. They were noticed, really, only when they came under attack. The newspaper of Fort Niles Island, which folded soon after the granite industry left, had run occasional editorials fulminating against the Italians.

From *The Fort Niles Bugle* in February 1905: "These Garibaldians constitute the poorest, the most vile, creatures of Europe. Their children and wives are crippled and bent by the depravities of the Italian men."

"These Neapolitans," reads a later editorial, "give shocks to our children, who must pass them as they chatter and bark frightfully on our roads."

It was unthinkable that an Italian, a Garibaldian, a Neapolitan, could have gained access to the Ellis household. Still, when interrogated by the Ellis family about the father of her child, Ruth Thomas's grandmother would reply only, "He is Italian."

There was some talk of action. Dr. Jules Ellis wanted Jane to be immediately dismissed, but his wife reminded him that it would be difficult and a trifle rude to dismiss a woman who was, after all, not an employee but a legal member of the family.

"Disown her, then!" thundered Vera Ellis's brothers, but Vera would not hear of it. Jane had lapsed, and Vera felt betrayed, but, still, Jane was indispensable. No, there was no way around it: Jane must stay with the family because Vera Ellis could not live without her. Even Vera's brothers had to admit this was a good point. Vera, after all, was impossible, and without the constant tending of Jane, she would have been a murderous little harpy. So, yes, Jane should stay.

What Vera did demand, instead of punishment for Jane, was a measure of punishment for the Italian community on Fort Niles. She was probably unfamiliar with the expression "lynch mob," but that was not far from what she had in mind. She asked her father whether it would be too much trouble to round up some Italians and have them beaten, or have a peanut house or two burned down, don't you know. But Dr. Jules Ellis wouldn't hear of it. Dr. Ellis was far too shrewd a businessman to interrupt work at the quarry or injure his good laborers, so it was decided to hush up the entire matter. It would be handled as discreetly as possible.

Jane Smith-Ellis remained with the Ellis family during her pregnancy, performing her chores for Miss Vera. Her baby was born on the island in June of 1926, on the very night the Ellis family arrived on Fort Niles for the summer. No one had considered altering the schedule to accommodate the hugely pregnant Jane. Jane shouldn't have been anywhere near a boat in her condition, but Vera had her travel out there, nine months pregnant. The baby was practically delivered on the Fort Niles dock. And the little girl was named Mary. She was the illegitimate daughter of an orphan and an immigrant, and she was Ruth's mother.

Miss Vera gave Ruth's grandmother one week's respite from her duties after the difficult delivery of Mary. At the end of the week, Vera summoned Jane and said, almost tearfully, "I need you, darling. The baby is lovely, but I need you to help me. I simply can't do without you. You'll have to tend to *me* now."

Thus Jane Smith-Ellis began her schedule of staying up all night to care for her baby and working all day for Miss Vera — sewing, dressing, plaiting hair, drawing baths, buttoning and unbuttoning gown after gown. The servants of Ellis House tried to look after the baby during the day, but they had their own chores to attend to. Ruth's mother, although legally and rightfully an Ellis, spent her infancy in the servants' quarters, pantries, and root cellars, passed from hand to hand, quietly, as though she were contraband. It was just as bad in the winter, when the family returned to Concord. Vera gave Jane no relief.

In early July of 1927, when Mary was just over a year old, Miss Vera Ellis became ill with the measles and developed a high fever. A doctor, who was one of the family's summer guests on Fort Niles, treated Vera with morphine, which eased her discomfort and caused her to sleep for long hours each day. These hours provided Jane Smith-Ellis with the first period of rest she had since coming to Ellis House as a child. This was her first taste of leisure, her first reprieve from duty.

And so, one afternoon, while Miss Vera and baby Mary were both sleeping, Ruth's grandmother strolled down the steep cliff path on the eastern shore of the island. Was this her first outing? The first free hours of her life? Probably. She carried her knitting with her, in a black bag. It was a lovely clear day, and the ocean was calm. Down at the shore, Jane Smith-Ellis climbed up on a large rock jutting into the sea, and there she perched, quietly knitting. The waves rose and fell evenly and mildly far below her. Gulls circled. She was alone. She continued to knit. The sun shone.

Back at Ellis House, after several hours, Miss Vera awoke and rang her bell. She was thirsty. A housemaid came to her room with a tumbler of water, but Miss Vera would not have it.

"I want Jane," she said. "You are a *darling*, but I want my sister Jane. Will you summon her? Wherever could she be?"

The housemaid passed the request to the butler. The butler sent for a young assistant gardener and told him to fetch Jane Smith-Ellis. The young gardener walked along the cliffs until he saw Jane, sitting below on her rock, knitting.

"Miss Jane!" he shouted down, and waved.

She looked up and waved back.

"Miss Jane!" he shouted. "Miss Vera wants you!"

She nodded and smiled. And then, as the young gardener later testified, a great and silent wave rose from the sea and completely covered the enormous rock on which Jane Smith-Ellis was perched. When the gigantic wave receded, she was gone. The tide resumed its easy motion, and there was no sign of Jane. The gardener called for the other servants, who rushed down the cliff path to search for her, but they found not so much as a shoe. She was gone. She had simply been removed by the sea.

"Nonsense," Miss Vera Ellis declared when she was told that Jane had vanished. "Of course she has not vanished. Go and find her. Now. Find her."

The servants searched and the citizens of Fort Niles Island searched, but nobody found Jane Smith-Ellis. For days, the search parties scoured the shores, but no trace was discovered.

"Find her," Miss Vera continued to command. "I need her. No one else can help me."

And so she continued for weeks, until her father, Dr. Jules Ellis, came to her room with all four of her brothers and carefully explained the circumstances.

"I'm very sorry, my dear," Dr. Ellis said to his only natural-born daughter. "I'm sorry indeed, but Jane is gone. It is pointless for anyone to search further."

Miss Vera set her face in a stubborn scowl. "At the very least, can't someone find her *body?* Can't someone *dredge* for it?"

Miss Vera's youngest brother scoffed. "One cannot *dredge* the sea, Vera, as though it were a *fishpond.*"

"We shall postpone the funeral service as long as we can," Dr. Ellis assured his daughter. "Perhaps Jane's body will emerge in time. But you must stop telling the servants to find Jane. It's a waste of their time, and the household must be tended."

"You see," explained Vera's eldest brother, Lanford, "they will not find her. Nobody will ever find Jane."

The Ellis family held off on a funeral service for Jane Smith-Ellis until the first week of September. Then, because they had to return to Concord within a few days, they could delay the event no further. There was no talk of waiting until they returned to Concord, where they could put a marker on the family plot; there was no place for Jane there. Fort Niles seemed to be as good a place as any for Jane's funeral. With no corpse to bury, Ruth's grandmother's funeral was more a memorial service than a funeral. Such a service is not uncommon on an island, where drowning victims often are not recovered. A stone was placed in the Fort Niles cemetery, carved from Fort Niles black granite. It read:

JANE SMITH-ELLIS
? 1884–JULY 10, 1927
SORELY MISSED

Miss Vera resignedly attended the service. She did not yet accept that Jane had abandoned her. She was, in fact, rather angry. At the end of the service, Miss Vera asked some of the servants to bring Jane's baby to her. Mary was just over a year old. She would grow up to be Ruth Thomas's mother, but at this time she was a tiny little girl. Miss Vera took Mary Smith-Ellis in her arms and rocked her. She smiled down at the child and said, "Well, little Mary. We shall now turn our attention to you."

5

> The popularity of the lobster extends far beyond the limits of our island, and he travels about all parts of the known world, like an imprisoned spirit soldered up in an airtight box.
>
> —*Crab, Shrimp, and Lobster Lore*
> W. B. Lord
> 1867

CAL COOLEY made the arrangements for Ruth Thomas to visit her mother in Concord. He made the arrangements and then called Ruth and told her to be on her porch, with her bags packed, at six o'clock the next morning. She agreed, but just before six o'clock that morning, she changed her mind. She had a short moment of panic, and she bolted. She didn't go far. She left her bags on the porch of her father's house and ran next door to Mrs. Pommeroy.

Ruth guessed that Mrs. Pommeroy would be up and guessed that she might get breakfast out of the visit. Indeed, Mrs. Pommeroy was up. But she wasn't alone and she wasn't making breakfast. She was painting her kitchen. Her two older sisters, Kitty and Gloria, were helping her. All three were wearing black garbage bags to protect their clothes, their heads and arms pushed through the plastic. It was immediately obvious to Ruth that the three women had been up all night. When Ruth stepped into the house, the women lunged toward her at the same time, crushing her between them and leaving paint marks all over her.

"Ruth!" they shouted. "Ruthie!"

"It's six o'clock in the morning!" Ruth said. "Look at you!"

"Painting!" Kitty shouted. "We're painting!"

Kitty swiped at Ruth with a paintbrush, streaking more paint across Ruth's shirt, then dropped to her knees, laughing. Kitty was drunk. Kitty was, in fact, a drunk. ("Her grandmother was the same kind of person," Senator Simon had once told Ruth. "Always lifting the gas caps off old Model Ts and sniffing the fumes. Staggered around this island in a daze her whole life.") Gloria helped her sister to stand. Kitty put her hand over her mouth, delicately, to stop laughing, then put her hands to her head, in a ladylike motion, to fix her hair.

All three Pommeroy sisters had magnificent hair, which they wore piled on their heads in the same fashion that had made Mrs. Pommeroy such a famous beauty. Mrs. Pommeroy's hair grew more silvery every year. It had silvered to the point that, when she turned her head in the sunlight, she gleamed like a swimming trout. Kitty and Gloria had the same gorgeous hair, but they weren't as attractive as Mrs. Pommeroy. Gloria had a heavy, unhappy face, and Kitty had a damaged face; there was a burn scar on one cheek, thick as a callus, from an explosion at a canning factory many years earlier.

Gloria, the oldest, had never married. Kitty, the next one, was off-and-on married to Ruth's father's brother, Ruth's reckless Uncle Len Thomas. Kitty and Len had no children. Mrs. Pommeroy was the only one of the Pommeroy sisters to have children, that huge batch of sons: Webster and Conway and Fagan and so on and so on. By now, 1976, the boys were grown. Four had left the island, having found lives elsewhere on the planet, but Webster, Timothy, and Robin were still at home. They lived in their old bedrooms in the huge house next to Ruth and her father. Webster, of course, had no job. But Timothy and Robin worked on boats, as sternmen. The Pommeroy boys only found temporary work, on other people's boats. They had no boats of their own, no real means of livelihood. All signs pointed to Timothy and Robin being hired hands forever. That morning, both were already out fishing; they'd been gone since before daylight.

"What are you doing today, Ruthie?" Gloria asked. "What are you doing up so early?"

"Hiding from somebody."

"Stay, Ruthie!" said Mrs. Pommeroy. "You can stay and watch us!"

"Watch *out* for you is more like it," Ruth said, pointing to the paint on her shirt. Kitty dropped to her knees again at this joke, laughing and laughing. Kitty always took jokes hard, as if she'd been kicked by them. Gloria waited for Kitty to stop laughing and again helped her to stand. Kitty sighed and touched her hair.

Every object in Mrs. Pommeroy's kitchen was piled on the kitchen table or hidden beneath sheets. The kitchen chairs were in the living room, tossed on the sofa, out of the way. Ruth got a chair and sat in the middle of the kitchen while the three Pommeroy sisters resumed painting. Mrs. Pommeroy was painting windowsills with a small brush. Gloria was painting a wall with a roller. Kitty was scraping old paint off another wall in absurd, drunken lunges.

"When did you decide to paint your kitchen?" Ruth asked.

"Last night," Mrs. Pommeroy said.

"Isn't this a disgusting color, Ruthie?" Kitty asked.

"It's pretty awful."

Mrs. Pommeroy stepped back from her windowsill and looked at her work. "It is awful," she admitted, not unhappily.

"Is that buoy paint?" Ruth guessed. "Are you painting your kitchen with buoy paint?"

"I'm afraid it is buoy paint, honey. Do you recognize the color?"

"I can't believe it," Ruth said, because she did recognize the color. Astonishingly, Mrs. Pommeroy was painting her kitchen the exact shade that her dead husband had used to paint his trap buoys—a powerful lime green that chewed at the eyes. Lobstermen always use garish colors on their pot buoys to help them spot the traps against the flat blue of the sea, in any kind of weather. It was thick industrial paint, wholly unsuited to the job at hand.

"Are you afraid of losing your kitchen in the fog?" Ruth asked.

Kitty hit her knees laughing. Gloria frowned and said, "Oh, for Christ's sake, Kitty. Get a-hold of yourself." She pulled Kitty up.

Kitty touched her hair and said, "If I had to live in a kitchen this color, I'd vomit all over the place."

"Are you allowed to use buoy paint indoors?" Ruth asked. "Aren't you supposed to use indoor paint for indoor painting? Is it going to give you cancer or something?"

"I don't know," Mrs. Pommeroy said. "I found all these cans of paint in the toolshed last night, and I thought to myself, better not to waste it! And it reminds me of my husband. When Kitty and Gloria came over for dinner, we started giggling, and the next thing I knew, we were painting the kitchen. What do you think?"

"Honestly?" Ruth asked.

"Never mind," Mrs. Pommeroy said. "I like it."

"If I had to live in this kitchen, I'd vomit so much, my head would fall off," Kitty announced.

"Watch it, Kitty," Gloria said. "You might have to live in this kitchen soon enough."

"I will fucking *not!*"

"Kitty is welcome to stay in this house anytime," Mrs. Pommeroy said. "You know that, Kitty. You know that, too, Gloria."

"You're so mean, Gloria," said Kitty. "You're so fucking mean."

Gloria kept painting her wall, her mouth set, her roller layering clean, even strokes of color.

Ruth asked, "Is Uncle Len throwing you out of your house again, Kitty?"

"Yes," Gloria said, quietly.

"No!" Kitty said. "No, he's not throwing me out of the *house*, Gloria! You're so fucking mean, Gloria!"

"He says he'll throw her out of the house if she doesn't stop drinking," Gloria said, in the same quiet tone.

"So why doesn't *he* stop fucking drinking?" Kitty demanded. "Len tells me I have to stop drinking, but nobody drinks as much as he does."

"Kitty's welcome to move in with me," Mrs. Pommeroy said.

"Why does *he* still get to be fucking drinking every fucking day?" Kitty shouted.

"Well," Ruth said, "because he's a nasty old alcoholic."

"He's a prick," Gloria said.

"He's got the biggest prick on this island; that's for sure," Kitty said.

Gloria kept painting, but Mrs. Pommeroy laughed. From upstairs came the sound of a baby crying.

"Oh, dear," Mrs. Pommeroy said.

"Now you've done it," Gloria said. "Now you've woken up the goddamn baby, Kitty."

"It wasn't me!" Kitty shouted, and the baby's cry became a wail.

"Oh, dear," Mrs. Pommeroy repeated.

"God, that's a loud baby," Ruth said, and Gloria said, "No shit, Ruth."

"I guess Opal's home, then?"

"She came home a few days ago, Ruth. I guess she and Robin made up, so that's good. They're a family now, and they should be together. I think they're both pretty mature. They're both growing up real nice."

"Truth is," Gloria said, "her own family got sick of her and sent her back here."

They heard footsteps upstairs and the cries diminished. Soon after, Opal came down, carrying the baby.

"You're always so loud, Kitty," Opal whined. "You always wake up my Eddie."

Opal was Robin Pommeroy's wife, a fact that was still a source of wonder to Ruth: fat, dopy, seventeen-year-old Robin Pommeroy had a wife. Opal was from Rockland, and she was seventeen, too. Her father owned a gas station there. Robin had met her on his trips to town when he was filling gas cans for his truck on the island. She was pretty enough ("A cute dirty little slut," Angus Addams pronounced), with ash-blond hair worn in sloppy pigtails. This morning, she was wearing a housecoat and dingy slippers, and she shuffled her feet like an old woman. She was fatter than Ruth remembered, but Ruth hadn't seen her since the previous summer. The baby was in a heavy diaper and was wearing one sock. He took his fingers out of his mouth and grabbed at the air.

"Oh, my God!" Ruth exclaimed. "He's huge!"

"Hey, Ruth," Opal said shyly.

"Hey, Opal. Your baby's huge!"

"I didn't know you were back from school, Ruth."

"I've been back almost a month."

"You happy to be back?"

"Sure I am."

"Coming back to Fort Niles is like falling off a horse," Kitty Pommeroy said. "You never forget how."

Ruth ignored that. "Your baby's enormous, Opal! Hey, there, Eddie! Hey, Eddie boy!"

"That's right!" Kitty said. "He's our great big baby boy! Aren't you, Eddie? Aren't you our great big boy?"

Opal stood Eddie down on the floor between her legs and gave him her two index fingers to hold. He tried to lock his knees and swayed like a drunk. His belly stuck out comically over his diaper, and his thighs were taut and plump. His arms seemed to be assembled in segments, and he had several chins. His chest was slick with drool.

"Oh, he's so big!" Mrs. Pommeroy smiled widely. She knelt in front of Eddie and pinched his cheeks. "Who's my great big boy? How big are you? How big is Eddie?"

Eddie, delighted, shouted, "Gah!"

"Oh, he's big, all right," Opal said, pleased. "I can't hardly lift him anymore. Even Robin says Eddie's getting too heavy to carry around. Robin says Eddie'd better learn to walk pretty soon, I guess."

"Look who's gonna be a great big fisherman!" Kitty said.

"I don't think I ever saw such a big, healthy boy," Gloria said. "Look at those legs. That boy's going to be a football player for sure. Isn't that the biggest baby you ever saw, Ruth?"

"That's the biggest baby I ever saw," Ruth agreed.

Opal blushed. "All the babies in my family are big. That's what my mom says. And Robin was a big baby, too. Isn't that right, Mrs. Pommeroy?"

"Oh, yes, Robin was a great big baby boy. But not as big as great big Mr. Eddie!" Mrs. Pommeroy tickled Eddie's belly.

"Gah!" he shouted.

Opal said, "I can't hardly feed him enough. You should see him at mealtimes. He eats more than I do! Yesterday he had five strips of bacon!"

"Oh, my God!" Ruth said. Bacon! She couldn't stop staring at the kid. He didn't look like any baby she had ever seen. He looked like a fat bald man, shrunken down to two feet high.

"He's got a great big appetite, that's why. Don't you? Don't you, you great big boy?" Gloria picked up Eddie with a grunt and covered his cheek with kisses. "Don't you, chubby cheeks? You have a great big healthy appetite. Because you're our little lumberjack, aren't you? You're our little football player, aren't you? You're the biggest little boy in the whole world."

The baby squealed and kicked Gloria heftily. Opal reached out. "I'll take him, Gloria. He's got a ca-ca diaper." She took Eddie and said, "I'll go upstairs and clean him up. I'll see you all later. See you later, Ruth."

"See you later, Opal," Ruth said.

"Bye-bye, big boy!" Kitty called, and waved bye-bye at Eddie.

"Bye-bye, you great big handsome boy!" Gloria called.

The Pommeroy sisters watched Opal head up the stairs, and they grinned and waved at Eddie until they lost sight of him. Then they heard Opal's footsteps in the bedroom above and all stopped grinning at the same moment.

Gloria brushed off her hands, turned to her sisters, and said, sternly, "That baby's too big."

"She feeds him too much," Mrs. Pommeroy said, frowning.

"Not good for his heart," Kitty pronounced.

The women returned to their painting.

Kitty immediately started talking again about her husband, Len Thomas.

"Oh, yeah, he hits me, sure," she said to Ruth. "But I'll tell you something. He can't give anything to me any worse than I can give anything back to him."

"What?" Ruth said. "What's she trying to say, Gloria?"

"Kitty's trying to say Len can't hit her any harder than she can hit him."

"That's right," Mrs. Pommeroy said with pride. "Kitty has a real good swing on her."

"That's right," Kitty said. "I'll put his head right through the fucking door if I feel like it."

"And he'll do the same to you, Kitty," Ruth said. "Nice arrangement."

"Nice marriage," Gloria said.

"That's right," Kitty said, satisfied. "It is a nice marriage. Not like you'd know anything about *that*, Gloria. And nobody's kicking anybody out of anybody's house."

"We'll see," Gloria said, real low.

Mrs. Pommeroy had been a romp as a young girl, but she'd quit drinking when Mr. Pommeroy drowned. Gloria had never been a romp. Kitty had been a romp as a young girl, too, but she'd kept at it. She was a lifetime boozer, a grunt, a dozzler. Kitty Pommeroy was the example of what Mrs. Pommeroy might have become if she had stayed on the bottle. Kitty had lived off-island for a while, back when she was younger. She'd worked in a herring-canning factory for years and years and saved up all her money to buy a fast convertible. And she'd had sex with dozens of men—or so Gloria reported. Kitty had had *abortions*, Gloria said, which was why Kitty couldn't have babies now. After the explosion in the canning factory, Kitty Pommeroy returned to Fort Niles. She took up with Len Thomas, another prime drunk, and the two of them had been beating each other up ever since. Ruth couldn't stand her Uncle Len.

"I have an idea, Kitty," Ruth said.

"Oh, yeah?"

"Why don't you kill Uncle Len in his sleep some night?"

Gloria laughed, and Ruth continued, "Why don't you club him to death, Kitty? I mean, before he does it to you. Get a jump on him."

"Ruth!" Mrs. Pommeroy exclaimed, but she was also laughing.

"Why not, Kitty? Why not bludgeon him?"

"Shut up, Ruth. You don't know anything."

Kitty was sitting on the chair Ruth had brought in, lighting a cigarette, and Ruth went over and sat on her lap.

"Get off my goddamn lap, Ruth. You got a bony ass, just like your old man."

"How do you know my old man has a bony ass?"

"Because I fucked him, stupid," Kitty said.

Ruth laughed as if this was a big joke, but she had a chilling sense that it may have been true. She laughed to cover her discomfort, and she jumped off Kitty's lap.

"Ruth Thomas," Kitty said, "you don't know a thing about this island anymore. You don't live here anymore, so you have no right to say anything. You aren't even *from* here."

"Kitty!" Mrs. Pommeroy exclaimed. "That's nasty!"

"Excuse me, Kitty, but I do so live here."

"For a few months a year, Ruth. You live here like a tourist, Ruth."

"I hardly think that's my fault, Kitty."

"That's right," Mrs. Pommeroy said. "It isn't Ruth's fault."

"You think nothing is ever Ruth's fault."

"I think I wandered into the wrong house," Ruth said. "I think I wandered into the house of hate today."

"No, Ruth," Mrs. Pommeroy said. "Don't get upset. Kitty's just teasing you."

"I'm not upset," said Ruth, who was getting upset. "I think it's funny; that's all."

"I am *not* teasing anyone. You don't know anything about this place anymore. You haven't practically *been* here in four goddamn years. A lot changes around a place in four years, Ruth."

"Yeah, especially a place like this," Ruth said. "Big changes, everywhere I look."

"Ruth didn't want to go away," Mrs. Pommeroy said. "Mr. Ellis sent her away to school. She didn't have any choice, Kitty."

"Exactly," Ruth said. "I was banished."

"That's right," Mrs. Pommeroy said, and went over to nudge Ruth. "She was banished! They took her away from us."

"I wish a rich millionaire would banish me to some millionaire's private school," Kitty muttered.

"No, you don't, Kitty. Trust me."

"I wish a millionaire would have banished *me* to private school," Gloria said, in a voice a little stronger than her sister had used.

"OK, Gloria," Ruth said. "You might wish that. But Kitty doesn't wish that."

"What the fuck is that supposed to mean?" Kitty barked. "What? I'm too stupid for school?"

"You would have been bored to death at that school. Gloria might have liked it, but you'd have hated it."

"What's *that* supposed to mean?" Gloria asked. "That I wouldn't have been bored? Why not, Ruth? Because I'm boring? Are you calling me boring, Ruth?"

"Help," Ruth said.

Kitty was still muttering that she was plenty goddamn smart for any goddamn school, and Gloria was staring Ruth down.

"Help me, Mrs. Pommeroy," Ruth said, and Mrs. Pommeroy said, helpfully, "Ruth isn't calling anyone dumb. She's just saying that Gloria is a little bit smarter than Kitty."

"Good," said Gloria. "That's right."

"Oh, my God, save me," Ruth said, and she ducked under the kitchen table as Kitty came at her from across the room. Kitty bent down and started whacking at Ruth's head.

"Ow," Ruth said, but she was laughing. It was ridiculous. She'd only come over for breakfast! Mrs. Pommeroy and Gloria were laughing, too.

"I'm not fucking stupid, Ruth!" Kitty slapped her again.

"Ow."

"You're the stupid one, Ruth, and you aren't even from here anymore."

"Ow."

"Quit your bitching," Kitty said. "You can't take a slap to the head? I got five concussions in my life." Kitty let up on Ruth for a moment to tick off her concussions on her fingers. "I fell out of a highchair. I fell off a bicycle. I fell in a quarry, and I got two concussions from Len. And I got blown up in a factory explosion. And I got eczema. So don't tell me you can't take a goddamn hit, girl!" She smacked Ruth again. Comically, now. Affectionately.

"Ow," Ruth repeated. "I'm a victim. Ow."

Gloria Pommeroy and Mrs. Pommeroy kept laughing. Kitty finally quit and said, "Someone at the door."

Mrs. Pommeroy went to answer the door. "It's Mr. Cooley," she said. "Good morning, Mr. Cooley."

A low drawl came through the room: "Ladies . . ."

Ruth stayed under the table, her head cradled in her arms.

"It's Cal Cooley, everyone!" Mrs. Pommeroy called.

"I'm looking for Ruth Thomas," he said.

Kitty Pommeroy lifted a corner of the sheet from the table and shouted, "Ta-da!" Ruth waggled her fingers at Cal in a childish wave.

"There's the young woman I'm looking for," he said. "Hiding from me, as ever."

Ruth crawled out and stood up.

"Hello, Cal. You found me." She wasn't upset to see him; she felt relaxed. It was as if Kitty had knocked her head clear.

"You certainly seem busy, Miss Ruth."

"I actually am a little busy, Cal."

"It seems you forgot about our appointment. You were supposed to be waiting for me at your house. Maybe you were too busy to keep your appointment?"

"I was delayed," Ruth said. "I was helping my friend paint her kitchen."

Cal Cooley took a long look around the room, noting the dreadful green buoy paint, the sloppy sisters wrapped in garbage bags, the sheet hastily tossed on the kitchen table, the paint on Ruth's shirt.

"Old Cal Cooley hates to take you away from your work," Cal Cooley drawled.

Ruth grinned. "I hate to be taken away by old Cal Cooley."

"You're up early, buster," Kitty Pommeroy said, and punched Cal in the arm.

"Cal," Ruth said, "I believe you know Mrs. Kitty Pommeroy? I believe you two have met? Am I correct?"

The sisters laughed. Before Kitty married Len Thomas—and for several years after—she and Cal Cooley had been lovers. This was a piece of information that Cal Cooley hilariously liked to imagine was top secret, but every last person on the island knew it. And everyone knew they were still occasional lovers, despite Kitty's marriage. Everyone but Len Thomas, of course. People got a big laugh out of that.

"Nice to see you, Kitty," Cal said flatly.

Kitty fell to her knees laughing. Gloria helped Kitty up. Kitty touched her mouth and then her hair.

"I hate to take you away from your hen party, Ruth," Cal said, and Kitty cackled fiercely. He winced.

"I have to go now," Ruth said.

"Ruth!" Mrs. Pommeroy exclaimed.

"I'm being banished again."

"She's a victim!" Kitty shouted. "You watch yourself with that one, Ruth. He's a rooster, and he'll always be a rooster. Keep your legs crossed." Even Gloria laughed at this, but Mrs. Pommeroy did not. She looked at Ruth Thomas—concerned.

Ruth hugged all three sisters. When she got to Mrs. Pommeroy, she gave her a long hug and whispered into her ear, "They're making me visit my mother."

Mrs. Pommeroy sighed. Held Ruth close. Whispered in her ear, "Bring her back here with you, Ruth. Bring her back here, where she belongs."

Cal Cooley often liked to affect a tired voice around Ruth Thomas. He liked to pretend that she made him weary. He often sighed, shook his head, as though Ruth could not begin to appreciate the suffering she caused him. And so, as they walked to his truck from Mrs. Pommeroy's house, he sighed and shook his head and said, as though defeated by exhaustion, "Why must you always hide from me, Ruth?"

"I wasn't hiding from you, Cal."

"No?"

"I was just evading you. Hiding from you is futile."

"You always blame me, Ruth," Cal Cooley lamented. "Stop smiling, Ruth. I'm serious. You always have blamed me."

He opened the door of the truck and paused. "You don't have any luggage?" he asked.

She shook her head and got into the truck.

Cal said, with dramatic fatigue, "If you bring no clothes to Miss Vera's house, Miss Vera will have to buy you new clothes."

When Ruth did not answer, he said, "You know that, don't you? If this is a protest, it will backfire in your pretty face. You inevitably make things harder for yourself than you have to."

"Cal," Ruth whispered conspiratorially, and leaned toward him in the cab of the truck. "I don't like to bring luggage when I go to Concord. I don't like anyone at the Ellis mansion to think I'll be staying."

"Is that your trick?"

"That's my trick."

They drove toward the wharf, where Cal parked the truck. He said to Ruth, "You look very beautiful today."

Now it was Ruth who sighed dramatically.

"You eat and eat," Cal continued, "and you never get heavier. That's marvelous. I always wonder when your big appetite's going to catch up to you and you'll balloon on us. I think it's your destiny."

She sighed again. "You make me so goddamn tired, Cal."

"Well, you make me goddamn tired, too, sweetheart."

They got out of the truck, and Ruth looked down the wharf and across the cove, but the Ellises' boat, the *Stonecutter*, was not there. This was a surprise. She knew the routine. Cal Cooley had been ferrying Ruth around for years, to school, to her mother. They always left Fort Niles in the *Stonecutter*, courtesy of Mr. Lanford Ellis. But this morning Ruth saw only the old lobster boats, bobbing. And a strange sight: there was the *New Hope*. The mission boat sat long and clean on the water, her engine idling.

"What's the *New Hope* doing here?"

"Pastor Wishnell is giving us a ride to Rockland," Cal Cooley said.

"Why?"

"Mr. Ellis doesn't want the *Stonecutter* used for short trips anymore. And he and Pastor Wishnell are good friends. It's a favor."

Ruth had never been on the *New Hope*, though she'd seen it for years, cruising. It was the finest boat in the area, as fine as Lanford Ellis's yacht. The boat was Pastor Toby Wishnell's pride. He may have forsworn the great fishing legacy of the Wishnell family in the name of God, but he had kept his eye for a beautiful boat. He'd restored the *New Hope* to a forty-foot glass-and-brass enchantress, and even the men on Fort Niles Island, all of whom loathed Toby Wishnell, had to admit that the *New Hope* was a looker. Although they certainly hated to see her show up in their harbor.

They didn't see her much, though. Pastor Toby Wishnell was rarely around. He sailed the coast from Casco to Nova Scotia, ministering to every island along the way. He was nearly always at sea. And, though he was based directly across the channel on Courne Haven Island, he did not often visit Fort Niles. He came for funerals and for weddings, of course. He came for the occasional baptism, although most Fort Niles citizens skipped that particular procedure to avoid asking for him. He came to Fort Niles only when he was invited, and that was seldom.

So Ruth was indeed surprised to see his boat.

On that morning, a young man was standing at the end of the Fort Niles dock, waiting for them. Cal Cooley and Ruth Thomas walked toward him, and Cal shook the boy's hand. "Good morning, Owney."

The young man did not answer but climbed down the wharf ladder to a neat little white rowboat. Cal Cooley and Ruth Thomas climbed down after him, and the rowboat rocked delicately under their weight. The young man untied his line, seated himself in the stern, and rowed out to the *New Hope.* He was big—maybe twenty years old, with a large, squarish head. He had a thick square body, with hips as wide as his shoulders. He wore oilskins, like a lobsterman, and had on fisherman's tall rubber boots. Though he was dressed like a lobsterman, his oilskins were clean and his boots did not smell of bait. His hands on the oars were square and thick like a fisherman's hands, yet they were clean. He had no cuts or knobs or scars. He was in a fisherman's costume, and he had a fisherman's body, but he was obviously not a fisherman. When he pulled the oars, Ruth saw his huge forearms, which bulged like turkey legs and were covered with blond hairs scattered as light as ash. He had a homemade crew cut and yellow hair, a color never seen on Fort Niles Island. Swedish hair. Light blue eyes.

"What's your name again?" Ruth asked the boy. "Owen?"

"Owney," Cal Cooley answered. "His name is Owney Wishnell. He's the pastor's nephew."

"Owney?" Ruth said. "Owney, is it? Really? Hello there, Owney."

Owney looked at Ruth but did not greet her. He rowed quietly all the way out to the *New Hope.* They climbed a ladder, and Owney hoisted the rowboat up behind him and stowed it on deck. This was the cleanest boat Ruth had ever seen. She and Cal Cooley walked back to the cabin, and there was Pastor Toby Wishnell, eating a sandwich.

"Owney," Pastor Wishnell said, "let's get moving."

Owney hauled up the anchor and set the boat in motion. He sailed them out of the harbor, and they all watched him, although he did not seem aware of them. He sailed out of the shallows around Fort Niles and passed buoys that rocked on the waves with warning bells. He passed close to Ruth's father's lobster boat. It was early in the morning still, but Stan Thomas had been out for three hours. Ruth, leaning over the rail, saw her father hook a trap buoy with his long wooden gaff. She saw Robin Pommeroy in the stern, cleaning out a trap, tossing short lobsters and crabs back into the sea with a flick of his wrist. Fog circled them like a spook. Ruth did not call out. Robin Pommeroy stopped his work for a moment and looked up at the *New Hope.* It clearly gave him a shock to see Ruth. He stood for a moment, with his mouth hanging open, staring up at her. Ruth's father did not look up at all. He was not interested in seeing the *New Hope* with his daughter aboard.

Farther out, they passed Angus Addams, fishing by himself. He did not look up, either. He kept his head down, pushing rotting herring into bait bags, furtively, as if he were stuffing loot into a sack during a bank robbery.

When Owney Wishnell was fully on track and heading on the open sea toward Rockland, Pastor Toby Wishnell finally addressed Cal Cooley and Ruth Thomas. He regarded Ruth silently. He said to Cal, "You were late."

"I'm sorry."

"I said six o'clock."

"Ruth wasn't ready at six o'clock."

"We were to leave at six in order to be in Rockland by early afternoon, Mr. Cooley. I explained that to you, didn't I?"

"It was the young lady's fault."

Ruth listened to the conversation with some pleasure. Cal Cooley was usually such an arrogant prick; it was engaging to see him defer to the minister. She'd never seen Cal defer to anyone. She wondered whether Toby Wishnell was really going to chew Cal a new asshole. She would very much like to watch that.

But Toby Wishnell was finished with Cal. He turned to speak to his nephew, and Cal Cooley glanced at Ruth. She raised an eyebrow.

"It *was* your fault," he said.

"You're a brave man, Cal."

He scowled. Ruth turned her attention to Pastor Wishnell. He was still an exceedingly handsome man, now in his mid-forties. He had probably spent as much time at sea as any Fort Niles or Courne Haven fisherman, but he did not look like any of the fishermen Ruth had known. There was a fineness about him that matched the fineness of his boat: beautiful lines, an economy of detail, a polish, a finish. His blond hair was thin and straight, and he wore it parted on the side and brushed smooth. He had a narrow nose and pale blue eyes. He wore small, wire-framed glasses. Pastor Toby Wishnell had the look of an elite British officer: privileged, cool, brilliant.

They sailed for a long time without any further conversation. They left in the worst kind of fog, the cold fog that sits on the body like damp towels, hurtful to lungs, knuckles, and knees. Birds don't sing in the fog, so there were no gulls screaming, and it was a quiet ride. As they sailed farther away from the island, the fog diminished and then vanished, and the day turned clear. But it was, nonetheless, an odd day. The sky was blue, the wind was slight, but the sea was a churning mass—huge round swells, rough and constant. This sometimes happens when there's a storm much farther out at sea. The sea gets the aftermath of the violence, but there's no sign in the sky of the storm. It's as though the sea and the sky are not on terms of communication. They take no notice of each other, as if they've never been introduced. Sailors call this a "ground sea." It's disorienting to be on so rough an ocean under a picnic-day blue sky. Ruth stood against the rail and watched the water seethe and fume.

"You don't mind the rough sea?" Pastor Toby Wishnell asked Ruth.

"I don't get seasick."

"You're a lucky girl."

"I don't think we're lucky today," Cal Cooley drawled. "Fishermen say it's bad luck to have women or clergy on a boat. And we got both."

The pastor smiled wanly. "Never begin a trip on a Friday," he recited. "Never go on a ship that had an unlucky launch. Never go on a boat if her name has been changed. Never paint anything on a boat blue. Never whistle on a boat, or you'll whistle up a wind. Never bring women or clergy aboard. Never disturb a bird's nest on a boat. Never say the number *thirteen* on a boat. Never use the word *pig*."

"Pig?" Ruth said. "I never heard that one."

"Well, it's been said twice now," Cal Cooley said. "Pig, pig, pig.

We've got clergy; we've got women; we've got people shouting *pig*. So now we are doomed. Thank you to all who participated."

"Cal Cooley is such an old salt," Ruth said to Pastor Wishnell. "Being from *Missourah* and all, he's just *steeped* in the lore of the sea."

"I am an old salt, Ruth."

"Actually, Cal, I believe you're a farm boy," Ruth corrected. "I believe you are a cracker."

"Just because I was born in Missourah doesn't mean I can't be an island man at heart."

"I don't think the other island men would necessarily agree, Cal."

Cal shrugged. "A man can't help where he's born. A cat can have kittens in the oven, but that don't make 'em biscuits."

Ruth laughed, although Cal Cooley did not. Pastor Wishnell was looking closely at Ruth.

"Ruth?" he said. "Is that your name? Ruth Thomas?"

"Yes, sir," Ruth said, and stopped laughing. She coughed into her fist.

"You have a familiar face, Ruth."

"If I look familiar, that's only because I look exactly like everyone else on Fort Niles. We all look alike, sir. You know what they say about us—we're too poor to buy new faces, so we share the same one. Ha."

"Ruth is much prettier than anyone else on Fort Niles," Cal contributed. "Much darker. Look at those pretty dark eyes. That's the Italian in her. That's from her Eye-talian grandpappy."

"Cal," Ruth snapped, "stop talking now." He always seized the opportunity to remind her of her grandmother's shame.

"Italian?" Pastor Wishnell said, with a frown. "On Fort Niles?"

"Tell the man about your grandpap, Ruth," Cal said.

Ruth disregarded Cal, as did the pastor. Pastor Wishnell was still looking at Ruth with great attention. At last he said, "Ah . . ." He nodded. "I know now how it is that I recognize you. I believe I buried your father, Ruth, when you were a little girl. That's it. I believe I presided over your father's funeral. Didn't I?"

"No, sir."

"I'm quite sure of it."

"No, sir. My father's not dead."

Pastor Wishnell considered this. "Your father did not drown? Almost ten years ago?"

"No, sir. I believe you're thinking of a man named Ira Pommeroy. You presided over Mr. Pommeroy's funeral about ten years ago. We passed my father baiting lobster as we left the harbor. He's very much alive."

"He was found caught up in another man's fishing lines, that Ira Pommeroy?"

"That's right."

"And he had several children?"

"Seven sons."

"And one daughter?"

"No."

"But you were there, weren't you? At the funeral?"

"Yes, sir."

"So I was not imagining it."

"No, sir. I was there. You were not imagining it."

"You certainly seemed to be a member of the family."

"Well, I'm not, Pastor Wishnell. I'm not a member of that family."

"And that lovely widow . . . ?"

"Mrs. Pommeroy?"

"Yes. Mrs. Pommeroy. She's not your mother?"

"No, sir. She's not my mother."

"Ruth is a member of the Ellis family," Cal Cooley said.

"I am a member of the Thomas family," Ruth corrected. She kept her voice level, but she was mad. What exactly was it about Cal Cooley that brought to her such immediate thoughts of homicide? She never had this reaction to anyone else. All Cal had to do was open his mouth, and she started imagining trucks running over him. Incredible.

"Ruth's mother is Miss Vera Ellis's devoted niece," Cal Cooley explained. "Ruth's mother lives with Miss Vera Ellis in the Ellis mansion in Concord."

"My mother is Miss Vera Ellis's handmaid," Ruth said, her voice level.

"Ruth's mother is Miss Vera Ellis's devoted niece," Cal Cooley repeated. "We're going to visit them now."

"Is that so?" said Pastor Wishnell. "I was certain that you were a Pommeroy, young lady. I was certain that the lovely young widow was your mother."

"Well, I'm not. And she's not."

"Is she still on the island?"

"Yes," Ruth said.

"With her sons?"

"A few of her sons joined the Army. One's working on a farm in Orono. Three live at home."

"How does she survive? How does she make money?"

"Her sons send her money. And she cuts people's hair."

"She can survive on that?"

"Everyone on the island gets their hair cut by her. She's excellent at it."

"Perhaps I should get a haircut from her someday."

"I'm sure you'd be satisfied," Ruth said, formally. She couldn't believe the way she was talking to this man. *I'm sure you'd be satisfied?* What was she *saying?* What did she care about Pastor Wishnell's hair-related satisfaction?

"Interesting. And what about your family, Ruth? Is your father a lobsterman, then?"

"Yes."

"A terrible profession."

Ruth did not respond.

"Savage. Brings out the greed in a man. The way they defend their territory! I have never seen such greed! There have been more murders on these islands over lobster boundaries . . ."

The pastor trailed off. Ruth again did not answer. She'd been watching his nephew, Owney Wishnell, whose back was to her. Owney, standing at the wheel, was still sailing the *New Hope* toward Rockland. It would have been easy to assume that Owney Wishnell was deaf, the way he had disregarded them all morning. Yet now that Pastor Wishnell had begun to talk about lobstering, a change seemed to come over Owney's body. His back seemed to draw steady, like that of a hunting cat. A subtle ripple of tension. He was listening.

"Naturally," Pastor Wishnell resumed, "you would not see it as I do, Ruth. You see only the lobstermen of your island. I see many. I see men like your neighbors all up and down this coast. I see these savage dramas played out on—how many islands is it, Owney? How many islands do we minister to, Owney? How many lobster wars have we seen? How many of those lobster territory disputes have I mediated in the last decade alone?"

But Owney Wishnell did not reply. He stood perfectly still, his paint-can–shaped head facing forward, his big hands resting on the wheel of the *New Hope*, his big feet—big as shovels—planted in his clean, high lobsterman's boots. The boat in his command beat down the waves.

"Owney knows how dreadful the lobstering life is," Pastor Wishnell said after a while. "He was a child in 1965, when some of the fishermen on Courne Haven tried to form a collective. Do you remember that incident, Ruth?"

"I remember hearing about it."

"It was a brilliant idea, of course, on paper. A fishermen's collective is the only way to thrive in this business instead of starving. Collective bargaining with wholesalers, collective bargaining with bait dealers, price setting, agreements on trap limits. It would have been a very wise thing to do. But tell that to those blockheads who fish for a living."

"It's hard for them to trust each other," Ruth said. Ruth's father was dead against any idea of a fishermen's collective. As was Angus Addams. As was Uncle Len Thomas. As were most of the fishermen she knew.

"As I said, they are blockheads."

"No," Ruth said. "They're independent, and it's hard for them to change their ways. They feel safer doing things the way they always have, taking care of themselves."

"Your father?" Pastor Wishnell said. "How does he get his lobster catch to Rockland?"

"He takes it on his boat." She wasn't sure how this conversation had turned into an interrogation.

"And how does he get his bait and fuel?"

"He brings them back from Rockland on his boat."

"And so do all the other men on the island, right? Each man in his own little boat, chugging away to Rockland alone because they can't trust one another enough to combine the catch and take turns making the trip. Correct?"

"My dad doesn't want everyone in the world to know how much lobster he's catching, or what kind of price he's getting. Why should he want everyone to know that?"

"So he's enough of a blockhead never to go into partnership with his neighbors."

"I prefer not to think of my father as a blockhead," Ruth said, quietly. "Besides, nobody has the capital to start a cooperative."

Cal Cooley snorted. "Shut up, Cal," Ruth added, less quietly.

"Well, my nephew Owney saw, close up, the war that came of that last collective attempt, didn't he? It was Dennis Burden who tried to form the cooperative on Courne Haven. He put his life out for it. And it was Dennis Burden's little children to whom we brought food and clothing after his neighbors—his *own* neighbors—set his boat on fire and the poor man could no longer make a living."

"I heard that Dennis Burden had made a secret deal with the Sandy Point wholesaler," Ruth said. "I heard he cheated his neighbors." She paused, then, imitating the pastor's inflection, added, "His *own* neighbors."

The pastor frowned. "That is a myth."

"That's not what I heard."

"Would you have burned the man's boat?"

"I wasn't there."

"No. You were not there. But I was there and Owney was there. And it was a good lesson for Owney on the realities of the lobster business. He's seen these medieval battles and disputes on every island from here to Canada. He understands the depravity, the danger, the greed. And he knows better than to become involved in such a profession."

Owney Wishnell made no comment.

At last, the pastor said to Ruth, "You're a bright girl, Ruth."

"Thank you."

"It seems you've had a good education."

Cal Cooley put in, "Too much of an education. Cost a fucking fortune."

The pastor gave Cal such a hard look, it almost made Ruth wince. Cal turned his face. Ruth sensed that this was the last time she'd be hearing the word *fuck* spoken on the *New Hope*.

"And what will become of you, Ruth?" Pastor Toby Wishnell asked. "You have good sense, don't you? What will you do with your life?"

Ruth Thomas looked at the back and the neck of Owney Wishnell, who, she could tell, was still listening closely.

"College?" Pastor Toby Wishnell suggested.

What urgency there was in Owney Wishnell's posture!

So Ruth decided to engage. She said, "More than anything else, sir, I would like to become a lobster fisherman."

Pastor Toby Wishnell gazed at her, coolly. She returned the gaze.

"Because it's such a noble calling, sir," she said.

That was the end of the conversation. Ruth had shut it right up. She couldn't help herself. She could never help herself from mouthing off. She was mortified at the way she had spoken to this man. Mortified, and a little proud. Yeah! She could sass the best of them! But, good God, what an awkward silence. Maybe she should have minded her manners.

The *New Hope* rocked and bumped on the rough sea. Cal Cooley looked pallid, and he quickly went out on deck, where he clung to the railing. Owney sailed on, silent, the back of his neck flushed plum. Ruth Thomas was deeply uncomfortable alone in the presence of Pastor Wishnell, but she hoped that her discomfort was not apparent. She tried to look relaxed. She did not try to converse further with the pastor. Although he did have one last thing to say to her. They were still an hour from Rockland when Pastor Toby Wishnell told Ruth one last thing.

He leaned toward her and said, "Did you know that I was the first man in the Wishnell family not to become a lobster fisherman, Ruth? Did you know that?"

"Yes, sir."

"Good," he said. "Then you'll understand when I tell you this. My nephew Owney will be the second Wishnell not to fish."

He smiled, leaned back, and watched her carefully for the rest of the trip. She maintained a small, defiant smile. She wasn't going to show this man her discomfort. No, sir. He fixed his cool, intelligent gaze on her for the next hour. She just smiled away at him. She was miserable.

Cal Cooley drove Ruth Thomas to Concord in the two-tone Buick the Ellis family had owned since Ruth was a little girl. After telling Cal she was tired, she lay down on the back seat and pretended to sleep. He literally whistled "Dixie" during the entire drive. He knew Ruth was awake, and he knew he was annoying her intensely.

They arrived in Concord around dusk. It was raining lightly, and the Buick made a sweet hissing sound on the wet macadam—a sound that Ruth never heard on a Fort Niles dirt road. Cal turned into the long driveway of the Ellis mansion and let the car coast to a stop. Ruth still pretended to be asleep, and Cal pretended to wake her up. He twisted around in the front seat and poked her hip.

"Try to drag yourself back into consciousness."

She opened her eyes slowly and stretched with great drama. "Are we here already?"

They got out of the car, walked to the front door, and Cal rang the bell. He put his hands in his jacket pockets.

"You are so goddamned pissed off about being here," Cal said, and laughed. "You hate me so much."

The door opened, and there was Ruth's mother. She gave a little gasp and stepped out on the doorstep to put her arms around her daughter. Ruth laid her head on her mother's shoulder and said, "Here I am."

"I'm never sure if you'll really come."

"Here I am."

They held each other.

Ruth's mother said, "You look wonderful, Ruth," although, with her daughter's head lying on her shoulder, she could not really see.

"Here I am," Ruth said. "Here I am."

Cal Cooley coughed decorously.

6

> The young animals that issue from the eggs of the lobster are distinct in every way, including shape, habits, and mode of transportation, from the adult.
>
> —William Saville-Kent
> 1897

MISS VERA ELLIS had never wanted Ruth's mother to marry.

When Mary Smith-Ellis was a little girl, Miss Vera would say, "You know how difficult it was for me when your mother died."

"Yes, Miss Vera," Mary would say.

"I barely survived without her."

"I know, Miss Vera."

"You look so much like her."

"Thank you."

"I can't do a thing without you!"

"Yes, I know."

"My helpmate!"

"Yes, Miss Vera."

Ruth's mother had a most peculiar life with Miss Vera. Mary Smith-Ellis never had close friends or sweethearts. Her life was circumscribed by service—mending, corresponding, packing, shopping, braiding, reassuring, aiding, bathing, and so on. She had inherited the very workload that once burdened her mother and had been raised into servitude, exactly as her mother had been.

Winters in Concord, summers on Fort Niles. Mary did go to school, but only until she was sixteen, and only because Miss Vera did not want a complete idiot as a companion. Other than those years of schooling, Mary Smith-Ellis's life consisted of chores for Miss Vera. In this manner, Mary passed through childhood and adolescence. Then she was a young woman, then one not so young. She had never had a suitor. She was not unattractive, but she was busy. She had work to do.

It was at the end of the summer of 1955 that Miss Vera Ellis decided to give a picnic for the people of Fort Niles. She had guests visiting Ellis House from Europe, and she wanted to show them the local spirit, so she planned to have a lobster bake on Gavin Beach, to which all the residents of Fort Niles were to be invited. The decision was without precedent. There had never before been social occasions attended by the locals of Fort Niles and the Ellis family, but Miss Vera thought it would be a delightful event. A novelty.

Mary, of course, organized everything. She spoke with the fishermen's wives and arranged for them to bake the blueberry pies. She had a modest, quiet manner, and the fishermen's wives liked her well enough. They knew she was from Ellis House, but they didn't hold that against her. She seemed a nice girl, if a bit mousy and shy. Mary also ordered corn and potatoes and charcoal and beer. She borrowed long tables from the Fort Niles grammar school, and arranged to have the pews moved from the Fort Niles church down to the beach. She talked to Mr. Fred Burden of Courne Haven, who was a decent enough fiddler, and hired him to provide music. Finally, she needed to order several hundred pounds of lobster. The fishermen's wives suggested that she discuss this with Mr. Angus Addams, who was the most prolific fisherman on the island. She was told to wait for his boat, the *Sally Chestnut*, at the dock in the middle of the afternoon.

So Mary went down to the dock on a windy August afternoon and picked her way around the tossed stacks of wrecked wooden lobster traps and nets and barrels. As each fisherman came past her, stinking in his high boots and sticky slicker, she asked, "Excuse me, sir? Are you Mr. Angus Addams? Excuse me? Are you the skipper of the *Sally Chestnut*, sir?"

They all shook their heads or grunted crude denials and passed right by. Even Angus Addams himself passed right by, with his head down. He had no idea who the hell this woman was and what the hell she wanted, and he had no interest in finding out. Ruth Thomas's father was another of the men who passed Mary Smith-Ellis, and when she asked, "Are you Angus Addams?" he grunted a denial like that of the other men. Except that, after he passed, he slowed down and turned to take a look at the woman. A good long look.

She was pretty. She was nice-looking. She wore tailored tan trousers and a short-sleeved white blouse, with a small round collar decorated with tiny embroidered flowers. She did not wear makeup. She had a thin silver watch on her wrist, and her dark hair was short and neatly waved. She carried a notepad and a pencil. He liked her slim waist and her clean appearance. She looked tidy. Stan Thomas, a fastidious man, liked that.

Yes, Stan Thomas really looked her over.

"Are you Mr. Angus Addams, sir?" she was asking Wayne Pommeroy, who was staggering by with a broken trap on his shoulder. Wayne looked embarrassed and then angry at his embarrassment, and he hustled past without answering.

Stan Thomas was still looking her over when she turned and caught his eye. He smiled. She walked over, and she was smiling, as well, with a sort of sweet hopefulness. It was a nice smile.

"You're sure *you're* not Mr. Angus Addams?" she asked.

"No. I'm Stan Thomas."

"I'm Mary Ellis," she said, and held out her hand. "I work at Ellis House."

Stan Thomas didn't respond, but he didn't look unfriendly, so she continued.

"My Aunt Vera is giving a party next Sunday for the whole island, and she'd like to purchase several hundred pounds of lobster."

"She would?"

"That's right."

"Who's she want to buy it from?"

"I don't suppose it matters. I was told to look for Angus Addams, but it doesn't matter to me."

"I could sell them to her, but she'd have to pay the retail price."

"Have you got that much lobster?"

"I can get it. It's right out there." He waved his hand at the ocean and grinned. "I just have to pick it up."

Mary laughed.

"It would have to be retail price, though," he repeated. "If I sell it to her."

"Oh, I'm sure that would be fine. She wants to be certain there's plenty of it."

"I don't want to lose any money on the deal. I got a distributor in Rockland who expects a certain amount of lobster from me every week."

"I'm sure your price will be fine."

"How you plan on cooking the lobster?"

"I suppose . . . I'm sorry . . . I don't know, really."

"I'll do it for you."

"Oh, Mr. Thomas!"

"I'll build a big fire on the beach and boil them in garbage cans, with seaweed."

"Oh, my goodness! Is that how?"

"That's how."

"Oh, my goodness! Garbage cans! You don't say."

"The Ellis family can buy new ones. I'll order them for you. Pick them up in Rockland couple days from now."

"Really?"

"The corn goes right on top. And the clams. I'll do the whole thing for you. Sister, that's the only way!"

"Mr. Thomas, we'll certainly pay you for all that and would be very grateful. I actually had no idea how to do it."

"No need," Stan Thomas said. "Hell, I'll do it for free." He surprised himself with this tossed-off line. Stan Thomas had never done anything for free in his life.

"Mr. Thomas!"

"You can help me. How about that, Mary? You can be my helper. That would be pay enough for me."

He put his hand on Mary's arm and smiled. His hands were filthy and reeked of rotting herring bait, but what the hell. He liked the shade of her skin, which was darker and smoother than he was used to seeing around the island. She wasn't as young as he'd thought at first. Now that he was up close, he could see she was no kid. But she was slim and had nice round breasts. He liked her serious, nervous little frown. A pretty mouth, too. He gave her arm a squeeze.

"I think you'll be a real good helper," he said.

She laughed. "I help all the time!" she said. "Believe me, Mr. Thomas, I'm a very good helper!"

It poured rain on the day of the picnic, and that was the last time the Ellis family tried entertaining the whole island. It was a miserable day. Miss Vera stayed down at the beach for only an hour and sat under a tarp, griping. Her European guests went for a walk along the beach and lost their umbrellas to the wind. One of the gentlemen from

Austria complained that his camera was destroyed by the rain. Mr. Burden the fiddler got drunk in someone's car, and played his fiddle in there, with the windows up and the doors locked. They couldn't get him out for hours. Stan Thomas's fire pit never really took off, what with the soaked sand and the driving rain, and the women of the island held their cakes and pies close against their bodies, as if they were protecting infants. The affair was a disaster.

Mary Smith-Ellis bustled around in a borrowed fisherman's slicker, moving chairs under trees and covering tables with bed sheets, but there was no way to salvage the day. The party had been her event to organize, and it was a calamity, but Stan Thomas liked the way she took defeat without shutting down. He liked the way she kept moving around, trying to maintain cheer. She was a nervous woman, but he liked her energy. She was a good worker. He liked that a great deal. He was a good worker himself, and he scorned idleness in any man or woman.

"You should come to my house and warm up," he told her as she rushed past him at the end of the afternoon.

"Oh, no," she said. "You should come with me to Ellis House and warm up."

She repeated this invitation later, after he had helped her return the tables to the school and the pews to the church, so he drove her up to Ellis House at the top of the island. He knew where it was, of course, although he'd never been inside.

"That sure must be a nice place to live," he said.

They were sitting in his truck in the circular driveway; the window glass was fogged from their breath and their steaming wet clothes.

"Oh, they stay here only for the summer," Mary said.

"What about you?"

"Of course I stay here, too. I stay wherever the family stays. I take care of Miss Vera."

"You take care of Miss Vera Ellis? All the time?"

"I'm her helpmate," Mary said, with a wan smile.

"And what's your last name again?"

"Ellis."

"Ellis?"

"That's right."

He couldn't figure this out exactly. He couldn't figure out who this woman was. A servant? She sure acted like a servant, and he'd seen the way that Vera Ellis bitch harped at her. But how come her last name was Ellis? Ellis? Was she a poor relative? Who ever heard of an Ellis hauling chairs and pews all over the place and bustling around in the rain with a borrowed slicker. He thought about asking her what the hell her story was, but she was a sweetheart, and he didn't want to antagonize her. Instead, he took her hand. She let him take it.

Stan Thomas, after all, was a good-looking young man, with a trim haircut and handsome dark eyes. He wasn't tall, but he had a fine, lean figure and an appealing intensity, a directness, that Mary liked very much. She didn't mind his taking her hand at all, even after so short an acquaintance.

"How long are you going to be around?" he asked.

"Until the second week of September."

"That's right. That's when they—you—always leave."

"That's right."

"I want to see you again," he said.

She laughed.

"I'm serious," he said. "I'm going to want to do this again. I like holding your hand. When can I see you again?"

Mary thought silently for a few minutes and then said, in an open way, "I'd like to see you some more, too, Mr. Thomas."

"Good. Call me Stan."

"Yes."

"So when can I see you?"

"I'm not sure."

"I'm probably going to want to see you tomorrow. What about tomorrow? How can I see you tomorrow?"

"Tomorrow?"

"Is there any reason I can't see you tomorrow?"

"I don't know," Mary said, and turned to him suddenly with a look of near panic. "I don't know!"

"You don't know? Don't you like me?"

"Yes, I do. I like you, Mr. Thomas. Stan."

"Good. I'll come by for you tomorrow around four o'clock. We'll go for a drive."

"Oh, my goodness."

"That's what we're going to do," said Stan Thomas. "Tell whoever you have to tell."

"I don't know that I have to tell anybody, but I don't know whether I'll have time to go for a drive."

"Do whatever you have to do, then. Figure out a way. I really do want to see you. Hey! I insist on it!"

"Fine!" She laughed.

"Good. Am I still invited inside?"

"Of course!" Mary said. "Please do come inside!"

They got out of the truck, but Mary did not head up the walk to the grand front door. Dashing through the rain, she went around the side, and Stan Thomas chased her. She ran along the granite edge of the house, under the protection of the great eaves, and ducked inside a plain wooden door, holding it open for Stan. They were in a back hallway, and she took his slicker and hung it on a wall peg.

"We'll go to the kitchen," she said, and opened another door. A set of spiral iron stairs twisted down to a huge, old-fashioned cellar kitchen. There was a massive stone fireplace with iron hooks and pots and crevices that looked as though they were still being used for baking bread. One wall was lined with sinks, another with stoves and ovens. Bundled herbs hung from the ceilings, and the floor was clean worn tile. At the wide pine table in the center of the room sat a tiny middle-aged woman with short red hair and a keen face, nimbly snipping beans into a silver bowl.

"Hello, Edith," said Mary.

The woman nodded her hello and said, "She wants you."

"She does!"

"She keeps calling down for you."

"Since what time?"

"Since all afternoon."

"Oh, but I was busy returning all the chairs and tables," Mary said, and she rushed over to one of the sinks, washed her hands in a speedy blur, and patted them dry on her slacks.

"She doesn't know you're back yet, Mary," said the woman named Edith, "so you may as well have a cup of coffee and a seat."

"I should really see what she needs."

"What about your friend here?"

"Stan!" Mary said, and spun to look at him. Clearly, she had forgotten he was there. "I'm sorry, but I won't be able to sit here and warm up with you, after all."

"Have a cup of coffee and a seat, Mary," said Edith, still snipping the beans. Her voice was commanding. "She doesn't know you're back yet."

"Yes, Mary, have a cup of coffee and a seat," said Stan Thomas, and Edith the bean-snipper flashed him a sidelong look. It was a fast snatch of a look, but it took in a whole lot of information.

"And why don't you have a seat, sir?" Edith said.

"Thank you, ma'am, I will." He sat.

"Get your guest a cup of coffee, Mary."

Mary winced. "I can't," she said. "I have to check on Miss Vera."

"She won't die if you sit here for five minutes and dry off," Edith said.

"I can't!" Mary said. She flashed past Stan Thomas and Edith, right out the kitchen door. They heard her quick footsteps fluttering up the stairs as she called out, "Sorry!" and she was gone.

"I guess I can get the coffee for myself," Stan Thomas said.

"I'll get it for you. This is my kitchen."

Edith left the beans and poured Stan a cup of coffee. Without asking how he took it, she added a splash of cream and did not offer any sugar, which was fine with him. She made herself a cup of the same.

"Are you courting her?" she asked, after she sat down. She was looking at him with a suspicion she made no attempt to mask.

"I only just met her."

"Are you interested in her?"

Stan Thomas did not answer, but he raised his eyebrows in ironic surprise.

"I don't have any advice for you, you know," Edith said.

"You don't have to give me any advice."

"Somebody should."

"Somebody like who?"

"You know, she's already married, Mr. — ?"

"Thomas. Stan Thomas."

"She's already married, Mr. Thomas."

"No. She doesn't wear a ring. She didn't say anything."

"She's married to that old bitch up there." Edith thrust a thin yellow thumb at the ceiling. "See how she scampers away even before she's called?"

"Can I ask you a question?" Stan said. "Who the hell is she?"

"I don't like your mouth," Edith said, although her tone did not suggest she minded it all that much. She sighed. "Mary is technically Miss Vera's niece. But she's really her slave. It's a family tradition. It was the same thing with her mother, and that poor woman only got out of the slavery by drowning. Mary's mother was the one who got swept off by the wave back in twenty-seven. They never found her body. You heard about that?"

"I heard about that."

"Oh, God, I've told this story a million times. Dr. Ellis adopted Jane as a playmate for his little girl—who is now that screaming pain-in-my-hole upstairs. Jane was Mary's mother. She got pregnant by some Italian quarry worker. It was a scandal."

"I heard something about it."

"Well, they tried to keep it quiet, but people do like a good scandal."

"They sure like a good one around here."

"So she drowned, you know, and Miss Vera took over the baby and raised that little girl to be her helper, to replace the mother. And that's who Mary is. And I, for one, cannot believe that the people who watch out for children allowed it."

"What people who watch out for children?"

"I don't know. I just can't believe it's legal for a child to be born into slavery in this day and age."

"You don't mean slavery."

"I know exactly what I mean, Mr. Thomas. We all sat here in this house watching it come to pass, and we asked ourselves why nobody put a stop to it."

"Why didn't you put a stop to it?"

"I'm a cook, Mr. Thomas. I'm not a police officer. And what do you do? No, I'm sure I know. You live here, so of course you're a fisherman."

"Yes."

"You make good money?"

"Good enough."

"Good enough for what?"

"Good enough for around here."

"Is your job dangerous?"

"Not too bad."

"Would you like a real drink?"

"I sure would."

Edith the cook went to a cabinet, moved around some bottles, and came back with a silver flask. She poured amber liquid from it into two clean coffee cups. She gave one to Stan. "You're not a drunk, are you?" she asked.

"Are you?"

"Very funny, with my workload. Very funny." Edith stared at Stan Thomas narrowly. "And you never married anyone from around here?"

"I never married anyone from around anywhere," Stan said, and he laughed.

"You seem good-natured. Everything's a big joke. How long have you been courting Mary?"

"Nobody's courting anybody, ma'am."

"How long have you been interested in Mary?"

"I only met her this week. I guess this is a bigger deal than I thought. I think she's a nice girl."

"She is a nice girl. But don't they have nice girls right here on your island?"

"Hey, now take it easy."

"Well, I think it's unusual that you're not married. How old are you?"

"I'm in my twenties. My late twenties." Stan Thomas was twenty-five.

"A good-looking, good-natured man like you with a good business? Who isn't a drunk? And not married yet? My understanding is that people marry young around here, especially the fishermen."

"Maybe nobody around here likes me."

"Smart mouth. Maybe you have bigger ambitions."

"Listen, all I did was drive Mary around to do some errands."

"Do you want to see her again? Is that your idea?"

"I was thinking about it."

"She's almost thirty years old, you know."

"I think she looks swell."

"And she is an Ellis—legally an Ellis—but she doesn't have any money, so don't go getting any ideas about that. They'll never give her a dime except to keep her dressed and fed."

"I don't know what kind of ideas you think I have."

"That's what I'm trying to figure out."

"Well, I can see you're trying to figure something out. I can see that pretty clear."

"She doesn't have a mother, Mr. Thomas. She is considered important around this house because Miss Vera needs her, but nobody in this house looks out for Mary. She's a young woman without a mother to watch over her, and I'm trying to find out your intentions."

"Well, you don't talk like a mother. All respect to you, ma'am, but you talk like a father."

This pleased Edith. "She doesn't have one of those, either."

"That's a tough break."

"How do you think you'll go about seeing her, Mr. Thomas?"

"I think I'll pick her up and take her for a drive sometimes."

"Will you?"

"What do you make of that?"

"It's none of my business."

Stan Thomas laughed right out loud. "Oh, I'll bet you can make just about anything your business, ma'am."

"Very funny," she said. She took another swig of hooch. "Everything's a big joke with you. Mary's leaving in a few weeks, you know. And she won't be back until next June."

"Then I'll have to pick her up and take her for a drive every day, I guess."

Stan Thomas treated Edith to his biggest smile, which was most winning.

Edith pronounced, "You're in for a heap of trouble. Too bad, because I don't dislike you, Mr. Thomas."

"Thank you. I don't dislike you, either."

"Don't you mess up that girl."

"I don't plan to mess up anybody," he said.

Edith evidently thought their conversation was over, so she got back to the beans. Since she did not ask Stan Thomas to leave, he sat there in the kitchen of Ellis House for a while longer, hoping Mary would come back and sit with him. He waited and waited, but Mary did not return, so he finally went home. It was dark by then, and still raining. He figured he'd have to see her another day.

They were married the next August. It wasn't a hasty wedding. It wasn't an unexpected wedding, in that Stan told Mary back in June of 1956—the day after she returned to Fort Niles Island with the Ellis family—that they were going to get married by the end of that summer. He told her that she was going to stay on Fort Niles with him from now on and she could forget about being a slave to goddamn Miss Vera Ellis. So it had all been arranged well in advance. Still, the ceremony itself had the marks of haste.

Mary and Stan were married in Stan Thomas's living room by Mort Beekman, who was then the traveling pastor for the Maine islands. Mort Beekman preceded Toby Wishnell. He was, at the time, the skipper of the *New Hope*. Unlike Wishnell, Pastor Mort Beekman was well liked. He had an air about him of not giving a shit, which was fine with everyone concerned. Beekman was no zealot, and that too put him in good standing with the fishermen in his far-flung parishes.

Stan Thomas and Mary Smith-Ellis had no witnesses at their ceremony, no rings, no attendants, but Pastor Mort Beekman, true to his nature, went right ahead with the ceremony. "What the hell do you need a witness for, anyhow?" he asked. Beekman happened to be on the island for a baptism, and what did he care about rings or attendants or witnesses? These two young people certainly looked like adults. Could they sign the certificate? Yes. Were they old enough to do this without anyone's permission? Yes. Was it going to be a big hassle? No.

"Do you want all the praying and Scriptures and stuff?" Pastor Beekman asked the couple.

"No, thanks," Stan said. "Just the wedding part."

"Maybe a little praying . . ." Mary suggested hesitantly.

Pastor Mort Beekman sighed and scraped together a marriage ceremony with a little praying, for the sake of the lady. He couldn't help noticing that she looked like hell, what with all the paleness and all the trembling. The whole ceremony was over in about four minutes. Stan Thomas slipped the pastor a ten-dollar bill on his way out the door.

"Much appreciated," Stan said. "Thanks for coming by."

"Sure enough," said the pastor, and headed down to the boat so that he could get off the island before dark; there was never any decent lodging for him on Fort Niles, and he wasn't about to stay overnight on that inhospitable rock.

It was the least ostentatious wedding in the history of the Ellis family. If, that is, Mary Smith-Ellis could be considered a member of the Ellis family, a matter now seriously in question.

"As your aunt," Miss Vera had told Mary, "I must tell you that I think marriage would be a mistake for you. I think it a big mistake for you to handcuff yourself to this fisherman and to this island."

"But you love this island," Mary had said.

"Not in February, darling."

"But I could visit you in February."

"Darling, you'll have a husband to look after, and there will be no time for visiting. I had a husband once myself, and I know. It was most *restrictive*," she declared, although it had not in the least been restrictive.

To the surprise of many, Miss Vera did not put up further argument against Mary's wedding plans. For those who had witnessed Vera's violent outrage over Mary's mother's pregnancy thirty years earlier, and her tantrums at Mary's mother's death twenty-nine years earlier (not to mention her daily bouts of temper over sundry insignificant matters), this calm in the face of Mary's news was a mystery. How could Vera stand for this? How could she lose another helpmate? How could she tolerate this disloyalty, this abandonment?

Perhaps nobody was more surprised by this reaction than Mary herself, who had lost ten pounds over the course of that summer from anxiety about Stan Thomas. What to do about Stan Thomas? He was not pressing her to see him, he was not taking her away from her responsibilities, but he persistently insisted that they would marry by the end of the summer. He'd been saying so since June. There did not seem to be room for negotiation.

"You think it's a good idea, too," he reminded her, and she did think so. She did like the idea of marrying. It wasn't something she had thought about much before, but now it seemed exactly right. And he was so handsome. And he was so confident.

"We're not getting any younger," he reminded her, and indeed they were not.

Still, Mary vomited twice on the day she had to tell Miss Vera she was to marry Stan Thomas. She couldn't put it off any longer and finally broke the news in the middle of July. But the conversation, surprisingly, was not difficult at all. Vera did not become enraged, although she had frequently become enraged over much smaller issues. Vera made her "this is a big mistake" statement as a concerned aunt, and then resigned herself to the idea entirely, leaving Mary to ask all the panicky questions.

"What will you do without me?" she asked.

"Mary, you sweet, sweet girl. Don't let it cross your mind." This was accompanied by a warm smile, a pat on the hand.

"But what will I do? I've never been away from you!"

"You are a lovely, capable young woman. You'll be fine without me."

"But you don't think I should do this, do you?"

"Oh, Mary. What does it matter what I think?"

"You think he'll be a bad husband."

"I have never spoken a word against him."

"But you don't like him."

"You're the one who has to like him, Mary."

"You think I'll end up poor and alone."

"Oh, you never will, Mary. You'll always have a roof over your head. You'll never end up selling matches in the city or something dreadful like that."

"You think I won't make friends here on the island. You think I'll be lonely, and you think I'll go crazy in the winter."

"Who wouldn't make friends with you?"

"You think I'm loose, running around with a fisherman. You think I'm turning out to be like my mother."

"The things I think!" Miss Vera said, and laughed.

"I will be happy with Stan," Mary said. "I *will.*"

"Then I couldn't be happier for you. A happy bride is a radiant bride."

"But where should we get married?"

"At a church of God, I dearly hope."

Mary fell silent, as did Miss Vera. It was a tradition for Ellis brides to marry in the gardens of Ellis House, attended by the Episcopal Bishop of Concord, boated in for the occasion. Ellis brides had lavish weddings, witnessed by every available member of the Ellis family and by all the family's dearest friends. Ellis brides had elegant receptions at Ellis House. So when Miss Vera Ellis suggested a marriage at an unnamed "church of God," Mary had reason to be silent.

"But I want to get married here, at Ellis House."

"Oh, Mary. You don't want that headache. You should have a simple ceremony and get it over with."

"But will you be there?" Mary asked, after a long while.

"Oh, darling."

"Will you?"

"I would only cry and cry, darling, and spoil your special day."

Later that afternoon, Mr. Lanford Ellis—Vera's older brother and the reigning patriarch of the family—called Mary Smith-Ellis to his room to congratulate her on her forthcoming marriage. He expressed his hope that Stan Thomas was an honorable young man. He said, "You should buy yourself a pretty wedding gown," and he passed her an envelope. She picked at the flap, and he said, "Don't open it here." He gave her a kiss. He gave her a squeeze on the hand and said, "We have always had the fondest feelings for you." And he did not say more.

Mary didn't open the envelope until she was alone in her room that evening. She counted out a thousand dollars in cash. Ten hundred-dollar bills, which she slipped under her pillow. That was a great deal of money for a wedding gown in 1956, but, in the end, Mary was married in a flowered cotton dress that she had sewn for herself two summers earlier. She didn't want to spend the money. Instead, she decided to hand the envelope and its contents to Stan Thomas.

That money was what she brought to the marriage, along with her clothing and the sheets from her bed. These were all her possessions, after decades of service to the Ellis family.

In the Ellis mansion in Concord, Ruth Thomas's mother showed her to her room. They had not seen each other for some time. Ruth didn't like to visit Concord and rarely did. There had been some Christmases, in fact, when Ruth had elected to stay in her room at boarding school. She liked that more than being in Concord and the Ellis mansion. Last Christmas, for instance.

"You look wonderful, Ruth," her mother said.

"Thank you. You look good, too."

"Don't you have any bags?"

"No. Not this time."

"We put up new wallpaper for you."

"It looks nice."

"And here's a picture of you when you were a little girl."

"Look at that," Ruth said, and leaned toward the framed photograph hanging on the wall next to the dresser. "That's me?"

"That's you."

"What do I have in my hands?"

"Pebbles. Pebbles from the Ellises' driveway."

"Boy, look at those fists!"

"And there I am," Ruth's mother said.

"There you are."

"I'm trying to get you to hand me the pebbles."

"It doesn't look as if you're going to get them."

"No, it doesn't. I'll bet I didn't get them."

"How old was I?"

"About two. So adorable."

"And how old were you?"

"Oh. Thirty-three or so."

"I never saw that picture before."

"No, I don't think you have."

"I wonder who took it."

"Miss Vera took it."

Ruth Thomas sat down on the bed, a handsome brass heirloom covered with a lace spread. Her mother sat beside her and asked, "Does it smell a bit musty in here?"

"No, it's fine."

They sat quietly for a time. Ruth's mother stood and raised the window shades. "We may as well let in some light," she said, and sat down again.

"Thank you," Ruth said.

"When I bought that wallpaper, I thought it was cherry blossoms, but now that I look at it, I think it's apple blossoms. Isn't that funny? I don't know why I didn't see that at first."

"Apple blossoms are nice."

"It doesn't make any difference, I suppose."

"Either way is nice. You did a good job with the wallpapering."

"We paid a man to do it."

"It looks really pretty."

After another long silence, Mary Smith-Ellis Thomas took her daughter's hand and asked, "Should we go see Ricky now?"

. . .

Ricky was in a baby's crib, although he was nine years old. He was the size of a small child, a three-year-old, perhaps, and his fingers and toes were curled like talons. His hair was black and short, matted in the back because of the way he swiveled his head back and forth, back and forth. He was forever grinding his head against the mattress, forever flipping his face from side to side, as though searching desperately for something. And his eyes, too, rolled to the left and to the right, always seeking. He made screeching sounds and high-pitched whines and howls, but when Mary approached, he settled into a steady muttering.

"Here's Mama," she said. "Here's Mama."

She lifted him out of the crib and placed him, on his back, on a sheepskin mat on the floor. He could not sit up or hold up his head. He could not feed himself. He could not speak. On the sheepskin mat, his small, crooked legs flopped to one side and his arms to the other. Back and forth he swung his head, back and forth, and his fingers waved and tensed, fluttering in the air the way sea plants flutter in the water.

"Is he getting any better?" Ruth asked.

"Well," her mother said, "I think so, Ruth. I always think he's getting a little better, but nobody else ever sees it."

"Where's his nurse?"

"Oh, she's around. She may be down in the kitchen, taking a break. She's a new woman, and she seems very nice. She likes to sing to Ricky. Doesn't she, Ricky? Doesn't Sandra sing to you? Because she knows you like it. Doesn't she?"

Mary spoke to him the way mothers speak to newborns, or the way Senator Simon Addams spoke to his dog Cookie, in a loving voice with no expectation of reply.

"Do you see your sister?" she asked. "Do you see your big sister? She came to visit you, little boy. She came to say hello to Ricky."

"Hello there, Ricky," said Ruth, trying to follow the cadence of her mother's voice. "Hello there, little brother."

Ruth felt sick. She bent over and patted Ricky's head, which he whipped away from under her palm, and she felt his matted hair slip away in a flash — gone. She pulled back her hand, and he let his head rest for a moment. Then he flipped it with a suddenness that made Ruth start.

Ricky was born when Ruth was nine years old. He was born in a hospital in Rockland. Ruth never saw him when he was a baby, because her mother didn't return to the island after Ricky was born. Her father went to Rockland with his wife when the baby was due, and Ruth stayed with Mrs. Pommeroy next door. Her mother was supposed to come back with a baby, but she never did. She didn't come back, because something was wrong with the baby. Nobody had expected that.

According to what Ruth had heard, her father, from the moment he saw the severely retarded infant, started laying out the blame, fast and mean. He was disgusted and he was angry. Who had done this to his son? He immediately decided that the baby had inherited the sad condition from Mary's ancestors. After all, what did anyone know of the Bath Naval Hospital orphan or of the Italian immigrant? Who knew what monsters had lurked in that dark past? Stan Thomas's ancestors, on the other hand, were accounted for back to ten generations, and nothing of this sort had ever appeared. There had never been any freaks in Stan's family. Obviously, Stan said, this is what you get for marrying someone whose background isn't known. Yes, this is what you get.

Mary, still exhausted in her hospital bed, came back with her own demented defense. She was not normally a fighter, but she fought this time. She fought back dirty. Oh, yes, she said, all Stan's ancestors could be accounted for, precisely because they were all *related* to one another. They were all siblings and first cousins, and it doesn't take a genius to realize that, after enough generations of inbreeding and incest, this is what you get. This child, this Ricky-boy with the flippy head and the clawed hands.

"This is *your* son, Stan!" she said.

It was an ugly, wretched fight, and it upset the nurses in the maternity ward, who heard every cruel word. Some of the younger nurses cried. They had never heard anything like it. The head nurse came on duty at midnight and led Stan Thomas away from his wife's room. The head nurse was a big woman, not easily intimidated, even by a tough-mouthed lobsterman. She hustled him away while Mary was still screaming at him.

"For the love of God," the nurse snapped at Stan, "the woman needs her rest."

A few afternoons later, a visitor came to see Mary and Stan and the new baby in the hospital; it was Mr. Lanford Ellis. Somehow, he had heard the news. He had sailed over to Rockland on the *Stonecutter* to pay his respects and to offer Mary and Stan the Ellis family's condolences on their tragic situation. Stan and Mary were coolly reconciled by this time. At least they could be in the same room.

Lanford Ellis told Mary of a conversation he'd had with his sister Vera, and of their consensus. He and his sister had discussed the immediate problem and had agreed that Mary should not take the baby to Fort Niles Island. Mary would have no medical support there, no professional help for Ricky. The doctors had already announced that he would need round-the-clock care for the rest of his life. Did Mary and Stan have a plan?

Mary and Stan admitted that they did not. Lanford Ellis was sympathetic. He understood that this was a difficult time for the couple, and he had a suggestion. Because of the Ellis family's attachment to Mary, they were prepared to help. Lanford Ellis would pay for Ricky's care at an appropriate institution. For life. No matter the cost. He had heard of an excellent private facility in New Jersey.

"New Jersey?" Mary Thomas said, incredulous.

New Jersey did seem far away, Lanford Ellis conceded. But the home was said to be the best in the country. He had spoken with the administrator that morning. If Stan and Mary weren't comfortable with the arrangement, there was one other possibility . . .

Or . . .

Or what?

Or, if Mary and her family moved to Concord, where Mary could resume her position as companion to Miss Vera, the Ellis family would provide Ricky with private care right there, at the Ellis mansion. Lanford Ellis would have part of the servants' wing converted into a comfortable area for young Ricky. He would pay for good private nurses and for the finest medical care. For life. He would also find Stan Thomas a good job and would send Ruth to a good school.

"Don't you fucking dare," Stan Thomas said, in a dangerously low voice. "Don't you fucking dare try to take my wife back."

"It is merely a suggestion," said Lanford Ellis. "The decision is yours." And he left.

"Did you people fucking poison her?" Stan Thomas shouted after Lanford as the old man walked away, down the hospital hall. Stan followed him. "Did you poison my wife? Did you people make this happen? Answer me! Did you goddamn people set this whole fucking thing up just to get her back?"

But Lanford Ellis had no more to say, and the big nurse stepped in once more.

Naturally, Ruth Thomas never knew the details of the argument her parents had following Mr. Ellis's offer. But she did know that a few points were made immediately clear, right there in the hospital room. There was no way on earth that Mary Smith-Ellis Thomas, child of an orphan, was going to put her son, no matter how disabled, into an institution. And there was no way on earth that Stan Thomas, tenth-generation islander, was going to move to Concord, New Hampshire. Nor would he allow his daughter to move there, where she might be turned into a slave of Miss Vera Ellis, like her mother and her grandmother before her.

These points having been established, there was little room for negotiation. And whatever the severity of the argument, the decision was quick and final. Mary went to Concord with her son. She returned to the Ellis mansion and to her position with Vera Ellis. Stan Thomas went back to the island to join his daughter, alone. Not immediately, however. He went missing for a few months.

"Where did you go?" Ruth asked him when she was seventeen years old. "Where did you run off to for all that time?"

"I was angry," he replied. "And it's none of your business."

"Where's my mother?" Ruth asked her father, back when she was nine years old and he finally came back to Fort Niles, alone. His explanation was a disaster—something about what didn't matter and what wasn't worth asking about and what should be forgotten. Ruth puzzled over this, and then Mr. Pommeroy drowned, and she thought—it made perfect sense—that her mother may have drowned, too. Of course. That was the answer. A few weeks after reaching this conclusion, Ruth began receiving letters from her mother, which was confusing. She thought for a time that the letters came from heaven. As she grew older, she more or less pieced the story together. Eventually, Ruth felt she understood the event completely.

Now, in Ricky's room, which smelled of his medicines, Ruth's mother took a bottle of lotion from the dresser and sat on the floor beside her son. She rubbed the lotion into his strange feet, massaging and stretching his toes and pressing her thumbs into his curled arches.

"How's your father?" she asked.

Ricky shrieked and muttered.

"He's well," Ruth said.

"Is he taking good care of you?"

"Maybe I'm taking good care of him."

"I used to worry about your not getting enough love."

"I got enough."

Ruth's mother looked so concerned, though, that Ruth tried to think of something to reassure her, some loving incident related to her father. She said, "On my birthdays, when he gives me presents, he always says, 'Now, don't go using your x-ray vision on it, Ruth.' "

"X-ray vision?"

"Before I open the present, you know? When I'm looking at the box? He always says that. 'Don't go using your x-ray vision on it, Ruth.' He's pretty funny."

Mary Smith-Ellis Thomas nodded slowly, without looking the slightest bit less concerned.

"He gives you nice birthday presents?"

"Sure."

"That's good."

"On my birthdays when I was little he used to stand me up on a chair and say, 'Do you feel any bigger today? You sure look bigger.' "

"I remember him doing that."

"We have a real good time," Ruth said.

"Is Angus Addams still around?"

"Oh, sure. We see Angus about every day."

"He used to scare me. I once saw him beating a child with a buoy. Back when I was first married."

"No kidding. A child?"

"Some poor boy who was working on his boat."

"Oh, not a child, then. His sternman, probably. Some lazy teenager. Angus is a tough boss, that's for sure. He can't fish with anyone these days. He doesn't get along with anyone."

"I don't think he ever thought much of me."

"He doesn't like to let on that he thinks much of anybody."

"You have to understand, Ruth, that I had never met people like that. You know, it was the first winter I was on Fort Niles that Angus Addams lost his finger while he was fishing. Do you remember hearing about that? It was such cold weather, and he wasn't wearing gloves, so his hands got frozen. And I guess he caught his finger in — what is it?"

"The winch head."

"He caught his finger in the winch head and it got twisted in some rope and was pulled right off. The other man on the boat said Angus kicked the finger overboard and kept fishing the rest of the day."

"The way I heard it," Ruth said, "he cauterized his hand with the lit end of his cigar so he could keep fishing all day."

"Oh, Ruth."

"I don't know if I believe it, though. I've never once seen Angus Addams with a cigar in his mouth that was actually lit."

"Oh, Ruth."

"One thing's for sure. He's definitely missing a finger."

Ruth's mother said nothing. Ruth looked down at her hands. "Sorry," she said. "You were trying to make a point?"

"Just that I'd never been around people who were so rough."

Ruth thought to point out that many people found Miss Vera Ellis pretty rough, but she bit her tongue and said, "I see."

"I'd been on the island only a year, you know, when Angus Addams came over to our house with Snoopy, his cat. He said, 'I'm sick of this cat, Mary. If you don't take it off my hands, I'll shoot it right here in front of you.' And he was carrying a gun. You know how big his voice is, how angry he always sounds? Well, I believed him, so of course I took the cat. Your father was furious; he told me to give the cat back, but Angus threatened again to shoot it in front of me. I didn't want to see that cat get shot. Your dad said he wouldn't do it, but I couldn't be sure. She was a pretty cat. Do you remember Snoopy?"

"I think so."

"Such a pretty, big white cat. Your father said Angus was playing a trick on us, his way to unload the cat. I guess it was a trick, because a few weeks later Snoopy had five kittens, and those kittens were our problem. Then I was the one who got angry, but your father and Angus thought it was a big joke. And Angus thought it was clever of him to trick me like that. He and your father teased me about it for months. Your father, you know, ended up drowning the kittens."

"That's too bad."

"It was. But I think there was something wrong with those kittens, anyway."

"Yeah," Ruth said. "They couldn't swim."

"Ruth!"

"I'm just kidding. Sorry. It was a stupid joke." Ruth hated herself.

She was amazed once again at how swiftly she reached this point with her mother, this point of making a cruel joke at the expense of a woman who was so fragile. Despite her best intentions, she would, within minutes, say something that hurt her mother. In the company of her mother, Ruth could feel herself turn into a charging rhinoceros. A rhinoceros in a china shop. But why was her mother so easy to wound? Why was her mother such a china shop in the first place? Ruth wasn't used to women like her. She was used to women like the Pommeroy sisters, who strode through life as though they were invincible. Ruth was more comfortable around tough people. Tough people made Ruth feel less like a . . . rhinoceros.

Mary rubbed her son's legs and gently rotated each of his feet, stretching the ankle. "Oh, Ruth," she said, "I was so hurt the day the kittens were drowned."

"I'm sorry," Ruth said, and she truly was. "I'm sorry."

"Thank you, sweetheart. Do you want to help with Ricky? Will you help me rub him?"

"Sure," Ruth said, although she could think of nothing less appealing.

"You can rub his hands. They say it's good to keep them from getting too twisted, poor little guy."

Ruth poured some lotion into her palm and started to rub one of Ricky's hands. Immediately, she felt a movement in her stomach, a building wave like seasickness. Such an atrophied, lifeless little hand!

Ruth was once fishing with her father when he pulled up a trap with a molting lobster. It was not unusual, in the summertime, to find lobsters with new, soft shells only days old, but this lobster had probably molted an hour or so before. Its perfect and empty shell lay beside it in the trap, useless now, hollow armor. Ruth had held the naked lobster in her palm, and handling it had given her the same seasickness she now experienced in handling her brother. A lobster with no shell was boneless meat; when Ruth picked it up, the limp lobster hung on her hand, offering no more resistance than a wet sock. It hung there like something melting, as if it would eventually drip from her fingers. It was nothing like a normal lobster, nothing like one of those snappy fierce little tanks. And yet she could feel its life in her hand, its blood whirring in her palm. Its flesh was a bluish jelly, like a raw scallop. She had shuddered. Just by handling it, she had begun to kill it, leaving her fingerprints on its thin-skinned organs. She had flung it over the side of the boat and watched it sink, translucent. It didn't have a chance. It didn't have a chance in the world. Something probably ate it before it even touched bottom.

"There," said Ruth's mother. "That's good of you."

"Poor little guy," Ruth made herself say, working the lotion into her brother's strange fingers, his wrist, his forearm. Her voice sounded strained, but her mother seemed not to notice. "Poor little guy."

"Did you know that when your father was a little boy in the Fort Niles school, back in the forties, the teachers taught the children to tie knots? That was an important part of the curriculum on the island. And they were taught how to read tidal charts, too. In school! Can you imagine?"

"It was probably a good idea," Ruth said. "It makes sense for island kids to know those things. Especially back then. They were going to be fishermen, right?"

"But in *school*, Ruth? Couldn't they first teach the children to read and leave the knots till the afternoon?"

"I'm sure they learned to read, too."

"That's why we wanted to send you to private school."

"Dad didn't want it."

"I meant the Ellises and I. I'm very proud of you, Ruth. I'm proud of how well you did. Eleventh in the class! And I'm proud that you learned French. Will you say something in French for me?"

Ruth laughed.

"What?" her mother asked. "What's funny?"

"Nothing. It's just that whenever I speak French around Angus Addams, he says, 'What? Your *what* hurts?' "

"Oh, Ruth." She sounded sad. "I'd hoped you would speak some French to me."

"It's not worth it, Mom. I have a stupid accent."

"Well. Whatever you want, honey."

They were quiet for a spell, and then Ruth's mother said, "Your father probably wished you'd stayed on the island and learned to tie knots!"

"I'm sure that's exactly what he wished," Ruth said.

"And tides! I'm sure he wanted you to learn tides. I could never learn them, though I tried. Your father tried to teach me how to operate a boat. Driving the boat was easy, but somehow I was supposed to know where all the rocks and ledges were, and which ones popped up during which tides. They had practically no buoys out there, and the ones they had were always drifting off course, and your father would yell at me if I tried to navigate according to them. He didn't trust the buoys, but how was I to know? And currents! I thought you were supposed to point the boat and pull the throttle. I didn't know anything about currents!"

"How could you know?"

"How could I know, Ruth? I thought I knew about island life, because I'd spent my summers there, but I didn't know a thing. I had no idea about how bad the wind gets in the winter. Did you know that some people lost their minds from it?"

"I think most people on Fort Niles did," Ruth said and laughed.

"It doesn't stop! My first winter there, the wind started blowing at the end of October and didn't die down until April. I had the strangest dreams that winter, Ruth. I kept dreaming that the island was about to blow away. The trees on the island had long, long roots that reached right down to the ocean floor, and they were the only thing keeping the island from drifting away in the wind."

"Were you scared?"

"I was terrified."

"Wasn't anybody nice to you?"

"Yes. Mrs. Pommeroy was nice to me."

There was a knock at the door, and Ruth's mother started. Ricky started, too, and began flipping his head back and forth. He screeched; it was a terrible sound, like the screech of an old car's bad brakes.

"Shhh," his mother said. "Shhh."

Ruth opened the nursery door, and there stood Cal Cooley.

"Catching up?" he asked. He came in and bent his tall frame into a rocking chair. He smiled at Mary but did not look at Ricky.

"Miss Vera wants to go for a drive," he said.

"Oh!" Mary exclaimed, and jumped to her feet. "I'll fetch the nurse. We'll get our coats. Ruth, go get your coat."

"She wants to go shopping," Cal said, still smiling, but looking at Ruth now. "She heard that Ruth arrived with no luggage."

"And how did she hear that, Cal?" Ruth asked.

"Beats me. All I know is she wants to buy you some new clothes, Ruth."

"I don't need anything."

"Told you so," he said, with the greatest satisfaction. "I told you to bring your own clothes or Miss Vera would end up buying you new things and pissing you off."

"Look, I don't care," Ruth said. "Whatever you people feel like making me do, I don't care. I do not give a shit. Just get it over with."

"Ruth!" exclaimed Mary, but Ruth didn't care. The hell with all of them. Cal Cooley didn't seem to care, either. He just shrugged.

They drove to the dress shop in the old two-tone Buick. It took Mary and Cal nearly an hour to get Miss Vera dressed and bundled up and down the stairs to the car, where she sat in the front passenger seat with her beaded purse on her lap. She had not been out of the house for several months, Mary said.

Miss Vera was so small; she was like a bird perched in the front seat. Her hands were tiny, and she trembled her thin fingers lightly across her beaded purse, as though reading Braille or praying with an endless rosary. She had lace gloves with her, which she set beside her on the seat. Whenever Cal Cooley turned a corner, she would put her left hand on the gloves, as though she were afraid they would slide away. She gasped at every turn, although Cal was driving at approximately the speed of a healthy pedestrian. Miss Vera wore a long mink coat and a hat with a black veil. Her voice was very quiet, with a slight waver. She smiled when she spoke, pronounced her words with a trace of a British accent, and delivered her every line wistfully.

"Oh, to go on a drive . . ." she said.

"Yes," agreed Ruth's mother.

"Do you know how to drive, Ruth?"

"I do," said Ruth.

"Oh, how clever of you. I was never proficient, myself. I would always *collide* . . ." The memory set Miss Vera to tittering. She put her hand to her mouth, as shy girls do. Ruth had not remembered Miss Vera to be a giggler. It must have come with age, a late affectation. Ruth looked at the old woman and thought about how, back on Fort Niles Island, Miss Vera made the local men working on her yard drink from the garden hose. She wouldn't allow them into the kitchen for a glass of water. Not on the hottest day. That practice of hers was so hated that it gave rise to an expression on the island: *Drinking out of the hose.* It indicated the lowest depth of insult. *My wife got the house and the kids, too. That bitch really left me drinking out of the hose.*

Cal Cooley, at a four-way intersection, paused at a stop sign and let another car pass through. Then, as he started to move, Miss Vera cried, "Wait!"

Cal stopped. There were no other cars in sight. He started up again.

"Wait!" repeated Miss Vera.

"We have the right of way," Cal said. "It's our turn to go."

"I think it more prudent to wait. Other cars may be coming."

Cal shifted into park and waited at the stop sign. No other cars appeared. For several minutes they sat in silence. Eventually a station wagon pulled up behind the Buick and the driver honked one short burst. Cal said nothing. Mary said nothing. Miss Vera said nothing. Ruth sank down into her seat and thought how full the world was of assholes. The station wagon driver honked again, twice, and Miss Vera said, "So rude."

Cal rolled down his window and waved the station wagon by. It passed. They sat in the Buick at the stop sign. Another car pulled up behind them, and Cal waved it past, too. A red, rusted pickup truck passed them from the other direction. Then, as before, there were no cars to be seen.

Miss Vera clenched her gloves in her left hand and said, "Go!"

Cal drove slowly through the intersection and continued to the highway. Miss Vera giggled again. "An exploit!" she said.

They drove into the center of Concord, and Mary directed Cal Cooley to park in front of a ladies' dress shop. The name, Blaire's, was painted in gold on the window in elegant cursive.

"I won't go in," Miss Vera said. "It is too much effort. But tell Mr. Blaire to come here. I shall tell him what we need."

Mary went into the shop and soon reappeared with a young man. She looked apprehensive. The young man walked to the passenger side of the car and tapped on the window. Miss Vera frowned. He grinned and gestured for her to roll down her window. Ruth's mother stood behind him in a posture of overriding anxiety.

"Who the *devil?*" Miss Vera said.

"Maybe you should roll down your window and see what he wants," Cal suggested.

"I'll do no such thing!" She glared at the young man. His face shone in the morning sun, and he smiled at her, again making the window-rolling gesture. Ruth slid over in the back seat and rolled down her window.

"Ruth!" Miss Vera exclaimed.

"Can I help you?" Ruth asked the man.

"I'm Mr. Blaire," the young man said. He reached his hand through the window to shake Ruth's.

"Nice to meet you, Mr. Blaire," she said. "I'm Ruth Thomas."

"He is not!" Miss Vera declared. She spun in her seat with a sudden and shocking agility and glared fiercely at the young man. "You are not Mr. Blaire. Mr. Blaire has a silver mustache!"

"That's my father, ma'am. He's retired, and I run the store."

"Tell your father that Miss Vera Ellis wishes to speak to him."

"I'd be happy to tell him, ma'am, but he's not here. My father lives in Miami, ma'am."

"Mary!"

Ruth's mother rushed over to the Buick and stuck her head in Ruth's window.

"Mary! When did this happen?"

"I don't know. I don't know anything about it."

"I don't need any clothes," Ruth said. "I don't need anything. Let's go home."

"When did your father retire?" Ruth's mother asked the young Mr. Blaire. She was pale.

"Seven years ago, ma'am."

"Impossible! He would have informed me!" Miss Vera said.

"Can we go someplace else?" Ruth asked. "Isn't there another shop in Concord?"

"There is no shop in Concord but Blaire's," Miss Vera said.

"Well, we're happy to hear that you think so," said Mr. Blaire. "And I'm sure we can help you, ma'am."

Miss Vera did not reply.

"My father taught me everything he knew, ma'am. All his customers are now my customers. As satisfied as ever!"

"Take your head out of my car."

"Ma'am?"

"Remove your damn head from my car."

Ruth started laughing. The young man pulled his head from the Buick and walked stiffly and quickly back into his shop. Mary followed, trying to touch his arm, trying to mollify him, but he shook her off.

"Young lady, this is not amusing." Miss Vera turned again in her seat and leveled an evil glare at Ruth.

"Sorry."

"Imagine!"

"Shall we head back home, Miss Vera?" Cal asked.

"We shall wait for Mary!" she snapped.

"Naturally. That's what I meant."

"That is not, however, what you said."

"Pardon me."

"Oh, the *nitwits!*" Miss Vera exclaimed. "Everywhere!"

Mary came back and sat silently beside her daughter. Cal pulled away from the curb, and Miss Vera said, with exasperation, "Careful! Careful, careful, careful."

Nobody spoke on the drive home until they pulled up to the house. There, Miss Vera turned and smiled yellowly at Ruth. She giggled once again. She had composed herself. "We have a nice time, your mother and I," she said. "After all those years of living with men, we are at last alone together. We don't have husbands to tend to or brothers or fathers looking over us. Two independent ladies, and we do as we choose. Isn't that right, Mary?"

"Yes."

"I missed your mother when she ran off and married your father, Ruth. Did you know that?"

Ruth said nothing. Her mother looked at her nervously and said, in a low voice, "I'm sure Ruth knows that."

"I remember her walking out of the house after she told me she was marrying a fisherman. I watched her walk away. I was upstairs in my bedroom. You know that room, Ruth? How it looks out over the front walk? Oh, my little Mary looked so small and brave. Oh, Mary. Your little shoulders were so square, as if to say, *I can do anything!* You dear girl, Mary. You poor, dear, sweet girl. You were so brave."

Mary closed her eyes. Ruth felt an appalling, bilious anger rising in her throat.

"Yes, I watched your mother walk away, Ruth, and it made me cry. I sat in my room and shed tears. My brother came in and put his arm around me. You know how kind my brother Lanford is. Yes?"

Ruth could not speak. Her jaw was clenched so fiercely, she could not imagine releasing it to issue a single word. Certainly not a civil word. She might have let out a greased string of curses. She might have been able to do that for this wicked bitch.

"And my wonderful brother said to me, 'Vera, everything will be fine.' Do you know what I replied? I said, 'Now I know how poor Mrs. Lindbergh felt!' "

They sat in silence for what seemed a year, letting that sentence hang over them. Ruth's mind roiled. Could she hit this woman? Could she step out of this ancient car and walk back to Fort Niles?

"But now she is with me, where she belongs," Miss Vera said. "And we do as we please. No husbands to tell us what to do. No children to look after. Except Ricky, of course. Poor Ricky. But he doesn't ask much, heaven knows. Your mother and I are independent women, Ruth, and we have a good time together. We enjoy our independence, Ruth. We like it very much."

Ruth stayed with her mother for a week. She wore the same clothes every day, and no one said another word about it. There were no more shopping trips. She slept in her clothes and put them on again every morning after her bath. She did not complain.

What did she care?

This was her survival strategy: Fuck it.

Fuck all of it. Whatever they asked of her, she would do. Whatever outrageous act of exploitation she saw Miss Vera commit against her mother, she would ignore. Ruth was doing time in Concord. Getting it over with. Trying to stay sane. Because if she'd reacted to everything that galled her, she'd have been in a constant state of disgust and rage, which would have made her mother more nervous and Miss Vera more predatory and Cal Cooley more smug. So she sat on it. *Fuck it.*

Every night before she went to bed she kissed her mother on the cheek. Miss Vera would ask coyly, "Where's my kiss?" and Ruth would cross the room on steel legs, bend, and kiss that lavender cheek. She did this for her mother's sake. She did this because it was less trouble than throwing an ashtray across the room. She could see the relief it brought her mother. Good. Whatever she could do to help, fine. *Fuck it.*

"Where's *my* kiss?" Cal would ask every night.

And every night Ruth would mutter something like "Goodnight, Cal. Try to remember not to murder us in our sleep."

And Miss Vera would say, "Such hateful words for a child your age."

Yeah, Ruth thought. *Yeah, whatever.* She knew she should keep her mouth shut entirely, but she enjoyed getting a stab or two into Cal Cooley now and again. Made her feel like herself. Familiar, somehow. Comforting. She would carry the satisfaction to bed with her and curl up against it, as if it were a teddy bear. Her nightly poke at Cal would help Ruth Thomas go to sleep without stewing for hours over the eternal, nagging question: *What fate had shoved her into the lives of the Ellis family? And why?*

7

In every batch of segmenting lobster eggs, one is sure to meet with irregular forms, and in some cases, the greater number appear to be abnormal.

— *The American Lobster: A Study of Its Habits and Development*
Francis Hobart Herrick, Ph.D.
1895

AT THE END of the week, Cal Cooley and Ruth drove back to Rockland, Maine. It rained the whole time. She sat in the front seat of the Buick with Cal, and he did not shut up. He teased her about her one set of clothes and about the shopping trip to Blaire's, and he did grotesque imitations of her mother's servile attendance on Miss Vera.

"Shut up, Cal," Ruth said.

"Oh, Miss Vera, shall I wash your hair now? Oh, Miss Vera, shall I file your corns now? Oh, Miss Vera, shall I wipe your butt now?"

"Leave my mother alone," Ruth said. "She does what she has to do."

"Oh, Miss Vera, shall I lie down in traffic now?"

"You're worse, Cal. You kiss more Ellis ass than anyone. You play that old man for every penny, and you suck up like crazy to Miss Vera."

"Oh, I don't think so, sweetheart. I think your mother wins the prize."

"Up yours, Cal."

"So articulate, Ruth!"

"Up yours, you sycophant."

Cal burst out laughing. "That's better! Let's eat."

Ruth's mother had sent them off with a basket of bread and cheese and chocolates, and Ruth now opened it. The cheese was a small wheel, soft and wax-covered, and when Ruth cut into it, it released a deadly odor, like something rotting at the bottom of a damp hole. Specifically, it smelled like vomit at the bottom of that hole.

"Jesus fuck!" Cal shouted.

"Oh, my God!" Ruth said, and she stuffed the cheese back into the basket, slamming down the wicker cover. She pulled the top of her sweatshirt up over her nose. Two useless measures.

"Throw it out!" Cal shouted. "Get that out of here."

Ruth opened the basket, rolled down the window, and flung out the cheese. It bounced and spun on the highway behind them. She hung her head out of the window, taking deep breaths.

"What was that?" Cal demanded. "What *was* that?"

"My mom said it was sheep's milk cheese," Ruth said, when she caught her breath. "It's homemade. Somebody gave it to Miss Vera for Christmas."

"To murder her!"

"Apparently it's a delicacy."

"A delicacy? She said it was a delicacy?"

"Leave her alone."

"She wanted us to eat that?"

"It was a gift. She didn't know."

"Now I know where the expression 'cut the cheese' comes from."

"Oh, for Christ's sake."

"I never knew why they said that before, but now I know," Cal said. "*Cut the cheese.* Never thought about it."

Ruth said, "That's enough, Cal. Do me a favor and don't talk to me for the rest of the trip."

After a long silence, Cal Cooley said thoughtfully, "Where does the expression 'blow a fart' come from, I wonder?"

Ruth said, "Leave me alone, Cal. Please, for the love of God, just leave me alone."

When they arrived at the dock in Rockland, Pastor Wishnell and his nephew were already there. Ruth could see the *New Hope,* sitting on flat gray sea speckled with rain. There were no greetings.

Pastor Wishnell said, "Drive me to the store, Cal. I need oil, groceries, and stationery."

"Sure," Cal said. "No problem."

"Stay here," Pastor Wishnell said to Owney, and Cal, imitating the pastor's inflection, pointed at Ruth and said, "Stay here."

The two men drove off, leaving Ruth and Owney on the dock, in the rain. Just like that. The young man was wearing a brand-new yellow slicker, a yellow rain hat, and yellow boots. He stood still and broad, looking out to sea, his big hands clasped behind his back. Ruth liked the size of him. His body was dense and full of gravity. She liked his blond eyelashes.

"Did you have a good week?" Ruth asked Owney Wishnell.

He nodded.

"What did you do?"

He sighed. He grimaced, as if he were trying hard to think. "Not much," he finally said. His voice was low and quiet.

"Oh," Ruth said. "I went to see my mother in Concord, New Hampshire."

Owney nodded, frowned, and took a deep breath. He seemed about to say something, but, instead, he clasped his hands behind his back again and was silent, his face blank. *He's incredibly shy,* Ruth thought. She found it charming. *So big and so shy!*

"To tell you the truth," Ruth said, "it makes me sad to see her. I don't like it on the mainland; I want to get back to Fort Niles. What about you? Would you rather be out there? Or here?"

Owney Wishnell's face turned pink, bright cherry, pink again, then back to normal. Ruth, fascinated, watched this extraordinary display and asked, "Am I bothering you?"

"No." He colored again.

"My mother always presses me to get away from Fort Niles. Not really presses, but she made me go to school in Delaware, and now she wants me to move to Concord. Or go to college. But I like it out there." Ruth pointed at the ocean. "I don't want to live with the Ellis family. I want them to leave me alone." She didn't understand why she was rambling on to this huge, quiet, shy young man in the clean yellow slicker; it occurred to her that she sounded like a child or a fool. But when she looked at Owney, she saw that he was listening. He wasn't looking at her as if she were a child or a fool. "You're sure I'm not bothering you?"

Owney Wishnell coughed into his fist and stared at Ruth, his pale blue eyes flickering with his effort. "Um," he said and coughed again. "Ruth."

"Yes?" It thrilled her to hear him say her name. She hadn't known that he was aware of it. "Yes, Owney?"

"Do you want to see something?" he asked. He blurted out this line as if it were a confession. He said it most urgently, as if he were about to reveal a cache of stolen money.

"Oh, yes," Ruth said, "I'd love to."

He looked uncertain, strained.

"Show me," Ruth said. "Show me something. Sure. Show me whatever you want to show me."

"Have to hurry," Owney said, and he snapped alive. He rushed to the end of the dock, and Ruth rushed after him. He hustled down the ladder and into a rowboat, untied it in a flash, and gestured for Ruth to follow. He was already rowing, it seemed, as she tumbled into the boat. He pulled at the oars with beautiful, solid strokes—*swish, swish, swish*—and the boat shimmied across the waves.

He rowed past the *New Hope*, past all the other boats docked in the harbor, never easing his pace. His knuckles on the oars were white, and his mouth was a tight, concentrated line. Ruth held on to both sides of the boat, once again amazed at his strength. This was not at all what she'd expected to be doing about thirty seconds ago, when she was standing on the dock. Owney rowed until they were out of the protected cove, and the waves had become swells that bounced and rocked against the little rowboat. They reached a huge granite rock—a small granite island, really—and he steered the boat behind it. They were completely out of sight of the shore. Waves lapped at the rock.

Owney stared ahead at the ocean, frowning and breathing heavily. He rowed away from the island, into the sea about forty feet, and stopped. He stood up in the rowboat and peered into the water, then sat down and rowed another ten feet, and peered into the water again. Ruth leaned over but saw nothing.

Owney Wishnell reached to the bottom of the rowboat for a fishing gaff, a long stick with a hook at one end. Slowly, he dipped it in the water and started to pull, and Ruth saw that he'd snagged the gaff on a buoy, like the ones lobstermen used for marking where they'd set traps. But this buoy was plain white, with none of the lobstermen's bright identifying colors. And instead of bobbing on the surface, the buoy was on a short line, which kept it hidden several feet below. Nobody could have found it without knowing exactly, precisely, where to look.

Owney threw the buoy into the boat and then, hand over hand, pulled the line it was attached to until he reached the end. And there was a handmade wooden lobster trap. He heaved it aboard; it was packed with huge, snapping lobsters.

"Whose trap is that?" Ruth asked.

"Mine!" Owney said.

He flicked open the trap door and pulled out the lobsters, one by one, holding up each for Ruth to see and then tossing it into the water.

"Hey!" she said after the third one. "Don't throw them back! They're good!"

He threw them back, every one. The lobsters were indeed good. They were enormous. They were packed in that trap like fish in a deep-sea net. They were, however, behaving oddly. When Owney touched them, they didn't snap or fight. They lay still in his hand. Ruth had never seen anything like these obedient lobsters. And she'd never seen anything close to this many in a single trap.

"Why are there so many? Why don't they fight you?" she asked.

"Because they don't," he said. He tossed another one in the ocean.

"Why don't you keep them?" Ruth said.

"Can't!" Owney cried.

"When did you set the trap?"

"Last week."

"Why do you keep the buoy under water, where you can't see it?"

"Hiding it."

"From who?"

"Everyone."

"How did you find the trap, then?"

"I just knew where it was," he said. "I know where they are."

" 'They'?"

He threw the last of the lobsters into the sea and tossed the trap over the side with a mighty splash. As he wiped his hands on his overalls, he said, with tragic urgency, "I know where the lobsters are."

"You know where the lobsters are."

"Yes."

"You really are a Wishnell," she said. "Aren't you?"

"Yes."

"Where are your other traps, Owney?"
"Everywhere."
"Everywhere?"
"All over the coast of Maine?"
"Yes."
"Your uncle knows?"
"No!" He looked aghast, horrified.
"Who built the traps?"
"Me."
"When?"
"At night."
"You do all this behind your uncle's back."
"Yes."
"Because he'd kill you, right?"
No answer.
"Why do you throw them back, Owney?"
He put his hands over his face, then let them drop. He looked as if he was about to cry. He could only shake his head.
"Oh, Owney."
"I know."
"This is crazy."
"I know."
"You could be rich! My God, if you had a boat and some gear, you could be rich!"
"I can't."
"Because somebody—"
"My uncle."
"—would find out."
"Yes."
"He wants you to be a minister or something pathetic like that, right?"
"Yes."
"Well, that's a big fucking waste, isn't it?"
"I don't want to be a minister."
"I don't blame you, Owney. I don't want to be a minister, either. Who else knows about this?"
"We have to go," Owney said. He grabbed the oars and spun the boat around, his broad, straight back toward the shore, and started to

pull through the water in his beautiful long strokes, like a gorgeous machine.

"Who else knows, Owney?"

He stopped rowing and looked at her. "You."

She looked right back at him, right at his big, square blond head, at his blue Swedish eyes.

"You," he repeated. "Only you."

8

> As the lobster increases in size, it grows bolder and retires farther from shore, although it never really loses its instinct for digging, and never abandons the habit of concealing itself under stones when the necessity arises.
>
> — *The American Lobster: A Study of Its Habits and Development*
> Francis Hobart Herrick, Ph.D.
> 1895

GEORGES BANK, at the end of the Ice Age, was a forest, lush and thick and primeval. It had rivers, mountains, mammals. Then it was covered by the sea and became some of the finest fishing ground on earth. The transformation took millions of years, but it didn't take the Europeans long to find the place once they reached the New World, and they fished the hell out of it.

The big boats sailed out with nets and lines for every kind of fish—redfish, herring, cod, mackerel, whales of many varieties, squid, tuna, swordfish, dogfish—and there were draggers, too, for scallops. By the end of the nineteenth century, the bank had became an international city afloat; German, Russian, American, Canadian, French, and Portuguese boats all pulled up tons of fish. Each boat had men aboard to shovel the flopping fish into the holds as thoughtlessly as men shovel coal. Each vessel stayed out there for a week, even two weeks at a stretch. At night, the lights from the hundreds of ships shone on the water like the lights of a small city.

The boats and ships out there, stuck in the open sea, a day from any shore, were sitting targets for bad weather. The storms came up fast and mean and could wipe out a whole fleet, devastating the community it came from. A village might send a few fishing boats out on a routine trip to Georges Bank and a few days later find itself a village of widows and orphans. The newspapers listed the dead men and their surviving dependents, too. This was perhaps the crux of the tragedy. It was imperative to count who was left, to estimate how many souls remained on shore without fathers, brothers, husbands, sons, uncles to support them. What was to become of them?

46 DEAD, the headline would read. 197 DEPENDENTS LEFT BEHIND.

That was the truly sad number. That was the number everyone needed to know.

Lobster fishing is not like this, though, and never was. It is dangerous enough, but it isn't as deadly as deep-sea fishing. Not by a long shot. Lobster towns don't lose men in battalions. Lobstermen fish alone, are rarely out of sight of shore, are generally home by early afternoon to eat pie and drink beer and sleep with their boots on the couch. Widows and orphans are not created in crowds. There are no unions of widows, no clutches of widows. Widows in lobster-fishing communities appear one at a time, through random accidents and freak drownings and strange fogs and storms that come and go without doing other havoc.

Such was the case of Mrs. Pommeroy, who, in 1976, was the only widow in Fort Niles; that is, the only fisherman's widow. She was the only woman who had lost her man to the sea. What did this status afford her? Very little. The fact that her husband had been a drunk who fell overboard on a calm sunny day lessened the catastrophic dimensions of the event, and as the years went by her tragedy was by and large forgotten. Mrs. Pommeroy was something of a calm sunny day herself, and she was so lovely that people had difficulty remembering to pity her.

Besides, she had managed well without a husband to support her. She had survived without Ira Pommeroy, and did not show the world any signs of suffering from her loss. She had her big house, which had been built and paid for long before she was born and was constructed so solidly that it required little upkeep. Not that anyone cared about upkeep. She had her garden. She had her sisters, who were irritating but devoted. She had Ruth Thomas for daughterly companionship. She had her sons, who, though pretty much a pack of deadbeats, were no worse deadbeats than anyone else's sons, and they did contribute to their mother's support.

The Pommeroy boys who stayed on the island had small incomes, of course, because they could work only as sternmen on other people's boats. The incomes were small because the Pommeroy boats and Pommeroy territory and Pommeroy fishing gear had all been lost at the death of their father. The other men on the island had bought everything up for a pittance, and it could never be recovered. Because of this, and because of their natural laziness, the Pommeroy boys had no future on Fort Niles. They couldn't, once they were grown men, start to assemble a fishing business. They grew up knowing this, so it came as no surprise that a few of them had left the island for good. And why not? They had no future at home.

Fagan, the middle child, was the only Pommeroy son with ambitions. He was the only one with a goal in life, and he pursued it successfully. He was working on a squalid little potato farm in a remote, landlocked county of northern Maine. He had always wanted to get away from the ocean, and that's what he had done. He had always wanted to be a farmer. No seagulls, no wind. He sent money home to his mother. He called her every few weeks to tell her how the potato crop was doing. He said he hoped to be the foreman of the farm someday. He bored her senseless, but she was proud of him for having a job, and she was happy to get the money he sent.

Conway and John and Chester Pommeroy had joined the military, and Conway (a Navy man all the way, as he liked to say, as though he were an admiral) was lucky enough to have caught the last year or so of action in the Vietnam War. He was a sailor on a river patrol boat in a nasty area of contention. He had two tours of duty in Vietnam. He passed the first without injury, though he sent boastful and crude letters to his mother explaining in explicit detail how many of his buddies had bought it and exactly what stupid mistakes those idiots had made that caused them to buy it. He also described for his mother what his buddies' bodies looked like after they'd bought it, and assured her that he would never buy it because he was too smart for that shit.

In 1972, Conway, on his second tour of duty, nearly bought it himself, with a bullet near the spine, but he got fixed up after six months in an Army hospital. He married the widow of one of his idiot buddies who really did buy it back on the river patrol boat, and he moved to Connecticut. He used a walking stick to get around. He collected disability. Conway was fine. Conway was not a drain on his widowed mother.

John and Chester had joined the Army. John was sent to Germany, where he stayed on after his Army service was over. What a Pommeroy boy could do with himself in a European country was beyond the imagination of Ruth Thomas, but nobody heard from John, so everyone assumed he was fine. Chester did his time in the Army, moved to California, indulged in a lot of drugs, and took up with some weirdoes who considered themselves fortunetellers. They called themselves the Gypsy Bandoleer Bandits.

The Gypsy Bandoleer Bandits traveled around in an old school bus, making money by reading palms and tarot cards, though Ruth heard they really made their money by selling marijuana. Ruth was pretty interested in that part of the story. She'd never tried marijuana herself, but was interested in it. Chester came back to visit the island once—without his Gypsy Bandit brothers—when Ruth Thomas was home from school, and he tried to give her some of his famous spiritual advice. This was back in 1974. He was wasted.

"What kind of advice do you want?" Chester asked. "I can give you all kinds." He ticked off the different kinds on his fingers. "I can give you advice about your job, advice about your love life, advice about what to do, special advice, or regular advice."

"Do you have any pot?" Ruth asked.

"Oh, yeah."

"Can I try it? I mean, do you sell it to people? I have money. I could buy some."

"I know a card trick."

"I don't think so, Chester."

"Yes, I do know a card trick." He shoved a pack of cards in Ruth's face and slurred, "Pig a card."

She wouldn't pick one.

"Pig a card!" shouted Chester Pommeroy, the Gypsy Bandoleer Bandit.

"Why should I?"

"Pig a fuggin' card! Come on! I already planted the fuggin' card, and I know it's the three of hearts, so pig the fuggin' card, will ya?"

She wouldn't. He threw the deck at the wall.

She asked, "Can I please try some pot now?"

He scowled and waved her out of his face. He kicked a table and called her a stupid bitch. He had really turned into a freak, Ruth decided, so she stayed out of his way the rest of the week. That all happened when Ruth was sixteen, and it was the last time she saw Chester Pommeroy. She heard he had a bunch of children but wasn't married to anybody. She never did get any of his marijuana.

With four of the Pommeroy boys off the island for good, that left three living at home. Webster Pommeroy, who was the oldest and smartest, was small, stunted, depressed, shy, and gifted only at plowing through the mudflats for artifacts for Senator Simon Addams's future Museum of Natural History. Webster brought no income to his mother, but he didn't cost much. He still wore the clothes of his childhood and barely ate a thing. Mrs. Pommeroy loved him the most and worried about him the most, and didn't care that he made no contribution to the family, as long as he wasn't spending day after day on the couch with a pillow over his head, sighing mournfully.

At the other end was the well-known idiot Robin Pommeroy, the youngest. At seventeen, he was married to Opal from town and father of the enormous baby Eddie. Robin worked as a sternman on Ruth's father's boat. Ruth's father more or less hated Robin Pommeroy because the kid would not shut up all day. Since overcoming his speech defect, Robin had become a ceaseless motor mouth. And he wouldn't talk just to Ruth's father, who was the only one there. He would talk to himself, too, as well as the lobsters. He'd get on the radio during breaks and talk to all the other lobster boats. Whenever he saw another lobster boat cruising nearby, he'd grab the radio and say to the approaching skipper, "Don't you look pretty, coming along?" Then he'd turn off the microphone and wait for a reply, which was usually along the lines of "Stuff it, kid." Sadly, he'd ask Ruth's father, "How come nobody ever tells us *we* look pretty coming along?"

Robin was always dropping things off the boat accidentally. He'd somehow let the gaff slide out of his hands, and then he'd run down the length of the boat to catch it. Too late. This didn't happen every day; it happened almost every day. It was a real annoyance to Ruth's father, who'd back the boat and try to catch up with the tool. Ruth's father had taken to keeping spares of all his tools, just in case. Ruth suggested that he attach a small buoy to each tool so that at least it would float. She called this "Robin-proofing."

Robin was tiresome, but Ruth's father tolerated the kid because he was cheap, cheap, cheap. Robin accepted much less money than any other sternman. He had to accept less money, because nobody wanted to work with him. He was dumb and lazy, but he was strong enough to do the job, and Ruth's father was saving a lot of money off Robin Pommeroy. He tolerated the kid because of the bottom line.

That left Timothy. Always the quietest, Timothy Pommeroy was never a bad child, and he grew up to be a pretty decent guy. He didn't bother anybody. He looked like his father, with the heavy doorknob fists and the tight muscles and the black hair and squinty eyes. He worked on the boat of Len Thomas, Ruth Thomas's uncle, and he was a good worker. Len Thomas was a windbag and a hothead, but Timothy quietly pulled up traps, counted lobsters, filled bait bags, and stood in the stern while the boat was moving, facing away from Len and keeping his thoughts to himself. It was a good arrangement for Len, who usually had trouble finding sternmen who'd put up with his legendary temper. He once came at a sternman with a wrench and knocked the kid out for the whole afternoon. But Timothy did not provoke Len's anger. He made a pretty respectable living, Timothy did. He gave it all to his mother except the portion he used to buy his whiskey, which he drank, all by himself, every night, in his bedroom, with the door firmly closed.

All of which is to say that Mrs. Pommeroy's many sons did not turn out to be a financial burden on her and, indeed, were kind enough to pass along some money. Everything considered, they'd turned out fine, except for Webster. Mrs. Pommeroy subsidized the money her sons passed her way by cutting hair.

She was good at cutting hair. She had a gift. She curled and colored the hair of women and seemed to have a natural instinct for shape, but she specialized, as it were, in men's hair. She cut the hair of men who had previously had only three kinds of haircuts in their lives: haircuts from their mothers, haircuts from the Army, haircuts from their wives. These were men who had no interest in style, but they let Mrs. Pommeroy do frivolous things with their hair. They sat under her hand with pure vanity, enjoying the attention as much as any starlet.

The fact was, she could make a man look wonderful. Mrs. Pommeroy magically hid baldness, encouraged beards for the weak-chinned, thinned the wild brush of uncontrollable curls, and tamed the most headstrong cowlicks. She flattered and joked with each man, nudging him and teasing him as she worked his hair, and the flirtation immediately made the guy more attractive, brought color to the cheek and a shine to the eye. She could almost rescue men from true ugliness. She could even make Senator Simon and Angus Addams look respectable. When she was through with an old crank like Angus, even he would be blushing right up the back of his neck from the pleasure of her company. When she was through with a naturally good-looking man like Ruth's father, he would be embarrassingly handsome, movie-matinee-idol handsome.

"Go hide," she'd tell him. "Get on out of here, Stan. If you start walking around town looking like that, it's your own fault if you get raped."

Surprisingly, the ladies of Fort Niles didn't mind letting Mrs. Pommeroy groom their husbands. Perhaps it was because the results were so nice. Perhaps it was because they wanted to help a widow, and this was the easy way to do it. Perhaps the women felt guilty around Mrs. Pommeroy for even *having* husbands, for having men who had thus far managed to avoid getting drunk and falling overboard. Or perhaps the women had come to loathe their husbands so much over the years that the thought of personally dragging their own fingers through the dirty hair of those stinking, greasy, shiftless fishermen was sickening. They'd just as soon let Mrs. Pommeroy do it, since she seemed to like it so much, and since it put their men in a good goddamn mood, for once.

So it was that when Ruth returned from visiting her mother in Concord, she went right to Mrs. Pommeroy's house, and found her cutting the hair of the entire Russ Cobb family. Mrs. Pommeroy had all the Cobbs there: Mr. Russ Cobb, his wife, Ivy, and their youngest daughter, Florida, who was forty years old and still living with her parents.

They were a miserable family. Russ Cobb was almost eighty, but he still went out fishing every day. He'd always said he would fish as long as he could throw his leg over the boat. The previous winter, he'd lost half his right leg at the knee, amputated because of his diabetes, or "sugars," as he called it, but he still went fishing every day, throwing what remained of that leg over the boat. His wife, Ivy, was a disappointed-looking woman who painted holly sprigs, candles, and Santa Claus faces on sand dollars and tried to sell them to her neighbors as Christmas ornaments. The Cobbs' daughter, Florida, never said a word. She was devastatingly silent.

Mrs. Pommeroy had already set Ivy Cobb's frothy white hair in curlers and was tending to Russ Cobb's sideburns when Ruth came in.

"So thick!" Mrs. Pommeroy was telling Mr. Cobb. "Your hair is so thick, you look like Rock Hudson!"

"Cary Grant!" he bellowed.

"Cary Grant!" Mrs. Pommeroy laughed. "OK! You look like Cary Grant!"

Mrs. Cobb rolled her eyes. Ruth walked across the kitchen and kissed Mrs. Pommeroy on the cheek. Mrs. Pommeroy took her hand, held it for a long moment. "Welcome home, sweetheart."

"Thank you." Ruth felt she was home.

"Did you have a good time?"

"I had the worst week of my life." Ruth meant to say this in a sarcastic, joking manner, but it accidentally came out of her mouth as the unadorned truth.

"There's pie."

"Thank you very much."

"Did you see your father?"

"Not yet."

"I'll be done here in a bit," Mrs. Pommeroy said. "You take a seat, sweetheart."

So Ruth took herself a seat, next to silent Florida Cobb, on a chair that had been painted that dreadful trap-buoy green. The kitchen table and the corner cupboard had also been painted that frightening green, so the whole kitchen matched terribly. Ruth watched Mrs. Pommeroy perform her usual magic on ugly Mr. Cobb. Her hands were constantly at work in his hair. Even when she wasn't cutting, she was stroking his head, fingering his hair, patting him, tugging at his ears. He leaned his head back into her hands like a cat rubbing against a favorite person's leg.

"Look how nice," she murmured, like an encouraging lover. "Look how nice you look."

She trimmed his sideburns and shaved his neck in arcs through foamy suds and wiped him down with a towel. She pressed her body against his back. She was as affectionate with Mr. Cobb as if he were the last person she would ever touch, as if his ugly skull was to be her final human contact on this earth. Mrs. Cobb, in her steel gray curlers, sat watching, her gray hands in her lap, her steel eyes on her husband's ruined face.

"How are things, Mrs. Cobb?" Ruth asked.

"We got goddamn raccoons all over our goddamn yard," Mrs. Cobb said, demonstrating her remarkable trick of talking without moving her lips. When Ruth was a child, she used to lure Mrs. Cobb into conversation only to watch this trick. In truth, at the age of eighteen Ruth was luring her into conversation for the same reason.

"Sorry to hear that. Did you ever have trouble with raccoons before?"

"Never had them at all."

Ruth stared at the woman's mouth. It honestly didn't budge. Incredible. "Is that right?" she asked.

"I'd like to shoot one."

"Wasn't a raccoon on this island until 1958," Russ Cobb said. "Had them on Courne Haven, but not here."

"Really? What happened? How did they get here?" Ruth asked, knowing exactly what he was about to say.

"They brought 'em over here."

"Who did?"

"Courne Haven people! Threw some pregnant raccoons in a sack. Rowed 'em over. Middle of the night. Dumped 'em on our beach. Your great-uncle David Thomas saw it. Walking home from his girl's house. Seen strangers on the beach. Seen 'em letting something out of a bag. Seen 'em row away. Few weeks later, raccoons everywhere. All over the goddamn place. Eating people's chickens. Garbage. Everything."

Of course, the story Ruth had heard from family members was that it was Johnny Pommeroy who had seen the strangers on the beach, right before he went off to get killed in Korea in 1954, but she let it slide.

"I had a pet baby raccoon when I was a little girl," Mrs. Pommeroy said, smiling at the memory. "That raccoon bit my arm, come to think of it, and my father killed him. I think it was a him. I always called it a him, anyway."

"When was that, Mrs. Pommeroy?" Ruth asked. "How long ago?"

Mrs. Pommeroy frowned and rubbed her thumbs deep into Mr. Cobb's neck. He groaned, so happy. She said innocently, "Oh, I guess that was the early 1940s, Ruth. Goodness, I'm so old. The 1940s! Such a long time ago."

"Wasn't a raccoon, then," Mr. Cobb said. "Couldn't have been."

"Oh, it was a little raccoon, all right. He had a striped tail and the cutest little mask. I called him Masky!"

"Wasn't a raccoon. Couldn't have been. Wasn't a raccoon on this island until 1958," Mr. Cobb said. "Courne Haven folks brought 'em over in 1958."

"Well, this was a *baby* raccoon," Mrs. Pommeroy said, by way of explanation.

"Probably a skunk."

"I'd like to shoot a raccoon!" Mrs. Cobb said with such force that her mouth actually moved, and her silent daughter, Florida, actually started.

"My father sure shot Masky," Mrs. Pommeroy said.

She toweled off Mr. Cobb's hair and brushed the back of his neck with a tiny pastry brush. She patted talcum powder under his frayed shirt collar and rubbed oily tonic into his wiry hair, shaping it into an excessively curved pompadour.

"Look at you!" she said, and gave him an antique silver hand mirror. "You look like a country music star. What do you think, Ivy? Isn't he a handsome devil?"

"Silly," said Ivy Cobb, but her husband beamed, his cheeks shiny as his pompadour. Mrs. Pommeroy took the sheet off him, gathering it up carefully so as not to spill his hair all over her glaring green kitchen, and Mr. Cobb stood up, still admiring himself in the antique mirror. He turned his head slowly from side to side and smiled at himself, grinning like a handsome devil.

"What do you think of your father, Florida?" Mrs. Pommeroy asked. "Doesn't he look fine?"

Florida Cobb blushed deeply.

"She won't say nothing," Mr. Cobb said, suddenly disgusted. He plunked the hand mirror down on the kitchen table and dug some money out of his pocket. "Never says a goddamn word. Wouldn't say shit if she had a mouthful of it."

Ruth laughed and decided to get herself a piece of pie after all.

"I'll take those curlers out for you now, Ivy," Mrs. Pommeroy said.

Later, after the Cobbs had gone, Mrs. Pommeroy and Ruth sat on the front porch. There was an old couch out there, upholstered in big bleeding roses, that smelled as if it had been rained on, or worse. Ruth drank beer and Mrs. Pommeroy drank fruit punch, and Ruth told Mrs. Pommeroy about visiting her mother.

"How's Ricky?" Mrs. Pommeroy asked.

"Oh, I don't know. He's just, you know . . . He flops around."

"That was the saddest thing, when that baby was born. You know, I never saw that poor baby."

"I know."

"I never saw your poor mother after that."

Yah po-ah mothah . . . Ruth had missed Mrs. Pommeroy's accent.

"I know."

"I tried to call her. I *did* call her. I told her to bring her baby back here to the island, but she said he was much too sick. I made her describe what was wrong with him, and, I'll tell you something; it didn't sound too bad to me."

"Oh, it's bad."

"It didn't sound to me like something we couldn't take care of out here. What did he need? He didn't need much. Some medicine. That's easy. Jesus, Mr. Cobb takes medicine every single day for his sugars, and he manages. What else did Ricky need? Someone to watch him. We could have done that. That's a person's *child;* you find a place for him. That's what I told her. She cried and cried."

"Everyone else said he should be in an institution."

"Who said? Vera Ellis said that. Who else?"

"The doctors."

"She should have brought that baby here to his home. He would've been just fine out here. She still could bring him out here. We'd take care of that child as good as anyone else."

"She said you were her only friend. She said you were the only person out here who was nice to her."

"That's sweet. But it's not true. Everyone was nice to her."

"Not Angus Addams."

"Oh, he loved her."

"Loved? *Loved?*"

"He liked her as much as he likes anyone."

Ruth laughed. Then she said, "Did you ever meet someone named Owney Wishnell?"

"Who's that? From Courne Haven?"

"Pastor Wishnell's nephew."

"Oh, yes. That great big blond boy."

"Yes."

"I know who he is."

Ruth didn't say anything.

"Why?" Mrs. Pommeroy asked. "Why do you ask?"

"Nothing," Ruth said.

The porch door swung open, kicked by Robin Pommeroy's wife, Opal, whose hands were so full of her huge son that she couldn't operate the doorknob. The baby, on seeing Mrs. Pommeroy, let out a crazy holler, like a delighted gorilla toddler.

"There's my baby grandson," Mrs. Pommeroy said.

"Hey, Ruth," Opal said shyly.

"Hey, Opal."

"Didn't know you were here."

"Hey, big Eddie," Ruth said to the baby. Opal brought the child over and bent down, heaving a bit, so that Ruth could kiss the boy's enormous head. Ruth slid over on the sofa to make space for Opal, who sat down, lifted her T-shirt, and gave a breast to Eddie. He lunged for it and set to sucking with concentration and a lot of wet noise. He sucked at that breast as if he were drawing breath through it.

"Doesn't that hurt?" Ruth asked.

"Yeah," said Opal. She yawned without covering her mouth, showing off a mine of silver fillings.

The three women on the couch all stared at the big baby locked so fiercely onto Opal's breast.

"He sucks like a regular old bilge pump," Ruth said.

"Bites, too," said the laconic Opal.

Ruth winced.

"When did you feed him last?" Mrs. Pommeroy asked.

"I don't know. An hour ago. Half hour."

"You should try to keep him on a schedule, Opal."

She shrugged. "He's always hungry."

"Of course he is, sweetheart. That's because you *feed* him all the time. Builds his appetite. You know what they say. If the mama's a-willin', the baby's a-takin'."

"They say that?" Ruth asked.

"I just made it up," Mrs. Pommeroy said.

"It's nice how you made it rhyme like that," Ruth said, and Mrs. Pommeroy grinned and punched her. Ruth had missed the delight of teasing people without being afraid they'd burst into tears on her. She punched Mrs. Pommeroy back.

"My idea is, I let him eat whenever he wants," Opal said. "I figure if he's eating, he's hungry. He ate three hot dogs yesterday."

"Opal!" Mrs. Pommeroy exclaimed. "He's only ten months old!"

"I can't help it."

"You can't *help* it? He got the hot dogs himself?" Ruth asked. Mrs. Pommeroy and Opal laughed, and the baby suddenly popped himself off the breast with the loud sound of a tight seal breaking. He lolled his head like a drunk, and then he laughed, too.

"I told a baby joke!" Ruth said.

"Eddie likes you," Opal said. "You like Roof? You like your Auntie Roof, Eddie?" She set the baby on Ruth's lap, where he grinned crookedly and spat up yellow soup on her pants. Ruth handed him back to his mother.

"Oops," said Opal. She heaved the baby up and went into the house, coming out a moment later to toss a bathroom towel at Ruth. "I think it's nap time for Eddie," she said, and disappeared into the house again.

Ruth wiped the hot, foamy puddle off her leg. "Baby barf," she said.

"They feed that baby too much," Mrs. Pommeroy said.

"He makes the necessary adjustments, I'd say."

"She was feeding him chocolate fudge sauce the other day, Ruth. With a spoon. Right out of the jar. I saw it!"

"That Opal isn't very smart."

"She's got great big boobs, though."

"Oh, lucky her."

"Lucky baby Eddie. How could she have such big boobs when she's only seventeen? I didn't even know what boobs were when I was seventeen."

"Yes, you did. Jesus, Mrs. Pommeroy, you were already married when you were seventeen."

"Yes, that's right. But I didn't know what boobs were when I was twelve. I saw my sister's chest and asked her what those big things were. She said it was baby fat."

"Gloria said that?"

"Kitty said that."

"She should've told you the truth."

"She probably didn't know the truth."

"Kitty? Kitty was born knowing the truth."

"Imagine if she'd told me the truth? Imagine if she said, 'They're tits, Rhonda, and someday grown men will want to suck on them.' "

"Grown men and young boys, too. And other people's husbands, knowing Kitty."

"Why did you ask me about Owney Wishnell, Ruth?"

Ruth gave Mrs. Pommeroy a quick glance, then looked out at the yard. She said, "No reason."

Mrs. Pommeroy watched Ruth for a long moment. She tilted her head. She waited.

"It's not true that you were the only person on this island who was nice to my mother?" Ruth said.

"No, Ruth, I told you. We all liked her. She was wonderful. She was a little *sensitive*, though, and sometimes had trouble understanding the way some people are."

"Angus Addams, for instance."

"Oh, a lot of them. She couldn't understand all the drinking. I used to tell her, Mary, these men are cold and wet ten hours a day their whole lives. That can really *chafe* a person. They need to drink, or there's no way to deal with it."

"My dad didn't ever drink so much."

"He didn't talk to her so much, either. She was lonely out here. She couldn't stand the winters."

"I think she's lonely in Concord."

"Oh, I'm sure of it. Does she want you to move there with her?"

"Yeah. She wants me to go to college. She says that's what the Ellises want. She says Mr. Ellis'll pay for it, of course. Vera Ellis thinks if I stay here much longer, I'll get pregnant. She wants me to move to Concord and then go to some small, respectable women's college, where the Ellises know the president."

"People do get pregnant out here, Ruth."

"I think Opal has a big enough baby to go around for all of us. And besides, a person has to have sex to get pregnant these days. So they say."

"You should be with your mother if that's what she wants. There's nothing keeping you here. People out here, Ruth, they're not really your people."

"I'll tell you what. I'm not going to do a single thing with my life that the Ellises want me to do. That's my plan."

"That's your plan?"

"For now."

Mrs. Pommeroy took off her shoes and put her feet up on the old wooden lobster trap she used for a table on the porch. She sighed. "Tell me some more about Owney Wishnell," she said.

"Well, I met him," Ruth said.

"And?"

"And he's an unusual person."

Again, Mrs. Pommeroy waited, and Ruth looked out at the front yard. A seagull standing on a child's toy truck stared back at her. Mrs. Pommeroy was staring at her, too.

"What?" Ruth asked. "What's everyone staring at?"

"I think there's more to tell," Mrs. Pommeroy said. "Why don't you tell me, Ruth?"

So Ruth started to tell Mrs. Pommeroy about Owney Wishnell, although it hadn't been her original intention to tell anyone about him. She told Mrs. Pommeroy about Owney's clean fisherman's outfit and his ease with boats and about his rowing her out behind the rock to show her his lobster traps. She told about Pastor Wishnell's threatening speeches on the evils and immoralities of lobster fishing and about Owney's nearly crying when he showed her his packed, useless trap of lobsters.

"That poor child," Mrs. Pommeroy said.

"Not exactly a child. I think he's about my age."

"Bless his heart."

"Can you believe it? He's got traps all along the coast, and he tosses the lobsters back. You should see how he handles them. It's the strangest thing. He sort of puts them in a trance."

"He looks like a Wishnell, right?"

"Yes."

"Handsome, then?"

"He has a big head."

"They all do."

"Owney's head is really huge. It looks like a weather balloon with ears."

"I'm sure he's handsome. They all have big chests, too, the Wishnells, except Toby Wishnell. Lots of muscles."

"Maybe it's baby fat," Ruth said.

"Muscle," said Mrs. Pommeroy, and smiled. "They're all big old Swedes. Except the pastor. Oh, how I used to want to marry a Wishnell."

"Which one?"

"Any of them. Any Wishnell. Ruth, they make so much money. You've seen their houses over there. The prettiest houses. The prettiest yards. They always have these sweet little flower gardens . . . I don't think I ever talked to a Wishnell, though, when I was a girl. Can you believe that? I'd see them in Rockland sometimes, and they were so handsome."

"You should have married a Wishnell."

"How, Ruth? Honestly. Regular people don't marry Wishnells. Besides, my family would have killed me if I'd married someone from Courne Haven. Besides, I never even *met* a Wishnell. I couldn't tell you which one I wanted to marry."

"You could've had your pick of them," Ruth said. "A sexy looker like you?"

"I loved my Ira," Mrs. Pommeroy said. But she patted Ruth's arm for the compliment.

"Sure you loved your Ira. But he was your cousin."

Mrs. Pommeroy sighed. "I know. But we had a good time. He used to take me over to the sea caves on Boon Rock, you know. With the stalactites, or whatever they were, hanging down everywhere. God, that was pretty."

"He was your *cousin!* People shouldn't marry their cousins! You're lucky your kids weren't born with dorsal fins!"

"You're terrible, Ruth! You're terrible!" But she laughed.

Ruth said, "You wouldn't believe how scared of Pastor Wishnell that Owney is."

"I believe everything. Do you like that Owney Wishnell, Ruth?"

"Do I like him? I don't know. No. Sure. I don't know. I think he's . . . interesting."

"You never talk about boys."

"I never meet any boys to talk about."

"Is he handsome?" Mrs. Pommeroy asked again.

"I told you. He's big. He's blond."

"Are his eyes very blue?"

"That sounds like the title of a love song."

"Are they very blue or not, Ruth?" She sounded slightly annoyed.

Ruth changed her tone. "Yes. They are very blue, Mrs. Pommeroy."

"Do you want to know something funny, Ruth? I always secretly hoped you'd marry one of my boys."

"Oh, Mrs. Pommeroy, *no.*"

"I know. I know."

"It's just—"

"I know, Ruth. Look at them. What a bunch! You couldn't end up with any of them. Fagan is a farmer. Can you imagine that? A girl like you could never live on a potato farm. John? Who knows about John? Where is he? We don't even know. Europe? I can hardly remember what John's like. It's been so long since I've seen him, I can hardly remember his face. Isn't that a terrible thing for a mother to say?"

"I can hardly remember John either."

"You're not his mother, Ruth. And then there's Conway. Such a violent person, for some reason. And now he walks with a limp. You'd never marry a man with a limp."

"No limpers for me!"

"And Chester? Oh, boy."

"Oh, boy."

"Thinks he can tell fortunes? Rides around with those hippies?"

"Sells dope."

"Sells dope?" Mrs. Pommeroy said, surprised.

"Just kidding," Ruth lied.

"He probably does." Mrs. Pommeroy sighed. "And Robin. Well, I have to admit I never thought you'd marry Robin. Not even when you were both little. You never thought much of Robin."

"You probably thought he wouldn't be able to ask me to marry him. He wouldn't be able to pronounce it. It'd be like *Would you pwease mawwey me, Woof?* It would have been embarrassing for everyone."

Mrs. Pommeroy shook her head and wiped her eyes quickly. Ruth noticed the gesture and stopped laughing.

"What about Webster?" Ruth asked. "That leaves Webster."

"That's the thing, Ruth," Mrs. Pommeroy said, and her voice was sad. "I always thought you'd marry Webster."

"Oh, Mrs. Pommeroy." Ruth moved over on the couch and put her arm around her friend.

"What happened to Webster, Ruth?"

"I don't know."

"He was the brightest one. He was my brightest son."

"I know."

"After his father died . . ."

"I know."

"He didn't even *grow* any more."

"I know. I know."

"He's so *timid.* He's like a *child.*" Mrs. Pommeroy wiped tears off both cheeks with the back of her hand—a fast, smooth motion. "Me and your mom both have a son that didn't grow, I guess," she said. "Oh, brother. I'm such a crybaby. How about that?" She wiped her nose on her sleeve and smiled at Ruth. They brought their foreheads together for a moment. Ruth put her hand on the back of Mrs. Pommeroy's head, and Mrs. Pommeroy closed her eyes. Then she pulled back and said, "I think something was taken from my sons, Ruthie."

"Yes."

"A lot was taken from my sons. Their father. Their inheritance. Their boat. Their fishing ground. Their fishing gear."

"I know," Ruth said, and she felt a rush of guilt, as she had for years, whenever she thought of her father on his boat with Mr. Pommeroy's traps.

"I wish I could have another son for you."

"What? For me?"

"To marry. I wish I could have one more son, and make him normal. A good one."

"Come on, Mrs. Pommeroy. All your sons are good."

"You're sweet, Ruth."

"Except Chester, of course. He's no good."

"In their way, they're good enough. But not good enough for a bright girl like you. I'll bet I could get it right, you know, if I had another go at it." Mrs. Pommeroy's eyes teared up again. "Now, what a thing for me to say, a woman with seven kids."

"It's OK."

"Besides, I can't expect you to wait around for a baby to grow up, can I? Listen to me."

"I am listening."

"I'm talking crazy now."

"A little crazy," Ruth admitted.

"Oh, things don't always work out, I guess."

"Not always. I think they must work out sometimes."

"I guess. Don't you think you should go live with your mother, Ruth?"

"No."

"There's nothing out here for you."

"That's not true."

"Truth is, I like having you around, but that's not fair. There's nothing here for you. It's like a prison. It's your little San Quentin. I always thought, 'Oh, Ruth will marry Webster,' and I always thought, 'Oh, Webster will take over his dad's lobster boat.' I thought I had it all figured out. But there's no boat."

And there's barely a Webster, Ruth thought.

"Don't you ever think you should live out there?" Mrs. Pommeroy stretched out her arm and pointed. She had clearly intended to point west, toward the coast and the country that lay beyond it, but she was pointing in the dead-wrong direction. She was pointing toward the open sea. Ruth knew what she was trying to say, though. Mrs. Pommeroy, famously, did not have a great sense of direction.

"I don't need to marry one of your sons to stay here with you, you know," Ruth said.

"Oh, Ruth."

"I wish you wouldn't tell me I should go. I get that enough from my mom and Lanford Ellis. I belong on this island as much as anyone. Forget about my mother."

"Oh, Ruth. Don't say that."

"All right, I don't mean forget about her. But it doesn't matter where she lives or who she lives with. It doesn't matter to me. I'll stay here with you; I'll go where you go." Ruth was smiling as she said this, and nudging Mrs. Pommeroy the way Mrs. Pommeroy often nudged her. A teasing little poke, a loving one.

"But I'm not going anywhere," Mrs. Pommeroy said.

"Fine. Me neither. It's decided. I'm not budging. This is where I stay from now on. No more trips to Concord. No more bullshit about college."

"You can't make a promise like that."

"I can do whatever I want. I can make even bigger promises."

"Lanford Ellis would kill you if he heard you talking like that."

"Hell with it. The hell with *them.* From now on, whatever Lanford Ellis says to do, I do the opposite. Fuck the Ellises. Watch me! Watch me, world! Look out, baby!"

"But why do you want to spend your life on this crappy island? These aren't your people out here, Ruth."

"Sure they are. Yours and mine. If they're your people, they're my people!"

"Listen to you!"

"I'm feeling pretty grand today. I can make big promises today."

"I guess so!"

"You don't think I mean any of it."

"I think you say the sweetest things. And I think, in the end, you'll do whatever you want."

They sat out there on the porch couch for another hour or so. Opal wandered out a few more times in a bored and aimless way with Eddie, and Mrs. Pommeroy and Ruth took turns heaving him onto their laps and trying to bounce him around without hurting themselves. The last time Opal left, she didn't go into the house; she wandered down toward the harbor, to go "downstreet to the store," she said. Her sandals flip-flopped against her soles, and her big baby smacked his lips as he sat, heavy, on her right hip. Mrs. Pommeroy and Ruth watched the mother and baby descend the hill.

"Do you think I look old, Ruth?"

"You look like a millions bucks. You'll always be the prettiest woman out here."

"Look at this," Mrs. Pommeroy said, and she lifted her chin. "My throat's all droopy."

"It is not."

"It is, Ruth." Mrs. Pommeroy tugged at the loose flesh under her chin. "Isn't that horrible, how it hangs there? I look like a pelican."

"You do not look like a pelican."

"I look like a pelican. I could carry a whole salmon in here, like a ratty old pelican."

"You look like a very young pelican," Ruth said.

"Oh, that's better, Ruth. Thank you very much." Mrs. Pommeroy stroked her neck, and asked, "What were you thinking when you were alone with Owney Wishnell?"

"Oh, I don't know."

"Sure you do. Tell me."

"I don't have anything to tell."

"Hmm," said Mrs. Pommeroy. "I wonder." She pinched the skin on the back of her hand. "Look how dry and saggy I am. If I could change anything about myself, I'd try to get my old skin back. I had beautiful skin when I was your age."

"Everyone has beautiful skin when they're my age."

"What would you change about your appearance if you could, Ruth?"

Without hesitating, Ruth replied, "I wish I was taller. I wish I had smaller nipples. And I wish I could sing."

Mrs. Pommeroy laughed. "Who said your nipples were too big?"

"Nobody. Come on, Mrs. Pommeroy. Nobody's ever seen them but me."

"Did you show them to Owney Wishnell?"

"No," Ruth said. "But I'd like to."

"You should, then."

That little exchange took both of them by surprise; they'd shocked each other. The idea lingered on the porch for a long, long time. Ruth's face burned. Mrs. Pommeroy was quiet. She seemed to be thinking very carefully about Ruth's comment. "OK," she said at last, "I guess you want him."

"Oh, I don't know. He's weird. He hardly ever talks —"

"No, you want him. He's the one you want. I know about these things, Ruth. So we'll have to get him for you. We'll figure it out somehow."

"Nobody has to figure anything out."

"We'll figure it out, Ruth. Good. I'm happy that you want someone. That's appropriate for a girl your age."

"I'm not ready for anything stupid like that," Ruth said.

"Well, you'd better *get* ready."

Ruth didn't know what to say to that. Mrs. Pommeroy swung her legs up on the couch and put her bare feet on Ruth's lap. "Feet on you, Ruth," she said, and she sounded deeply sad.

"Feet on me," Ruth said, and felt a sudden and sharp awkwardness about her admission. She felt guilty about everything she'd said: guilty about her frank sexual interest in a Wishnell, guilty about leaving her mother, guilty about her weird promise never to leave Fort Niles, guilty about confessing that she'd never in a million years marry one of Mrs. Pommeroy's sons. God, it was true, though! Mrs. Pommeroy could have a son every year for the rest of her life, and Ruth would never marry one of them. Poor Mrs. Pommeroy!

"I love you, you know," she said to Mrs. Pommeroy. "You're my favorite person."

"Feet on you, Ruth," Mrs. Pommeroy said quietly, by way of reply.

Later that afternoon, Ruth left Mrs. Pommeroy and wandered over to the Addams house to see what the Senator was up to. She didn't feel like going home yet. She didn't feel like talking to her father when she was blue, so she thought she'd talk to the Senator instead. Maybe he'd show her some old photographs of shipwreck survivors and cheer her up. But when she reached the Addams house, she found only Angus. He was trying to thread a length of pipe, and he was in an appalling mood. He told her the Senator was down at Potter Beach again with that skinny goddamn nitwit Webster Pommeroy, looking for a goddamn elephant's tusk.

"No," Ruth said, "they already found the elephant's tusk."

"For Christ's sake, Ruthie, they're looking for the goddamn other tusk." He said it as if he was mad at *her* for some reason.

"Jeez," she said. "Sorry."

When she got down to Potter Beach, she found the Senator pacing unhappily on the rocky sand, with Cookie close at his heels.

"I don't know what to do with Webster, Ruth," the Senator said. "I can't talk him out of it."

Webster Pommeroy was far out in the mudflats, scrambling around awkwardly, looking unsettled and panicky. Ruth might not have recognized him. He looked like a kid floundering around out there, a stupid little kid in big trouble.

"He won't quit," the Senator said. "He's been like this all week. It was pissing rain two days ago, and he wouldn't come in. I'm afraid he's going to hurt himself. He cut his hand yesterday on a tin can, digging around out there. It wasn't even an old tin can. Tore his thumb right open. He won't let me look at it."

"What happens if you leave?"

"I'm not leaving him out there, Ruth. He'd stay out there all night. He says he wants to find the other tusk, to replace the one Mr. Ellis took."

"So go up to Ellis House and demand that tusk back, Senator. Tell those fuckers you need it."

"I can't do that, Ruth. Maybe Mr. Ellis is holding on to the tusk while he decides about the museum. Maybe he's having it appraised or something."

"Mr. Ellis probably never even saw the thing. How do you know that Cal Cooley didn't keep it?"

They watched Webster flail around some more.

The Senator said, quietly, "Maybe you could go up to Ellis House and ask about it?"

"I'm not going up there," Ruth said. "I'm never going up there ever again."

"Why'd you come down here today, Ruth?" the Senator asked, after a painful silence. "Do you need something?"

"No, I just wanted to say hello."

"Well, hello, Ruthie." He wasn't looking at her; he was watching Webster with an expression of intense concern.

"Hello to you. This isn't a good time for you, is it?" asked Ruth.

"Oh, I'm fine. How's your mother, Ruth? How was your trip to Concord?"

"She's doing OK, I guess."

"Did you send her my regards?"

"I think I did. You could write her a letter if you really wanted to make her day."

"That's a fine idea, a fine idea. Is she as pretty as ever?"

"I don't know how pretty she ever was, but she looks fine. I think she's lonely there, though. The Ellises keep telling her they want me to go to college; they'd pay for it."

"Mr. Ellis said that?"

"Not to me. But my mom talks about it, and Miss Vera, and even Cal Cooley. It's coming, Senator. Mr. Ellis will be making an announcement about it soon, I bet."

"Well, that sounds like a pretty good offer."

"If it came from anyone else, it would be a great offer."

"Stubborn, stubborn."

The Senator paced the length of the beach. Ruth followed him, and Cookie followed Ruth. The Senator was hugely distracted.

"Am I bothering you?" Ruth asked.

"No," the Senator said. "No, no. But you can stay. You can stay here and watch."

"Don't worry about it. It's nothing," Ruth said. But she couldn't stand watching Webster beating around in the mud so painfully. And she didn't want to follow the Senator around if all he was going to do was pace up and down the beach, wringing his hands. "I was heading home anyway."

So she headed home. She was out of ideas, and there was nobody else on Fort Niles she wanted to talk to. There was nothing on Fort Niles she wanted to do. She might as well check in with her father, she decided. She might as well make some dinner.

9

If tossed into the water back or head first, the animal, unless exhausted, immediately rights itself, and, with one or two vigorous flexations of the tail, shoots off obliquely toward the bottom, as if sliding down an inclined plane.

—*The American Lobster: A Study of Its Habits and Development*
Francis Hobart Herrick, Ph.D.
1895

THE SECOND Courne Haven–Fort Niles lobster war took place between 1928 and 1930. It was a pathetic war, not worth discussing.

The third Courne Haven–Fort Niles lobster war was an ugly, short, four-month affair that raged in 1946 and had a greater effect on some islanders than the bombing of Pearl Harbor. This war prevented the island men from fishing in a year that saw the largest total catch of lobsters known in the fisheries of Maine: six thousand licensed fishermen took in a record nineteen million pounds of lobster that year. But the men on Fort Niles and Courne Haven missed the bounty because they were too busy fighting.

The fourth Courne Haven–Fort Niles lobster war began in the mid-1950s. The cause of this war was not clearly defined. There was no single instigation, no one angry event that lit the fuse. So how did it begin? With pushing. With slow, typical, everyday pushing.

According to the laws of Maine, any man with a lobstering license may put a trap anywhere in Maine waters. That's what the laws say. The reality is different. Certain families fish certain territories because they have always done so; certain areas belong to certain islands because they always have; certain waterways are under the control of certain people because they always have been. The ocean, though not marked by fences and deeds, is strictly marked by traditions, and it would serve a novice well to pay attention to those traditions.

The barriers, though invisible, are real, and they are constantly being tested. It is the nature of man to try to extend his property, and lobstermen are no exception. They push. They see what they can get away with. They shove and bump the boundaries whenever they can, trying to move each empire a foot here, a foot there.

Maybe Mr. Cobb has always stopped his line of traps at the mouth of a certain inlet. But what would happen if, one day, Mr. Cobb decided to set a few traps a few dozen feet farther in, to a spot where Mr. Thomas has traditionally fished? What harm could there be in a few dozen feet? Maybe the move would go unnoticed. Mr. Thomas isn't as diligent as he once was, thinks Mr. Cobb. Perhaps Mr. Thomas has been ill or has had a bad year or has lost his wife and isn't paying as close attention as he used to, and maybe — just maybe — the push will go unnoticed.

And it may. Mr. Thomas might not feel the crunch. Or, for whatever reasons, he may not care enough to challenge Mr. Cobb. Then again, maybe he will care. Maybe he'll be immensely annoyed. Maybe Mr. Thomas will send a message of dissatisfaction. Maybe when Mr. Cobb goes to pull his traps the next week, he'll find that Mr. Thomas has tied a half-hitch knot in the middle of each line, as a warning. Maybe Mr. Thomas and Mr. Cobb are neighbors who've never had any conflict in the past. Maybe they're married to sisters. Maybe they're good friends. Those harmless knots are Mr. Thomas's way of saying, "I see what you're trying to do here, friend, and I ask you to please back the hell out of my territory while I still have patience with you."

And perhaps Mr. Cobb will back away, and that will be the end of it. Or perhaps he won't. Who knows what reasons he may have for persisting? Perhaps Mr. Cobb is resentful that Mr. Thomas feels entitled to such a big piece of the ocean in the first place, when Mr. Thomas isn't even that gifted a fisherman. And maybe Mr. Cobb is angry because of a rumor he heard that Mr. Thomas is keeping illegal short lobsters, or maybe Mr. Thomas's son has looked in a lecherous manner at Mr. Cobb's attractive thirteen-year-old daughter on more than one occasion. Perhaps Mr. Cobb has had troubles of his own at home and needs more money. Perhaps Mr. Cobb's grandfather once laid claim to that same inlet, and Mr. Cobb is taking back what he believes rightfully belongs to his family.

So next week he sets his traps in Mr. Thomas's territory again, only now he doesn't think of it as Mr. Thomas's territory but as free ocean and his own property as a free American man. And he's a little pissed off, to tell you the truth, at that greedy bastard Thomas for tying knots in a man's fishing lines, for Christ's sake, when all a man is trying to do is make a goddamn living. What the hell was that supposed to mean, tying knots in his lines? If Mr. Thomas has a problem, why doesn't he talk about it like a man? And by now Mr. Cobb doesn't care if Mr. Thomas tries cutting his traps away, either. Let him cut! The hell with it! Let him try. He'll clobber the bastard.

And when Mr. Thomas finds his neighbor's pot buoys floating in his territory again, he has to make a choice. Cut the traps away? Mr. Thomas wonders how serious Cobb is. Who are Cobb's friends and allies? Can Thomas afford to lose traps if Cobb retaliates by cutting them? Is it such great territory, after all? Worth fighting for? Did any Cobb ever have a legitimate claim to it? Is Cobb being malicious or is he ignorant?

There are so many reasons that can lead a man to set traps accidentally in another man's area. Did these traps happen to drift there in a storm? Is Cobb a young hothead? Should a man protest every affront? Must a man be on constant guard against his neighbors? On the other hand, should a man sit in silence while some greedy bastard eats from his dinner plate, for Christ's sake? Should a man be deprived of his means for making a living? What if Cobb decides to take over the whole area? What if Cobb pushes Thomas into someone else's traps and causes more trouble for Thomas? Must a man spend hours of his every working day making such decisions?

In fact, he must.

If he is a lobsterman, he must make these decisions every day. It's the way of the business. And over the years, a lobsterman develops a policy, a reputation. If he's fishing for a living, fishing to feed his family, he cannot afford to be passive, and in time he'll come to be known as either a pusher or a cutter. It's hard to avoid becoming one or the other. He must fight to extend his territory by pushing another man's trap line, or he must fight to defend his territory by cutting away the traps of anyone who pushes in on his.

Both *pusher* and *cutter* are derogatory terms. Nobody wants to be called either one, but nearly every lobsterman is one or the other. Or both. In general, pushers are young men, and cutters are older. Pushers have few traps in their fleet; cutters have many. Pushers have little to lose; cutters have everything to defend. The tension between pushers and cutters is constant, even within a single community, even within a single family.

On Fort Niles Island, Angus Addams was the most famous resident cutter. He cut away anybody and everybody who came near him, and he boasted about it. He said, of his cousins and neighbors, "They've been pushing my fanny around for fifty years, and I've cut away every last one of those bastards." As a rule, Angus cut without warning. He didn't waste time tying friendly warning knots in the lines of a fisherman who, ignorantly or accidentally, may have strayed into his domain. He didn't care who the errant fisherman was or what his motives were. Angus Addams cut away with rage and consistency, cursing as he sawed through the wet, seaweed-slick rope, cursing those who were trying to take what was rightfully his. He was a good fisherman; he knew he was constantly being followed and watched by lesser men who wanted a piece of what he had. For the love of Christ, he wasn't going to hand it to them.

Angus Addams had even cut away Ruth's father, Stan Thomas, who was his best friend in the world. Stan Thomas was not much of a pusher, but he had once set traps past Jatty Rock, where the only buoys that ever bobbed were the yellow-and-green–striped buoys of Angus Addams. Stan observed that Angus hadn't laid a trap there for months and thought he'd give it a try. He didn't think Angus would notice. But Angus noticed. And Angus cut away every last trap in the line of his best friend, pulled up the severed red-and-blue Thomas buoys, tied them together with a yard of rope, and quit fishing for the day, he was so goddamn mad. He set out to find Stan Thomas. He motored all over the inlets and islands in and out of Worthy Channel until he saw the *Miss Ruthie* floating ahead, surrounded with seagulls greedy for the bait. Angus sped up to the boat. Stan Thomas stopped his work and looked over at his friend.

"Something wrong, Angus?" Stan asked.

Angus Addams threw the severed buoys onto Stan's deck without saying a word. He threw the buoys down with a triumphant gesture, as if they were the severed heads of his worldly enemies. Stan looked at the buoys impassively.

"Something wrong, Angus?" he repeated.

"You push me again," Angus said, "the next thing I'll cut is your goddamn throat."

That was Angus's standard threat. Stan Thomas had heard it a dozen times, sometimes directed to a malefactor and sometimes in the gleeful retelling of a story over beers and cribbage. But Angus had never before directed it at Stan. The two men, the two best friends, looked at each other. Their boats bobbed below them.

"You owe me for twelve traps," Stan Thomas said. "Those were brand-new. I could tell you to sit down and make me twelve brand-new traps, but you can give me twelve of your old ones, and we'll forget about it."

"You can jump up my ass."

"You haven't set any traps there all spring," Stan said.

"Don't you fucking think you have any play with me because we have a goddamn *history*, Stan."

Angus Addams was purple around his neck, but Stan Thomas stared him down without showing any anger. "If you were anyone else," Stan said, "I'd punch you in the teeth right now for the way you're talking to me."

"Don't give me no special goddamn treatment."

"That's right. You didn't give me any."

"That's right. And I won't ever give you none, neither, so keep your goddamn traps the hell away from my ass."

And he pulled his boat away, giving Stan Thomas the finger as he sped off. Stan and Angus did not speak to each other for nearly eight months. And that encounter was between good friends, between two men who ate dinner together several nights a week, between two neighbors, between a teacher and his protégé. That was an encounter between two men who did not believe that the other was working day and night to destroy him, which was what the men of Fort Niles Island and Courne Haven Island happen to believe of each other. Correctly, for the most part.

It's a dicey business. And it was that sort of pushing and cutting that brought about the fourth lobster war, back in the late 1950s. Who started it? Hard to say. Hostility was in the air. There were men back from Korea who wanted to take up fishing again and found that their territory had been eaten away. There were, in the spring of 1957, several young men who had just come of age and had bought their own boats. They were trying to find a place for themselves. The fishing had been good the year before, so everyone had enough money to buy more traps and bigger boats with bigger engines, and the fishermen were pressing against one another.

There was some cutting on both sides; there was some pushing. Curses were shouted over the bows of some boats. And, over the course of several months, the rancor grew more intense. Angus Addams got tired of cutting away Courne Haven traps in his territory, so he started messing with the enemy in more imaginative ways. He took all his household garbage aboard, and when he found alien traps in his way, he'd pull them up and stuff them with garbage. Once, he stuffed an old pillow into someone's trap so that no lobsters could get in, and he wasted one entire afternoon driving nails through a trap; it ended up looking like a spiked instrument of torture. Angus had another trick; he'd stuff someone's straying trap with rocks and throw it back into the sea. It was a lot of work, that trick. He had to load the rocks on his own boat, with sacks and a wheelbarrow, which took a lot of time. But Angus considered it time well spent. He liked to think of the Courne Haven bastard straining and struggling to pull up a trap, only to find it full of rubble.

Angus got a big kick out of these games until the day he pulled up one of his own traps and found in it a child's doll, with a rusty pair of scissors stuck in its chest. That was an alarming, violent message to pull from the sea. Angus Addams's sternman shrieked like a girl when he saw it. The doll horrified even Angus. Its blond hair was wet and slathered across its face, which was cracked china. The doll's stiff lips formed a shocked O. A crab had found its way into the trap and was clinging to the doll's dress.

"What the fuck is this?" Angus shouted. He pulled the stabbed doll from his trap and yanked out the scissors. "What the fuck is this, some kind of fucking threat?"

He brought the doll back to Fort Niles and showed it around, thrusting it into people's faces in a manner that was pretty damned unsettling. The people on Fort Niles were generally dismissive of Angus Addams's rages, but this time they paid attention. There was something about the savagery of the stabbed doll that angered everyone. A doll? What the hell was that supposed to mean? Garbage and nails were one thing, but a murdered doll? If someone on Courne Haven had a problem with Angus, why couldn't that person say it to his face? And whose doll was it? It probably belonged to some fisherman's poor daughter. What kind of a man would stab his little girl's doll, just to make a point? And what exactly *was* the point?

Those people over on Courne Haven were animals.

The next morning, many of the Fort Niles lobstermen gathered at the dock much earlier than usual. It was more than an hour before sunrise, still dark. There were stars in the sky, and the moon was low and dim. The men set off toward Courne Haven in a small fleet. Their engines threw up a huge, stinking cloud of diesel fumes. They didn't have a particular intent, but they motored with determination over to Courne Haven and stopped their boats right outside the harbor. There were twelve of them, the fishermen of Fort Niles, a small blockade. Nobody spoke. A few of the men smoked cigarettes.

After about a half hour, they could see activity on the Courne Haven dock. The Courne Haven men coming down to begin their day of fishing looked out to the sea and saw the line of boats. They gathered in a small group on the dock and kept looking at the boats. Some of the men were drinking from thermoses of coffee, and wisps of steam rose among them. The group grew larger as more men came down to start their day of fishing and found the huddle on the dock.

Some of the men pointed. Some of them smoked cigarettes, too. After about fifteen minutes, it was clear they didn't know what to do about the blockade. No one made a move toward his boat. They all shuffled around, talking to each other. Across the water, the Fort Niles men in their boats could hear the watery distillations of Courne Haven conversation. Sometimes a cough or a laugh would carry clearly. The laughter was killing Angus Addams.

"Fucking pussies," he said, but only a few in the blockade could hear him, because he muttered it under his breath.

"What's that?" said the man in the boat beside him, Angus's cousin Barney.

"What's so funny?" asked Angus. "I'll show them funny."

"I don't think they're laughing at us," said Barney. "I think they're just laughing."

"I'll show them funny."

Angus Addams went to his helm and gunned his motor, powering his boat forward, right into the Courne Haven harbor. He sped among the boats, smacking up a mean wake in his path, then slowed down near the dock. It was low tide, and his boat was far, far below the gathered

Courne Haven fishermen. They moved to the edge of the dock to look down at Angus Addams. None of the other Fort Niles fishermen had followed him; they hung back at the mouth of the harbor. No one knew what to do.

"YOU PEOPLE LIKE PLAYING WITH DOLLS?" Angus Addams bellowed. His friends in their boats could hear him clear across the water. He held up and shook the murdered doll. One of the Courne Haven men said something that made his friends laugh.

"COME ON DOWN HERE!" Angus shouted. "COME ON DOWN AND SAY THAT!"

"What'd he say?" Barney Addams asked Don Pommeroy. "Did you hear what that guy said?"

Don Pommeroy shrugged.

Just then, a big man walked down the path to the dock and the fishermen parted to make way for him. He was tall and wide and wasn't wearing a hat on his gleaming head of blond hair. He had some ropes, neatly coiled, over his shoulder, and was carrying a tin lunchbox. The laughter on the Courne Haven dock stopped. Angus Addams said nothing; that is, nothing that his friends could hear.

The blond man, not looking at Angus, climbed down from the dock, his lunchbox tucked under his arm, and stepped into a rowboat. He released it from its post and began to row. His stroke was beautiful to behold: a long pull followed by a quick, muscular snap. In very little time, he reached his boat and climbed aboard. By now, the men at the mouth of the harbor could see that this was Ned Wishnell, a true high-line fisherman and the current patriarch of the Wishnell dynasty. They looked at his boat with envy. It was twenty-five feet long, immaculate, white, with a clean blue stripe all around it. Ned Wishnell started it up and headed out of the harbor.

"Where the hell's he going?" said Barney Addams.

Don Pommeroy shrugged again.

Ned Wishnell came right at them, right toward their blockade, as if it weren't there. The Fort Niles fishermen looked at each other warily, wondering whether they were supposed to stop this man. It didn't seem right to let him pass, but Angus Addams wasn't with them to give instructions. They watched, paralyzed, as Ned Wishnell sailed right through, passing between Don Pommeroy and Duke Cobb without looking left or right. The Fort Niles boats bobbed in his wake. Don had to grab his rail, or he would have fallen over. The men watched as Ned Wishnell sped off, smaller and smaller as he went out to sea.

"Where the hell's he going?" Barney apparently still expected an answer.

"I think he's going fishing," said Don Pommeroy.

"Hell of a note," said Barney. He squinted out at the ocean. "Didn't he see us?"

"Course he seen us."

"Why didn't he say anything?"

"What the hell did you think he'd say?"

"I don't know. Something like, 'Hey, fellas! What's going on?' "

"Shut up, Barney."

"I don't see why I should," said Barney Addams, but he did.

Ned Wishnell's impudence utterly dissolved any menace the Fort Niles men may have presented, so the rest of the Courne Haven fishermen, one at a time, climbed down their dock, got into their boats, and set out for a day of lobstering. Like their neighbor Ned, they passed through the Fort Niles blockade without looking to the left or right. Angus Addams screamed at them for a while, but this embarrassed the rest of the Fort Niles men, who, one at a time, turned around and headed home. Angus was the last to go. He was, as Barney reported later, "sweating bullets, cursing stars, sewing buttonholes, and everything else." Angus was outraged at being deserted by his friends, furious that what could have been a pretty decent blockade had turned comic and useless.

This might have been the end of the fourth Fort Niles–Courne Haven lobster war, right there. If the incidents that morning had closed the quarrel, in fact, it wouldn't even have been remembered as a lobster war; rather, just another in the long series of disputes and confrontations. As the summer went on, the pushing and cutting continued, but sporadically. For the most part, it was Angus Addams doing the cutting, and the men on both islands were used to that. Angus Addams held on to what was his like a bull terrier. For everyone else, new boundaries were set. Some territory got shifted; some new fishermen took over old areas; some old fishermen cut back on their workload; some fishermen home from the war resumed their profession. Everything settled down to a normal, tense peace.

For a few weeks.

At the end of April, Angus Addams happened to go to Rockland to sell his lobsters at the same time as Don Pommeroy. Don, a bachelor, was a known fool. He was the softer brother of Ira Pommeroy, the scowling, hard-knuckled husband of Rhonda Pommeroy, the father of Webster and Conway and John and Fagan and so on. Angus Addams didn't think much of either of the Pommeroys, but he ended up spending a night drinking with Don at the Wayside Hotel, because it was too rough and too dark to head back home, and he was bored. Angus might have preferred to drink alone in his hotel room, but that's not how things ended up. The men met at the wholesaler's place, and Don said, "Let's have a refresher, Angus," and Angus agreed.

There were some men from Courne Haven at the Wayside that night. Fred Burden the fiddler was there with his brother-in-law, Carl Cobb. Because it was a night of windy, icy rain, and because the Courne Haven men and the Fort Niles men were the only ones at the bar, they found themselves in conversation. It wasn't unfriendly conversation. In fact, it began when Fred Burden ordered a drink sent down to Angus Addams.

"That's to keep your strength up," Fred called over, "after a long day of cutting away our traps."

It was a hostile opening line, so Angus Addams called back, "You'd better send me the whole bottle, then. I cut away a hell of a lot more than one drink's worth today."

This was hostile, too, but it didn't lead to fighting. It led to laughing all around. The men had all had enough drinks to be jovial but not enough to start fighting. Fred Burden and Carl Cobb moved down the bar to sit next to their neighbors from Fort Niles. Of course they knew one another. They clapped each other on the back, ordered up some more beers and whiskeys, talked about their new boats and the new wholesaler and the newest trap design. They talked about the new fishing limitations the state was imposing, and what idiots the new wardens were. They had absolutely everything in common, so there was a lot to talk about.

Carl Cobb had been stationed in Germany during the Korean War, and he took out his wallet and showed off some German money. Everyone looked at Angus Addams's stump, where he'd lost his finger in the winch, and made him tell the story about kicking his finger overboard and searing the wound with his cigar. Fred Burden told the other men that the summer tourists on Courne Haven had decided the island was too rowdy and had pooled their money to hire a policeman for the months of July and August. The policeman was a redheaded teenager from Bangor, and he'd been beaten up three times in his first week on the island. The summer people had even got the kid a police car, which the stupid kid had flipped over in a high-speed chase across the island, trying to catch a guy with no license plate on his car.

"A high-speed chase!" Fred Burden said. "On an island four miles long! For Christ's sake, how far was the guy gonna go? Damn kid could've killed somebody."

As it was, Fred Burden went on, the dazed young policeman was dragged out of his wrecked car and beaten up again, this time by a neighbor, furious at finding a police car overturned in his garden. After three weeks, the young policeman went home to Bangor. The police car was still on the island. One of the Wishnells bought it and fixed it up for his kid to drive around. The summer tourists were enraged, but Henry Burden and everyone else told them that if they didn't like it on Courne Haven, they should go back to Boston, where they could have all the policemen they wanted.

Don Pommeroy said that was one good thing about Fort Niles—no summer tourists. The Ellis family owned damn near the whole island, and they wanted it all to themselves.

"That's one good thing about Courne Haven, though," Fred Burden said. "No Ellis family."

Everyone laughed. That was a good point.

Angus Addams told about the old days on Fort Niles, when the granite industry was still thriving. They'd had a policeman back then, and he was the perfect cop for an island. He was an Addams, first of all, so he knew everybody, and he knew how things operated. He left the islanders alone and mostly made sure the Italians didn't cause too much trouble. Roy Addams was his name; he'd been hired by the Ellis family to keep order. The Ellises didn't care what old Roy did as long as nobody was getting murdered or robbed. He had a squad car—a big Packard sedan, with wooden panels—but he never drove it. Roy had his own theory of policing. He'd sit in his house, listening to the radio, and if anything happened on the island, everyone would know where to find him. Once he heard about a crime, he'd go have a talk with the perpetrator. That was a good island policeman, Angus said. Fred and his brother-in-law agreed.

"There wasn't even a jail," Angus said. "You got in trouble, you had to sit in old Roy's living room for a while."

"That sounds about right," Fred said. "That's how it should be with police on an island."

"If there's going to be any police at all, that is," said Angus.

"That's right. If."

Angus then told the joke about the polar bear kid who wants to know if there's any koala blood in his family, and Fred Burden said that reminded him of the one about the three Eskimos in the bakery. And Don Pommeroy told the one about the Japanese guy and the iceberg, but he screwed it up, so Angus Addams had to tell it right. Carl Cobb said he'd heard it a different way, and he gave his whole version, and it was practically the same. That was a waste of time. Don contributed the joke about the Catholic lady and the talking frog, but he wrecked it pretty bad, too.

Angus Addams went off to the bathroom, and when he came back, Don Pommeroy and Fred Burden were arguing. They were really going at it. Someone had said something. Someone had started something. It sure hadn't taken long. Angus Addams went over to figure out what the fight was about.

"There's no way," Fred Burden was saying, his face red and his lips spitting when he talked. "No way you could! He'd *kill* you!"

"I'm just saying I could," Don Pommeroy said, slowly and with dignity. "I'm not saying it would be easy. I'm just saying I could do it."

"What's he talking about?" Angus asked Carl.

"Don bet Fred Burden a hundred bucks he could beat up a five-foot monkey in a fight," Carl said.

"What?"

"You'd get creamed!" Fred was shouting now. "You'd get *creamed* by a five-foot monkey!"

"I'm a good fighter," Don said.

Angus rolled his eyes and sat down. He felt sorry for Fred Burden. Fred Burden was from Courne Haven, but he didn't deserve to get into a stupid conversation like this with a known fool like Don Pommeroy.

"Have you ever *seen* a goddamn monkey?" Fred demanded. "The way a monkey is built? A five-foot monkey would have a six-foot arm span. You know how strong a monkey is? You couldn't beat up a *two*-foot monkey. You'd get *demolished!*"

"But he wouldn't know how to fight," Don said. "That's where my advantage is. I know how to fight."

"Now that's stupid. We're assuming he'd know how to fight."

"No we ain't."

"Then what are we talking about? How can we talk about fighting a five-foot monkey if the monkey can't even fight?"

"I'm just saying I could beat one if he *could* fight." Don was speaking very calmly. He was the prince of logic. "If a five-foot monkey could fight, I could beat him."

"What about the teeth?" Carl Cobb asked, genuinely interested now.

"Shut up, Carl," said his brother-in-law Fred.

"That's a good question," Don said, and nodded sagely. "The monkey wouldn't be allowed to use his teeth."

"Then he wouldn't be *fighting!*" Fred shouted. "That's how a monkey *would* fight! By biting!"

"No biting allowed," Don said, and his verdict was final.

"He would be boxing? Is that it?" Fred Burden demanded. "You're saying you could beat a five-foot monkey in a boxing match?"

"Exactly," said Don.

"But a monkey wouldn't *know* how to box," Carl Cobb observed, frowning.

Don nodded with composed satisfaction. "Exactly," he said, "why I would win."

This left Fred Burden with no choice but to punch Don out, so he did. Angus Addams said later he'd have done it himself if Don had said another goddamn word about boxing a five-foot monkey, but Fred was the first who couldn't take it any more, so he laid one across Don's ear. Carl Cobb looked so surprised that it really annoyed Angus, so Angus punched Carl. Then Fred punched Angus. Carl punched Angus, too, but not hard. Don came up off the floor and threw himself, bent over and howling, right into Fred's gut, sending Fred tumbling backward into some empty barstools, which clattered and wavered and fell.

The two men—Fred and Don—set to rolling on the floor of the bar. They had somehow got laid up against each other head to foot and foot to head, which was not an effective posture for fighting. They looked like a large clumsy starfish—all arms and legs. Fred Burden was on top, and he dug his boot tip into the floor and spun himself and Don in a circle, trying to get a grip.

Carl and Angus had stopped fighting. They hadn't had that strong an interest in it, anyway. Each had got in a punch, and that took care of that. Now they stood beside each other, backs to the bar, watching their friends on the floor.

"Get 'em, Fred!" Carl hooted, and shot a sheepish look at Angus.

Angus shrugged. He didn't particularly care if Don Pommeroy got beat up. He deserved it, the idiot. A five-foot monkey. For Christ's sake.

Fred Burden set his teeth into Don's shin and clamped. Don howled at the injustice, "No biting! No biting!" He was outraged, it seemed, because he'd made that rule perfectly clear with regard to the monkey fight. Angus Addams, standing at the bar, watched the awkward scramble on the floor for a while and then sighed, turned around, and asked the bartender if he could settle the tab. The bartender, a small, slight man with an anxious expression, was holding a baseball bat that was half his height.

"You don't need that," Angus said, nodding at the bat.

The bartender looked relieved and slid the bat back under the bar. "Should I call the police?"

"You don't need to worry. It's no big deal, buddy. Just let 'em fight it out."

"What are they fighting about?" the bartender asked.

"Ah, they're old friends," Angus said, and the bartender smiled with relief, as if that explained everything. Angus settled his bill and walked past the men (who were wrestling and grunting on the floor) to go upstairs and get some sleep.

"Where you going?" Don Pommeroy, on the floor, shrieked after Angus as he was leaving. "Where the hell you *going?*"

Angus had walked out on the fight because he thought it was nothing, but it turned out to be something after all.

Fred Burden was a tenacious bastard, and Don was as stubborn as he was stupid, and neither man let up on the other. The fight went on for a good ten minutes after Angus went to bed. The way Carl Cobb described it, Fred and Don were "two dogs in a field," biting, kicking, punching. Don tried to break a few bottles over Fred's head, and Fred broke a few of Don's fingers so fiercely, you could hear them snap. The bartender, a not very bright man who had been told by Angus not to worry about the fight, didn't.

Even when Fred was sitting on top of Don's chest, fistfuls of hair in his hands, pounding Don's head into the floor, the bartender did not intervene. Fred pounded until Don was unconscious, then sat back, heaving. The bartender was polishing an ashtray with his towel when Carl said, "Maybe you should call somebody." The bartender looked over the bar and saw that Don was not moving and that his face was mashed up. Fred was bloody, too, and one of his arms was hanging in a funny way. The bartender called the police.

Angus Addams didn't hear about any of this until the next morning, when he got up for breakfast and prepared to head back to Fort Niles. He learned that Don Pommeroy was in the hospital, and that things didn't look good. He hadn't woken up, Angus heard. He had some "internal damage," and the rumor was that a lung was punctured.

"Son of a bitch," Angus said, deeply impressed.

He'd never thought the fight would turn into something so serious. The police had questions for Angus, but they let him go. They were still holding Fred Burden, but he was so beat up himself that he hadn't yet been charged with anything. The police weren't sure what to do, because the bartender—their one sober, reliable witness—insisted that the two men were old friends who were only kidding around.

Angus arrived at the island late in the afternoon, and went looking for Don's brother Ira, but Ira had already heard the news. He'd received a telephone call from the Rockland police, informing him that his brother had been beaten into a coma by a Courne Haven fisherman in a bar. Ira went wild. He stormed around, flexing and unflexing his muscles and waving his fists in the air and shouting. His wife, Rhonda, tried to calm him down, but he wouldn't hear her. He was going to take a shotgun over to Courne Haven and "cause some trouble." He was going to "show somebody." He was going to "teach them a thing or two." He got together with some of his friends and worked them up into a serious froth. Nobody ended up taking any shotguns on board, but the tense peace that existed between the two islands was shattered, and the fourth Courne Haven lobster war was under way.

The daily details of this war are not significant; it was a typical lobster war. There was fighting, cutting, pushing, vandalism, theft, aggression, accusation, paranoia, intimidation, terror, cowardice, and threats. There was virtually no commerce. It's hard enough to make a living at fishing, but it's harder still when the fisherman has to spend his days defending his property or attacking the property of another man.

Ruth's father, with little fuss and no hesitation, took his traps out of the water, just as his father had done during the first Courne Haven–Fort Niles lobster war, back in 1903. He took his boat out of the water and stored it in his front yard. "I don't get involved in these things," he told his neighbors. "I don't care who did what to who." Stan Thomas had it all figured out. By sitting out the war, he would lose less money than his neighbors. He knew it wouldn't last forever.

The war lasted seven months. Stan Thomas used the time to fix up his boat, build new traps, tar his lines, paint his buoys. While his neighbors fought steadily and drove themselves and each other back into poverty, he polished his business apparatus to sparkling perfection. Sure, they took over his fishing territory, but he knew they'd burn themselves out and that he'd be able to take it all back—and more. They would be beaten. In the meantime, he fixed his gear and made every piece of brass and every barrel gorgeous. His brand-new wife, Mary, helped a great deal, and painted up his buoys very prettily. They had no trouble with money; the house had long been paid for, and Mary was wonderfully frugal. She'd lived her whole life in a room that was ten feet square and had never owned a thing. She expected nothing, asked for nothing. She could make a hearty stew out of a carrot and a chicken bone. She planted a garden, sewed patches into her husband's clothing, darned his socks. She was used to this kind of work. Not all that much difference between darning wool socks and pairing and matching silk stockings.

Mary Smith-Ellis Thomas tried, gently, to persuade her husband to take a job at Ellis House and not go back to lobstering, but he wouldn't hear of it. He didn't want to be near any of those assholes, he told her. "You could work in the stables," she said, "and you'd never see them." But he didn't want to shovel the shit of the horses of any of those assholes, either. So she let it drop. It had been a quiet fantasy of Mary's, that her husband and the Ellises would grow to love one another, and that she would be welcomed back at Ellis House. Not as a servant but as a member of the family. Maybe Vera Ellis would come to admire

Stan. Maybe Vera would invite Stan and Mary for luncheons. Maybe Vera would pour Stan a cup of tea and say, "I'm so happy Mary married such a resourceful gentleman."

One night in bed in her new home with her new husband, Mary started, in the meekest way, to hint at this fantasy. "Maybe we could go to visit Miss Vera . . ." she began, but her husband interrupted her with the information that he would eat his own feces before he would visit Vera Ellis.

"Oh," said Mary.

So she let it go. She put all her resourcefulness toward helping her husband through the dry months of the lobster war, and, in return, she received small, precious acknowledgments of her worth. He liked to sit in the living room and watch her sew curtains. The house was immaculate, and he found endearing her attempts at decoration. Mary set wildflowers on the windowsill in water glasses. She polished his tools. That was the most adorable thing.

"Come here," he'd tell her at the end of the day, and he'd pat his knee.

Mary would go over and sit on his lap. He'd open his arms. "Come in here," he'd say, and she'd fold up against him. When she dressed prettily, or styled her hair in a nice way, he called her Mint, because she looked freshly minted, shiny as a new coin.

"Come here, Mint," he'd say.

Or, while watching her iron his shirts, he'd say, "Nice work there, Mint."

They spent every day, all day, together, because he was not going out to sea. There was a feeling in their house that they were working together toward a common goal, and that they were a team, untainted by sordid quarrels of the rest of the world. The Courne Haven–Fort Niles lobster war raged around them, corroding everybody but them. They were Mr. and Mrs. Stan Thomas. They needed, Mary believed, only each other. They made their home stronger while the homes of others shook.

It was — those seven war months — the happiest time of their marriage. Those seven war months gave Mary Smith-Ellis Thomas a soaring joy, a sense that she had made the unquestionably right decision in leaving Vera Ellis to marry Stan. She had a true sense of worth. She was well accustomed to working, but was not at all accustomed to working for her own future, for her own benefit. She had a husband, and he loved her. She was essential to him. He told her so.

"You're a great kid, Mint."

After seven months of daily care, Stan Thomas's fishing gear was a paragon. He wanted to rub his hands together like a millionaire when he looked over his gear and his boat. He wanted to laugh like a tyrant as he watched his friends and neighbors fight themselves into ruin.

Fight it out, he silently urged the others. *Go ahead. Fight it out.*

The longer the others fought, the weaker they would become. All the better for Stan Thomas when, finally, he would put his boat back in the water. He willed the war to go on, but in November of 1957 the fourth Courne Haven–Fort Niles lobster war ended. Lobster wars tend to die down in the winters. Many fishermen stop working in November under the best of circumstances, because the weather is too rough. With fewer fishermen out there, the chance of confrontation eventually grows lower. The war might have run itself out because of the weather. Both islands might have sunk into their winter slumbers, and when spring came, the old disputes might have been dropped. But that's not how it happened in 1957.

On November 8, a young man from Courne Haven Island, by the name of Jim Burden, set out for a day of lobster fishing. He had meant to fuel up his boat first thing in the morning, but before he could get to the pumps, he found a stranger's buoys, painted a hideous, garish green, bobbing among his traps. They were the buoys of Ira Pommeroy, from Fort Niles Island. Jim recognized them immediately. And he knew who Ira Pommeroy was. Ira Pommeroy, wife of Rhonda, father of Webster and Conway and John and so on, was the brother of Don Pommeroy. Who was in a hospital in Rockland, learning how to walk again, an ability he had lost after being beaten by Fred Burden. Who was Jim Burden's father.

Ira Pommeroy had been harassing Fred Burden and young Jim for months, and Jim had had enough of it. Jim Burden had set these traps right off the north coast of Courne Haven only the day before. They were so near Courne Haven that Jim could practically see them from his house. They were in a place where a Fort Niles fisherman had no business. To set those rogue traps, Ira Pommeroy must have come over in the middle of the night. What would drive a man to do that? Didn't the man ever sleep?

It should be noted that the buoys Ira Pommeroy had set on Jim's little shoreline were dummies. There were no traps at the end of those lines; there were cement blocks. Ira Pommeroy's plan was not to take Jim Burden's lobsters. The plan was to drive Jim Burden nuts, and it worked. Jim, a mild-mannered nineteen-year-old who'd been pretty much intimidated by this lobster war, lost every shred of meekness in an instant and went after Ira Pommeroy. Jim was in a hot rage. He didn't usually curse, but as he sped his boat over the waves, he said under his breath things like "Damn it, damn it, damn it. Damn *him!*"

He got to Fort Niles and set out to look for Ira Pommeroy's boat. He didn't know for sure whether he'd recognize it, but he was damn sure set on finding it. He more or less knew his way around the waters near Fort Niles, but he still had a few close calls with rocky ledges he couldn't spot from behind the throttle. And he wasn't paying all that much attention to the bottom or to landmarks that would help get him back home. He wasn't thinking about getting back home. He was looking for any boat belonging to a Fort Niles fisherman.

He scanned the horizon for flocks of seagulls and followed the seagulls to the lobster boats. Whenever he found a boat, he would zoom right up to it, slow down, and peer at it, trying to see who was aboard. He didn't say anything to the fishermen, and they didn't say anything to him. They stopped their work and looked at him. *What's that kid up to? What the hell is the matter with that kid's face? He's purple, for Christ's sake.*

Jim Burden didn't say a word. He zoomed off, searching for Ira Pommeroy. He hadn't planned exactly what he was going to do once he found him, but his thoughts were somewhere along the lines of murder.

Unluckily for Jim Burden, he didn't think to look for Ira Pommeroy's boat in the Fort Niles harbor, which is where it sat, bobbing quietly. Ira Pommeroy had taken the day off. He was exhausted from a night spent dropping cement blocks near Courne Haven, and he'd slept in until eight in the morning. While Jim Burden was speeding around the Atlantic looking for Ira, Ira was in bed with his wife, Rhonda, making another son.

Jim Burden went *way* out. He went much farther out to sea than any lobster boat needs to go. He went past all the pot buoys of any kind. He followed what he thought was a flock of seagulls far, far out to sea, but the seagulls, as he came nearer, vanished. They dissolved into the sky like sugar in hot water. Jim Burden slowed his boat down and looked around. Where was he? He could see Fort Niles Island shimmering in the distance, a pale gray apparition. His anger was now frustration, and even that was beginning to wane, replaced with something like anxiety. The weather was getting bad. The sea was high. The sky was whipped with fast, black clouds, which had come up quickly. Jim wasn't sure at all where he was.

"Damn it," Jim Burden said. "Damn *him.*"

And then he ran out of gas.

"*Damn* it," he said again, and this time he meant it.

He tried to start up the engine, but there was no doing so. No going anywhere. It hadn't occurred to him that this could happen. He hadn't thought about the gas tank.

"Oh, boy," said nineteen-year-old Jim Burden.

He was now afraid as well as embarrassed. Some fisherman he was. Paying his gas tank no mind. How stupid could you get? Jim got on the radio and put out a staticky call for help. "Help," he said, "I'm out of gas." He wasn't sure if there was a more nautical way to say this. He didn't know all that much about boating, really. This was the first year he'd been out to haul by himself. He'd worked for years as a sternman for his father, so he thought he knew all about the ocean, but now he realized he'd been a mere passenger before. His dad had taken care of everything, while he'd just done the muscle work in the back of the boat. He hadn't been paying attention all those years, and now he was alone on a boat in the middle of nowhere.

"Help!" he said into the radio again. Then he remembered the word. "Mayday!" he said. "Mayday!"

The first voice to get back to him was that of Ned Wishnell, and it made young Jim wince. Ned Wishnell was the best fisherman in Maine, people said. Something like this would never happen to Ned Wishnell, to any Wishnell. Jim had been hoping somewhere in the back of his mind that he could get through this without Ned Wishnell's finding out.

"Is that Jimmy?" Ned's voice cracked.

"This is the *Mighty J,*" Jim replied. He thought it would make him sound more adult to name his boat. But he was immediately embarrassed by the name. *The Mighty J!* Yeah, right.

"Is that Jimmy?" Ned's voice came again.

"This is Jimmy," Jim said. "I'm out of gas. Sorry."

"Where are you, son?"

"I . . . uh . . . don't know." He hated to say it, hated to admit it. To Ned Wishnell, of all people!

"Didn't make that out, Jimmy."

"I don't know!" Jim shouted it now. Humiliating. "I don't know where I am!"

There was silence. Then an unintelligible gargle.

"Didn't make that out, Ned," Jim said. He was trying to sound like the older man, imitating his cadence. Trying to maintain some dignity.

"You see any landmarks?" Ned asked.

"Fort Niles is, um, maybe two miles to the west," Jimmy said, but as he said it, he realized he could no longer see that distant island. A fog had come up, and it was growing as dark as evening, although it was only ten in the morning. He didn't know which way he was pointing.

"Drop your anchor. Stay put," Ned Wishnell said, and signed off.

Ned found the kid. It took him several hours, but he found Jimmy. He had notified the other fishermen, and they'd all been looking for Jimmy. Even some fishermen from Fort Niles went out to look for Jim Burden. It was terrible weather. On a normal day, everyone would have headed in because of the weather, but they all stayed out, looking for young Jimmy. Even Angus Addams went out looking for Jim Burden. It was the right thing to do. The kid was only nineteen, and he was lost.

But it was Ned Wishnell who found him. How, nobody knew. But the guy was a Wishnell—a gifted fisherman, a hero on the water—so nobody was surprised that he found a small boat in the fog in the big ocean without the faintest clue about where to look. Everyone was accustomed to nautical miracles from Wishnells.

By the time Ned got to the *Mighty J*, the weather was really rough, and Jim Burden had been pulled—despite his little anchor—far away from where he'd sent his call for help. Not that Jim knew where he'd been in the first place. He heard Ned Wishnell's boat before he could see it. He heard the motor through the fog.

"Help!" he shouted. "Mayday!"

Ned circled him and emerged out of the fog in that huge, gleaming boat of his, with that handsome, manly face of his. Ned was angry. He was angry and silent. His day of fishing had been ruined. Jim Burden could see the anger immediately, and it shrank his guts. Ned Wishnell pulled his boat up right beside the *Mighty J*. It had begun to rain. It was warm for Maine in November, which meant that it was miserable and freezing and wet. The wind blew the rain sideways. In his gloves, Jim's hands were chapped and scarlet, but Ned Wishnell wasn't wearing gloves. He wasn't wearing a hat. Seeing this, Jim quickly took off his hat and dropped it at his feet. He immediately regretted this decision as the freezing rain pinged his scalp.

"Hi," he said, lamely.

Ned tossed a line over to Jim and said, "Latch on." His voice was tight with irritation.

Jim tied the boats together—his small, cheap boat up against that Wishnell beauty. *The Mighty J* bounced, silent and useless, as Ned's boat chugged and chugged in a competent idle.

"You sure it's the gas run out?" Ned asked.

"Pretty sure."

"Pretty sure?" Disgusted.

Jim did not reply.

"It's not another kind of engine trouble?"

"I don't think so," Jim said. But his voice had no authority. He knew he'd lost any right to sound knowledgeable.

Ned looked grim. "You don't know if your boat has run out of gas."

"I'm—I'm not sure."

"I'll take a look," Ned said.

He leaned over his rail to pull the *Mighty J* closer, to get it side by side with his boat. He used his fishing gaff to yank Jim's boat, and he did it with a jerky motion. He was really annoyed. He was usually gorgeously smooth with boats. Jim also leaned over to pull the boats closer. The boats bounced and bounced in the rough sea. They separated and smashed together. Ned put one booted foot on his rail and made a move to swing himself over to the *Mighty J*. It was a stupid move. It was a very stupid move for a high-line sailor like Ned Wishnell. But Ned was annoyed and was being careless. And something happened. The wind blew, a wave rose, a foot slipped, a hand lost its grip. Something happened.

Ned Wishnell was in the water.

Jim stared down at the man, and his first reaction was almost amusement. Ned Wishnell was in the water! It was the damnedest thing. Like seeing a nun naked. *Would you look at that?* Ned was soaked from the drop, and when he popped out of the water, he gasped, and his mouth made an unimpressive, weak little circle. Ned looked up at Jim Burden with panic, an expression wholly incongruous on a Wishnell. Ned Wishnell looked desperate, stricken. And this gave Jim Burden a moment to enjoy a second reaction, which was pride. Ned Wishnell needed Jim Burden's help. Now wasn't that a hell of a note?

Would you look at that?

Jim's reactions were fleeting, but they prevented him from taking the lightning-fast action that might have saved Ned Wishnell's life. If he'd grabbed a gaff and thrust it down to Ned immediately, if he'd reached down to save Ned even as the man was falling in, things might have been different. But Jim stood there for that quick moment of amusement and pride—and a swell came and knocked the two boats together. Smashed them together, with a force that almost threw Jim off his feet. Between the two boats was Ned Wishnell, of course, and when the boats separated after the collision, he was gone. He had sunk.

He must have been badly banged up. He was wearing long boots, and they had probably filled up with water, and he couldn't swim. Whatever had happened, Ned Wishnell was gone.

That was the end of the fourth Fort Niles–Courne Haven lobster war. That pretty much did it. Losing Ned Wishnell was tragic for both islands. The reaction on Fort Niles and Courne Haven was almost like the nationwide reaction a few years later, when Martin Luther King, Jr., was shot. A shocked citizenry faced an impossibility come true—and everyone felt changed by (perhaps even a little complicit in) the death. There was a sense on both islands that something was fundamentally wrong if this could happen, if the fight went so far that a man like Ned Wishnell died because of it.

It is not certain that the death of another fisherman could have stirred this feeling. Ned Wishnell was the patriarch of a dynasty that had seemed inviolable. He hadn't been participating in this lobster war. Not that he'd taken his gear out of the water, as Stan Thomas had done, but Ned Wishnell had always been above this kind of conflict, like Switzerland. What need did he have to push or cut? He knew where the lobsters were. Other fishermen tried to follow him around, tried to learn his secrets, but Ned didn't care. He didn't try to chase them off. He barely noticed them. They could never make the catches he made. He was intimidated by nobody. He had no malice. He could afford not to have any.

The fact that Ned Wishnell had drowned while trying to help a boy who'd been sucked into this war struck everyone as ugly. It horrified even Ira Pommeroy, who had basically been responsible for the tragedy. Ira started drinking hard, much harder than usual, and it was then that he turned from a regular drunk into a serious drunk. A few weeks after the drowning of Ned Wishnell, Ira Pommeroy asked his wife, Rhonda, to help him write a letter of condolence to Mrs. Ned Wishnell. But there was no way to reach the Widow Wishnell. She was no longer on Courne Haven Island. She had disappeared.

She wasn't from there to begin with. Like all Wishnells, Ned had married a beauty from away. Mrs. Ned Wishnell was a ginger-haired, leggy, intelligent girl from a prominent Northeastern family that had always summered at Kennebunkport, Maine. She was nothing like the wives of the other fishermen; that was for sure. Her name was Allison, and she'd met Ned when she was sailing with her family up the Maine coast. She'd seen this man in his fishing boat and been captivated by his looks, by his fascinating silence, by his competence. She encouraged her parents to follow his boat into the harbor at Courne Haven, and she approached him with great boldness. He excited her a good deal; he made her tremble. He was nothing like the men she knew, and she married him—to her family's astonishment—within weeks. She'd been crazy about the man, but there was nothing to keep her on Courne Haven Island after her husband drowned. She was mortified by the war, by the drowning.

The beautiful Allison Wishnell learned the details of her husband's death, and looked around her and wondered what the hell she was doing on this rock in the middle of the ocean. It was a ghastly feeling. It was like waking up in a stranger's dirty bed after a night of drinking. It was like waking up in jail in a foreign land. How had she got here? She looked around at her neighbors and decided they were animals. And what was this house, this fish-smelling house, in which she was living? And why was there only one store on the island, a store that sold nothing but dusty canned goods? And what was with this appalling weather? Whose idea was *that?*

Mrs. Ned Wishnell was very young, just over twenty, when her husband drowned. Immediately after the funeral, she went back to her parents. She dropped her married name. She became Allison Cavanaugh again and enrolled in Smith College, where she studied art history and never told anybody that she had been a lobster fisherman's wife. She left it all behind. She even left her son behind on the island. There didn't seem to be much negotiating involved in that decision, and even less trauma. People said Mrs. Ned Wishnell had never been all that attached to her boy anyway; that something about her child frightened her. The Wishnells on Courne Haven made a strong case that the baby should remain with the family, and that was that. She gave him up.

The boy was to be raised by his uncle, a young man who had just come out of the seminary, a young man who had ambitions to be a traveling minister for all the obscure Maine islands. The uncle's name was Toby. Pastor Toby Wishnell. He was the youngest brother of Ned Wishnell, and just as handsome, although in a more delicate way. Toby Wishnell was the first Wishnell not to be a fisherman. The baby—Ned Wishnell's little boy—would be his charge. The baby's name was Owney, and he was just one year old.

If Owney Wishnell missed his mother when she left, he didn't show it. If Owney Wishnell missed his drowned father, he didn't show that, either. He was a big, blond, quiet baby. He caused no one any trouble, except when he was taken out of the bath. Then he'd scream and fight, and his strength was a wonder. The only thing Owney Wishnell wanted, it seemed, was to be in the water all the time.

A few weeks after Ned Wishnell was buried, when it became evident that the lobster war was over, Stan Thomas put his boat back into the water and started fishing with supremacy. He fished with a single-mindedness that would soon earn him the nickname Greedy Number Two (the natural successor to Angus Addams, who had long been known as Greedy Number One). His little period of domesticity with his wife was over. Mary Smith-Ellis Thomas was clearly no longer his partner. His partner was whatever teenage boy was slaving away as his sternman.

Stan came home to Mary late every afternoon exhausted and absorbed. He kept a journal of each fishing day so that he could chart the abundance of lobsters in each area of the ocean. He spent long nights with maps and calculators, and he did not include Mary in this work.

"What are you doing?" she'd ask. "What are you working on?"

"Fishing," he'd say.

To Stan Thomas, any work related to fishing was itself the act of fishing, even if it took place on dry land. And since his wife was not a fisherman, her views were of no service to him. He stopped calling her over to his lap, and she would not have dared to climb there uninvited. It was a bleak time in her life. Mary was beginning to realize something about her husband that was not pleasant. During the lobster war, when he'd pulled his boat and gear out of the water, she'd interpreted his acts as those of a man of virtue. Her husband was staying out of the war, she thought, because he was a peaceful man. She had gravely misunderstood, and it was now becoming clear to her. He had stayed out of the war to protect his interests and to make a killing when the war was over and he could start fishing again. And now that he was making a killing, he could scarcely stop gloating for a minute.

He spent his evenings transcribing the notes he had taken on his boat into ledgers full of long, complicated figures. The records were meticulous and dated back for years. Some evenings, he would page backward through his ledgers and muse over exceptionally great batches of lobsters in days gone by. He would talk to his ledgers. "I wish it could be October all year round," he would tell the columns of figures.

Some nights, he'd talk to his calculator as he worked. He'd say, "I hear you, I hear you." Or "Quit teasing!"

In December, Mary told her husband she was pregnant.

"Way to go, Mint," he said, but he wasn't as excited as she hoped he'd be.

Mary secretly sent a letter to Vera Ellis, telling her of the pregnancy, but she got no response. That devastated her; she cried and cried. The only person, in fact, who was at all interested in Mary's pregnancy was her neighbor Rhonda Pommeroy, who, as usual, was pregnant herself.

"I'll probably have a boy," Rhonda said, tipsily.

Rhonda was drunk, as usual. Drunk in a charming way, as usual, as though she were a young girl and this was the first alcohol she had ever tasted. Drunk like *wheee!* "I'll probably have another boy, Mary, so you have to have a girl. Did you feel it when you got pregnant?"

"I don't think so," Mary said.

"I feel it every time. It's like *click!* And this one's a boy. I can always tell. And yours is going to be a girl. I'll bet it's a girl! How about that?

When she grows up, she can marry one of my boys! And we can be *related!*" Rhonda nudged Mary so hard, she almost knocked her over.

"We're already related," Mary said. "Through Len and Kitty."

"You're going to like having a baby," Rhonda said. "It's the funnest thing."

But it wasn't the funnest thing, not for Mary. She got stuck on the island for the delivery, and it was a living nightmare. Her husband couldn't take the screaming and all the women around, so he went fishing and left her to deliver the baby without his help. It was a cruel act on many levels. There had been bad storms all week, and none of the other men on the island had dared to put out their boats. On this day, Stan and his terrified sternman set out alone. He'd prefer to risk his life, it seemed, than help his wife or even listen to her pain. He'd been expecting a boy, but he was polite enough to conceal his disappointment when he came home from fishing and met his little girl. He didn't get to hold her at first, because Senator Simon Addams was there, hogging the baby.

"Oh, isn't she the dearest little baby?" Simon said, again and again, as the women laughed at his tenderness.

"What should we name her?" Mary asked her husband, quietly. "Do you like the name Ruth?"

"I don't care what you name her," Stan Thomas said, of his daughter, who was only an hour old. "Name her whatever you like, Mint."

"Do you want to hold her?" Mary asked.

"I have to wash up," he said. "I smell like a bait bag."

10

What say you to a ramble among the fairy rock pools, weed-covered ledges, and gem-decked parterres bordering the gardens of the sea?

— *Crab, Shrimp, and Lobster Lore*
W. B. Lord
1867

July arrived for Fort Niles. It was now the middle of the summer of 1976. It wasn't as exciting a month as it might have been.

The Bicentennial passed on Fort Niles without any outstanding revelry. Ruth thought she lived in the only place in America that wasn't getting its act together for a decent celebration. Her dad even went out to haul that day, although, out of some patriotic stirring, he gave Robin Pommeroy the day off. Ruth spent the holiday with Mrs. Pommeroy and her two sisters. Mrs. Pommeroy had tried to sew costumes for them all. She wanted the four of them to dress up as Colonial dames and march in the town parade, but she'd managed to finish only Ruth's costume by the morning of the Fourth, and Ruth refused to dress up alone. So Mrs. Pommeroy put the costume on Opal, and baby Eddie immediately vomited all over it.

"The dress looks more authentic now," Ruth said.

"He was eating pudding this morning," Opal said, shrugging. "Pudding always makes Eddie barf."

There was a short parade up Main Street, but there were more people in the parade than there were people to watch it. Senator Simon Addams recited the Gettysburg Address from memory, but he always recited the Gettysburg Address from memory, given any opportunity. Robin Pommeroy set off some cheap fireworks sent to him by his brother Chester. He burned his hand so severely that he would be unable to go fishing for two weeks. This made Ruth's father angry enough to fire Robin and hire a new sternman, Duke Cobb's ten-year-old grandson, who was skinny and weak as a third-grade girl and, unhelpfully, scared of lobsters. But the kid came cheap.

"You could've hired *me*," Ruth told her father. She sulked about it for a while, but she didn't really mean it, and he knew that.

So the month of July was almost passed, and then one afternoon Mrs. Pommeroy received a most unusual telephone call. The call came from Courne Haven Island. It was Pastor Toby Wishnell on the line.

Pastor Wishnell wanted to know whether Mrs. Pommeroy would be available to spend a day or two on Courne Haven. It seemed there was to be a big wedding on the island, and the bride had confided to the pastor that she was concerned about her hair. There were no professional hairdressers on Courne Haven. The bride wasn't young anymore, and she wanted to look her best.

"I'm not a *professional* hairdresser, Pastor," Mrs. Pommeroy said.

Pastor Wishnell said that was quite all right. The bride had hired a photographer from Rockland, at considerable cost, to document the wedding, and she wanted to look pretty for the pictures. She was relying on the pastor to help her out. It was a strange request to be made to a pastor, Toby Wishnell readily admitted, but he had received stranger ones. People expected their pastors to be fonts of information on all manner of subjects, Pastor Wishnell told Mrs. Pommeroy, and this lady was no exception. The pastor explained, further, that this bride felt somewhat more entitled than others to ask the pastor so unusual and personal a favor, because she was a Wishnell. She was actually Pastor Wishnell's second cousin, Dorothy Wishnell, known as Dotty. Dotty was to marry Fred Burden's oldest son, Charlie, on July 30.

In any case, the pastor went on, he had mentioned to Dotty that there was a gifted hair stylist right over on Fort Niles. That, at least, was what he had heard from Ruth Thomas. Ruth Thomas had told him that Mrs. Pommeroy was quite good with hair. Mrs. Pommeroy told the pastor that she was really nothing special, that she'd never been to *school* or anything.

The pastor said, "You'll do fine. And another thing . . ." Apparently, Dotty, having heard that Mrs. Pommeroy was so good at styling hair, wondered whether Mrs. Pommeroy would also cut the groom's hair. And the best man's, if she didn't mind. And the hair of the maid of honor, the mother of the bride, the father of the bride, the flower girls, and some members of the groom's family. If it wouldn't be too much trouble. And, said Pastor Wishnell, while he was thinking of it, he could use a little trim himself.

"Since the professional photographer who is coming is known to be expensive," the pastor continued, "and since almost everyone on the island will be at the wedding, they want to look their best. It's not often that a professional photographer comes here. Of course, the bride will pay you well. Her father is Babe Wishnell."

"Ooh," Mrs. Pommeroy said, impressed.

"Will you do it, then?"

"That's a whole lot of haircuts, Pastor Wishnell."

"I can send Owney to pick you up in the *New Hope*," the pastor said. "You can stay here as long as you are needed. It might be a nice way for you to make some extra money."

"I don't think I've ever cut so much hair at once. I don't know that I could do it all in one day."

"You could bring a helper."

"May I bring one of my sisters?"

"Certainly."

"May I bring Ruth Thomas?" Mrs. Pommeroy asked.

This gave the pastor a moment's pause. "I suppose so," he said, after a cool beat. "If she's not too busy."

"Ruth? *Busy?*" Mrs. Pommeroy found this idea hilarious. She laughed out loud, right into the pastor's ear.

At that very moment, Ruth was down at Potter Beach with Senator Simon Addams again. She was beginning to be depressed when she spent time down there, but she didn't know what else to do with herself. So she continued to stop at the beach a few hours every day to keep the Senator company. She also liked to keep an eye on Webster, for the sake of Mrs. Pommeroy, who constantly worried about her oldest, strangest boy. And she also went there because it was difficult to talk with anyone else on the island. She couldn't very well hang out with Mrs. Pommeroy *all* the time.

Not that watching Webster dig in the mud was still fun. It was painful and sad to watch. He'd lost all his grace. He floundered. He was searching for that second tusk as if he was both dying to find it and terrified of finding it. Ruth thought Webster might sink down in the mud one day and never show up again. She wondered whether that was, in fact, his plan. She wondered whether Webster Pommeroy was plotting the world's most awkward suicide.

"Webster needs a purpose in life," the Senator said.

The thought of Webster Pommeroy seeking a purpose in life depressed Ruth Thomas even more. "Isn't there anything else you can have him do with his time?"

"What else, Ruth?"

"Isn't there something he can do for the museum?"

The Senator sighed. "We have everything we need for the museum, except a building. Until we get that, there's nothing we can do. Digging in the mud, Ruth, is what he's good at."

"He's not so good at it anymore."

"He's having some trouble with it now, yes."

"What are you going to do if Webster finds the other tusk? Throw another elephant in there for him?"

"We'll take that as it comes, Ruth."

Webster hadn't found anything good in the mudflats lately. He hadn't turned up anything other than a lot of junk. He did find an oar, but it wasn't an old oar. It was aluminum. ("This is *magnificent!*" the Senator had raved to Webster, who looked frantic when he handed it over. "What a *rare oar* this is!") Also, Webster had uncovered a vast number of single boots under the mud, and single gloves, kicked and and tossed off by years of lobstermen. And bottles, too. Webster had found a lot of bottles in recent days, and not old ones. Plastic laundry detergent bottles. He hadn't, though, found anything worth all the time spent in that cold, loose mud. He looked thinner and more anxious every day.

"Do you think he'll die?" Ruth asked the Senator.

"I hope not."

"Could he snap completely and kill somebody?"

"I don't think so," the Senator said.

On the day Pastor Wishnell called Mrs. Pommeroy, Ruth had already been at Potter Beach with the Senator and Webster for several hours. She and the Senator were looking at a book, a book Ruth had purchased for the Senator at a Salvation Army store in Concord a month earlier. She'd given it to him as soon as she returned from visiting her mother, but he hadn't yet read it. He said he was finding it difficult to concentrate because he was so concerned about Webster.

"I'm sure it's a super book, Ruth," he said. "Thanks for bringing it down here today."

"Sure," she said. "I saw it sitting on your porch, and I thought you might want to look at it. You know, if you got bored or something."

The book was called *Hidden Treasure: How and Where to Find It. A Finder's Guide to the World's Missing Treasures.* It was something that, under normal circumstances, would have brought the Senator all sorts of excitement.

"You *do* like it?" Ruth asked.

"Oh, yes, Ruth. It's a swell book."

"Are you learning anything?"

"Not too much, Ruth, to be honest. I haven't finished it. I was expecting a little more information from the author, to tell you the truth. You'd think from the title," Senator Simon said, turning the book over in his hands, "that the author would tell you how to find specific treasures, but she doesn't give much information about that. So far, she says that if you do find anything, it's an accident. And she gives some examples of people who got lucky and found treasures when they weren't looking for anything. That doesn't seem to me like much of a system."

"How far have you read?"

"Just the first chapter."

"Oh. I thought you might like it because of the nice color illustrations. Lots of photographs of lost treasures. Did you see those? Did you see those pictures of the Fabergé eggs? I thought you'd like those."

"If there are photographs of the objects, Ruth, then they aren't really lost. Now, are they?"

"Well, Senator, I see what you mean. But the photographs are pictures of lost treasures that regular people already found, on their own. Like that guy who found the Paul Revere goblet. Did you get to that part yet?"

"Ah, not yet," the Senator said. He was shading his eyes and looking out over the mudflats. "I think it's going to rain. I hope it doesn't, because Webster won't come in when it rains. He's already got a terrible cold. You should hear his chest rattle."

Ruth took the book from the Senator. She said, "I saw a part in here—where is it? It says a kid found a marker in California that Sir Francis Drake left. It was made of iron, and it claimed the land as belonging to Queen Elizabeth. It had been there for, like, three centuries."

"Isn't that something?"

Ruth offered the Senator a stick of chewing gum. He refused it, so she chewed it herself. "The author says the greatest site of buried treasure anywhere in the world is on Cocos Island."

"That's what your book says?"

"It's *your* book, Senator. I was thumbing through it when I was coming back from Concord and I saw that thing about Cocos Island. The author says Cocos Island is a real bonanza for people looking for buried treasure. She says Captain James Cook stopped at Cocos Island all the time with loot. The great circumnavigator!

"The great circumnavigator."

"So did the pirate Benito Bonito. So did Captain Richard Davis and the pirate Jean Lafitte. I thought you'd be interested . . ."

"Oh, I am interested, Ruth."

"You know what I thought you'd be interested in? About Cocos Island, I mean? The island is only about as big as Fort Niles. How about *that?* Wouldn't that be ironic? Wouldn't you be right at home there? And with all that buried treasure to find. You and Webster could go there and dig it up together. How about that, Senator?"

It started to rain, big heavy drops.

"I bet the weather's better on Cocos Island, anyhow," she said, and laughed.

The Senator said, "Oh, Ruth, we're not going anywhere, Webster and I. You know that. You shouldn't say such things, even as a joke."

Ruth was stung. She recovered and said, "I'm sure you two would come home rich as kings if you ever got to Cocos Island."

He did not reply.

She wondered why she was pursuing this. Christ, how desperate she sounded. How starved for conversation. It was pathetic, but she missed sitting on the beach with the Senator for hours and hours of uninterrupted drivel, and she wasn't used to being ignored by him. She was suddenly jealous of Webster Pommeroy for getting all the attention. That's when she really started to feel pathetic. She stood and pulled up the hood of her jacket and asked, "Are you coming in?"

"It's up to Webster. I don't think he's noticed that it's raining."

"You don't have a waterproof jacket on, do you? Do you want me to get you one?"

"I'm fine."

"You and Webster should both come in before you get soaked."

"Sometimes Webster comes in when it rains, but sometimes he stays out there and gets wetter and wetter. It depends on his mood. I guess I'll stay until he wants to come in. I've got sheets on the line at home, Ruth. Would you take them in for me before they get wet?"

The rain was coming down now at a fast, slicing pace.

"I think the sheets are already wet, Senator."

"You're probably right. Forget it."

Ruth ran back to Mrs. Pommeroy's house through the rain, which was now pounding down. She found Mrs. Pommeroy with her sister Kitty, upstairs in the big bedroom, pulling clothes out of the closet. Kitty, watching her sister, was sitting on the bed. She was drinking coffee, which Ruth knew to be spiked with gin. Ruth rolled her eyes. She was getting fed up with Kitty's drinking.

"I should just sew something new," Mrs. Pommeroy was saying. "But I don't have the time!" Then, "There's my Ruth. Oh, you're soaking wet."

"What are you doing?"

"Looking for a pretty dress."

"What's the occasion?"

"I've been invited somewhere."

"Where?" Ruth asked.

Kitty Pommeroy started laughing, followed by Mrs. Pommeroy.

"Ruth," she said, "you'll never believe it. We're going to a wedding on Courne Haven. Tomorrow!"

"Tell her who said so!" Kitty Pommeroy shouted.

"Pastor Wishnell!" Mrs. Pommeroy said. "He's invited us over."

"Get out of here."

"I am getting out of here!"

"You and Kitty are going to Courne Haven?"

"Sure. And you, too."

"Me?"

"He wants you there. Babe Wishnell's daughter is getting married, and I'm doing her hair! And you two are my helpers. We're going to open a little temporary salon."

"Well, la-di-dah," Ruth said.

"Exactly," said Mrs. Pommeroy.

That night, Ruth asked her father whether she could go to Courne Haven for a big Wishnell wedding. He did not answer right away. They were talking less and less lately, the father and daughter.

"Pastor Wishnell invited me," she said.

"Do whatever you want," Stan Thomas said. "I don't care who you spend your time with."

Pastor Wishnell sent Owney to pick up everyone the next day, which was Saturday. At seven in the morning of Dotty Wishnell and Charlie Burden's wedding, Mrs. Pommeroy and Kitty Pommeroy and Ruth Thomas walked to the end of the dock and found Owney waiting for them. He rowed Kitty and Mrs. Pommeroy out to the *New Hope.* Ruth enjoyed watching him. He came back for her, and she climbed down the ladder and hopped into his rowboat. He was looking at the bottom of the boat, not at her, and Ruth could not think of a single thing to say to him. But she did like looking at him. He rowed toward his uncle's gleaming mission boat, where Mrs. Pommeroy and Kitty, leaning over the rail, were waving like tourists on a cruise. Kitty shouted, "Looking good, kid!"

"How's everything going?" Ruth asked Owney.

He was so startled by her question that he stopped rowing; he just let the oars sit on the water.

"I'm fine," he said. He was staring at her. He wasn't blushing, and he didn't seem embarrassed.

"Good," said Ruth.

They bobbed on the water for a moment.

"I'm fine, too," said Ruth.

"OK," said Owney.

"You can keep rowing if you want."

"OK," said Owney, and he started to row again.

"Are you related to the bride?" Ruth asked, and Owney stopped rowing.

"She's my cousin," Owney said. They bobbed on the water.

"You can row and talk to me at the same time," Ruth said, and now Owney did blush. He took her out to the boat without saying another word.

"He's cute," Mrs. Pommeroy whispered to Ruth when she climbed onto the deck of the *New Hope.*

"Look who's here!" Kitty Pommeroy shrieked, and Ruth turned around to see Cal Cooley stepping out of the captain's bridge.

Ruth let out a scream of horror that was only partly a joke. "For God's sake," she said. "He's everywhere."

Kitty threw her arms around her old lover, and Cal extricated himself. "That's quite enough."

"What the hell are you doing here?" Ruth asked.

"Supervising," Cal said. "And nice to see you, too."

"How did you get here?"

"Owney rowed me out earlier. Old Cal Cooley certainly did not swim."

It was a quick trip to Courne Haven Island, and when they got off the boat, Owney led them to a lemon-yellow Cadillac parked by the dock.

"Whose car is this?" Ruth asked.

"My uncle's."

It matched the house, as it turned out. Pastor Wishnell lived a short drive from the Courne Haven dock, in a beautiful house, yellow with lavender trim. It was a three-story Victorian with a tower and a circular porch; bright blooming plants hung from hooks, placed three feet apart, around the entire porch. The slate walkway to the house was lined with lilies. The pastor's garden, in the back of the house, was a little museum of roses, surrounded by a low brick wall. On the drive over, Ruth had noticed a few other homes on Courne Haven Island, equally nice. Ruth hadn't been to Courne Haven since she was a little girl, too young to notice the differences between it and Fort Niles.

"Who lives in the big houses?" she asked Owney.

"Summer people," Cal Cooley answered. "You're lucky not to have them on Fort Niles. Mr. Ellis keeps them away. One of the many nice things Mr. Ellis does for you. Summer people are vermin."

It was summer people, too, who owned the sailboats and the speedboats that surrounded the island. On the trip over, Ruth had seen two silvery speedboats darting across the water. They were so close to each other, the head of one boat seemed to be kissing the ass of the other. They looked like two dragonflies, chasing each other around, trying to have sex in the salty air.

Pastor Wishnell set up Mrs. Pommeroy to cut hair in his back garden, right in front of a white trellis of pink roses. He had brought out a stool and a small side table, where she placed her scissors and combs and a tall glass of water in which to dip the combs. Kitty Pommeroy sat on the low brick wall and had herself a few cigarettes. She buried the butts in the soil under the roses when she thought nobody was looking. Owney Wishnell was sitting on the steps of the back porch in his strangely clean fisherman's clothes, and Ruth went to sit beside him. He kept his hands on his knees, and she could see the curling gold filaments of hair on his knuckles. They were such clean hands. She wasn't used to seeing men with clean hands.

"How long has you uncle lived here?" she asked.

"Forever."

"This doesn't look like a house he'd live in. Does somebody else live here?"

"Me."

"Anyone else?"

"Mrs. Post."

"Who's Mrs. Post?"

"She takes care of the house."

"Shouldn't you be helping your friends over there?" Cal Cooley asked. He'd come up behind them on the porch without making a sound. Now he lowered his tall body and sat next to Ruth so that she was between the two men.

"I don't think they need any help, Cal."

"Your uncle wants you to head back over to Fort Niles, Owney," Cal Cooley said. "He needs you to pick up Mr. Ellis for the wedding."

"Mr. Ellis is coming to this wedding?" Ruth asked.

"He is."

"He never comes over here."

"Regardless. Owney, it's time to push off. I'm going with you."

"May I go with you?" Ruth asked Owney.

"You certainly may not," said Cal.

"I didn't ask you, Cal. May I go with you, Owney?"

But Pastor Wishnell was approaching, and when Owney saw him, he quickly jumped off the steps and said to his uncle, "I'm going. I'm going right now."

"Hurry," said the pastor as he walked up the steps and onto the porch. He looked over his shoulder and said, "Ruth, Mrs. Pommeroy is going to need your help."

"I'm not much help cutting hair," Ruth said, but the pastor and Owney were gone. One in each direction.

Cal looked at Ruth and lifted a satisfied eyebrow. "I wonder why you're so eager to hang around that boy."

"Because he doesn't annoy the fuck out of me, Cal."

"I annoy the fuck out of you, Ruth?"

"Oh, not *you*. I didn't mean *you*."

"I enjoyed our little trip to Concord. Mr. Ellis had a lot of questions for me when I got back. He wanted to know how you and your mother got along, and if you seemed at home there. I told him that you'd both got along swimmingly and that you seemed very much at home there, but I'm sure he'll want to talk to you about it. Come to think of it, perhaps you should write him a note when you get the chance, thanking him for having sponsored the trip. It's important to him that the two of you have a good relationship, considering how close your mother and grandmother have been to the Ellis family. And it's important to him that you get as much time off Fort Niles as possible, Ruth. I told him I'd be happy to take you to Concord at any time, and that we had a good time traveling together. I do enjoy it, Ruth." He was giving her his heavy-lidded stare now. "Although I can't get out of my head this idea that someday the two of us will end up in a motel along Route One having filthy sex together."

Ruth laughed. "Get it out of your head."

"Why are you laughing?"

"Because Old Cal Cooley is such a funny man," Ruth said. Which was not at all the truth. The truth was that Ruth was laughing because she had decided—as she often did, with varying degrees of success—that Old Cal Cooley was not going to get to her. She wouldn't allow it. He could heap upon her loads of his most insidious abuse, but she would not rise to it. Certainly not today.

"I know it's only a matter of time before you start having filthy sex with somebody, Ruth. All signs point to it."

"Now we're going to play a different kind of game," Ruth said. "Now you leave *me* alone for a while."

"And you should keep yourself away from Owney Wishnell, by the way," Cal said as he walked down the porch steps and wandered into the garden. "It's obvious that you're up to something with that boy, and nobody likes it."

"Nobody?" Ruth called after him. "Really, Cal? Nobody?"

"Get over here, you big old man," Kitty Pommeroy said to Cal when she saw him. Cal Cooley turned on his heel and walked stiffly in the other direction. He was going back to Fort Niles to get Mr. Ellis.

The bride, Dotty Wishnell, was a likable blonde in her mid-thirties. She'd been married before, but her husband died of testicular cancer. She and her daughter, Candy, who was six years old, were the first to have their hair done. Dotty Wishnell walked over to Pastor Wishnell's house in her bathrobe, her hair wet and uncombed. Ruth thought this was a pretty relaxed way for a bride to walk around on her wedding day, and it made Ruth like the woman right away. Dotty had an attractive enough face, but she looked exhausted. She had no makeup on yet, and she was chewing gum. She had deep lines across her forehead and around her mouth.

Dotty Wishnell's daughter was extremely quiet. Candy was going to be her mother's maid of honor, which Ruth thought an awfully serious job for a six-year-old, but Candy seemed up to it. She had a grown-up face for a child, a face that didn't belong anywhere near a child.

"Are you nervous about being the maid of honor?" Mrs. Pommeroy asked Candy.

"Obviously not." Candy had the firm mouth of the aging Queen Victoria. She wore a most judgmental expression, and those lips of hers were firmly set. "I was already a flower girl at Miss Dorphman's wedding, and we aren't even related."

"Who's Miss Dorphman?"

"Obviously she's my teacher."

"Obviously," Ruth repeated, and Kitty Pommeroy and Mrs. Pommeroy both laughed. Dotty laughed, too. Candy looked at the four women as if she were disappointed in the lot of them.

"Oh, great," Candy said, as if she had already had this kind of irritating day and wasn't looking forward to another. "So far, so bad."

Dotty Wishnell asked Mrs. Pommeroy to take care of Candy first and see whether she could give her thin brown hair some curls. Dotty Wishnell wanted her daughter to look "adorable." Mrs. Pommeroy said it would be easy to make such an adorable child look adorable, and she would do all she could to make everyone happy.

"I could give her the cutest little bangs," she said.

"No bangs," Candy insisted. "No way."

"She doesn't even know what bangs are," Dotty said.

"I do so, Mom," said Candy.

Mrs. Pommeroy set to work on Candy's hair while Dotty stood and watched. The two women talked comfortably with each other, although they'd never before met.

"The good thing is," Dotty told Mrs. Pommeroy, "that Candy doesn't have to change her name. Candy's daddy was a Burden, and her new daddy is a Burden, too. My first husband and Charlie were first cousins, believe it or not. Charlie was one of the ushers at my first wedding, and today he's the groom. Yesterday I said to him, 'You never know how things are going to turn out,' and he said, 'You never know.' He's going to adopt Candy, he said."

"I lost my first husband, too," Mrs. Pommeroy said. "Actually, he was my only husband. I was a young thing like you. It's true; you never know."

"How did your husband die?"

"He drowned."

"What was his last name?"

"It was Pommeroy, sweetheart."

"I think I remember that."

"It was in 1967. But we don't need to talk about that today, because today's a happy day."

"You poor thing."

"*You* poor thing. Oh, don't you worry about me, Dotty. What happened to me was a long, long time ago. But you lost your husband only last year, right? That's what Pastor Wishnell said."

"Last year," Dotty replied, staring ahead. The women were silent for a while. "March twentieth, 1975."

"My dad died," Candy said.

"We don't need to talk about that today," Mrs. Pommeroy said, forming another perfect ring in Candy's hair with her damp finger. "Today is a happy day. Today is your mommy's wedding."

"Well, I'm getting another husband today, that's for sure," said

Dotty. "I'm getting a new one. This island is no place to live without a husband. And you're getting a new daddy, Candy. Isn't that right?"

Candy did not express an opinion on this.

"Does Candy have other little girls to play with on Courne Haven?" Mrs. Pommeroy asked.

"No," Dotty said. "There are some teenage girls around, but they aren't too interested in playing with Candy, and next year they'll be going inland to school. Mostly, it's little boys around here."

"It was the same thing with Ruth when she was little! All she had were my boys to play with."

"Is that your daughter?" Dotty asked, looking at Ruth.

"She's practically my daughter," Mrs. Pommeroy said. *My daughtah* . . . "And she grew up with nothing but boys around."

"Was that hard on you?" Dotty asked Ruth.

"It was the worst," Ruth said. "It ruined me completely."

Dotty's face collapsed into worry. Mrs. Pommeroy said, "She's teasing. It was *fine.* Ruth loved my boys. They were like her brothers. Candy will be fine."

"I think Candy wishes she could be a girly-girl sometimes, and play girly games for a change," said Dotty. "I'm the only girl she can play with, and I'm no fun. I haven't been much fun all year."

"That's because my dad died," Candy said.

"We don't need to talk about that today, honey," Mrs. Pommeroy said. "Today your mommy's getting married. Today's a happy day, sweetheart."

"I wish there were some little boys *my* age around here," said Kitty Pommeroy. Nobody seemed to hear this but Ruth, who snorted in disgust.

"I always wanted a little girl," Mrs. Pommeroy said. "But I had a whole bunch of boys. Is it fun? Is it fun dressing Candy up all pretty? My boys wouldn't let me touch them. And Ruth always had short hair, so it wasn't fun to play with."

"You're the one who kept it short," Ruth said. "I wanted my hair to be just like yours, but you were always cutting it."

"You couldn't keep it combed, sweetheart."

"I can dress myself," Candy said.

"I'm sure you can, sweetheart."

"No bangs."

"That's right," Mrs. Pommeroy said. "We're not giving you any bangs, even though they'd be beautiful." She expertly circled the puff of curls she had created on top of Candy's head with a wide white ribbon. "Adorable?" she asked Dotty.

"Adorable," said Dotty. "Precious. You did a great job. I can never get her to sit still, and I don't know anything about styling hair. Obviously. I mean, look at me. This is about as good as I get."

"There you go. Thank you, Candy." Mrs Pommeroy bent over and kissed the little girl on the cheek. "You were very brave."

"Obviously," said Candy.

"Obviously," said Ruth.

"You're next, Dotty. We'll do the bride, and you can go get dressed, and then we'll do your friends. Somebody should tell them to start coming over. What do you want me to do with your hair?"

"I don't know. I guess I just want to look happy," Dotty instructed. "Can you do that for me?"

"You can't hide a happy bride, even under a bad hairstyle," Mrs. Pommeroy said. "I could wrap your head in a towel, and if you're happy, you'd still look beautiful, marrying your man."

"Only God can make a happy bride," Kitty Pommeroy said very seriously, for some reason.

Dotty considered this and sighed. "Well," she said, and spat her gum into a used tissue she'd fished out of her bathrobe pocket, "see what you can do for me. Just do your best."

Mrs. Pommeroy set to work on Dotty Wishnell's wedding day hair, and Ruth left the women and went to look more closely at Pastor Wishnell's house. She could not make any sense of its delicate, feminine style. She walked the length of the long, curving porch, with its wicker furniture and bright cushions. That must be the work of the mysterious Mrs. Post. She saw a bird feeder, shaped like a little house and cheerfully painted red. Knowing that she was trespassing, but overcome by curiosity, she let herself into the house through the French doors that opened from the porch. Now she was in a small parlor, a sitting room. Brightly covered books lay on end tables, and doilies covered the backs of the sofa and chairs.

She walked next through a living room papered in a print of pale green lilies. A ceramic Persian cat crouched next to the fireplace, and a real tabby cat reclined on the back of a rose-colored couch. The cat looked at Ruth and, unconcerned, went back to sleep. Ruth touched a handmade afghan on a rocking chair. Pastor Wishnell lived *here*? Owney Wishnell lived *here*? She walked on. The kitchen smelled of vanilla, and a coffee cake sat on the counter. She noticed stairs at the back of the kitchen. *What was upstairs?* She was out of her mind, to be snooping around like this. She'd be hard put to explain to anyone what she was doing upstairs in Pastor Toby Wishnell's house, but she was dying to find Owney's bedroom. She wanted to see where he slept.

She walked up the steep wooden stairs and, on the next floor, peered into an immaculate bathroom, with a potted fern hanging in the window and a small cake of lavender soap in a dish above the sink. There was a framed photograph of a small girl and a small boy, kissing. BEST FRIENDS, it read below in pink script.

Ruth moved to the doorway of a bedroom containing stuffed animals propped against the pillows. The next bedroom had a beautiful sleigh bed and its own bathroom. The last bedroom had a single bed with a rose-covered quilt. Where did Owney sleep? Not with the teddy bears, surely. Not on the sleigh bed. She couldn't picture that. She had no sense of Owney at all in this house.

But Ruth kept exploring. She climbed up to the third floor. It was hot, with sloping ceilings. Seeing a partly closed door, she naturally pushed it open. And walked in on Pastor Wishnell.

"Oh," Ruth said.

He looked at her from behind an ironing board. He was in his black trousers. He wasn't wearing a shirt. That's what he was ironing. His torso was long and seemed to have no muscle or fat or hair. He lifted his shirt off the ironing board, slid his arms into the starched sleeves, and fastened the buttons, bottom to top, slowly.

"I was looking for Owney," Ruth said.

"He's gone to Fort Niles to pick up Mr. Ellis."

"Oh, really? Sorry."

"You knew that very well."

"Oh, that's right. Yes, I did know that. Sorry."

"This is not your house, Miss Thomas. What made you think you were free to wander about it?"

"That's right. Sorry to have bothered you." Ruth backed into the hallway.

Pastor Wishnell said, "No, Miss Thomas. Come in."

Ruth paused, then stepped back into the room. She thought to herself, *Fuck*, and looked around. Well, this was certainly Pastor Wishnell's room. This was the first room in the house that made any sense. It was stark and blank. The walls and ceiling were white; even the bare wooden floor was whitewashed. The room smelled faintly of shoe polish. The pastor's bed was a narrow brass frame, with a blue woollen blanket and a thin pillow. Under the bed was a pair of leather slippers. The bedside table held no lamp or book, and the room's single window had only a window shade, no curtain. There was a dresser, and on it a small pewter plate holding a few coins. The dominant object in the room was a large, dark wooden desk, beside which was a bookcase filled with heavy volumes. The desk held an electric typewriter, a stack of paper, a soup can of pencils.

Hanging above the desk was a map of the coast of Maine, covered with pencil marks. Ruth looked for Fort Niles, instinctively. It was unmarked. She wondered what that meant. Unsaved? Ungrateful?

The pastor unplugged the iron, wrapped the cord around it, and set it on his desk.

"You have a pretty house," Ruth said. She put her hands in her pockets, trying to look casual, as if she'd been invited here. Pastor Wishnell folded the ironing board and placed it inside the closet.

"Were you named after the Ruth of the Bible?" he asked. "Have a seat."

"I don't know who I was named after."

"Don't you know your Bible?"

"Not too much."

"Ruth was a great woman of the Old Testament. She was the model of female loyalty."

"Oh, yeah?"

"You might enjoy reading the Bible, Ruth. It contains many wonderful stories."

Ruth thought, *Exactly. Stories. Action-adventure.* Ruth was an atheist. She had decided that the year before, when she learned the word. She was still having fun with the idea. She hadn't told anyone, but the knowledge gave her a thrill.

"Why aren't you helping Mrs. Pommeroy?" he asked.

"I'm going to do that right now," Ruth said, and thought about making a run for it.

"Ruth," Pastor Wishnell said, "sit down. You can sit on the bed."

There was no bed in the world that Ruth wanted less to sit on than Pastor Wishnell's. She sat down.

"Don't you ever get tired of Fort Niles?" he asked. He tucked his shirt into his pants, in four smooth strokes, with flat palms. His hair was damp, and she could see the tooth marks from a comb. His skin was pale as fine linen. He leaned against the side of the desk, folded his arms, and looked at her.

"I haven't been able to spend enough time there to get tired of it," Ruth said.

"Because of school?"

"Because Lanford Ellis is always sending me away," she said. She thought that statement made her sound a little pathetic, so she shrugged blithely, trying to indicate that it was no big deal.

"I think Mr. Ellis is interested in your well-being. I understand that he paid for your schooling and has offered to pay for your college education. He has vast resources, and he obviously cares what becomes of you. Not such a bad thing, is it? You are meant for better things than Fort Niles. Don't you think?"

Ruth did not reply.

"You know, I don't spend very much time on my island, either, Ruth. I'm hardly ever here on Courne Haven. In the last two months, I've preached twenty-one sermons, visited twenty-nine families, and attended eleven prayer meetings. I often lose count of weddings, funerals, and christenings. For many of these people, I am their only connection to the Lord. But I am also called upon to give worldly advice. They need me to read business papers for them or to help them find a new car. Many things. You'd be surprised. I settle disputes between people who would otherwise end up attacking each other physically. I am a peacemaker. It's not an easy life; sometimes I'd like to stay home and enjoy my nice house."

He made a gesture, indicating his nice house. It was a small gesture, though, and seemed to take in only his bedroom, which wasn't, as far as Ruth could see, much to enjoy.

"I do leave my home, though," Pastor Wishnell continued, "because I have duties, you see. I've been to every island in Maine in the course of my life. There are times when they all look the same to me, I must admit. Of all the islands I visit, though, I think Fort Niles is the most isolated. It is certainly the least religious."

That's because we don't like you, Ruth thought.

"Is that right?" she said.

"Which is a pity, because it is the isolated people of the world who most need fellowship. Fort Niles is a strange place, Ruth. They've had chances, over the years, to become more involved in the world beyond their island. But they are slow and suspicious. I don't know whether you're old enough to remember when there was talk of building a ferry terminal."

"Sure."

"So you know about that failure. Now, the only tourists who can visit these islands are those with their own boats. And every time someone needs to go into Rockland from Fort Niles, he has to take his lobster boat. Every penny nail, every can of beans, every shoelace on Fort Niles has to come on some man's lobster boat."

"We have a store."

"Oh, please, Ruth. Scarcely. And every time a lady from Fort Niles needs to do her grocery shopping or visit a doctor, she has to get a ride on some man's lobster boat."

"It's the same thing over on Courne Haven," Ruth said. She thought she'd already heard the pastor's view on this subject, and she wasn't interested in hearing it again. What did it have to do with her? He clearly enjoyed giving a little sermon. *Lucky me,* Ruth thought grimly.

"Well, Courne Haven's fortunes are closely tied to those of Fort Niles. And Fort Niles is slow to act; your island is the last to embrace any change. Most of the men on Fort Niles still make their own traps, because, without reason, they're suspicious of the wire ones."

"Not everyone."

"You know, Ruth, all over the rest of Maine, the lobstermen are starting to consider fiberglass boats. Just as an example. How long will it be before fiberglass comes to Fort Niles? Your guess is as good as mine. I can easily imagine Angus Addams's reaction to such an idea. Fort Niles always resists. Fort Niles resisted size limitations on lobsters harder than anyone in the state of Maine. And now there's talk all over the rest of Maine of setting voluntary trap limits."

"We'll never set trap limits," Ruth said.

"They may be set *for* you, young lady. If your fishermen will not do it voluntarily, it may become a law, and there will be wardens crawling all over your boats, just as there were when the size limits were set.

That's how innovation comes to Fort Niles. It has to be rammed down your stubborn throats until you choke on it."

Did he just say that? She stared at him. He was smiling slightly, and he had spoken in an even, mild tone. Ruth was appalled by his snide little speech, uttered with such ease. Everything he said was true, of course, but that haughty manner! She herself may have said some nasty things about Fort Niles in her time, but she had the right to speak critically of her own island and her own people. Hearing such condescension from someone so smug and unattractive was intolerable. She felt indignantly defensive, suddenly, of Fort Niles. How dare he!

"The world changes, Ruth," he went on. "There was a time when many of the men on Fort Niles were hakers. Now there's not enough hake left in the Atlantic to feed a kitty cat. We're losing redfish, too, and pretty soon the only lobster bait left will be herring. And some of the herring the men are using these days is so bad, even the seagulls won't eat it. There used to be a granite industry out here that made everyone rich, and now that's gone, too. How do the men on your island expect to make a living in ten, twenty years? Do they think every day for the rest of time will be the same? That they can count on big lobster catches forever? They're going to fish and fish until there's only one lobster left, and then they'll fight to the death over the last one. You know it, Ruth. You know how these people are. They'll never agree to do what's in their best interest. You think those fools will come to their senses and form a fishing cooperative, Ruth?"

"It'll never happen," Ruth said. *Fools?*

"Is that what your father says?"

"That's what everyone says."

"Well, everyone may be right. They've certainly fought it hard enough in the past. Your friend Angus Addams came to a cooperative meeting once on Courne Haven, back when our Denny Burden nearly bankrupted his family and got himself killed trying to form a collective between the two islands. I was there. I saw how Angus behaved. He came with a bag of popcorn. He sat in the front row while some more highly evolved individuals discussed ways that the two islands could work together for the benefit of everyone. Angus Addams sat there, grinning and eating popcorn. When I asked him what he was doing, he said, 'I'm enjoying the show. This is funnier than the talking pictures.'

Men like Angus Addams think they're better off working alone forever. Am I correct? Is that what every man thinks over on your island?"

"I don't know what every man on my island thinks," Ruth said.

"You're a bright young woman. I'm sure you know exactly what they think."

Ruth chewed on the inside of her lip. "I think I should go help Mrs. Pommeroy now," she said.

"Why do you waste your time with people like that?" Pastor Wishnell asked.

"Mrs. Pommeroy is my friend."

"I'm not talking about Mrs. Pommeroy. I'm talking about Fort Niles lobstermen. I'm talking about Angus Addams, Simon Addams —"

"Senator Simon is not a lobsterman. He's never even been in a boat."

"I'm talking about men like Len Thomas, Don Pommeroy, Stan Thomas —"

"Stan Thomas is my father, sir."

"I know perfectly well that Stan Thomas is your father."

Ruth stood up.

"Sit down," said Pastor Toby Wishnell.

She sat down. Her face was hot. She immediately regretted sitting down. She should have walked out of the room.

"You don't belong on Fort Niles, Ruth. I've been asking around about you, and I understand that you have other options. You should take advantage of them. Not everyone is so fortunate. Owney, for instance, does not have your choices. I know you have some interest in my nephew's life."

Ruth's face got hotter.

"Well, let's consider Owney. What will become of him? That's my worry, not yours, but let's think about it together. You're in a much better position than Owney is. The fact is, there is no future for you on your island. Every pigheaded fool who lives there ensures that. Fort Niles is doomed. There is no leadership over there. There is no moral core. My heavens, look at that rotted, run-down church! How was that allowed to happen?"

Because we fucking hate you, Ruth thought.

"The whole island will be abandoned in two decades. Don't look surprised, Ruth. That's what may well happen. I sail up and down this coast year after year, and I see communities trying to survive. Who on

Fort Niles even tries? Do you have any form of government, an elected official? Who is your leader? Angus Addams? That snake? Who's coming down the pike in the next generation? Len Thomas? Your father? When has your father ever considered anyone else's interests?"

Ruth was getting ambushed. "You don't know anything about my father," she said, trying to sound as measured as Pastor Wishnell, but sounding, in fact, somewhat shrill.

Pastor Wishnell smiled. "Ruth," he said, "mark my words. I know a great deal about your father. And I'll repeat my prediction. Twenty years from now, your island will be a ghost town. Your people will have brought it on themselves through stubbornness and isolation. Does twenty years seem far away? It isn't."

He leveled a cool gaze on Ruth. She tried to level one back.

"Don't think that because there have always been people on Fort Niles, there always will be. These islands are fragile, Ruth. Did you ever hear of the Isles of Shoals, from the early nineteenth century? The population got smaller and more inbred, and the society fell to pieces. The citizens burned down the meeting house, copulated with their siblings, hanged their only pastor, practiced witchcraft. When the Reverend Jedidiah Morse visited in 1820, he found only a handful of people. He married everyone immediately, to prevent further sin. It was the best he could do. A generation later, the islands were deserted. That could happen to Fort Niles. You don't think so?"

Ruth had no comment.

"One more thing," Pastor Wishnell said, "that came to my attention the other day. A lobsterman on Frenchman's Island told me that back when the state first introduced size limitations on lobsters, a certain lobsterman named Jim used to keep short lobsters and sell them to the summer people on his island. He had a nice little illegal business going, but word got around, because word always gets around, and someone notified the fishing warden. The fishing warden started following old Jim, trying to catch him with the shorts. He even inspected Jim's boat a few times. But Jim kept his shorts in a sack, weighted with a rock, that hung down from the stern of his boat. So he never got caught.

"One day, though, the fishing warden was spying on Jim with binoculars and saw him filling the sack and dumping it over the stern. So the warden chased Jim in his police boat, and Jim, knowing he was about to be caught, throttled his boat as fast as it could go, and took off for home. He drove it right up on the beach, grabbed the sack, and made a run for it. The warden chased him, so Jim dropped the sack and climbed up a tree. When the warden opened the sack, guess what he found, Ruth?"

"A skunk."

"A skunk. That's right. You've heard this story before, I gather."

"It happened to Angus Addams."

"It didn't happen to Angus Addams. It didn't happen to anyone. It's apocryphal."

Ruth and the pastor stared each other down.

"Do you know what apocryphal means, Ruth?"

"Yes, I know what apocryphal means," snapped Ruth, who, at just that moment, was wondering what apocryphal meant.

"They tell that story on all the islands in Maine. They tell it because it makes them feel good that an old lobsterman could outsmart the law. But that's not why I told it to you, Ruth. I told it to you because it's a good fable about what happens to anyone who snoops around too much. You haven't been enjoying our conversation, have you?"

She was not about to answer that.

"But you could have saved yourself this unpleasant conversation by staying out of my house. You brought it on yourself, didn't you, by poking around where you had no right to. And if you feel as though you've been sprayed by a skunk, you know where to lay the blame. Isn't that correct, Ruth?"

"I'm going to help Mrs. Pommeroy now," Ruth said. She stood up again.

"I think that's an excellent idea. And enjoy the wedding, Ruth."

Ruth wanted to run out of that room, but she didn't want to show Pastor Wishnell how agitated she was by his "fable," so she walked out with some dignity. Once outside the room, though, she took off down the hall and down the two flights of stairs, through the kitchen, through the living room, and out the parlor door. She sat down in one of the wicker chairs on the porch. *Fucking asshole*, she was thinking. *Unbelievable.*

She should have beat it out of that room the moment he started his little oration. What the hell was that all about? He didn't even know her. *I've been asking around about you, Ruth.* He had no business telling her who she should or shouldn't hang around with, telling her to stay away from her own father. Ruth sat on the porch in a private, angry chill. It was embarrassing, more than anything, to be lectured to by this minister. And strange, too, to watch him put on his shirt, to sit on his bed. Strange to see his empty little monkish room and his pathetic little ironing board. *Freak.* She should have told him she was an atheist.

Across the garden, Mrs. Pommeroy and Kitty were still at work on the women's hair. Dotty Wishnell and Candy were gone, probably getting dressed for the wedding. There was a small clutch of Courne Haven women still waiting for Mrs. Pommeroy's attention. They all had damp hair. Mrs. Pommeroy had instructed the women to wash their hair at home so that she could devote her time to cutting and setting it. There were a few men in the rose garden, too, waiting for their wives or, perhaps, waiting to have their hair cut.

Kitty Pommeroy was combing out the long blond hair of a pretty young teenager, a girl who looked about thirteen. There were so many blonds on this island! All those Swedes from the granite industry. Pastor Wishnell had mentioned the granite industry, as if anyone still gave a shit about it. So what if the granite industry was finished? Who cared anymore? Nobody on Fort Niles was starving because the granite industry was gone. It was all gloom and doom from that guy. Fucking *asshole.* Poor Owney. Ruth tried to imagine a childhood spent with that uncle. Grim, mean, hard.

"Where you *been?*" Mrs. Pommeroy called over to Ruth.

"Bathroom."

"You OK?"

"Fine," Ruth said.

"Come over here, then."

Ruth went over and sat on the low brick wall. She felt battered and slugged, and probably looked it. But nobody, not even Mrs. Pommeroy, took any notice. The group was too busy chatting. Ruth could see that she'd walked into the middle of a completely inane conversation.

"It's gross," said the teenage girl being tended to by Kitty. "He steps on all the urchins, and his whole boat gets covered with, like, guts."

"There's no need for that," Mrs. Pommeroy said. "My husband always threw urchins back in the water. Urchins don't harm anyone."

"Urchins eat bait!" said one of the Courne Haven men in the

rose garden. "They get up on your bait bag, they eat the bait and the bag, too."

"I got spikes in my fingers my whole life from goddamn urchins," said another man.

"But why does Tuck have to *step* on them?" asked the pretty teenager. "It's gross. And it takes time away from fishing. He gets all worked up about it; he has a really bad temper. He calls them whore's eggs." She giggled.

"Everyone calls them whore's eggs," said the fisherman with the spikes in his fingers.

"That's right," said Mrs. Pommeroy. "Having a bad temper takes time away from work. People should settle down."

"I hate those bottom feeders you pull up sometimes, and they're all bloated from coming up so fast," the girl said. "Those fish? With the big eyes? Every time I go out to haul with my brother, we get a ton of those."

"I haven't been out on a lobster boat in years," Mrs. Pommeroy said.

"They look like toads," said the girl. "Tuck steps on them, too."

"There's no reason to be cruel to animals," Mrs. Pommeroy said. "No reason at all."

"Tuck caught a shark once. He beat it up."

"Who's Tuck?" Mrs. Pommeroy asked.

"He's my brother," the teenage girl said. She looked at Ruth. "Who are you?"

"Ruth Thomas. Who are you?"

"Mandy Addams."

"Are you related to Simon and Angus Addams? The brothers?"

"Probably. I don't know. Do they live on Fort Niles?"

"Yeah."

"Are they cute?"

Kitty Pommeroy laughed so hard, she fell to her knees.

"Yeah," said Ruth. "They're adorable."

"They're in their seventies, dear," Mrs. Pommeroy said. "And, actually, they *are* adorable."

"What's the matter with her?" Mandy asked, looking at Kitty, who was wiping her eyes and being helped to her feet by Mrs. Pommeroy.

"She's drunk," Ruth said. "She falls down all the time."

"I am drunk!" Kitty shouted. "I *am* drunk, Ruth! But you don't have to tell everyone." Kitty got control of herself and went back to combing the teenager's hair.

"Jeez, I think my hair is combed enough," Mandy said, but Kitty kept combing, hard.

"Christ, Ruth," Kitty said. "You're such a blabbermouth. And I do *not* fall down all the time."

"How old are you?" Mandy Addams asked Ruth. Her eyes were on Ruth, but her head was pulling against the tug of Kitty Pommeroy's comb.

"Eighteen."

"Are you from Fort Niles?"

"Yeah."

"I've never seen you around."

Ruth sighed. She didn't feel like explaining her life to this dimwit. "I know. I went away to high school."

"I'm going away to high school next year. Where'd you go? Rockland?"

"Delaware."

"Is that in Rockland?"

"Not really," Ruth said, and as Kitty started to shake with laughter again, she added, "Take it easy, Kitty. It's going to be a long day. It's too early to start falling down every two minutes."

"Is that in Rockland?" Kitty wailed, and wiped her eyes. The Courne Haven fishermen and their wives, gathered in the Wishnell gardens around the Pommeroy sisters, all laughed, too. *Well, that's good,* Ruth thought. At least they know the little blond girl is an idiot. Or maybe they were laughing at Kitty Pommeroy.

Ruth remembered what Pastor Wishnell had said about Fort Niles disappearing in twenty years. He was out of his mind. There'd be lobsters enough forever. Lobsters were prehistoric animals, survivors. The rest of the ocean might be exterminated, but the lobsters wouldn't care. Lobsters can dig down into the mud and live there for months. They can eat rocks. *They don't give a shit,* Ruth thought, admiringly. Lobsters would thrive if there was nothing left in the sea to eat except other lobsters. The last lobster in the world would probably eat himself, if he was the only food available. There was no need to get all concerned about lobsters.

Pastor Wishnell was out of his mind.

"Your brother really beat up a shark?" Mrs. Pommeroy asked Mandy.

"Sure. Jeez, I don't think I ever had my hair combed so much in one day!"

"Everybody's caught a shark sometime," one of the fishermen said. "We all beat up a shark one time or another."

"You just kill them?" Mrs. Pommeroy said.

"Sure."

"There's no call for that."

"No call to kill a shark?" The fisherman sounded amused. Mrs. Pommeroy was a lady and a stranger (an attractive lady stranger), and all the men in the garden were in a good mood around her.

"There's no reason to be cruel to animals," Mrs. Pommeroy said. She spoke around a few bobby pins in the corner of her mouth. She was working on the head of a steel-haired old lady, who seemed utterly oblivious of the conversation. Ruth guessed she was the mother of the bride or the mother of the groom.

"That's right," said Kitty Pommeroy. "Me and Rhonda, we learned that from our father. He wasn't a cruel man. He never laid a hand on any of us girls. He stepped out on us plenty, but he never hit nobody."

"It's plain cruelty to pick on animals," Mrs. Pommeroy said. "All animals are God's creatures as much as any of us. I think it shows that there's something really wrong with you, if you have to be cruel to an animal for no reason."

"I don't know," said the fisherman. "I sure like eating them fine."

"Eating animals is different from picking on them. Cruelty to animals is unforgivable."

"That's right," repeated Kitty. "I think it's disgusting."

Ruth could not believe this conversation. It was the kind of conversation people on Fort Niles had all the time—dumb, circular, uninformed. Apparently it was the kind that people on Courne Haven liked, too.

Mrs. Pommeroy took a bobby pin from her mouth and set a small gray curl on the old lady in the chair. "Although," she said, "I have to admit I used to shove firecrackers in frogs' mouths and blow them up."

"Me, too," said Kitty.

"But I didn't know what it would *do*."

"Sure," said one of the amused Courne Haven fishermen. "How could you know?"

"Sometimes I throw snakes in front of the lawn mower and run over them," said Mandy Addams, the pretty teenager.

"Now that's downright cruel," said Mrs. Pommeroy. "There's no reason to do that. Snakes are good for keeping pests away."

"Oh, I used to do that, too," said Kitty Pommeroy. "Hell, Rhonda, we used to do that together, me and you. We were always chopping up snakes."

"But we were only children, Kitty. We didn't know any better."

"Yeah," said Kitty, "we were only children."

"We didn't know better."

"That's right," Kitty said. "Remember that time you found a nest of baby mice under the sink, and you drowned them?"

"Children don't know how to treat animals, Kitty," Mrs. Pommeroy said.

"You drowned each one in a different teacup. You called it a mouse tea party. You kept saying, 'Oh! They're so cute! They're so cute!' "

"I don't have such a big problem with mice," said one of the Courne Haven fishermen. "I'll tell you what I do have a big problem with. Rats."

"Who's next?" Mrs. Pommeroy asked brightly. "Whose turn is it to look pretty?"

Ruth Thomas got drunk at the wedding.

Kitty Pommeroy helped. Kitty made friends with the bartender, a fifty-year-old Courne Haven fisherman named Chucky Strachan. Chucky Strachan had earned the great honor of serving as bartender largely because he was a big drunk. Chucky and Kitty found each other right away, the way two garrulous drunks in a bustling crowd always find each other, and they set out to have a great time at the Wishnell wedding. Kitty appointed herself Chucky's assistant and made sure to match his customers, drink for drink. She asked Chucky to whip up something nice for Ruth Thomas, something to loosen up the little honey.

"Give her something fruity," Kitty instructed. "Give her something just as sweet as her." So Chucky whipped up for Ruth a tall glass of whiskey and a little tiny bit of ice.

"Now that's a drink for a lady," Chucky said.

"I meant a cocktail!" Kitty said. "That's going to taste gross to her! She's not used to it! She went to *private* school!"

"Let's see," said Ruth Thomas, and she drank down the whiskey Chucky gave her, not in one swallow, but pretty quickly.

"Very fruity," she said. "Very sweet."

The drink radiated a pleasant warmth in her bowels. Her lips felt bigger. She had another drink, and she started to feel incredibly affectionate. She gave Kitty Pommeroy a long, strong hug, and said, "You were always my favorite Pommeroy sister," which couldn't have been further from the truth but felt good to say.

"I hope things work out for you, Ruthie," Kitty slurred.

"Aw, Kitty, you're sweet. You've always been so sweet to me."

"We all want things to work out for you, hon. We're all just holding our fingers, hoping it all works out."

"Holding your fingers?" Ruth frowned.

"Crossing our breath, I mean," Kitty said, and they both nearly fell down laughing.

Chucky Strachan made Ruth another drink.

"Am I a great bartender?" he asked.

"You really know how to mix whiskey and ice in a glass," Ruth conceded. "That's for sure."

"That's my cousin getting married," he said. "We need to celebrate. Dotty Wishnell is my cousin! Hey! Charlie Burden is my cousin, too!"

Chucky Strachan leaped out from behind the bar and grabbed Kitty Pommeroy. He buried his face in Kitty's neck. He kissed Kitty all over her face, all over the good side of her face, the side that wasn't burn-scarred. Chucky was a skinny guy, and his pants dropped lower and lower over his skinny ass. Each time he bent over the slightest bit, he displayed a nice New England cleavage. Ruth tried to avert her eyes. A matronly woman in a floral skirt was waiting for a drink, but Chucky didn't notice her. The woman smiled hopefully in his direction, but he slapped Kitty Pommeroy's bottom and opened himself a beer.

"Are you married?" Ruth asked Chucky, as he licked Kitty's neck.

He pulled away, threw a fist in the air, and announced, "My name is Clarence Henry Strachan and I am married!"

"May I have a drink, please?" the matronly lady asked politely.

"Talk to the bartender!" shouted Chucky Strachan, and he took Kitty out on the plywood dance floor in the middle of the tent.

The wedding service itself had been insignificant to Ruth. She had barely watched it, barely paid attention. She was amazed by the size of Dotty's father's yard, amazed by his nice garden. Those Wishnells certainly had money. Ruth was used to Fort Niles weddings, where the guests brought casseroles and pots of beans and pies. After the wedding, there'd be a great sorting of the serving dishes. *Whose tray is this? Whose coffee machine is this?*

The wedding of Dotty Wishnell and Charlie Burden, on the other hand, had been catered by a mainland expert. And there was, as Pastor Wishnell had promised, a professional photographer. The bride wore white, and some of the guests who had been to Dotty's first wedding said this gown was even nicer than the last one. Charlie Burden, a stocky character with an alcoholic's nose and suspicious eyes, made an unhappy groom. He looked depressed to be standing there in front of everyone, saying the formal words. Dotty's little daughter, Candy, as maid of honor, had cried, and when her mother tried to comfort her, said nastily, "I'm *not* crying!" Pastor Wishnell went on and on about Responsibilities and Rewards.

And after it was over, Ruth got drunk. And after she got drunk, she set to dancing. She danced with Kitty Pommeroy and Mrs. Pommeroy and with the groom. She danced with Chucky Strachan, the bartender, and with two handsome young men in tan pants, who, she found out later, were summer people. Summer people at an island wedding! Imagine that! She danced with both of those men a few times, and she got the feeling that she was somehow making fun of them, though she couldn't later remember what she'd said. She dropped a lot of sarcastic comments that they didn't seem to get. She even danced with Cal Cooley when he asked her. The band played country music.

"Is the band from here?" she asked Cal, and he said that the musicians had come over on Babe Wishnell's boat.

"They're good," Ruth said. For some reason she was allowing herself to be held very close by Cal Cooley. "I wish I could play an instrument. I'd like to play the fiddle. I can't even sing. I can't play anything. I can't even play a radio. Are you having fun, Cal?"

"I'd have a lot more fun if you'd slide up and down my leg as if it were a greased fire pole."

Ruth laughed.

"You look good," he told Ruth. "You should wear pink more often."

"I should wear *pink* more often? I'm wearing yellow."

"I said you should *drink* more often. I like the way it makes you feel. All soft and yielding."

"What am I wielding?" Ruth said, but she was only pretending not to understand.

He sniffed her hair. She let him. She could tell he was sniffing her hair, because she could feel his puffs of breath on her scalp. He pressed himself against her leg, and she could feel his erection. She let him do that, too. What the hell, she figured. He ground himself against her. He rocked her slowly. He kept his hands low on her back and pulled her tight against him. She let him do all that. *What the hell,* she kept thinking. It was Old Cal Cooley, but it felt pretty good. He kissed her on the top of the head, and suddenly it was as if she woke up.

It was Cal Cooley!

"Oh, my God, I have to pee," Ruth said, and pulled herself away from Cal, which wasn't easy, because he made a fight to hold her. What was she doing dancing with *Cal Cooley?* Jesus Christ. She weaved her way out of the tent, out of the yard, and walked down the street until the street ended and the woods began. She stepped behind a tree, lifted her dress, and peed on a flat rock, proudly managing to not splatter her legs. She couldn't believe she had felt Cal Cooley's penis, even faintly, pressing through his pants. That was disgusting. She made a pact with herself to do anything she had to do for the rest of her life to forget that she had ever felt Cal Cooley's penis.

When she walked out of the woods, she took a wrong turn and ended up on a street marked FURNACE STREET. *They have street signs here?* she wondered. Like the other streets on Courne Haven, this one was unpaved. It was dusk. She passed a small white house with a porch; on the porch was an old woman in a flannel shirt. She was holding a fluffy yellow bird. Ruth peered at the bird and at the woman. She was feeling wobbly on her feet.

"I'm looking for Babe Wishnell's house," she said. "Can you tell me where it is? I think I'm lost."

"I've been taking care of my sick husband for years," the woman said, "and my memory's not what it ought to be."

"How's your husband doing, ma'am?"

"He doesn't have many good days anymore."

"Really sick, is he?"

"Dead."

"Oh." Ruth scratched a mosquito bite on her ankle. "Do you know where Babe Wishnell's house is? I'm supposed to be at a wedding there."

"I think it's right up the next street. After the greenhouse. Take a left," the woman said. "It's been some time since I was there."

"The greenhouse? You guys have a greenhouse on this island?"

"Oh, I don't think so, love."

Ruth was confused for a moment; then she figured it out. "Do you mean that I should take a left after the house that's *painted* green?"

"I think you should, yes. But my memory's not what it ought to be."

"I think your memory's just fine."

"Aren't you a love? Who's getting married?"

"Babe Wishnell's daughter."

"That little girl?"

"I guess so. Excuse me, ma'am, but is that a duckling you're holding?"

"This is a chick, love. Oh, it's awful soft." The woman grinned at Ruth, and Ruth grinned back.

"Well, then, thank you for your help," Ruth said. She headed up the street to the house that was green and found her way back to the wedding.

As she stepped into the tent, a hot, dry hand caught her by the arm. She said, "Hey!" It was Cal Cooley.

"Mr. Ellis wants to see you," he said, and before she could protest, Cal led her over to Mr. Ellis. Ruth had forgotten that he was coming to the wedding, but there he was, sitting in his wheelchair. He grinned up at her, and Ruth, who had been doing a lot of grinning lately, grinned back. Good God, he was thin. He couldn't have weighed a hundred and ten pounds, and he'd once been a tall, strong man. His head was a bald, yellow globe, burnished as the head of a well-used cane. He had no eyebrows. He wore an ancient black suit with silver buttons. Ruth was astonished, as always, at how poorly he had aged compared with his sister, Miss Vera. Miss Vera liked to affect frailty, but she was perfectly hale. Miss Vera was little, but she was sturdy as firewood. Her brother was a wisp. Ruth couldn't believe, when she'd seen him earlier in the spring, that he'd made the trip to Fort Niles this year from Concord. And now she could not believe that he had made the trip from

Fort Niles to Courne Haven for the wedding. He was ninety-four years old.

"It's nice to see you, Mr. Ellis," she said.

"Miss Thomas," he replied, "you look well. Your hair is very pretty away from your face." He squinted up at her with his rheumy blue eyes. He was holding her hand. "You will have a seat?"

She took a deep breath and sat down on a wooden folding chair beside him. He let go of her. She wondered whether she smelled of whiskey. One had to sit awfully close to Mr. Ellis so that he could hear and be heard, and she didn't want her breath to give her away.

"My granddaughter!" he said, and smiled a wide smile that threatened to crack his skin.

"Mr. Ellis."

"I can't hear you, Miss Thomas."

"I said, Hello, Mr. Ellis. Hello, Mr. Ellis"

"You haven't been to see me in some time."

"Not since I came over with Senator Simon and Webster Pommeroy." Ruth had some difficulty enunciating the words *Senator* and *Simon*. Mr. Ellis did not seem to notice. "But I've been meaning to come by. I've been busy. I'll come up to Ellis House very soon and see you."

"We shall have a meal."

"Thank you. That's very nice, Mr. Ellis."

"Yes. You'll come on Thursday. Next Thursday."

"Thank you. I look forward to it." *Thursday!*

"You haven't told me how you found your visit to Concord."

"It was lovely, thank you. Thank you for encouraging me to go."

"Wonderful. I received a letter from my sister saying as much. It might not be amiss for you to write her a note thanking her for her hospitality."

"I will," Ruth said, not even wondering how he knew that she hadn't done so. Mr. Ellis always knew things like that. Of course she would write a note, now that it had been suggested. And when she did write, Mr. Ellis would undoubtedly know of it even before his sister received the note. That was his way: omniscience. Mr. Ellis dug around in a pocket of his suit and came up with a handkerchief. He unfolded it and passed it, with a palsied hand, across his nose. "What do you suppose will come of your mother when my sister passes away?" he asked. "I ask only because Mr. Cooley raised the question the other day."

Ruth's stomach tightened as if it had been cinched. *What the hell was that supposed to mean?* She thought for a moment and then said what she certainly would not have said had she not been drinking.

"I only hope she will be taken care of, sir."

"Come again?"

Ruth did not reply. She was quite sure that Mr. Ellis had heard her. Indeed he had, because he finally said, "It is very expensive to take care of people."

Ruth was as uncomfortable as ever with Lanford Ellis. She never had a sense, when meeting with him, what the outcome would be: what he would tell her to do, what he would withhold from her, what he would give her. It had been this way since she was a child of eight and Mr. Ellis had called her into his study, handed her a stack of books, and said, "Read these in the order I have placed them, from top to bottom. You are to stop swimming in the quarries with the Pommeroy boys unless you wear a bathing suit." There had never been an implication of threat in these instructions. They were simply issued.

Ruth followed Mr. Ellis's commands because she knew the power this man had over her mother. He had more power over her mother than Miss Vera did, because he controlled the family money. Miss Vera exercised her control over Mary Smith-Ellis Thomas in petty daily cruelties. Mr. Ellis, on the other hand, had never once treated Ruth's mother in a cruel way. Ruth was aware of this. For some reason, this knowledge had always filled her with panic, not peace. And so, at the age of eight, Ruth read the books Mr. Ellis had given her. She did as she was told. He had not quizzed her on the books or asked her to return them. She did not acquire a bathing suit for her swims in the quarries with the Pommeroy boys; she merely stopped swimming with them. That seemed to have been an acceptable solution, because she heard no more about it.

Meetings with Mr. Ellis were also significant because they were rare. He called Ruth into his presence only twice a year or so, and began each conversation with an expression of fondness. He would then chastise her lightly for not coming to visit him on her own. He called her *granddaughter, love, dear.* She was aware, and had been from early childhood, that she was considered his pet and was therefore lucky. There were others on Fort Niles—grown men, even—who would have liked an audience with Mr. Ellis even once, but could not obtain one. Senator Simon Addams, for instance, had been trying for years to meet with him. Ruth was thought by many on Fort Niles to have some special influence with the man, though she scarcely ever saw him. For the most part, she heard of his requests and demands and displeasure or pleasure from Cal Cooley. When she did see Mr. Ellis, his instructions to her were usually simple and direct.

When Ruth was thirteen, he had summoned her to tell her that she would be attending private school in Delaware. He said nothing of how or why this was to be or whose decision it had been. Nor did he ask her opinion. He did say that her schooling was expensive but would be taken care of. He told her that Cal Cooley would drive her to school in early September and that she would be expected to spend her Christmas holiday with her mother in Concord. She would not return to Fort Niles until the following June. These were facts, not matters for discussion.

On a less momentous matter, Mr. Ellis summoned Ruth when she was sixteen to say that she was to wear her hair away from her face from now on. That was his only instruction to her for the year. And she followed it and had been doing so ever since, wearing it in a ponytail. He apparently approved.

Mr. Ellis was one of the only adults in Ruth's life who had never called her stubborn. This was surely because, in his presence, she was not.

She wondered whether he was going to tell her not to drink anymore tonight. Was that the point of this? Would he tell her to stop dancing like a trollop? Or was this something bigger, an announcement that it was time for her to go to college? Or move to Concord with her mother? Ruth wanted to hear none of these things.

In general, she avoided Mr. Ellis strenuously because she was terrified of what he would ask of her and of the certainty that she would obey. She had not yet heard directly from Mr. Ellis what her plans for the fall were to be, but she had a strong sense that she would be asked to leave Fort Niles. Cal Cooley had indicated that Mr. Ellis wanted her to go to college, and Vera Ellis had mentioned the college for women where the dean was a friend. Ruth was sure the subject would come up soon. She had even got a message about leaving from Pastor Wishnell, of all people, and the signs pointed to a decision soon from Mr. Ellis himself. There was nothing Ruth hated more in her character than her unquestioning obedience of Mr. Ellis. And while she had made up her mind that she would disregard his wishes from now on, she didn't feel up to asserting her independence tonight.

"How have you been spending your days lately, Ruth?" Mr. Ellis asked.

Wanting no instructions from him at all tonight, Ruth decided to divert him. This was a new tactic, a bold tactic. But she had been drinking and, as a consequence, felt bolder than usual.

"Mr. Ellis," she said, "do you remember the elephant tusk we brought you?"

He nodded.

"Have you had a chance to look at it?"

He nodded again. "Very well," he said. "I understand you have been spending a great deal of your time with Mrs. Pommeroy and her sisters."

"Mr. Ellis," Ruth said, "I wonder whether we can talk about that elephant tusk. For just a moment."

That's right. She would be the one to direct this conversation. How hard could that be? She certainly did it with everyone else. Mr. Ellis raised an eyebrow. That is to say, he raised the skin below where an eyebrow would be if he happened to have an eyebrow.

"It took my friend several years to find that tusk, Mr. Ellis. That young man, Webster Pommeroy, he's the one who found it. He worked hard. And my other friend, Senator Simon?" Ruth pronounced the name this time without a hitch. She felt dead sober now. "Senator Simon Addams? You know him?"

Mr. Ellis did not respond. He found his handkerchief again and made another pass at his nose.

Ruth went on. "He has many interesting artifacts, Mr. Ellis. Simon Addams has been collecting unusual specimens for years. He would like to open a museum on Fort Niles. To display what he has collected. He'd call it the Fort Niles Museum of Natural History and believes that the Ellis Granite Company Store building would be suitable for his museum. Since it is vacant. Perhaps you've heard about this idea? I think he has asked your permission for years . . . I think he . . . It may not seem like an interesting project to you, but it would mean everything to him, and he is a good man. Also, he would like the elephant tusk back. For his museum. If he can have a museum, that is."

Mr. Ellis sat in his wheelchair with his hands on his thighs. His thighs were not much wider than his wrists. Under his suit jacket, he wore a thick, black sweater. He reached into an inside pocket of his suit and pulled out a small brass key, which he held between his thumb and forefinger. It trembled like a divining rod. Handing it to Ruth, he said, "Here is the key to the Ellis Granite Company Store building."

Ruth gingerly took the key. It was cool and sharp and could not have been a greater surprise. She said, "Oh!" She was astonished.

"Mr. Cooley will bring the elephant tusk to your house next week."

"Thank you, Mr. Ellis. I appreciate this. You don't have to—"

"You will join me for dinner on Thursday."

"I will. Yes. Terrific. Should I tell Simon Addams . . . Um, what shall I tell Simon Addams about the building?"

But Mr. Ellis was finished talking to Ruth Thomas. He shut his eyes and ignored her, and she went away.

Ruth Thomas went to the other side of the tent, as far as she could get from Mr. Ellis. She felt sober and a little sick, so she made a quick stop at the card table that served as a bar and had Chucky Strachan mix her another glass of whiskey and ice. Between Pastor Wishnell and Mr. Ellis, this had been a day of strange conversations, and now she was wishing that she had stayed home with the Senator and Webster Pommeroy. She found a chair in the corner, behind the band, and claimed it. When she put her elbows on her knees and her face in her hands, she could hear her pulse in her head. At the sound of applause, she looked up. A man in his mid-sixties, with a blond-gray brush haircut and the face of an old soldier, was standing in the middle of the tent, a champagne glass raised in his hand. It was Babe Wishnell.

"My daughter!" he said. "Today is my daughter's wedding, and I'd like to say some words!"

There was more applause. Somebody shouted, "Go to it, Babe!" and everyone laughed.

"My daughter isn't marrying the best-looking man on Courne Haven, but, then, it isn't legal to marry her father! Charlie Burden? Where's Charlie Burden?"

The groom stood up, looking agonized.

"You got yourself a good Wishnell girl today, Charlie!" Babe Wishnell bellowed; more applause. Somebody shouted, "Go get her, Charlie!" and Babe Wishnell glared in the direction of the voice. The laughter stopped.

But then he shrugged and said, "My daughter's a modest girl. When she was a teenager, she was so modest, she wouldn't even walk over a potato patch. You know why? Because potatoes have eyes! They might have looked up her skirt!"

Here, he pantomimed a girl, daintily lifting her skirts. He fluttered his hand about in a feminine way. The crowd laughed. The bride, holding her daughter on her lap, blushed.

"My new son-in-law reminds me of Cape Cod. I mean, his nose reminds me of Cape Cod. Does anyone know why his nose reminds me of Cape Cod? Because it's a prominent projection!" Babe Wishnell roared at his own joke. "Charlie, I'm just playing with you. You can sit down now, Charlie. Let's have a hand for Charlie. He's a pretty goddamn good sport. Now, these two are going on a honeymoon. They're going to Boston for the week. I hope they have a good time."

More applause, and the same voice shouted, "Go get her, Charlie!" This time Babe Wishnell ignored the voice.

"I hope they have a hell of a good time. They deserve it. Especially Dotty, because she's had a tough year, losing her husband. So I hope you have a hell of a good time, Charlie and Dotty." He raised his glass. The guests murmured and raised their glasses, too. "Good for them to get away for a while," Babe Wishnell said. "Leaving the kid with Dotty's mother and me, but what the hell. We like the kid. Hiya, kid!"

He waved at the kid. The kid, Candy, on her mother's lap, was as regal and inscrutable as a lioness.

"But that reminds me of when I took Dotty's mother on our honeymoon."

Someone in the crowd whooped, and everyone laughed. Babe Wishnell shook his finger, like *tut-tut-tut*, and continued. "When I took Dotty's mother on our honeymoon, we went to Niagara Falls. This was back in the Revolutionary War! No, it was 1945. I was just out of the war. World War Two, that is! Now, I'd gotten stove up pretty bad in a wreck in the South Pacific. I'd seen some pretty serious action over there in New Guinea, but I was ready for action on my honeymoon! You bet! I was ready for a different kind of action!"

Everyone looked to Gladys Wishnell, who was shaking her head.

"So we went to Niagara Falls. We had to take that boat, *The Maid of the Mist.* Now, I didn't know if Gladys was the type to get seasick. I thought she might get all woozy on me under that waterfall, because you go—you know, you go right *under* the goddamn thing. So I went to the pharmacy, and I bought a bottle of—what's it called? A bottle of Drambuie? What's it called that you take for seasickness?"

"Dramamine!" Ruth Thomas called out.

Babe Wishnell peered through the darkening tent at Ruth. He gave her a stern, perceptive look. He didn't know who she was, but he accepted her answer.

"Dramamine. That's right. I bought a bottle of Dramamine from the pharmacist. And since I was there anyhow, I bought a package of rubbers, too."

This brought shrieks of joy and applause from the wedding guests. Everyone looked at Dotty Wishnell and her mother, Gladys, both of whom were wearing the same priceless expression of disbelief and horror.

"Yeah, I bought Dramamine and a package of rubbers. So the pharmacist gives me the Dramamine. He gives me the rubbers. He looks at me and he says, 'If it makes her so goddamn sick to her stomach, why do you keep doing it to her?' "

The wedding guests roared. They applauded and whistled. Dotty Wishnell and her mother both doubled over, laughing. Ruth felt a hand on her shoulder. She looked up. It was Mrs. Pommeroy.

"Hey," Ruth said.

"May I sit here?"

"Sure, sure." Ruth patted the seat next to her, and Mrs. Pommeroy sat down.

"Hiding?" she asked Ruth.

"Yeah. Tired?"

"Yeah."

"I know Charlie Burden thinks he's going to get rich, marrying a Wishnell girl," Babe Wishnell continued, as the laughter died down. "I know he thinks it's his lucky day. He probably has his eye on some of my boats and gear. Well, he may get it. He may get all my boats in the end. But there's one ship I'd never want Charlie and Dotty to have. Do you know what ship that is? *Hardship.*"

The crowd said, "Awww . . ." Gladys Wishnell wiped her eyes.

"My new son-in-law ain't the smartest guy on the island. I heard they were going to make him the master of the lighthouse over on Crypt Rock for a spell. Well, that didn't work out so great. Charlie turned the light off at nine o'clock. They asked him why, and he said, 'All good people should be in bed by nine o'clock.' That's right! Lights out, Charlie!"

The guests laughed heartily. Charlie Burden looked as if he might throw up.

"Yeah, let's have a hand for Charlie and Dotty. I hope they have a real good time. And I hope they stay on here on Courne Haven forever. They might like it over there in Boston, but I'm not one for cities. I don't like cities at all. Never have. There's only one city I like. It's the best city in the world. Do you know what city that is? *Generosity.*"

The crowd said "Awww . . ." again.

"He's a real joker," Ruth said to Mrs. Pommeroy.

"He likes those puns," she agreed.

Mrs. Pommeroy took Ruth's hand as they watched Babe Wishnell finish his toast with some more puns, some more jabs at his new son-in-law.

"That man could buy and sell every last one of us," Mrs. Pommeroy said, wistfully.

There were cheers for Babe Wishnell at the end of his toast, and he took a dramatic bow and said, "And now, I'm real honored because Lanford Ellis is here with us. He wants to say a couple words, and I think we all want to hear whatever he has to say. That's right. It's not too often we see Mr. Ellis. It's a real honor for me that he's come to my daughter's wedding. So there he is, over there. Let's keep it real quiet now, everyone. Mr. Lanford Ellis. A very important man. Going to say some words."

Cal Cooley rolled Mr. Ellis in his wheelchair to the center of the room. The tent became silent. Cal tucked Mr. Ellis's blanket tighter.

"I am a lucky man," Mr. Ellis began, "to have such neighbors." Very slowly, he looked around at all those in the tent. It was as if he were tallying each neighbor. A baby started to cry, and there was a rustle as the mother took the child out of the tent. "There is a tradition on this island—and on Fort Niles, too—of hard work. I remember when the Swedes on Courne Haven were making cobblestones for the Ellis Granite Company. Three hundred good quarrymen could each make two hundred cobblestones a day for five cents each. My family always appreciated the hard work."

"This is an interesting wedding toast," Ruth whispered to Mrs. Pommeroy.

Mr. Ellis went on. "Now you are all lobstermen. That's fine work, too. Some of you are Swedes, the descendants of Vikings. The Vikings used to call the ocean the Path of the Lobster. I am an old man. What will happen to Fort Niles and Courne Haven when I am gone? I am an old man. I love these islands."

Mr. Ellis stopped speaking. He was looking at the ground. He had no expression on his face, and an observer might have thought that the man had no idea where he was, that he had forgotten he was speaking to an audience. The silence lasted a long time. The wedding guests began to look at one another. They shrugged and looked at Cal Cooley, standing a few feet behind Mr. Ellis. But Cal did not appear concerned; he wore his usual expression of bored disgust. Somewhere, a man coughed. It was so quiet, Ruth could hear the wind in the trees. After a few minutes, Babe Wishnell stood up.

"We want to thank Mr. Ellis for coming all the way over to Courne Haven," he said. "How about that, everyone? That means a lot to us. How about a big hand for Mr. Lanford Ellis? Thanks a lot, Lanford."

The crowd broke into relieved applause. Cal Cooley wheeled his boss to the side of the tent. Mr. Ellis was still looking at the ground. The band started to play, and a woman laughed too loudly.

"Well, that was an unusual toast, too," said Ruth.

"Do you know who's over at Pastor Wishnell's house, sitting on the back steps of the house all by himself?" Mrs. Pommeroy asked Ruth.

"Who?"

"Owney Wishnell." Mrs. Pommeroy handed Ruth a flashlight. "Why don't you go find him? Take your time."

11

> From hunger to cannibalism is a short step, and although the lobster fry are kept from congregating, there still occur chances of individuals coming momentarily into contact with one another, and, if hungry, they make the most of their opportunities.
>
> —*A Method of Lobster Culture*
> A. D. Mead, Ph.D.
> 1908

RUTH, WITH HER WHISKEY in one hand and Mrs. Pommeroy's flashlight in the other, found her way over to Pastor Wishnell's house. There were no lights on inside. She walked to the back of the house and discovered, as Mrs. Pommeroy had said she would, Owney. He was sitting on the steps. He made a big shadow in the dark. As Ruth slowly moved the beam of the flashlight over him, she saw that he was wearing a gray sweatshirt with a zipper and a hood. She went over and sat beside him and turned off the flashlight. They sat in the dark for a while.

"Want some?" Ruth asked. She offered Owney her glass of whiskey. He accepted it and took a long swallow. The contents of the glass didn't seem to surprise him. It was as if he was expecting whiskey from Ruth Thomas at that moment, as if he'd been sitting here waiting for it. He handed her the glass, she drank some, and passed it back to him. The drink was soon gone. Owney was so quiet, she could scarcely hear him breathing. She set the glass on the step, near the flashlight.

"Do you want to go for a walk?" she asked.

"Yes," Owney said, and he stood up.

He offered her his hand, and she took it. A solid grip. He led her back through the garden, over the low brick wall, past the roses. She had left the flashlight on the steps of the house, and so they picked their way carefully. It was a clear night, and they could see their way.

They walked through a neighbor's yard, and then they were in the woods.

Owney led Ruth to a path. Now it was dark, because of the overhang, the shadow of spruces. The path was narrow, and Owney and Ruth walked single file. Because she didn't want to fall, she put her right hand on his right shoulder to balance herself. As she felt more confident, she took her hand off his shoulder, but reached for him whenever she was unsure.

They did not speak. Ruth heard an owl.

"Don't be afraid," Owney said. "The island's full of noises."

She knew those noises. The woods were at once familiar and disorienting. Everything smelled, looked, sounded like Fort Niles but wasn't Fort Niles. The air was sweet, but it was not her air. She had no idea where they were, until, suddenly, she sensed a great opening to her right, and she realized they were high up, along the edge of a gutted quarry. It was an old Ellis Granite Company scar, like the ones on Fort Niles. Now they moved with great caution, because the path Owney had chosen was only four feet or so from what seemed to be a serious drop. Ruth knew that some of the quarries were several hundred feet deep. She took baby steps because she was wearing sandals, and the soles were slippery. She was aware of a slickness beneath her feet.

They walked along the edge of the quarry for a while and then were back in the woods. The sheltering trees, the enclosed space, the embracing darkness was a relief, after the wide gape of the quarry. At one point they crossed an old railway. As they got deeper into the woods, it was hard to see, and after they had walked a half hour, in silence, the dark suddenly became thicker, and Ruth saw why. Just to her left was a shelf of granite reaching up into the darkness. It may have been a wall a hundred feet high of good black granite; it swallowed up the light. She reached out and brushed the surface with her fingers; it was damp and cool and mossy.

She said, "Where are we going?" She could really barely see Owney.

"For a walk."

She laughed, a quiet, nice sound that didn't travel at all.

"Is there a destination?" she asked.

"No," he said, and, to her great delight, he laughed. Ruth joined him; she liked the sound of their laughter in these woods.

Now they stopped. Ruth leaned back against the granite wall. It was slightly tilted, and she tilted with it. She could just make out Owney standing in front of her. She reached out to his arm and felt along it all the way down to his hand. Nice hand.

"Come here, Owney," she said, and laughed again. "Come in here." She pulled him close, and he put his arms around her, and there they stood. Against her back was the cold dark granite; against the front of her was Owney Wishnell's big warm body. She pulled him closer and pressed the side of her face to his chest. She really, really liked the way he felt. His back was wide. She didn't care if this was all they did. She didn't care if they held each other this way for hours and did nothing else.

No, actually; she did care.

Now everything was going to change, she knew, and she lifted her face and kissed him on the mouth. To be exact, she kissed him *in* the mouth, a thoughtful and long wet kiss and—what a nice surprise!—what a fat, excellent tongue Owney Wishnell had! God, what a lovely tongue. All slow and salty. It was a gorgeous tongue.

Ruth had kissed boys before, of course. Not many boys, because she didn't have access to many. Was she going to kiss the Pommeroy sons? No, there hadn't been many eligible boys in Ruth's life, but she'd kissed a few when she'd had the chance. She had kissed a strange boy on a bus to Concord one Christmas, and she had kissed the son of a cousin of Duke Cobb's who'd been visiting for a week from New Jersey, but those episodes were nothing like kissing Owney Wishnell's big soft mouth.

Maybe this was why Owney spoke so slowly all the time, Ruth thought; his tongue was too big and soft to form quick words. Well, what of it. She put her hands on the sides of his face and he put his hands on the sides of her face, and they kissed the hell out of each other. Each held the other's head firmly, the way you hold that of an errant child and get right in his face and say, "Listen!" And they kissed and kissed. It was great. His thigh was shoved so hard up into her crotch that it almost lifted her off the ground. He had a hard, muscled thigh. *Good for him,* Ruth thought. *Nice thigh.* She didn't care if they never did anything but kiss.

Yes, she did. She *did* care.

She took his hands off her face, took his big wrists in her own hands, and pushed his hands down to her body. She placed his hands on her hips, and he pushed himself even closer against her and—he was deep in her mouth now with that gorgeous sweet tongue—he moved his hands up her body until his palms were covering her breasts. Ruth realized that if she didn't get his mouth on her nipples soon she was going to die. *That's right*, she thought, *I will die.* So she unbuttoned the front of her sundress and pulled away the fabric and pushed his head down, and—he was brilliant! He made a touching, quiet little moan. It was as if her whole breast was in his mouth. She could feel it all the way to her lungs. She wanted to growl. She wanted to arch back into it, but there was no room to arch, with that rock wall behind her.

"Is there someplace we can go?" she asked.

"Where?"

"Someplace softer than this rock?"

"OK," he said, but it took them ages to separate from each other. It took them several tries, because she kept pulling him back, and he kept grinding his groin into hers. It went on and on. And when they finally did pull away from each other and headed up the trail, they raced. It was as if they were swimming under water, holding their breath and trying to make it to the surface. Forget about roots and rocks and Ruth's slippery sandals; forget about his helpful hand under her elbow. There was no time for those delicacies, because they were in a hurry. Ruth didn't know where they were off to, but she knew it was going to be a place where they could *continue*, and that knowledge set her pace and his. They had business to attend to. They practically ran for it. No talking.

They finally broke out of the woods onto a small beach. Ruth could see lights across the water and knew they were facing Fort Niles, which meant they were way on the other side of Courne Haven from the wedding party. Good. The farther away the better. There was a shed on a ridge above the level of sand, and it had no door, so they went right in there. Piles of old traps in the corner. An oar on the floor. A child's school desk, with the tiny kid's chair attached. A window covered with a wool blanket, which Owney Wishnell tore away without hesitation. He flipped the dust from the blanket, kicked away an old glass buoy from the middle of the floor, and spread out the blanket. Now moonlight came through the empty window.

As if this had been worked out well in advance, Ruth Thomas and Owney Wishnell stripped off their clothes. Ruth was faster, because all she had on was that sundress, which was already mostly unbuttoned. Off it came, then the blue cotton underpants and the sandals kicked away and—there!—she was done. But Owney took forever. Owney had to take off his sweatshirt and the flannel shirt that was under that (with buttons at the cuffs that had to be dealt with) and the undershirt beneath it all. He had to take off a belt, unlace his tall workboots, pull off his socks. He took off his jeans and—this was taking forever—finally his white underwear, and he was done.

They didn't exactly tackle each other, but they collected each other very quickly, and then realized this would be a whole lot easier if they were on the ground, so that happened pretty quickly, too. Ruth was on her back, and Owney was on his knees. He pushed her knees back against her chest and opened her legs, hands on her shins. She thought about all the people who would be outraged if they knew of this—her mother, her father, Angus Addams (if he knew she was *naked* with a *Wishnell!*), Pastor Wishnell (terrifying even to think of his reaction), Cal Cooley (he would lose his mind), Vera Ellis, Lanford Ellis (he would *kill* her! Hell, he would have them both killed!)—and she smiled and reached her hand forward through her legs and took his cock and helped him put it inside her. Just like that.

It is extraordinary what people can do even if they've never done it before.

Ruth had thought a lot in the last few years about what it would be like to have sex. Of all the things she'd thought about sex, though, she'd never considered that it might be so easy and so immediately *hot*. She'd thought of it as something to be puzzled out with difficulty and a lot of talking. And she could never really picture sex, because she couldn't picture who exactly she'd be puzzling it out with. She figured her partner would have to be much older, somebody who knew what he was doing and would be patient and instructive. *This goes here; no, not like that; try again, try again.* She'd thought that sex would be difficult at first, like learning to drive. She'd thought that sex was something that might grow on her slowly, after a great deal of grim practice, and that it would probably hurt a lot in the beginning.

Yes, it is truly extraordinary what people can do even if they've never done it before.

Ruth and Owney went at it like pros, right from the start. There, in that shack on the filthy woolen blanket, they were doing raunchy, completely satisfying things to each other. They were doing things it might take other partners months to figure out. She was on top of him; he was on top of her. There seemed no part of each other that they were not willing to put into the other's mouth. She was up on his face; he was leaning up against the child's desk while she crouched in front of him and sucked him as he clutched her hair. She was lying on her side, with her legs positioned like a runner in mid-stride while he fingered her. He was sliding his fingers into her slippy tight cracks and licking his fingers. Then he was sliding his fingers into her slippy tight cracks again and putting his fingers in her mouth, so that she could taste herself on his hands.

Incredibly, she was saying, "Yes, yes, fuck me, fuck me, fuck me."

He was flipping her over onto her stomach and lifting her hips into the air and, yes, yes, he was fucking her, fucking her, fucking her.

Ruth and Owney fell asleep, and when they woke, it was windy and cold. They hurried into their clothes and made the difficult hike back into town, through the woods and past the quarry. Ruth could see the quarry more clearly, now that the sky was starting to lighten. It was a huge hole, bigger than anything on Fort Niles. They must have made cathedrals out of that rock.

They came out of the woods in Owney's neighbor's yard, stepped over the low brick wall, and walked into Pastor Wishnell's rose garden. There was Pastor Wishnell on the steps of the porch, waiting for them. In one hand, he held Ruth's empty whiskey glass. In the other, Mrs. Pommeroy's flashlight. When he saw them coming, he shone the flashlight on them, although he really didn't need to. It was light enough outside now for him to see perfectly well who they were. No matter. He shone the flashlight on them.

Owney dropped Ruth's hand. She immediately thrust it into the pocket of her yellow sundress and clasped the key, the key to the Ellis Granite Company Store, the key Mr. Lanford Ellis had handed her only hours before. She hadn't thought about the key since taking off into the woods with Owney, but now it was extremely important that she locate it, that she confirm it had not been lost. Ruth held on to the key so tightly that it bit into her palm—as Pastor Wishnell came off the porch and walked toward them. She clung to the key. She could not have said why.

12

In severe winters, lobsters are either driven into deeper water, or, if living in harbors, seek protection by burrowing into the mud when this is available.

—*The American Lobster: A Study of Its Habits and Development*
Francis Hobart Herrick, Ph.D.
1895

RUTH SPENT MOST of the fall of 1976 in hiding. Her father had not expressly thrown her out of the house, but he did not make her feel welcome there after the incident. The incident was not that Ruth and Owney had been caught by Pastor Wishnell, hiking out of the Courne Haven woods at daybreak after Dotty Wishnell's wedding. That was unpleasant, but the incident occurred four days later, at dinner, when Ruth asked her father, "Don't you even want to know what I was doing in the woods with Owney Wishnell?"

Ruth and her father had been stepping around each other for days, not speaking, somehow managing to avoid eating meals together. On this night, Ruth had roasted a chicken and had it ready when her father came in from fishing. "Don't worry about me," he'd said, when he saw Ruth setting the table for two. "I'll pick some dinner up over at Angus's," and Ruth said, "No, Dad, let's eat here, you and me."

They didn't talk much over dinner. "I did a good job with this chicken, didn't I?" Ruth asked, and her father said that, sure, she'd done a real good job. She asked how things were working out with Robin Pommeroy, whom her father had recently hired back, and Stan said the kid was as stupid as ever, what did you expect? That sort of talk. They finished dinner quietly.

As Stan Thomas picked up his plate and headed to the sink, Ruth asked, "Dad. Don't you even want to know what I was doing in the woods with Owney Wishnell?"

"No."

"No?"

"How many times do I have to tell you? I don't care who you spend your time with, Ruth, or what you do with him."

Stan Thomas rinsed off his plate, came back to the table, and took Ruth's plate without asking whether she was finished with dinner and without looking at her. He rinsed her plate, poured himself a glass of milk, and cut himself a slice of Mrs. Pommeroy's blueberry cake, which was sitting on the counter under a sweaty tent of plastic wrap. He ate the cake with his hands, leaning over the sink. He wiped the crumbs on his jeans with both hands and covered the cake with the plastic wrap again.

"I'm heading over to Angus's," he said.

"You know, Dad," she said, "I'll tell you something." She didn't get up from her chair. "I think you should have an opinion about this."

"Well," he said, "I don't."

"Well, you should. You know why? Because we were having sex."

He picked his jacket off the back of his chair, put it on, and headed for the door.

"Where are you going?" Ruth asked.

"Angus's. Said that already."

"That's all you have to say? That's your opinion?"

"Don't have any opinion."

"Dad, I'll tell you something else. There's a lot of things going on around here that you should have an opinion about."

"Well," he said, "I don't."

"Liar," Ruth said.

He looked at her. "That's no way to talk to your father."

"Why? You are a liar."

"That's no way to talk to any person."

"I'm just a little tired of your saying you don't care what goes on around here. I think that's pretty damn weak."

"It doesn't do me any good to care about what's going on."

"You don't care if I go to Concord or stay here," she said. "You don't care if Mr. Ellis gives me money. You don't care if I work on a fishing boat forever or get hauled off to college. You don't care if I stay up all night having sex with a Wishnell. Really, Dad? You don't care about *that?*"

"That's right."

"Oh, come on. You're such a liar."

"Stop saying that."

"I'll say what I want to say."

"It doesn't matter what I care, Ruth. Whatever happens to you or your mother won't have anything to do with me. Believe me. I got nothing to do with it. I learned that a long time ago."

"Me or my *mother*?"

"That's right. I got no say in any decisions involving either one of you. So what the hell."

"My *mother*? What are you, kidding me? You could totally dominate my mother if you bothered. She's never in her life made a decision on her own, Dad."

"I got no say over her."

"Who does, then?"

"You know who."

Ruth and her father looked at each other for a long minute. "You could stand up to the Ellises if you wanted to, Dad."

"No, I couldn't, Ruth. And neither can you."

"Liar."

"I told you to stop saying that."

"Pussy," Ruth said, to her own immense surprise.

"If you don't watch your fucking mouth," Ruth's father said, and he walked out of the house.

That was the incident.

Ruth finished cleaning up the kitchen and headed over to Mrs. Pommeroy's. She cried for about an hour on her bed while Mrs. Pommeroy stroked her hair and said, "Why don't you tell me what happened?"

Ruth said, "He's just such a pussy."

"Where did you learn that word, hon?"

"He's such a fucking coward. It's pathetic. Why can't he be more like Angus Addams? Why can't he stand up for something?"

"You wouldn't really want Angus Addams for a father, would you, Ruth?"

This made Ruth cry harder, and Mrs. Pommeroy said, "Oh, sweetheart. You're sure having a tough time this year."

Robin came into the room and said, "What's all the noise? Who's blubbering?" Ruth shouted, "Get him out of here!" Robin said, "It's my house, bitch." And Mrs. Pommeroy said, "You two are like brother and sister."

Ruth stopped crying and said, "I can't believe this fucking place."

"What place?" Mrs. Pommeroy asked. "*What* place, hon?"

Ruth stayed at the Pommeroy house through July and August and on into the beginning of September. Sometimes she went next door to her house, to her father's house, when she knew he'd be out hauling, and picked up a clean blouse or a book to read, or tried to guess what he'd been eating. She had nothing to do. She had no job. She had given up even pretending that she wanted to work as a sternman, and nobody asked her anymore what plans she had. She was clearly never going to be offered work on a boat. And for people who didn't work on boats on Fort Niles in 1976, there wasn't a whole lot else to do.

Ruth had nothing to occupy herself. At least Mrs. Pommeroy could do needlepoint. And Kitty Pommeroy had her alcoholism for companionship. Webster Pommeroy had the mudflats to sift through, and Senator Simon had his dream of the Museum of Natural History. Ruth had nothing. Sometimes she thought she most resembled the oldest citizens of Fort Niles, the tiny ancient women who sat at their front windows and parted the curtains to see what was going on out there, on the rare instances that anyone walked past their homes.

She was sharing Mrs. Pommeroy's home with Webster and Robin and Timothy Pommeroy, and with Robin's fat wife, Opal, and their big baby, Eddie. She was also sharing it with Kitty Pommeroy, who'd been thrown out of her house by Ruth's Uncle Len Thomas. Len had taken up Florida Cobb, of all desperate women. Florida Cobb, Russ and Ivy Cobb's grown daughter, who rarely said a word and who'd spent her life gaining weight and painting pictures on sand dollars, was now living with Len Thomas. Kitty was in bad shape over this. She'd threatened Len with a shotgun, but he took it away from her and blasted it into her oven.

"I thought Florida Cobb was my goddamn friend," Kitty said to Ruth, although Florida Cobb had never been anyone's friend.

Kitty told Mrs. Pommeroy the whole sad story of her last night at home with Len Thomas. Ruth could hear the two women talking in

Mrs. Pommeroy's bedroom, with the door shut. She could hear Kitty sobbing and sobbing. When Mrs. Pommeroy finally came out, Ruth asked, "What did she say? What's the story?"

"I don't want to hear it twice, Ruth," Mrs. Pommeroy said.

"Twice?"

"I don't want to hear it once out of her mouth and once out of mine. Just forget it. She'll be staying here from now on."

Ruth was beginning to realize that Kitty Pommeroy woke up every day more drunk than most people would be in their entire lives. At night, she would cry and cry, and Mrs. Pommeroy and Ruth would put her to bed. She'd punch them as they struggled with her up the stairs. This happened nearly every day. Kitty even clocked Ruth in the face once and made her nose bleed. Opal was never any help in dealing with Kitty. She was afraid of getting hit, so she sat in the corner and cried while Mrs. Pommeroy and Ruth took care of everything.

Opal said, "I don't want my baby growing up around all this yelling."

"Then move into your own goddamn house," Ruth said.

"You move into your own goddamn house!" Robin Pommeroy said to Ruth.

"You all are just like brothers and sisters," Mrs. Pommeroy said. "Always teasing each other."

Ruth couldn't see Owney. She hadn't seen him since the wedding. Pastor Wishnell was making sure of that. The pastor had decided to spend the fall on a grand tour of the Maine islands, with Owney as his captain, sailing the *New Hope* to every dock in the Atlantic from Portsmouth to Nova Scotia, preaching, preaching, preaching.

Owney never called Ruth, but how could he? He had no number for her, no idea that she was living with Mrs. Pommeroy. Ruth didn't so much mind not being called; they'd probably have had little to say to each other on the phone. Owney wasn't much of a conversationalist in person, and she couldn't imagine dallying away hours with him over the line. They'd never had all that much to talk about. Ruth didn't want to talk to Owney, anyhow. She wasn't curious to catch up with Owney on local gossip, but that didn't mean she wasn't missing him or, rather, craving him. She wanted to be with him. She wanted him in the room with her so that she could feel again the comfort of his body and his silence. She wanted to have sex with him again, in the worst way. She wanted to be naked with Owney, and thinking about that filled up a good bit of her time. She thought about it while in the bathtub and in bed. She talked to Mrs. Pommeroy again and again about the one time she'd had sex with Owney. Mrs. Pommeroy wanted to hear all the different parts, everything the two of them had done, and she seemed to approve.

Ruth was sleeping on the top floor of the big Pommeroy house, in the bedroom Mrs. Pommeroy had first tried to give her when she was nine — the bedroom with the faint, rusty blood spatters on the wall where that long-ago Pommeroy uncle had taken his life with a shotgun blast in the mouth.

"As long as it doesn't bother you," Mrs. Pommeroy told Ruth.

"Not a bit."

There was a heating vent on the floor, and if Ruth lay with her head near it, she could hear conversations throughout the house. The eavesdropping brought her comfort. She could hide and pay attention. And, for the most part, Ruth's occupation that autumn was hiding. She was hiding from her father, which was easy, because he wasn't looking for her. She was hiding from Angus Addams, which was slightly more difficult, because Angus would cross the street if he saw her and tell her what a dirty little whore she was, fucking around with a Wishnell, trash-mouthing her father, slinking around town.

"Yeah," he'd say. "I heard about it. Don't think I didn't fucking hear about it."

"Leave me alone, Angus," Ruth would say. "It's none of your business."

"You slutty little slut."

"He's just teasing you," Mrs. Pommeroy would tell Ruth if she happened to be there, witnessing the insult. This made both Ruth and Angus indignant.

"You call that teasing?" Ruth would say.

"I'm not goddamn teasing anyone," Angus would say, equally disgusted. Mrs. Pommeroy, refusing to become upset, would say, "Of course you are, Angus. You're just a big tease."

"You know what we have to do?" Mrs. Pommeroy told Ruth again and again. "We have to let the dust settle. Everyone loves you here, but people are a little worked up."

The biggest portion of Ruth's hiding occupation during August involved Mr. Ellis, which meant she was hiding from Cal Cooley. More than anything else, she did not want to see Mr. Ellis, and she knew Cal would someday fetch her and bring her to Ellis House. She knew that Lanford Ellis would have a plan for her, and she wanted no part of it. Mrs. Pommeroy and Senator Simon helped her hide from Cal. When Cal came to the Pommeroy house looking for Ruth, Mrs. Pommeroy would tell him she was with Senator Simon, and when Cal asked for Ruth over at the Senator's, he was told she was at Mrs. Pommeroy's place. But the island was only four miles long; how long could that game last? Ruth knew that when Cal really wanted to catch her, he would. And he did catch her, one morning at the end of August, at the Ellis Granite Company Store building, where she was helping the Senator build display cases for his museum.

The inside of the Ellis Granite Company Store was dark and unpleasant. When the store was closed, almost fifty years earlier, everything had been stripped from the place, and now it was a gutted, dry building with boards over the windows. Still, Senator Simon couldn't have been happier with Ruth's strange gift to him, after the Wishnell wedding, of the key to the padlock that had kept him out of the place so long. He couldn't believe his fortune. He was so excited about creating the museum, in fact, that he temporarily abandoned Webster Pommeroy. He was willing to leave Webster down at Potter Beach alone to scour the mud for the last elephant tusk. He had no energy these days to worry about Webster. All his energy was devoted to fixing up the building.

"This is going to be a splendid museum, Ruth."

"I'm sure it will be."

"Mr. Ellis really said it was fine to make the place into a museum?"

"He didn't say that in so many words, but after I told him what you wanted, he gave me the key."

"So it must be fine with him."

"We'll see."

"He'll be delighted when he sees the museum," Senator Simon said. "He will feel like a patron."

Ruth was beginning to understand that a major part of Senator Simon's museum was going to be a library for his vast collection of books—books for which he had no more room in his house. The Senator had more books than artifacts. So the Senator had to build bookshelves. He'd already planned it. There was to be a section for books on shipbuilding, a section for books on piracy, a section for books on exploration. He was going to devote the entire downstairs for his museum. The storefront would be a gallery of sorts, for rotating exhibits. The old office rooms and storage rooms would have books and permanent displays. The basement would be for storage. ("Archives," he called it.) He had no plans for the top floor of the building, which was an abandoned three-room apartment where the manager of the general store had lived with his family. But the downstairs was all accounted for. The Senator was planning to dedicate an entire room to the "display and discussion" of maps. As far as Ruth could see, the display itself was not coming along very quickly. The discussion, though, was well advanced.

"What I wouldn't give," Senator Simon told Ruth that afternoon in August, "to see an original copy of the Mercator-Hondius map." He showed her a reproduction of that very map in a volume he'd ordered years earlier from an antiquarian book dealer in Seattle. This insistence of the Senator's to show Ruth every book he handled, to talk over every interesting illustration, was slowing down considerably the preparation of the museum. "Sixteen thirty-three. You can see they've got the Faroe Islands right, and Greenland. But what is this? Oh, dear. What could that land mass possibly be? Do you know, Ruth?"

"Iceland?"

"No, no. *That's* Iceland, Ruth. Right where it should be. This is a mythical island, called Frislant. It shows up on all kinds of old maps. There's no such place. Isn't that the strangest thing? It is drawn so distinctly, as if the cartographers were certain of it. It was probably a mistake in a sailor's report. That's where the mapmakers got their information, Ruth. They never left home. That's the remarkable thing, Ruth. They were just like me."

The Senator fingered his nose. "But they did get it wrong sometimes. You can see Gerhardus Mercator is still convinced that there's a Northeast Passage to the Orient. He obviously had no idea of the polar ice factor! Do you think the mapmakers were heroes, Ruth? I do."

"Oh, sure, Senator."

"I think they were. Look how they shaped a continent from the outside in. North Africa's sixteenth-century maps, for instance, are correct around the edges. They knew how to chart those coasts, the

Portuguese. But they didn't know what was going on inside, or how big the continent was. Oh, no, they sure didn't know that, Ruth."

"No. Do you think we could take some of these boards off the windows?"

"I don't want anyone to see what we're doing. I want it to be a surprise to everyone once we're finished."

"What *are* we doing, Senator?"

"Making a display." The Senator was paging through another one of his map books, and his face was soft and loving as he said, "Oh, for the love of mud, did they ever get that wrong. The Gulf of Mexico is *huge*."

Ruth looked over his shoulder at a reproduction of an ungainly, ancient map but couldn't make out any of the writing on the page. "We need to get more light in here, I think. Don't you think we should start cleaning this place a little, Senator?"

"I like the stories about how wrong they got it. Like Cabral. Pedro Cabral. Sailed west in 1520 trying to find India and ran right into Brazil! And John Cabot was trying to find Japan and ended up in Newfoundland. Verrazano was looking for a westward passage to the Spice Islands and ends up in New York Harbor. He thought it was a sea lane. The risks they took! Oh, how they tried!"

The Senator was in low-level ecstasy now. Ruth started to unpack a box marked SHIPWRECKS: PHOTOS/PAMPHLETS III. This was one of the many boxes containing items for the display the Senator planned to call either "Wages of Neptune" or "We Are Punished," a display entirely devoted to accidents at sea. The first item she pulled out was a folder, labeled *Medical* in Senator Simon's remarkable, antique script. She knew exactly what it was. She remembered looking through it when she was a little girl, peering at the ghastly pictures of shipwreck survivors, as Senator Simon told her the story of each man and each wreck.

"This could happen to you, Ruth," he'd say. "This could happen to anyone in a boat."

Now Ruth opened the folder and looked at each familiar old nightmare: the infected bluefish bite; the dinner plate–size leg ulcer; the man whose buttocks had rotted away after he'd sat on a wet coil of rope for three weeks; the saltwater boils; the blackening sunburns; the feet swollen with water bite; the amputations; the mummified corpse in the lifeboat.

"Here's a lovely print!" Senator Simon said. He was looking through another box, this one marked SHIPWRECKS: PHOTOS/PAMPHLETS VI. From a file labeled *Heroes*, the Senator pulled an etching of a woman on a beach. Her hair was in a loose bun, and a heavy length of rope was slung over one shoulder.

"Mrs. White," he said fondly. "Hello, Mrs. White. From Scotland. When a ship wrecked on the rocks near her home, she had the sailors on board throw her a rope. Then she dug her heels into the sand and pulled the sailors to shore, one at a time. Doesn't she look hale?"

Ruth agreed that Mrs. White looked hale, and dug further through the *Medical* file. She found index cards scribbled with brief notes in Simon's handwriting.

One card read only: "Symptoms: shivers, headaches, reluctance to move, drowsiness, torpor, death."

Another read: "Thirst: drink urine, blood, fluid of own blisters, spirit fluid of compass."

Another: "Dec. 1710, *Nottingham* wrecked Boon Island. 26 days. Crew ate ship's carpenter."

Another: "Mrs. Rogers, stewardess of *Stella*. Helped ladies into lifeboat, gave up own vest. DIES! GOES DOWN WITH SHIP!"

Ruth handed that last card to Senator Simon and said, "I think this one belongs in the *Heroes* file." He squinted at the card and said, "You're absolutely right, Ruth. How did Mrs. Rogers ever get in the *Medical* file? And look what I just found in the *Heroes* file that doesn't belong there at all."

He handed Ruth an index card reading: "*Augusta M. Gott*, capsized, Gulf Stream, 1868. Erasmus Cousins (of BROOKSVILLE, MAINE!) selected by lot to be eaten. Saved only by sight of rescue sail. E. Cousins had bad stammer rest of life; E. Cousins—NEVER RETURNED TO SEA!"

"Do you have a cannibalism file?" Ruth asked.

"This is much more poorly organized than I thought," said Senator Simon, mournfully.

It was at that moment that Cal Cooley stepped through the front door of the Ellis Granite Company Store building, without knocking.

"*There's* my Ruth," he said.

"Shit," Ruth said, simply and with dread.

Cal Cooley hung around a long time in the Ellis Granite Company

Store that afternoon. He rifled through Senator Simon's belongings, taking things out of order and putting things back in the wrong place. He agitated Senator Simon no end by handling some of the artifacts quite rudely. Ruth tried to keep her mouth shut. Her stomach hurt. She tried to be quiet and stay out of the way so that he wouldn't talk to her, but there was no avoiding him on his mission. After an hour of being a nuisance, Cal said, "You never went to see Mr. Ellis for dinner in July, as he invited you to do."

"Sorry about that."

"I doubt it."

"I forgot. Tell him I'm sorry."

"Tell him yourself. He wants to see you."

Senator Simon brightened and said, "Ruth, maybe you can ask Mr. Ellis about the basement!"

Senator Simon had recently found row upon row of locked file cabinets in the basement of the Ellis Granite Company Store. They were full, Senator Simon was sure, of fascinating Ellis Granite Company documents, and the Senator wanted permission to go through them and perhaps display a few of the choice items in the museum. He had written Mr. Ellis a letter requesting permission but had received no response.

"I can't make it up there today, Cal," Ruth said.

"Tomorrow's fine."

"I can't make it up there tomorrow, either."

"He wants to talk to you, Ruth. He has something to tell you."

"I'm not interested."

"I think it would be to your benefit to stop by. I'll give you a ride, if that makes it easier."

"I'm not going, Cal," Ruth said.

"Why don't you go see him, Ruth?" Senator Simon said. "You could ask him about the basement. Maybe I could come with you . . ."

"How does this weekend look? Maybe you can come for dinner Friday night. Or breakfast on Saturday?"

"I'm not going, Cal."

"How does next Sunday morning sound? Or the Sunday after that?"

Ruth thought for a moment. "Mr. Ellis will be gone by the Sunday after that."

"What makes you think so?"

"Because he always leaves Fort Niles on the second Saturday of September. He'll be back in Concord the Sunday after next."

"No, he won't. He made it very clear to me that he's not leaving Fort Niles until he sees you."

This shut Ruth up.

"My goodness," Senator Simon said, aghast. "Mr. Ellis isn't planning on spending the winter here, is he?"

"I guess that's up to Ruth," Cal Cooley said.

"But that would be astonishing," Senator Simon said. "That would be unheard of! He's never stayed here." Senator Simon looked at Ruth with panic. "What would that mean?" he said. "My goodness, Ruth. What are you going to *do?*"

Ruth had no answer, but she didn't need one, because the conversation was abruptly ended by Webster Pommeroy, who charged into the Ellis Granite Company Store building with a hideous object in his hands. He was covered with mud from the chest down, and his face was so contorted that Ruth thought he must have found the second elephant tusk. But, no, it was not a tusk he was carrying. It was a round, filthy object that he thrust at the Senator. It took Ruth a moment to see what it was, and when she did, her body turned cold. Even Cal Cooley blanched when he realized that Webster Pommeroy was carrying a human skull.

The Senator turned it around and around in his doughy hands. The skull was intact. There were still teeth in the jaw, and a rubbery, shriveled skin, with long, muddy hairs hanging from it, covered the bone. It was a horror. Webster was shaking savagely.

"What's that?" Cal Cooley asked, and for once his voice was free of sarcasm. "Who the hell is that?"

"I have no idea," the Senator said.

But he did have an idea, as it turned out. Several days later—after the Rockland police came out on a Coast Guard boat to examine the skull and take it away for forensic tests—a distraught Senator Simon told the horrified Ruth Thomas of his supposition.

"Ruthie," he said, "I'll bet you any money in the world that's the skull of your grandmother, Jane Smith-Ellis. That's what they're going to find out if they find out anything. The rest of her is probably still out there in the mudflats, where she's been rotting since the wave took her in 1927." He clutched Ruth's shoulders in an uncommonly fierce grip. "Don't you ever tell your mother I said that. She would be devastated."

"So why did you tell *me?*" Ruth demanded. She was outraged.

"Because you're a strong girl," the Senator said. "And you can take it. And you always want to know exactly what's going on."

Ruth started crying; her tears came sudden and hard. "Why don't you all just leave me alone?" she shouted.

The Senator looked crushed. He hadn't meant to upset her. And what did she mean, *you all?* He tried to console Ruth, but she wasn't having it. He was sad and confused by her lately; she was edgy all the time. He couldn't make any sense of Ruth Thomas these days. He couldn't figure out what she wanted, but she did seem awfully unhappy.

It was a hard fall. The weather got cold overly fast, taking everyone by surprise. The days grew shorter too quickly, locking the whole island in a state of irritation and misery.

Just as Cal Cooley had predicted, the second weekend of September came and went and Mr. Ellis didn't budge. The *Stonecutter* stayed in the harbor, rocking about where everyone could see it, and word soon spread across the island that Mr. Ellis was not leaving and the reason had something to do with Ruth Thomas. By the end of September, the *Stonecutter* was a distressing presence. Having the Ellis boat sitting in the harbor so late into the fall was weird. It was like an anomaly of nature—a total eclipse, a red tide, an albino lobster. People wanted answers. How long did Mr. Ellis intend to stick around? What was he asking for? Why didn't Ruth deal with him and get it over with? What were the *implications?*

By the end of October, several local fishermen had been hired by Cal Cooley to take the *Stonecutter* out of the water, clean it, store it on land. Obviously, Lanford Ellis was going nowhere. Cal Cooley didn't come looking for Ruth Thomas again. She knew the terms. She had been summoned, and she knew that Mr. Ellis was waiting for her. And the whole island knew it, too. Now the boat was up on land in a wooden cradle where every man on the island could see it when he went down to the dock each morning to haul. The men didn't stop to look at it, but they were aware of its presence as they walked by. They felt its large, expensive oddity. It made them skittish, the way a new object in a familiar trail unnerves a horse.

The snow began in the middle of October. It was going to be an early winter. The men pulled their traps out of the water for good much earlier than they liked to, but it was getting harder to go out there and deal with the ice-caked gear, the frozen hands. The leaves were off the trees, and everyone could see Ellis House clearly on the top of the hill. At night, there were lights in the upstairs rooms.

In the middle of November, Ruth's father came over to Mrs. Pommeroy's house. It was four in the afternoon, and dark. Kitty Pommeroy, already blindly drunk, was sitting in the kitchen, staring at a pile of jigsaw puzzle pieces on the table. Robin and Opal's little boy, Eddie, who had recently learned to walk, was standing in the middle of the kitchen in a soggy diaper. He held an open jar of peanut butter and a large wooden spoon, which he was dipping into the jar and then sucking. His face was covered with peanut butter and spit. He was wearing one of Ruth's T-shirts—it looked like a dress on him—that read VARSITY. Ruth and Mrs. Pommeroy had been baking rolls, and the shocking-green kitchen radiated heat and smelled of bread, beer, and wet diapers.

"I'll tell you," Kitty was saying. "How many years was I married to that man and I never once refused him. That's what I can't understand, Rhonda. Why'd he have to step out on me? What'd Len want that I couldn't give him?"

"I know, Kitty," Mrs. Pommeroy said. "I know, honey."

Eddie dipped his spoon into the peanut butter and then, with a squeal, threw it across the kitchen floor. It skidded under the table.

"Jesus, Eddie," said Kitty. She lifted the tablecloth, looking for the spoon.

"I'll get it," Ruth said, and got down on her knees and ducked under the table. The tablecloth fluttered down behind her. She found the spoon, covered with peanut butter and cat hair, and also found a full pack of cigarettes, which must have been Kitty's.

"Hey, Kit," she started to say, but stopped, because she heard her father's voice, greeting Mrs. Pommeroy. Her father had actually come over! He hadn't come over in months. Ruth sat up, under the table, leaned against its center post, and was very quiet.

"Stan," Mrs. Pommeroy said, "how nice to see you."

"Well, it's about the fuck time you stopped by and saw your own goddamn daughter," said Kitty Pommeroy.

"Hey, Kitty," Stan said. "Is Ruth around?"

"Somewhere," Mrs. Pommeroy said. "Somewhere. She's always around somewhere. It is nice to see you, Stan. Long time. Want a hot roll?"

"Sure. I'll give one a try."

"Were you out to haul this morning, Stan?"

"I had a look at 'em."

"Keep any?"

"I kept a few. I think this is about it for everyone else, though. But I'll probably stay out there for the winter. See what I can find. How's everything over here?"

There was an attention-filled silence. Kitty coughed into her fist. Ruth made herself as small as she could under the large oak table.

"We've missed having you come by for dinner," Mrs. Pommeroy said. "You been eating with Angus Addams these days?"

"Or alone."

"We always have plenty to eat over here, Stan. You're welcome any time you like."

"Thanks, Rhonda. That's nice of you. I miss your cooking," he said. "I was wondering if you know what Ruthie's plans might be."

Ruthie. Hearing this, Ruth had a touch of heartache for her father.

"I suppose you should talk to her about that yourself."

"She say anything to you? Anything about college?"

"You should probably talk to her yourself, Stan."

"People are wondering," Stan said. "I got a letter from her mother."

Ruth was surprised. Impressed, even.

"Is that right, Stan? A letter. That's been a long time coming."

"That's right. She said she hasn't heard from Ruth. She said she and Miss Vera were disappointed Ruth hadn't made a decision about college. Has she made a decision?"

"I couldn't say, Stan."

"It's too late for this year, of course. But her mother said maybe she could start after Christmas. Or maybe she could go next fall. It's up to Ruth, I don't know. Maybe she has other plans?"

"Should I leave?" Kitty asked. "You want to tell him?"

"Tell me what?"

Under the table, Ruth felt queasy.

"Kitty," Mrs. Pommeroy said. "Please."

"He doesn't know, right? You want to tell him in private? Who's telling him? Is she going to tell him?"

"That's OK, Kitty."

"Tell him what?" Stan Thomas asked. "Tell me what in private?"

"Stan," Mrs. Pommeroy said, "Ruth has something to tell you. Something you're not going to like. You need to talk to her soon."

Eddie staggered over to the kitchen table, lifted a corner of the tablecloth, and peeked in at Ruth, who was sitting with her knees pulled up to her chest. He squatted over his huge diaper and stared at her. She stared back. His baby face had a puzzled look.

"I'm not going to like *what?*" Stan said.

"It's really something Ruth should talk to you about, Stan. Kitty spoke too freely."

"About what?"

Kitty said, "Well, guess what, Stan. What the hell. We think Ruth's going to have a baby."

"Kitty!" Mrs. Pommeroy exclaimed.

"What? Don't holler at me. Christ's sake, Rhonda, Ruth doesn't have the guts to tell him. Get it the hell over with. Look at the poor guy, wondering what the hell's going on."

Stan Thomas said nothing. Ruth listened. Nothing.

"She hasn't told anyone but us," Mrs. Pommeroy said. "Nobody knows about it, Stan."

"They'll know soon enough," Kitty said. "She's getting fat as all hell."

"Why?" Stan Thomas asked blankly. "Why do you think my daughter's having a baby?"

Eddie crawled under the kitchen table with Ruth, and she handed him his filthy peanut butter spoon. He grinned at her.

"Because she hasn't had her period in four months and she's getting *fat!*" Kitty said.

"I know this is upsetting," Mrs. Pommeroy said. "I know it's hard, Stan."

Kitty snorted in disgust. "Don't worry about Ruth!" she put in, loudly, firmly. "This is no big deal!"

Silence hung in the room.

"Come on!" Kitty said. "There's nothing to having a baby! Tell him,

Rhonda! You had about twenty of 'em! Easy breezy! Anyone with clean hands and common sense can do it!"

Eddie stuck the spoon in his mouth, pulled it out, let forth a delighted howl. Kitty lifted the tablecloth and peered in. She started to laugh.

"Didn't even know you was there, Ruth!" Kitty shouted. "Forgot all about you!"

EPILOGUE

Giants are met with in all the higher groups of animals. They interest us not only on account of their absolute size, but also in showing to what degree individuals may surpass the mean average of their race. It may be a question whether lobsters which weigh from 20–25 pounds are to be regarded as giants in the technical sense, or simply as sound and vigorous individuals on whose side fortune has always fought in the struggle of life. I am inclined to the latter view, and to look upon the mammoth lobster simply as a favorite of nature, who is larger than his fellows because he is their senior. Good luck has never deserted him.

—*The American Lobster: A Study of Its Habits and Development*
Francis Hobart Herrick, Ph.D.
1895

BY THE SUMMER OF 1982, the Skillet County Fishing Cooperative was doing a pretty good business for the three dozen lobstermen of Fort Niles Island and Courne Haven Island who had joined it. The office of the cooperative was located in the sunny front room of what had once been the Ellis Granite Company Store but was now the Intra-Island Memorial Museum of Natural History. The cooperative's founder and manager was a competent young woman named Ruth Thomas-Wishnell. Over the past five years, Ruth had bullied and cajoled her relatives and most of her neighbors into entering the delicate network of trust that made the Skillet County Co-op successful.

To put it simply, this had not been simple.

The idea for the cooperative had come to Ruth the first time she saw her father and Owney's uncle Babe Wishnell in the same room together. This was at the christening of Ruth and Owney's son, David, in early June of 1977. The christening took place in the living room of Mrs. Pommeroy's home, was performed by the cheerless Pastor Toby Wishnell, and was witnessed by a handful of glum-looking residents of both Fort Niles and Courne Haven. Baby David had thrown up all over his borrowed antique christening gown only moments before the ceremony, so Ruth had taken him upstairs to change him into something less elegant but much cleaner. While she was changing him, he'd begun to cry, so she sat with him for a while in Mrs. Pommeroy's bedroom, letting him nurse at her breast.

When, after a quarter of an hour, Ruth came back to the living room, she noticed that her father and Babe Wishnell—who had not so much as looked at each other all morning, and were sitting sullenly on opposite sides of the room—had each produced a small notebook from somewhere on his person. They were scribbling in these notebooks with identical stubs of pencils and looked utterly absorbed, frowning and silent.

Ruth knew exactly what her father was doing, because she'd seen him do it a million times, so she had no trouble guessing what Babe Wishnell was up to. They were calculating. They were taking care of their lobster business. They were shuffling numbers around, comparing prices, planning where to drop traps, adding expenses, *making money*. She kept an eye on them both during the brief, unemotional ceremony, and neither man once looked up from his rows of figures.

Ruth got to thinking.

She got to thinking even harder a few months later, when Cal Cooley appeared unannounced at the Natural History Museum, where Ruth and Owney and David were now living. Cal climbed the steep stairs to the apartment above the growing clutter of Senator Simon's massive collection and knocked on Ruth's door. He looked miserable. He told Ruth he was on a mission for Mr. Ellis, who, it seemed, had an offer to make. Mr. Ellis wanted to give Ruth the gleaming French Fresnel lens from the Goat's Rock lighthouse. Cal Cooley could scarcely deliver this news without crying. Ruth got a big kick out of that. Cal had spent months and months polishing every inch of brass and glass on that precious lens, but Mr. Ellis was adamant. He wanted Ruth to have it. Cal could not imagine why. Mr. Ellis had specifically instructed Cal to tell Ruth that she could do whatever she wanted with the thing. Although, Cal said, he suspected Mr. Ellis would like to see the Fresnel lens displayed as the centerpiece of the new museum.

"I'll take it," Ruth said, and immediately asked Cal to please leave.

"By the way, Ruth," Cal said, "Mr. Ellis is still waiting to see you."

"Fine," Ruth said. "Thank you, Cal. Out you go."

After Cal left, Ruth considered the gift she had just been offered. She wondered what it was all about. No, she still had not been up to see Mr. Ellis, who had remained on Fort Niles the entire previous winter. If he was trying to lure her up to Ellis House, she thought, he could forget it; she wasn't going. Although she did not feel entirely comfortable with the idea of Mr. Ellis hanging about, waiting for her to visit. She knew it upset the chemistry of the island, having Mr. Ellis on Fort Niles as a permanent resident, and she knew her neighbors were aware that she had something to do with it. But she wasn't going up there. She had nothing to say to him and was not interested in anything he had to say to her. She would, however, accept the Fresnel lens. And, yes, she would do whatever she wanted with it.

That night she had a long conversation with her father, Senator Simon, and Angus Addams. She told them about the gift, and they tried to imagine what the thing was worth. They didn't have a clue, though. The next day, Ruth started calling auction houses in New York City, which took some research and gumption, but Ruth did it. Three months later, after intricate negotiations, a wealthy man from North Carolina took possession of the Goat's Rock lighthouse Fresnel lens, and Ruth Thomas-Wishnell had in her hands a check for $22,000.

She had another long conversation.

This one was with her father, Senator Simon, Angus Addams, and Babe Wishnell. She had lured Babe Wishnell over from Courne Haven with the promise of a big Sunday dinner, which Mrs. Pommeroy ended up cooking. Babe Wishnell didn't much like coming to Fort Niles, but it was hard to refuse the invitation of a young woman who was, after all, now a relative. Ruth said to him, "I had such a good time at your daughter's wedding, I feel I should thank you with a nice meal," and he could not turn her down.

It was not the most relaxed meal, but it would have been a good deal less relaxed had Mrs. Pommeroy not been there to flatter and pamper everyone. After dinner, Mrs. Pommeroy served hot rum drinks. Ruth sat at the table, bouncing her son on her lap and laying her idea before

Babe Wishnell, her father, and the Addams brothers. She told them she wanted to become a bait dealer. She said she would put up the money for a building to be constructed on the Fort Niles dock, and she would buy the scales and freezers, as well as the heavy boat needed to transport the bait every few weeks from Rockland to the island. She showed them the numbers, which she had been juggling for weeks. She had everything figured out. All she wanted from her father and Angus Addams and Babe Wishnell was their commitment to buy her bait if she gave them a good low price. She could save them ten cents on the bushel right away. And she could save them the trouble of having to cart the bait from Rockland every week.

"You three are the most respected lobstermen on Fort Niles and Courne Haven," she said, running a light finger over her son's gums, feeling for a new tooth. "If everyone sees you doing it, they'll know it's a good deal."

"You're out of your fucking mind," Angus Addams said.

"Take the money and move to Nebraska," Senator Simon said.

"I'm in," Babe Wishnell said, without the slightest hesitation.

"I'm in, too," said Ruth's father, and the two high-line fishermen exchanged a glance of recognition. They got it. They understood the concept immediately. The numbers looked good. They weren't idiots.

After six months, when it was clear that the bait dealership was hugely successful, Ruth founded the cooperative. She made Babe Wishnell the president but kept the office on Fort Niles, which satisfied everyone. She hand-picked a council of directors, composed of the sanest men from both Fort Niles and Courne Haven. Any man who became a member of the Skillet County Cooperative could get special deals on bait and could sell his lobster catch to Ruth Thomas-Wishnell, right there on the Fort Niles dock. She hired Webster Pommeroy to run the scales. He was so simple, nobody ever accused him of cheating. She appointed her father to set the daily lobster prices, which he arrived at by haggling over the telephone with dealers as far away as Manhattan. She hired someone completely neutral—a sensible young man from Freeport—to operate the pound Ruth had had built for storing the lobster catch before it was carted over to Rockland.

There was a good payout for anyone who joined up, and it saved weeks out of each man's year not to have to haul the catch to Rockland. There were some holdouts at first, of course. Ruth's father had rocks thrown through the windows of his house, and Ruth got some cold stares on the street, and someone once threatened to burn down the Natural History Museum. Angus Addams did not speak to Ruth or her father for over two years, but, in the end, even he joined. These were, after all, islands of followers, and once the high-liners were on board, it was not difficult to find members. The system was working. It was all working out just fine. Mrs. Pommeroy did all the secretarial tasks in the Skillet Co-op office. She was good at it, patient and organized. She was also great at calming down the lobstermen when they got too worked up or too paranoid or too competitive. Whenever a lobsterman stormed into the office, howling that Ruth was ripping him off or that someone had sabotaged his traps, he was sure to walk out happy and pacified—and with a nice new haircut, besides.

Ruth's husband and her father were making a fortune fishing together. Owney was Stan's sternman for two years; then he bought his own boat (a fiberglass boat, the first one on either island; Ruth had talked him into it), but he and Stan still shared profits. They formed their own corporation. Stan Thomas and Owney Wishnell made a dazzling couple. They were fishing wizards. There weren't enough hours in the day for all the lobsters they were pulling out of the ocean. Owney was a gifted fisherman, a natural fisherman. He came home to Ruth every afternoon with a sort of a glow, a hum, a low buzz of contentment and success. He came home every afternoon satisfied and proud and wanting sex in the worst way, and Ruth liked that. She liked that a lot.

As for Ruth, she too was content. She was satisfied and enormously proud of herself. As far as she was concerned, she pretty much kicked ass. Ruth loved her husband and her little boy, but mostly she loved her business. She loved the lobster pound and bait dealership, and she was pleased as punch with herself for having put together the co-op and for having convinced those big strong lobstermen to join it. All those men, who'd never before had a good word to say about one another! She'd offered them something so smart and efficient that even they had seen the worth of it. And business was great. Now Ruth was thinking about setting up fuel pumps on the docks of both islands. It would be an expensive investment, but it was sure to pay off fast. And she could afford it. She was making a lot of money. She was proud of that, too. She wondered, more than a little smugly, what had become of all her horsey classmates from that ridiculous school in Delaware. They'd probably just got out of college and were getting engaged to pampered idiots at this very moment. Who knew? Who cared?

More than anything, Ruth had a big sense of pride when she thought of her mother and the Ellises, who had tried so hard to drive her away from this place. They had insisted that there was no future for Ruth on Fort Niles, when, as things had turned out, Ruth *was* the future here. Yes, she was pretty content.

Ruth got pregnant again in the early winter of 1982, when she was twenty-four and David was a quiet five-year-old who spent most of his day trying not to get clobbered by Opal and Robin Pommeroy's enormous son, Eddie.

"We're going to have to move out of the apartment now," Ruth said to her husband when she was sure she was pregnant. "And I don't want to live in any of the old crappers down on the harbor. I'm sick of being cold all the time. Let's build our own house. Let's build a house that makes sense. A big one."

She knew exactly where she wanted it to be. She wanted to live way up on Ellis Hill, way up at the top of the island, above the quarries, looking out over Worthy Channel and Courne Haven Island. She wanted a grand house and wasn't ashamed to admit it. She wanted the view and the prestige of the view. Of course, Mr. Ellis owned the land. He owned pretty much all the good land on Fort Niles, so Ruth would have to talk to him if she was serious about building up there. And she was serious. As her pregnancy went on and the apartment began to feel smaller and smaller, Ruth grew even more serious.

Which is why, seven months pregnant and with her little boy in tow, Ruth Thomas-Wishnell drove her father's truck all the way up the Ellis Road one afternoon in June of 1982, finally seeking a meeting with Mr. Lanford Ellis.

Lanford Ellis had turned a century old that year. His health was hardly robust. He was all alone in Ellis House, that massive structure of black granite, fit for a mausoleum. He hadn't left Fort Niles in six years. He spent his days by the fireplace in his bedroom, with a blanket around his legs, sitting in the chair that had belonged to his father, Dr. Jules Ellis.

Every morning, Cal Cooley set up a card table near Mr. Ellis's chair and brought over his stamp albums, a strong lamp, and a powerful magnifying lens. Some of the stamps in the albums were old and valuable and had been collected by Dr. Jules Ellis. Every morning, Cal would make a fire in the fireplace, no matter the season, because Mr. Ellis was always cold. So that was where he was sitting the day Cal Cooley ushered in Ruth.

"Hello, Mr. Ellis," she said. "It's nice to see you."

Cal directed Ruth to a plush chair, stirred up the fire, left the room. Ruth lifted her little boy onto her lap, which was not easy, because she didn't have much of a lap these days. She looked at the old man. She could hardly believe he was alive. He looked dead. His eyes were shut. His hands were blue.

"Granddaughter!" Mr. Ellis said. His eyes snapped open, grotesquely magnified behind enormous, insectoid glasses.

Ruth's son, who was not a coward, flinched. Ruth took a lollipop from her bag, unwrapped it, and put it in David's mouth. Sugar pacifier. She wondered why she'd brought her son to see this specter. That may have been a mistake, but she was used to taking David with her everywhere. He was such a good kid, so uncomplaining. She should have thought this out better. Too late now.

"You were supposed to come to dinner on Thursday, Ruth," said the old man.

"Thursday?"

"A Thursday in July of 1976." He cracked a sly grin.

"I was busy," Ruth said, and smiled winningly, or so she hoped.

"You've cut your hair, girl."

"I have."

"You've put on weight." His head bobbed faintly all the time.

"Well, I have a pretty good excuse. I'm expecting another child."

"I've not yet met your first."

"This is David, Mr. Ellis. This is David Thomas Wishnell."

"Nice to meet you, young man." Mr. Ellis stretched out a trembling arm toward Ruth's boy, offering to shake hands. David scrunched against his mother in terror. The lollipop fell out of his shocked mouth. Ruth picked it up and popped it back in. Mr. Ellis's arm retreated.

"I want to talk to you about buying some land," Ruth said. What she really wanted was to get this meeting behind her as quickly as possible.

"My husband and I would like to build a house here on Ellis Hill, right near here. I have a reasonable sum to offer . . ."

Ruth trailed off because she was alarmed. Mr. Ellis was suddenly coughing with a strangling sound. He was choking, and his face was turning purple. She didn't know what to do. Should she get Cal Cooley? She had a quick and calculating thought: she didn't want Lanford Ellis to die before the land deal was settled.

"Mr. Ellis?" she said, and started to get up.

The trembling arm stretched out again, waving her away. "Sit down," he said. He took a deep breath, and the coughing started again. No, Ruth realized, he wasn't coughing. He was laughing. How perfectly horrible.

He stopped, at last, and wiped his eyes. He shook his old turtle head. He said, "You certainly aren't afraid of me any longer, Ruth."

"I never was afraid."

"Nonsense. You were petrified." A small, white spit-dot flew from his lips and landed on one of his stamp albums. "But no longer. And good for you. I must say, Ruth, I am pleased with you. I am proud of all you've accomplished here on Fort Niles. I have been watching your progress with great interest."

He pronounced the last word in three exquisite syllables.

"Um, thank you," Ruth said. This was a strange turn. "I know it was never your intent that I stay here on Fort Niles . . ."

"Oh, it was precisely my intent."

Ruth looked at him without blinking.

"It was always my hope that you would stay here and organize these islands. Bring some sense to them. As you have done, Ruth. You look surprised."

She was. Then again, she was not. She thought back.

Her mind slowed, picking around carefully for an explanation, looking closely at the details of her life. She reviewed some ancient conversations, some ancient meetings with Mr. Ellis. What exactly had he expected of her? What were his plans for her when her schooling was over? He had never said.

"I always understood that you wanted me to get off this island and go to college." Ruth's voice sounded calm in the big room. And she was calm. She was vitally involved in the conversation now.

"I said no such thing, Ruth. Did I ever talk to you about college? Did I ever say I wanted you to live elsewhere?"

Indeed he had not, she realized. Vera had said it; her mother had said it; Cal Cooley had said it. Even Pastor Wishnell had said it. But not Mr. Ellis. How very interesting.

"I'd like to know something," Ruth asked, "since we are being so candid. Why did you make me go to school in Delaware?"

"It was an excellent school, and I expected you to hate it."

She waited, but he did not elaborate.

"Well," she said, "that explains everything. Thanks."

He let out a rattling sigh. "Taking into account both your intelligence and your obstinacy, I imagined the school would serve two purposes. It would educate you and would drive you back to Fort Niles. I should not have to spell this out for you, Ruth."

Ruth nodded. That did explain everything.

"Are you angry, Ruth?"

She shrugged. Oddly, she was not. *Big deal,* she thought. So he'd been manipulating her whole life. He'd manipulated the life of everyone he had sway over. It was no surprise, really; in fact, it was edifying. And in the end—*what of it?* Ruth came to this conclusion rapidly and with no fuss. She liked knowing at last what had been going on all these years. There are moments in a person's life when the big understanding arrives in a snap, and this was such a moment for Ruth Thomas-Wishnell.

Mr. Ellis spoke again. "You could not possibly have married better, Ruth."

"My, my, my," she said. *On came the surprises!* "Well, how do you like that?"

"A Wishnell and a Thomas? Oh, I like it very much. You have founded a dynasty, young lady."

"Have I, now?"

"You have. And it would have given my father supreme satisfaction to see what you've accomplished here in the last few years with the co-operative, Ruth. No other local could have pulled it off."

"No other local ever had the capital, Mr. Ellis."

"Well, you were clever enough to acquire that capital. And you've spent it wisely. My father would have been proud and delighted at the success of your business. He was always concerned for the future of these islands. He loved them. As do I. As does the entire Ellis family. And after all my family has invested into these islands, I would not want to see Fort Niles and Courne Haven sink for lack of a worthy leader."

"I'll tell you something, Mr. Ellis," Ruth said, and for some reason she could not help smiling. "It was never my intent to make your family proud. Believe me. I have never been interested in serving the Ellis family."

"Regardless."

"Yeah, I suppose." Ruth felt strange and light—and thoroughly comprehending. "Regardless."

"But you've come to speak of business."

"So I have."

"You have some money."

"So I do."

"And you want me to sell you my land."

Ruth hesitated.

"No-o," she said, and she drew the word out. "No, not exactly. I don't want you to sell me your land, Mr. Ellis. I want you to give it to me."

Now it was Mr. Ellis who stopped blinking. Ruth tilted her head and returned his gaze.

"Yes?" she said. "Do you understand?"

He did not answer. She gave him time to think about what she'd said, and then explained it, with careful patience. "Your family owes a great debt to my family. It is important and proper that your family make some restitution to my family for the lives of my mother and my grandmother. And for my life, too. Surely you understand?"

Ruth was pleased with that word—*restitution.* It was exactly the right word.

Mr. Ellis thought this over for some time and then said, "You aren't threatening me with legal action, are you, Miss Thomas?"

"Mrs. Thomas-Wishnell," Ruth corrected. "And don't be absurd. I'm not threatening anybody."

"I rather thought not."

"I'm only explaining that you have an opportunity here, Mr. Ellis, to right some of the wrongs that your family inflicted on my family over the years."

Mr. Ellis did not reply.

"If you ever felt like cleaning up your conscience a bit, this might be your big chance."

Mr. Ellis still did not reply.

"I shouldn't have to spell this out for you, Mr. Ellis."

"No," he said. He sighed again, took off his glasses, and folded them. "You should not have to."

"You understand then?"

He nodded once and turned his head to regard the fire.

Ruth said, "Good."

They sat in silence. David was asleep by now, and his body made a hot, damp imprint against Ruth's body. He was heavy. And yet Ruth was comfortable. She thought this brief and forthright exchange with Mr. Ellis was both important and proper. And true. It had gone well. *Restitution.* Yes. And it was about time. She felt quite at ease.

Ruth watched Mr. Ellis as he watched the fire. She was not angry or sad. Nor did he appear to be so. She felt no resentment toward him. It was a nice fire, she thought. It was unusual, but not unpleasant, to have such a big, Christmasy fire blazing away in the middle of June. With the draperies drawn over the windows, with the smell of woodsmoke in the room, there was no way to know that the day was bright. It was a beautiful fireplace, the pride of the room. It was made of heavy, dark wood—mahogany, perhaps—decorated with nymphs and grapes and dolphins. It was capped by a marble mantelpiece of greenish hue. Ruth admired the workmanship of the fireplace for some time.

"I'll take the house, too," she said, at last.

"Of course," said Mr. Ellis. His hands were clasped on the card table in front of him. His hands were spotty and papery, but now they did not tremble.

"Good."

"Fine."

"You're with me?"

"Yes."

"And you do understand what all this means, Mr. Ellis? It means you'll have to leave Fort Niles." Ruth did not say this in an unkind manner. She was simply correct. "You and Cal should both return to Concord now. Don't you think?"

He nodded. He was still looking at the fire. He said, "When the weather is good enough to set sail in the *Stonecutter* . . ."

"Oh, there's no hurry. You don't have to leave here today. But I don't want you dying in this house, do you understand? And I do *not* want you dying on this island. That would not be appropriate, and it would unsettle everyone too much. I don't want to have to deal with that. So you do have to leave. And there's no immediate hurry. But sometime over the next few weeks, we'll pack you up and move you out of here. I don't think it'll be too hard."

"Mr. Cooley can take care of all that."

"Of course," Ruth said. She smiled. "That'll be a perfect job for Cal."

They sat for another long time in silence. The fire crackled and shimmered. Mr. Ellis unfolded his eyeglasses and returned them to his face. He turned his gaze upon Ruth.

"Your little boy is sleepy," he said.

"Actually, I think he's sleep*ing*. I should get him home to his father. He likes to see his father in the afternoons. Waits for him, you know, to come home from fishing."

"He's a handsome boy."

"We think so. We love him."

"Naturally you do. He is your son."

Ruth sat up straighter. Then she said, "I should get back to the harbor now, Mr. Ellis."

"You won't have a cup of tea?"

"No. But we are in agreement, yes?"

"I am enormously proud of you, Ruth."

"Well." she smiled broadly and made an ironic little flourish with her left hand. "It's all part of the service, Mr. Ellis."

With some effort, Ruth got herself up out of the deep chair, still holding David. Her son made a small noise of protest, and she shifted his weight, trying to hold him in a way that would be comfortable for them both. At this point in her pregnancy, she shouldn't have been carrying him around, but she enjoyed it. She liked holding David, and knew she only had a few more years of it, before he got too big and too independent to permit it. Ruth smoothed back her boy's fair hair and picked up her canvas bag, which was filled with snacks for David and co-op files for herself. Ruth started toward the door and then changed her mind.

She turned around to confirm a suspicion. She looked over at Mr. Ellis, and, yes, just as she had expected, he was grinning and grinning.

He made no attempt to hide his grin from her. Indeed, he let it grow wider. As she saw this, Ruth felt the oddest, the most unaccountable fondness for the man. So she did not walk out. Not just yet. Instead, she walked to Mr. Ellis's chair and—leaning awkwardly around the weight of her son and her pregnancy—bent down and kissed the old dragon right on the forehead.

ACKNOWLEDGMENTS

I WOULD LIKE to thank the New York Public Library for offering me the essential sanctuary of the Allen Room. I also extend my appreciation to the staff of the Vinalhaven Historical Society for helping me sift through that island's remarkable history. While I consulted many books during this project, I was most helped by *The Lobster Gangs of Maine*, *Lobstering and the Maine Coast*, *Perils of the Sea*, *Fish Scales and Stone Chips*, the collected works of Edwin Mitchell, the unpublished but thorough "Tales of Matinicus Island," and a disturbing 1943 volume called *Shipwreck Survivors: A Medical Study*.

Thanks to Wade Schuman for giving me the idea in the first place; to Sarah Chalfant for nudging it along; to Dawn Seferian for picking it up; to Janet Silver for seeing it through; and to Frances Apt for straightening it out. I am profoundly grateful to the residents of Matinicus Island, Vinalhaven Island, and Long Island for taking me into their homes and onto their boats. Special appreciation goes to Ed and Nan Mitchell, Barbara and David Ramsey, Ira Warren, Stan MacVane, Bunky MacVane, Donny MacVane, Katie Murphy, Randy Wood, Patti Rich, Earl Johnson, Andy Creelman, Harold Poole, Paula Hopkins, Larry Ames, Beba Rosen, John Beckman, and the legendary Ms. Bunny Beckman. Thank you, Dad, for attending U. of M. and for remembering your friends after all those many years. Thank you, John Hodgman, for taking time from your work to help me in the final moments of mine. Thank you, Deborah Luepnitz, for going lobster-by-lobster with me, right from the beginning. And God Bless the Fat Kids.